THE SEX ON THE BEACH BOOK CLUB

JENNIFER APODACA

BRAVA

KENSINGTON PUBLISHING CORP.
http://www.kensingtonbooks.com

THE SEX ON THE BEACH BOOK CLUB

Acknowledgments

Kate Duffy, thank you for believing and for the tremendous amount of work you do on every book. Working with you is a pleasure!

Natalie Collins, thank you for being there through every doubt and crisis, for forcing me to think through the problems, and most of all, for being a friend. All the Instant Messages that made me laugh saved my sanity while writing this book!

Louise Knott Ahern, thank you for the research information and your generous support. Your insights helped me build the character, and your friendship helped me believe in the book.

Karen Solem, thank you for keeping me focused on the writing while you worry about the bigger picture.

Chapter 1

Holly Hillbay was the best damned private investigator in Goleta, California, but you couldn't tell it from the week she was having. Losing her bread-and-butter client, whom she did routine new-hire background checks for, was bad enough. But she knew Brad the Cad, her ex-fiancé, had something to do with that, which made her furious.

She channeled her frustration into her new case—going undercover in a book club. That was what brought her to the Books on the Beach bookstore on a Tuesday evening. Pausing outside the door, she inhaled a breath of the damp, salty air from the nearby ocean. The preppy, probably over-educated bookstore owner Wes Brockman, and the very married Tanya Shaker, were about to have their sordid little affair exposed like a celebrity biography.

That thought cheered her up and she went inside. The ringing bell over the door still echoed as she quickly scanned the bookstore. The first thing she saw was an inviting sitting area done in white wicker with ocean blue cushions. That was bookended by a checkout counter with a coffee and beverage station next to it on her right, and a wall-sized bookcase featuring new releases directly across from the door. Beyond the sitting area were rows of dark bookcases. The whole atmosphere exuded sophisticated comfort where readers could leisurely browse until they selected the books they wanted to buy.

A deep voice from behind her asked, "Can I help you?"

Holly turned around and felt a slap of lust that could have been right out of a romance novel. Since she wasn't a big romance reader, she was going to have to blame it on the man—he was hot. Sun-streaked brown hair and vivid green eyes set in a face that had a little George Clooney going on. His mouth was full and oozed sensual promises. His jaw wore just enough of a shadow to make her want to run her hand along his cheek to feel the texture.

Oh yeah, he could help her end her long dry spell in the bedroom. She blinked and reminded her deprived hormones that she was on the job. *Damn it.* "Hi, I'm Holly. I'm here for the book club." She hoped her week had taken a turn for the better, and this guy turned out to be anyone but Wes Brockman.

He smiled, crinkling the skin around his green eyes. "I'm Wes. Book club is just getting started." He held a hand up toward a door that opened on the left side of the store.

It figured. She revised her opinion of the bookstore owner: *Sexy as hell, preppy and probably over-educated. Oh, and he screwed married women, probably because he could.* Her hormone levels banked down to a mere sizzle. Managing to look past her lust, she saw his expensive clothes mixed with the self-confidence that came with money and success. Holly immediately pegged the bookstore as his hobby and not the career that made him rich and sophisticated.

Tearing her gaze from him, she turned and headed toward the room he indicated. It was about the size of the master bedroom in her condo, and had four long tables set in a rectangle shape. She estimated about eighteen people gathered around it. Thermoses of coffee and plates of cookies were set out on the tables. A brief look around showed her a door that led to a small bathroom and another door that was closed—

probably a storage area or office. There were poster-sized book covers on the walls, adding color and energy to the room.

She scanned the more than a dozen women and three men, and spotted Tanya Shaker. She looked just like the picture Holly had of her, shoulder-length blond hair, lots of makeup, and an industrial-strength bra that pushed her breasts up to her chin in her low-cut black T-shirt. She sat with a lifeguard-handsome man on her right and an empty chair on her left.

Perfect.

"Holly, take a seat anywhere," Wes said next to her. His hand brushed her arm then was gone.

A warm shiver rolled down her spine, catching her off guard. *Must be a full moon or something.* Clearly her libido had not gotten the message that Wes was a player. She didn't date rich men who indiscriminately screwed women. In fact, she didn't date much at all these days. Men were a trouble-some distraction from her career.

Pulling her thoughts back to the job, she walked over to Tanya, slid into the seat next to her, and said, "Hi, I'm Holly. Have you belonged to the book club long?" In Holly's expe-rience, women talked more than men—usually because they mixed up sex and love.

Tanya did the girl-to-girl scan and said, "About a month."

Holly got to work. "I just heard about the book club. Thought I'd give it a try. Only three men, huh?" There was Wes Brockman at the end of the tables on her right. A guy sit-ting next to him who was a little older, darker, wearing blue-tinted glasses that didn't mask the deep suspicion in his dark eyes. Then there was the man on the other side of Tanya, who leaned forward and looked at Holly.

"I'm Cullen. Would you like to use my book?" He pushed the book toward her. "I'm sure Tanya will let me share with her."

Holly took the book and glanced at the title. *"Wicked" Women Whodunit.*

Tanya grinned at her. "It's good. I read it and I'm not much of a reader."

Holly swallowed the urge to ask what the hell she was doing at a book club if she didn't read. But she knew why Tanya was there. What really surprised her was how careful Tanya was being. Women usually gave it away long before the men did. Especially the player types like Wes Brockman. They were used to woman after woman moving through their beds and seldom gave them a thought outside of the sheets. "Yeah, I read it. Love those women who go after what they want." She *had* actually read the book.

Tanya turned to look the other way. "Me, too."

Holly presumed Tanya was looking down the table at Wes. *A secret lover's look?*

"Holly," Wes said from his end of the table. "Did I hear you say you read this book?"

She felt it again—that zing as his gaze met hers. What kind of crap was that? It was like a drippy movie moment and she refused to acknowledge it. She focused on her answer instead. "Yes, I did. I guess I'm surprised that your book club picked a book like this."

He arched his eyebrows. "Like what?"

She knew a challenge when she heard one. This was more comfortable territory for her. "This blatantly sexy. The heroines in this book get caught up in a mystery and are aggressive about solving it. And they aren't shy about sleeping with the man they choose."

Cullen, sitting on the other side of Tanya, said, "My kind of woman."

Wes cut his gaze from Holly to him. "Why is that, Cullen?"

Cullen flashed a boyish grin. "I don't see why men should always have to chase women. I don't mind being chased. Or caught."

Laughter rolled down both sides of the table.

Except, Holly noticed, for the three women who sat across from her. They looked at one another, all three of them wearing tight-lipped expressions. She could almost feel their collective reaction to Cullen. What was that about? What had Cullen done to annoy or embarrass those three?

One of the women spoke up. "The stories in this anthology are not just about sex. They're about a relationship developing when a man and woman are thrown together in mysterious circumstances."

"Very well stated, Nora," Wes said.

Holly looked at Nora, seeing a woman who had home-dyed brown hair, brown eyes, and a gentle manner. Maybe she'd been a romantic when she was younger and still believed just a little bit.

The woman next to Nora said, "The men just want sex."

"That's a little harsh, Maggie," Wes answered.

Maggie wore a tailored suit and constantly checked her cell phone—probably because she was text-messaging. She glared at Cullen before she dropped her gaze to her cell phone.

All kinds of undercurrents were going on in this book club, the kinds of undercurrents that usually had to do with sex. Was this a book club or a sex club? The women all seemed pretty easygoing with Wes. It was Cullen who was causing reactions.

And guess who was sitting next to Cullen? Had Holly's client, Tanya's husband Phil, been wrong about who Tanya was doing the sheet tango with?

Just as an awkward silence was ready to engulf the room, Wes tossed out another question. "Does murder break down social expectations and up the stakes so that the characters are more likely to come together sexually?"

The man was smooth. Holly snorted and looked up at Wes.

He asked, "Did you say something, Holly?"

What did she care? She was here to do a job and when it was done, she would never see these people again. So she told the truth. "That's crap. It's lust, pure and simple. Lust has been around for centuries. Women feel lust, too."

"Oh yeah," Tanya whispered in a low sexy voice, and leaned, boobs first, into Cullen on the other side of her.

Whoa, Holly thought. *Had Phil gotten his wires crossed about who his wife was sleeping with?*

Wes recaptured her attention when he asked, "What about love? Traditionally, women have searched for love."

She couldn't look away from him. She knew everyone had turned to watch her, but she didn't want to break the connection between her and Wes. There was something deep and mysterious about him, and it called to all Holly's instincts to find out the answers. What brought a man like Wes to owning a bookstore in a beach town? His question tugged at her old wounds, but she lifted her chin and told him her truth, a truth she learned the hard way. "I prefer lust over love. Lust is simple and straightforward."

Wes had no idea how he'd gotten through the remainder of the book club. Holly's "lust over love" comment had burrowed into his brain and taken up residence in his sex drive. There was something incredibly sexy about the newest member of his book club.

Watching Holly as she got up from the table, he thought she looked a little like the character Lilly Rush, from the *Cold Case* TV show. She had her hair tucked up in that same casual-messy style, though it was a darker blonde. Since he'd had the pleasure of walking up behind her, he got an eye full of her long lean figure and her mouthwatering ass. But when she'd turned around, it had been her blue eyes that captured his attention. Gray-blue, the color was hard to define—a bit of clear blue sky mixed with the churning waters of a stormy ocean.

Oh yeah, she'd caught his interest. She'd made him feel *something* when he hadn't felt *anything* in a hell of a long time.

So yeah, she was sexy, he was interested—but he was also wary, more from habit than anything. Holly seemed to have more interest in the people of the club than the book. He hadn't seen her in the bookstore before and no one else in the room seemed to recognize her. So how had she found out about the book club? Or had being in hiding for three years just made him paranoid?

Gazing around the room, he saw that Helene Essex had cornered Cullen, while Tanya looked daggers at them. He knew the torrid situation was going to explode; he just hoped it didn't happen in his bookstore. He didn't need the attention and headaches it would bring.

Cullen was the kind of man Wes despised. He used and discarded women, notching his belt as he went along. Wes had nothing against honest sex for the sake of sex alone. Over the last few years, it had been the only sex he had. But he never lied to the women, never let them believe he loved them. Tearing his gaze from them, he looked for the woman who was occupying his thoughts.

He spotted Holly holding a copy of *"Wicked" Women Whodunit* and talking to a couple of women, then she broke away. He intercepted her. "Hey," he said, watching as she turned to him, settling her smoke-blue gaze on him. His gut clenched with a thread of desire. He really liked her eyes, liked the way she looked right at him. But he didn't know if that was real or a phony sincerity. Wes had spent years ferreting out exactly what people's intentions were. Surely he could handle one young woman. He pulled out his most charming smile. "So how did you find out about our book club?"

"Word of mouth." She grinned. "But this isn't what I expected from a book club."

"No?" Leaving his answer open-ended to see how she'd reply, he noted her vague answer and change of subject. His interest kept ramping up, but the instincts that kept him at the top of his game in his old job told him that Holly was interested in more than just his book club. She was almost too alert, and she didn't volunteer anything about herself.

She shook her head. "I expected Oprah books."

"Ah. The realistic, and predominately tragic, endings. I've had enough of those in my life, how about you?" He didn't let his thoughts stray to the tragic endings, or the deadly mistakes he'd made. He lived with the guilt, but he didn't wallow in it.

Her eyes hardened. "Who doesn't?"

She wasn't going to spill her guts in the first minute. Damn, she was a challenge. He decided to try a little flirting. "So you don't like books with tragic endings. But you do like sexy anthologies."

She leaned her hips back against the table. "Fast-paced and sexy are more my style. You?"

Hell, yeah. Looking at her, with her breasts pushing against that tank top, and her intense gaze, he was completely and one hundred percent into fast-paced and sexy. If flirting, companionship, and maybe sex was what she wanted, he was on board and ready. "Fast-paced and sexy work for me. Are you free tonight to get a drink or coffee?"

Her blue eyes shaded to nearly gray. "I would think someone like you would have plans."

Wes narrowed his gaze. What was her game? Her remark had come out more like an accusation. "Nope. No plans once I close up the store." He left the ball in her court.

She smiled, but her gaze roamed around the room then down to her watch. "Can I have a rain check? I have to run. Thank you for an interesting evening."

Ice water chased out the heat in his gut as suspicion climbed up over his sex drive. She was up to something. "You're in a hurry?"

She started moving away. "Afraid so."

Wes followed her to the front of the store to see what she had been watching. As she opened the door and left, he caught sight of Tanya and Cullen walking ahead of her.

What was Holly doing? It appeared to him she was following Cullen and Tanya. Why? Could she be one of Cullen's castoffs? But Cullen hadn't acted as if he knew her. Wes was so intent on watching her walk away, he nearly jumped at the voice behind him.

"Check her out before you get in her pants."

Wes turned to look at George, whom he considered his best friend. These days, George played the retired business-man. He fudged the facts on the business he retired from and other minor details—like his name, rank, and social security number. But then, who was he to complain? George was the one who helped Wes obtain his new name and social security number. "She look dangerous to you?"

"Hell, yes. That woman instantly drained the blood from your head to your dick. That's the kind of shit that can get you killed."

Wes laughed. "I must be getting old if I'm that obvious." He sobered up. "But that woman is up to something. She seemed surprised at what book the club is reading, so why did she want to be in our book club?"

George looked over his glasses at Wes. "Want me to find out?"

Oh no, this one was all his. Wes was going to get to the bottom of sexy Holly. "No, I want you to stay here and watch the store. I'm going to go see just what Ms. Lust Over Love is up to."

Since Wes knew where Cullen and Tanya were going, if Holly really was following them, it shouldn't be hard to catch up to her.

Holly stood on the docks a mile away from the bookstore and watched as the boat motored away, carrying Tanya and Cullen under the full moon. There was no two ways about it. She was screwed. She had done her preliminary research on Tanya Shaker and Wes Brockman.

But she had the wrong guy. Judging by the hand-holding, giggling, and Cullen's hand on Tanya's ass, Tanya was having an extramarital affair with Cullen, not Wes. Her client had been so sure his wife was cheating with the bookstore owner, Wes. "Shit," she muttered to herself.

"Problem?"

Holly jumped as she watched Wes walk out from the shadows between two stores on the other side of the dock. Had he been spying on her? *What the hell?* She glared at him. "What are you doing here? And why are you sneaking up on me?"

He leaned against the wood rail. "Following you, which requires a certain stealth."

She studied Brockman. The evening was cool, the moon was full, and there was a spill of lights from surrounding businesses now that he had emerged from the shadows. He looked dangerous, sexy, and very Bond-like in his expensive clothes and casual demeanor. As if following a woman he just met was perfectly acceptable for a guy who owned a bookstore. Not in Holly's world. Who was this guy? "What are you, some kind of stalker?"

His eyes crinkled, but he didn't quite smile. His full lips did a slight, sarcastic curve. "Call me curious. Why did you follow Cullen and Tanya?"

Seriously, what did he care? She tried to control her annoyance enough to fix a sincere smile on her face. "I wanted to return his book." She raised her hand to show him the book Cullen had loaned her, then had forgotten in his hurry to get Tanya out to sea and naked.

Wes dropped his gaze to the book then looked back to her face. He pushed off the rail and took a long step toward her. "Give the book to me. I'll return it to him."

Inhaling, she caught his scent, something very woodsy mixed with male heat. Sensual. A little quiver danced in her stomach. She blinked and made herself focus. Her target wasn't Brockman, it was Cullen, who had just sailed off for an evening of moonlit sex. Experience taught her that the illicit lovers wouldn't be back for a couple of hours. In the meantime, Wes knew Cullen so she could get the information she needed from him. "I'd really like to thank Cullen myself. What's his last name? I'll look him up."

He leaned down and said in a low tone, "And how do I know you're not a stalker with murder on her mind?"

Oh boy, she was getting a bad case of poor judgment. Wes was a little mysterious and a little dark, two qualities that made her very curious. Why would he follow her to the docks? Because she turned down his invitation for drinks? Or another reason? And damn it, did he have to be so powerfully male? Sexy? He had that deep, passionate quality in a man that made a woman think that when she was naked with him, he'd be solely focused on her. Maybe her hormones needed a dip in the ocean. To Wes, she answered, "Why would I be stalking Cullen? I just want to return his book."

Wes moved close enough to touch her, to make her feel like he *might* touch her. But he didn't. "Guess you'll have to find another way." He turned and walked away.

Holly stood there, a little stunned. Was that payback for her turning him down in the bookstore? Shaking it off, she put Wes out of her mind. She could find out Cullen's last name on her own. She went around to a couple of the businesses, and stopped people on the docks, asking questions. But she drew a big fat zero in her quest for information on Cullen.

After twenty minutes, Holly knew she was wasting her time. She needed Cullen's last name to start doing research on him, and for her reports. Her client needed pictures and detailed reports—including Cullen's last name—to prove Tanya was cheating on him. Phil needed those to invoke a clause in the prenuptial agreement that would significantly reduce the amount of money Tanya would get.

She was sure that Wes knew Cullen's last name. All she had to do was convince him to tell her. Holly hurried through the cool night and reached the bookstore just in time to see Wes come outside, turn around, and lock the door.

Slowing her pace, she walked up. "Hi." Damn, he was still sexy in that overbearing male way.

He pulled his key out of the lock, then turned his gaze on her. "Change your mind?" He glanced down at the book in her hand. "Want me to return Cullen's book?" He added a grin that should be labeled as dangerous.

Holly leaned against the side of the bookstore and shrugged. "I have time to kill. Thought I'd see if you still wanted to get a drink. Unless"—she opened her eyes wide—"you really are afraid that I'm a stalker with murder on my mind."

A small smile tugged at his mouth as he shoved his keys into his pants pocket. "If not murder, then what—sex?"

Oh yeah. Wait, no! God, she was weak tonight. Maybe it was her bad week. She decided to change tactics. "I asked you out for a drink, Brockman. All you have to say is that you aren't interested." She turned and started to walk away.

"Does that work?" he called after her.

She'd only gone a couple feet and turned back. "What?"

"The offensive. Does it work?"

She couldn't help smiling. "Usually. But then, I don't usually have to beg men for their company."

He directed his gaze in a slow examination down her body, clad in a burgundy tank top and form-fitting jeans, then back to her face. His green eyes darkened. "Tell me more about this begging."

Down, girl. What was it about him? She shot back, "For that, you'd have to buy the drinks."

He stepped closer, throttling his voice down to a dangerous rumble. "Sex on the Beach?"

She swore the ocean roared in her head. Her hormones surged up into huge waves of longing, washing over her. "You're offering me sex on the beach?"

His grin widened, crinkling his gorgeous eyes. "The drink. What did you think I meant?"

Her thighs tightened in response. *Get a grip, Hillbay—it's just a reaction to a handsome man and a long dry spell of no sex.* Holly was all for sex, but on her terms. She always kept her emotions in check. She was the cool one—the one that walked away when the relationship had played out. It was time to take back the power. She said, "That information will cost you more than the price of a drink."

He didn't hesitate. "Name your price."

"Steak." She was hungry. And food might keep her from thinking about sex.

"Done. You can follow me in your car."

She was practically dizzy from the pace he set. Or maybe that was pent-up lust breaking free. "Follow you where?"

"My house. On the beach. I'll make the drinks and we'll grill some steaks out on my deck and watch the waves. Or maybe listen to the waves, since it's dark out." His grin suggested more than wave-watching.

She thought about that, but in the end, Wes had what she wanted. Information on Cullen.

Not sex.

She lifted her chin. "I'll follow you. I can spare an hour or so."

He nodded like it was no more than he expected.

Annoyed, she said, "I'm not sleeping with you."

He moved up to her until she felt the brush of his breath. "No?"

She felt a tremor in her belly that spread wet heat. *Keep control of the situation,* she reminded herself. "I don't go to bed on the first date."

He reached down and picked up her free hand in his larger one. "Kiss on the first date?"

She should put a stop to this. But the feel of his hand wrapped around hers was warm and sensual. She opened her mouth to tell him they weren't dating, but ended up saying, "If I like the man."

He ran his thumb over her palm. "You like me. Make out?"

Regaining her wits, she jerked her hand away. "Ain't gonna happen, book boy."

His face blanked at the nickname, then a grin spread out over his face. "Why don't we go to my house and take these rules of yours for a test drive?"

She was playing with fire. She knew it but couldn't stop herself. Wes was not the man she expected when she walked into his bookstore. There was so much more, and she had a strange compulsion to peel back the layers and find out just who this man was.

Could she do that and keep her clothes on? Or maybe do it naked, but keep her emotions in check?

She was going to find out. "Lead on, book boy."

Chapter 2

Wes flipped the steaks on the grill, then turned to watch Holly walk out the sliding glass door holding two drinks. She had volunteered to make the drinks in his kitchen while he cooked the steaks. He grinned. "Sex on the Beach?"

She handed him a glass. "Is that a fixation for you?"

Wes put down his tongs, then took her drink and set both glasses down on the table. He stepped closer to see if she'd move away. "Sex? Or doing it on the beach?"

She held her ground. "On the beach."

"No." The roar of the waves mixed with the crackle of flames in the fire pit and the sizzle of the steak on the barbeque. He put his hands on her wrists, then ran his palms up her bare arms to her shoulders. "But I'm fixated on you at the moment." Her skin felt smooth and he wanted more. He couldn't remember the last time he'd been so attracted to a woman. What had she been doing following Cullen out to the dock? That was part of the attraction, trying to figure her out. "Who are you, Holly? Why did you come to my book club tonight?"

She stared at him. "I've been looking for a new hobby."

He nearly laughed. "I don't think so. I think you're after something, but I can't put my finger on what it is."

She grinned. "You haven't figured it out by now? It's the steak. I've been looking for a man to cook for me."

He knew they were playing a game, knew he should push her harder to find out what she was really after. But her skin felt so good, her body was so close, and he wanted her. "Yeah? Do you find that sexy in a man, Holly?"

She tilted her head slightly. "It's on my list."

"Ah, the list. If I remember correctly, this was on your list, too." He lowered his head slowly, giving her time to turn away. But she didn't and Wes kissed her. Her mouth was soft and welcoming. He slid one hand around her back and another behind her neck. When she didn't object, he pulled her closer to his body. She tasted hot and slightly sweet from the drink. His blood pressure shot up. He wanted more of her, and slid his tongue deep in her mouth. She put her arms around him and Wes went hard and ready.

Holly pulled back. "Is that the steaks burning?"

He blinked. "Hell." Letting her go, he rescued the steaks. *Unbelievable.* A single kiss had rattled him. He carried the steaks into the house, added a baked potato from the microwave, and took a deep breath. Then he went back out and put the plates on the table.

Holly sat down. She appeared relaxed, but the flush across her face suggested that was a lie. She better damn well be as overheated as he was. Cutting into his steak, he said, "We can check off the kiss."

She looked at him blankly.

Thank God—she was rattled. He grinned, feeling a little more in control. "Your first date list."

"Right." She set to work eating her steak.

He watched her, enjoying the view. Then he asked, "Do I get to know your last name?"

"Hillbay. What's Cullen's last name?" Holly took a drink of her Sex on the Beach, then fixed her gaze on him.

"Vail."

"That easy?" She looked surprised.

Wes shrugged. "I don't care about Cullen. But you interest me."

"Don't get too interested." She took a bite of her baked potato, then asked, "Is that Cullen's boat he and Tanya went out on?"

But she did care about Cullen for some reason. What was she after? "You're very interested in Cullen."

She looked up from cutting another piece of steak. "If it's his boat, I'll know where to return the book."

She was a good liar, but it made no sense. She wouldn't go to this much trouble when all she had to do was leave the book with him and he'd return it. That's what most women would do. "Let's talk about you. What kind of work do you do?"

"I'm in real estate. The steak is good. You're not a bad cook, Brockman."

He noted the slip of calling him by his last name. It was the second time tonight. Most women didn't do that, unless they were in certain fields, like physical education or police work. Wes was not a fan of cops. To cover his thoughts, he nodded at her compliment and said, "Want some coffee?"

She opened her mouth to answer when a weak, pathetic bark caught their attention. It sounded like it was right below Wes's deck. A wretched little whimper followed. Wes frowned, wondering what that noise was from.

Holly matched his frown. "Do you have a dog?"

He shook his head. "No, but whatever it is sounds sick or hurt." He got up, went into the kitchen, and found a flashlight. When he went back out, Holly stood at the edge of his deck, looking over the rail. "See anything?"

She shook her head. "I hear crying, though. Like a puppy." Turning her head, she met his gaze. "It does sound hurt."

To back her up, the creature whimpered again.

Wes opened the gate and started down the stairs. He stopped, turned, and got an eyeful of Holly's breasts. She was right behind him, one step up. He sucked in a breath, catching her slightly spicy citrus scent. It was a real effort to angle his gaze from her full breasts to her face. "I was going to tell you to stay on the deck."

"Enjoying the view?" She looked down at him.

He wanted to drop the flashlight, pick her up, and go to his bedroom. Grinning, he said, "I'm alive and male, so hell yes." Just as he was thinking of getting her naked, he heard the cry again. He sighed and made his way down the steps. Once on the sand, he followed the sounds and swung the flashlight beam under his deck.

The shaft of light caught a pair of golden eyes in a little fur face. He ran the beam over the animal. It looked like a little ball of misery with eyes.

"A puppy," Holly said softly. She had dropped to her knees. "He's all wet and shivering. Is that blood?"

Crouched down beside her, Wes could see the little guy was terrified. And hurt. Blood appeared to be seeping from one ear. "Looks like someone tried to drown it."

Holly stiffened beside him. "Bastards."

"Yeah." There were a lot of bastards out there. He noticed that Holly didn't argue with him or deny that someone would try to drown a puppy. She looked at the facts—a puppy rarely ended up in the ocean all by himself. "Hold the light and I'll try to get under there and coax him out."

"You hold it, I'll get him."

Before he could argue, Holly started forward on all fours. "He's hurt, Holly, he might bite. Get back here—"

"Shut up, Brockman, you'll scare him."

She was halfway to the pup. Wes closed his mouth and kept the light on the shivering little dog. But his gaze went to her very shapely ass, wiggling as she made her way to the animal. The sight made his blood rush to his dick.

Her voice floated back. "It's okay, little guy. I'm not going to hurt you."

She stopped a foot from the puppy and kept talking to him. The puppy cried, wriggled, and finally went right to her. She scooped him up in one arm and crawled back out.

Lucky dog, Wes thought. Holly had nestled him up to her breasts.

"He's soaking wet," she said as she shimmied out from under the deck and she stood up. "His ear is bloody and he's shaking."

Wes conceded that the puppy deserved her body heat, but he was still envious. Putting his hand on her shoulder, he said, "Let's get him inside." They walked up the stairs and into his house.

She stopped in the kitchen and looked around blankly. "Do you have a first aid kit?"

Even holding a bedraggled, wet dog, he was attracted to her. But she was right, they needed to take care of the puppy. "I have one in my bathroom, come on." He led the way through his living room with his large fish tank on the left. Once he reached the front door, he turned left down a short hallway that opened to his bedroom. He had French doors that led to the deck so he could let in the ocean breeze. He ignored that, and his king-sized bed with its burgundy comforter which matched Holly's top, to make a right into his master bathroom.

Holly followed him into the bathroom. The puppy had stopped crying and nestled up against her chest. Her shirt was soaked. Wes leaned down and took a closer look at the puppy. He appeared to be a Golden Retriever mix. Clearly, he was smart enough to save himself from drowning. His right ear had a cut that had stopped bleeding. One of his back legs also had a minor cut. Mostly, Wes thought he was scared, exhausted from swimming in the ocean, and probably hungry.

He went to the cupboard and got out his first aid kit, a couple towels, and a washcloth. He heard Holly running water into the sink. When he turned around, she had talked the dog into letting her stand him in the sink full of water and rinse the sand and blood off him. For a dog that almost drowned, that was damned surprising. "What did you do, hypnotize him?"

She was bent over, putting her very fine ass next to his hips. Then she looked up in the mirror. "He's too tired to fight me, I think."

Wes set the first aid stuff on the counter and held open a thick towel. "Let's dry him off."

Holly lifted the dog from the water and Wes wrapped him up in the towel, gently rubbing his fur. The warm water seemed to have stopped his shivering. Finally they had him as dry as they could get him. He said, "Hold him while I put first aid cream on his cuts."

She nestled the puppy to her chest. Wes leaned over, trying to ignore her boobs in his face, and put the cream on the dog.

He licked Wes's face.

Holly laughed, her breasts bouncing in his face. The temperature in the bathroom shot up to sizzling.

He stepped back, grabbed the cap to the tube, and said the first thing he thought of. "Your shirt is all wet and has blood on it. I'll get you one of mine." He left the bathroom, and felt a little cooler when he stepped into his bedroom. Going to his dresser, he opened a drawer and pulled out a T-shirt.

Holding the shirt, he turned around to see Holly standing by his bed cradling the puppy and smoothing her hand over his head.

Clearly, he was a smart dog. Wes said, "I'll hold him while you change."

Her gaze went to his face. He saw a gentle, almost naked longing, an expression that locked his breath in his chest. Without any real decision, he walked up to her, feeling the damp puppy between them. "He'll be okay. We'll feed him, he'll get some sleep and be good as new. But he's going to need a home." He reached out to push back a piece of hair that had fallen from her clip. "Want a dog?"

Her eyes hardened. "No. I don't have time for a dog. Or any animals." She shoved the dog at him and took the shirt. Then she went into the bathroom and closed the door.

Holly had to get herself under control. *Stupid puppy.* She had just felt sorry for it. What kind of monster tried to drown a puppy? But she knew, she'd been a cop for over five years and had seen plenty of monsters. Ripping off her shirt, she realized that her bra was also wet. She undid the clasp and took that off, too.

Then she pulled on the soft black T-shirt Wes had given her. It smelled like him. Without her bra on, the shirt rubbed her nipples and made her feel restless and hot.

Horny.

She looked at her flushed face in the mirror. *Be honest,* she told herself, *a man rescuing a puppy is sexy. Big deal. Get over it.* She needed to find out all she could about Cullen and get the hell out of Wes Brockman's house. She was here to do a job. Nothing else. She reached up, took the clip from her hair, and finger-combed it. She tried to blank out the way Wes had looked when he asked her if she wanted the dog. Like he wanted to give her whatever she desired.

Holly didn't need animals or men in her life. She knew exactly what she was—an excellent PI. Her life was her work. She'd learned the hard way that love and a family of her own weren't for her. She didn't make those kinds of commitments anymore.

Not even to a dog.

She expertly twisted her hair back up, then picked up her shirt. Wes was right, there was blood on it. She rinsed all the dog hair and sand out of the sink, and washed the blood out of her shirt and bra. After drying them the best she could, she finally balled them up to stuff in her purse.

Having stamped out her moment of weakness, she left the bathroom to go find Wes. She went through the living room and into the kitchen but both he and the puppy were missing. Weird. She looked out on the deck and didn't see him there either.

Holly turned back and looked around the kitchen. There were two doorways, the one she had come through from the living room, and a second one that was closer to the sliding glass door.

A dining room, maybe?

There was a light burning so Holly walked into the room. On the left was a beautiful bay window that had a built-in seat to watch the waves during the day. Tonight she got a view of the full moon reflecting off the ocean. There was an entire wall of bookshelves across the room. To separate this room from the living room was a big aquarium that hummed and gurgled while colorful fish swam. A doorway to the living room opened up on the left of the fish tank. She could make a big circle, going right into the kitchen, then right again, and end up back in this room. Next to the fish tank were two deep recliners with a table and lamp between them. A baseball and a book sat on the table.

Certainly not a dining room, she guessed it was Wes's reading room or library. She walked to the massive bookcase. Right away she could see that he liked mysteries and autobiographies on sports stars.

She whirled around at the sound of footsteps. Wes filled the doorway, holding the puppy and a plastic bowl. He lifted the bowl and said, "Dog food from a neighbor."

She tried to look casual. "I wondered where you went."

He bent over and set the puppy on the floor with the bowl of food. Once the puppy stuck his face into the bowl and started chowing down, Wes stood up to his full height of at least six feet. He dropped his gaze over her, slow and measured, then said, "You look hot in my T-shirt."

To keep her mind off the heat in his green eyes, she glanced over her shoulder at the bookshelf behind her. "Uh, you really do like to read."

"Ever since I can remember." Wes walked into the room and went to the table to scoop up the baseball. He tossed it back and forth in his hands with a practiced ease, even while looking at her. "Do you like to read?"

"I like movies better, but sure, I read." It was mesmerizing to watch him toss the ball back and forth. "Play much?"

"What's that?"

She realized he wasn't really aware of what he was doing with the ball. "Baseball," she said dryly.

He looked down at his hands, then tossed the ball into one of the chairs and walked toward her. "I played a bit when I was a kid."

Her mystery man was back, and standing too close, making her restless. Time to find out what she needed to know and leave. Holding her spine straight, she said, "You never answered me. Was that Cullen's boat he and Tanya got on tonight?"

His full mouth tilted in a sexy, rueful grin. "Real estate, huh?"

"What?" She frowned and tried to follow him. After a second, she said, "Oh, my job? Yeah. Why?"

He put one hand on the bookcase just over her head. "Because you're after something, Hillbay."

The challenge crackled in the tiny space between them. She could not have looked away from him if the house were on fire. He returned her stare with a similar concentration. He couldn't know she was a private investigator or he'd lord it over her. Press his advantage. So what was up? Did Wes Brockman have something to hide? She met his challenge with, "And you aren't the average bookstore owner, Brockman."

His green eyes grew secretive and, yet, even sexier. "I love books. Look at my library."

She couldn't look at his library because she was looking at him. "Nope. You only opened the bookstore three years ago. This has to be your second career. What was your first?" The one she guessed he'd made a lot of money at. He looked like money, and she didn't need to be a real estate agent to know that this beach house wasn't cheap.

The silence stretched out. She could hear the puppy pushing the bowl on the wood floor as he ate. She could hear the waves from the ocean outside. She could hear the thump of her heart beating.

Finally Wes said, "It's Cullen's boat." Then he slid his hand down the side of the bookcase, over her shoulder, and wrapped it around the back of her neck. "Truce for tonight? No more questions?"

He had the most incredible eyes. But she had work to do. "I need to go."

"Stay." It came out a rough whisper.

His fingers on her neck were warm and solid. Needy little tremors started again deep in her belly. Beneath his shirt her nipples hardened. His mouth was two inches from hers. She could see the shadow on his jaw, knew if she rubbed her face against him, she'd feel the rough beginnings of a beard. What made her so powerfully attracted to him? She had never felt anything like it. Was it his secrets, or his sex appeal? "I need to—"

He lowered his mouth another inch. His rubbed his hand over the bare skin just below her hairline on the back of her neck. "Tell me what you need, Holly."

Hot sex, now. Her heartbeat ramped up, pumping her blood into a painful throb. "You're trying to seduce me." Had it been that long since a man had seduced her? Yeah, it had.

"Trying, my ass. I'm succeeding." Using his hand on the back of her neck, he pulled her a half inch closer and brushed his mouth over hers. Then he made a thick sound in his throat and wrapped his other arm around her, pulling her hard into a deep, wet kiss.

She felt his strength and felt herself surrendering to it. His body heat sank deep into her skin. He shifted his mouth and teased her tongue with his. Everything heated, and Holly met his tongue play. She ran her hands under his shirt, feeling his hot skin, pulled smooth and tight over hard muscles.

She wanted to lose herself in Wes.

The realization shocked her. Holly pulled back.

Wes let her go. Dropping his arms to his side, he looked down. "Afraid?"

More like pissed. Pissed that he could overwhelm her like that. Make her forget herself. "Get over yourself, Brockman. I told you I don't sleep with men on the first date." *Date. Too personal.* She hurried around him, putting distance between them. "And this wasn't a date." She went into the kitchen, grabbed her purse, damp shirt, and bra off the table.

The puppy woke up from his nap and jumped up to dash around her feet, barking and whining.

Behind her, Wes said, "He wants you to pick him up."

She looked down. The little guy was wiggling his entire body, making funny little whiny noises, then jumping up on his back legs.

She longed to pick him up. She longed to stay and get naked with Wes. But she had a job to do. Her work was her life, not a silly puppy and an overwhelming man. She took a breath. "Thanks for dinner. 'Bye, Wes." She moved around the puppy and walked to the front door.

Wes caught her arm before she reached the door. "Hey."

She turned around, ready to smack him. Or maybe shoot him. Anything to get free. "What?"

He grinned. "It was a date. You know where to find me when you're ready for date number two."

Chapter 3

Holly was just pouring her first cup of morning coffee, and trying to think of anything but Wes Brockman, when someone knocked on her front door.

"Damn." She had spent a couple hours working last night after leaving Wes's house, had gotten to bed after midnight, and dragged her tired ass out of bed for a run this morning. She hoped whoever it was would go away, but then she heard the key in the lock.

Figured. She knew who it was. Her two brothers, fraternal twins and the bane of her childhood, let themselves into her house. They both hovered around the six-foot mark, had sandy brown hair and blue eyes. Joe was a little taller and thinner, and tended to actually think things out once in a while. Seth had more bulk, charisma to spare, and a hair-trigger temper that he'd learned to control. Nearly ten years as sheriff's deputies had smoothed out some of their rough edges.

Joe came into the kitchen first, carrying a pink box that smelled like heaven. "Better be coffee. I brought donuts."

That made her suspicious. "What do you want?"

Seth came into the kitchen with a smirk. Reaching over her head to get a couple of mugs down from the cupboard, he said, "We're here to check up on you, AP."

Holly worked hard not to react to the nickname. AP stood for Anti-Princess. She was the youngest of the three of them.

Her mom had wanted a little princess, but she'd gotten Holly instead. By the time Holly was seven, her mom figured out she wasn't cut out for parenting two rough and tumble boys and a girl who was more hellion than princess. They'd only seen their mom a handful of times since then. She turned her attention to figuring out why both her brothers had paid her a morning visit with donuts. "You two looking for some extra work?" Sometimes her brothers moonlighted for her when she had the work for them. She added, "I don't have any work for you right now."

Joe dumped the box of donuts on Holly's table at the end of the kitchen overlooking her small patio. He walked back to pour his coffee. Looking down at her, he said, "Maybe we wanted to hang out with our little sister."

Holly snorted and went to the table. Lucky for her brothers, she found a chocolate donut. "You don't bring me chocolate donuts unless you want something." She looked at Joe and Seth. "Which one of you is in trouble?"

Seth went to the table and fished out a donut with sprinkles. "We're not in trouble, are you?"

She had spent nearly three years working her ass off to build her private investigation agency, *Hillbay Investigations*. For the most part, Holly was a one-woman show and liked it that way. But her brothers were damn good cops and they heard things in the community. They'd probably heard she lost a client. "Nope. No trouble I can't handle."

Joe leaned back against the counter by the coffeemaker. "You know, Seth, sometimes I think Holly believes we're stupid."

"Duh," Holly said.

Seth managed to swallow the better part of his donut, then sighed. "Now that's not nice, AP. Joe and me are here to help you."

Argh. She lifted her gaze to Seth's matching blue stare.

"I lose one client and you two suddenly think I need the cavalry?" That was just insulting. "I signed a new client yesterday that will help offset the loss. Now go catch some bad guys and leave me alone."

Seth frowned. "What client? You lost a client?"

Well, crap. She was tired, she hadn't been able to take a breath without thinking about Wes since last night, and now she'd just told her brothers information she'd intended to keep to herself. "And got a new client," she snapped.

Joe set down his coffee cup and locked his gaze on her. "What happened, Holly?"

She shrugged. "A client I did routine new-hire backgrounds for went with another PI. No big deal." Except that she thought that Brad the Cad was behind it, but that was her problem, not her brothers'. She didn't dare let her brothers know her suspicions.

Seth's voice dropped to pissy. "See, Joe, she thinks we're dumb."

Joe kept his slow and steady gaze on her. "Holly, been on any dates lately?"

Startled at the change of subject, she knew her eyes went wide. "What's that?"

"Dates?" Joe said with a smirk. "With a guy. You know, go out, have drinks, make out. That kind of thing?"

What? Immediately her evening with Wes the night before swam up in her brain. Had they been spying on her? Holly pulled herself together. She was being ridiculous. "No. Are you two so hard up for dates that you have to live vicariously through my social life?"

Seth grinned. "Checked your e-mail lately?"

She shot back, "Why? Are you out of Viagra?"

Joe roared out laughing. "She got you with that one."

Seth leaned down toward Holly. "Do you like the taste of soap, baby sister?"

She sipped some coffee and made a quick decision. Whatever mysterious thing that had brought her brothers to her house must have something to do with e-mail. She shoved her elbow into Seth's rib cage to push him away from her, then walked through the kitchen and turned left into the living room. Left of that was her dining room, which she used as a home office. Her computer was already booted up. She sat in her chair and signed onto her Internet server.

Joe and Seth followed her into the room.

She scanned her inbox and her gaze caught on an e-mail from The O'Man. He had a blog—the correct term was Web log—which was a Web site where people could keep sort of a public diary. Holly opened the blog and looked around, quickly discovering that the O'Man was some kind of sexist Neanderthal. He had a special feature where if a person signed up with their e-mail address, he would send the day's blog to that e-mail address. Holly hadn't signed up. Obviously her brothers had signed her up. Her soon-to-be-bleeding brothers.

On the blog, she read the latest entry: *The ball-buster. You know the type. The kind of anti-princess type of woman who carries a gun, maybe even a badge, and thinks she can take down a man. Maybe, deep down, she wants to be a man.*

Penis Envy, some doc had said.

But I'm The O'Man, and I can make these ball-buster women heel. And beg. And cry out, "O'Man!"

Holly lifted her gaze, first looking at Joe, then Seth. Growing up, her brothers had teased her about being a tomboy. These days, they harped on her recent lack of boyfriends while building her PI business. But this didn't seem like their style. She leaned back in her chair and studied them. "Why did you send this to me?"

Joe slapped his coffee cup on her desk. Even with her desk between them, she could feel his anger. His blue eyes were cold as steel. "Do you know who this guy is, Hol?"

She realized that she had misjudged the situation. Her brothers weren't there to harass her or pick up some extra work. They were pissed. "No. Why, what's up?"

Seth glanced at Joe, then at Holly. "Don't act dense. That's you he's talking about, Holly. I recognized you when I read his blog last night, which is why I sent it to you. Do you think it's Brad?"

It finally slammed into her. Oh God, they thought her ex-boyfriend was behind this blog. Holly had dated Bradley Knoll a few years ago; in fact, she'd been engaged to him. It had ended badly. Brad did his best to badmouth Holly and her family whenever he could. "Brad the Cad didn't do this Web site. He's too intent on being a defender of women and children to risk it." Brad used his law degree to sue everyone he could for any perceived offense against women and children. Truth and justice were flexible ideals in Brad's world. What mattered to him were money, prestige, and face time on TV.

Seth stood up from where he'd parked his butt on the side of her desk, his handsome face hardening to pure cop. "Anti-Princess. Where'd this guy on the Web site get that? Only Joe and I ever call you that and Brad knew it."

Joe leaned forward, putting his elbows on his knees, and zeroed his stern gaze in on her. "Is it someone else? Some guy you dated?"

Holly rolled her eyes. Every now and again, Seth and Joe had a rush of testosterone which sparked the asinine idea that they needed to protect her. "It's not me that guy's talking about. I don't have the slightest idea who this yahoo is. But"—she glared at both of them—"if I did know him, and he was talking about me, I wouldn't need your help setting him straight."

Seth opened his mouth, but Joe cut him off. "That's the truth?"

Tamping down on her exasperation, she put herself in their places for a moment. What if a woman had used one of her brothers then made fun of him on a Web site? Would Holly go after her?

Damn right she would.

She kept her answer simple. "Yes."

Seth moved around the desk, put his hand on the back of

Holly's chair, and leaned down. "I know you can take care of yourself, AP. But Joe and me, we're family. You would come to us if some guy screwed you over, right?"

Only if she wanted to bail her brothers out of jail. Cops didn't do well in jail, so that wasn't an option. Besides, she didn't need her brothers to do that whole knight-in-shining-armor crap. Holly liked to do her own ass-kicking when the situation called for it. She met Seth's gaze. "Absolutely."

Joe laughed. "She's lying. We'd have to lock her in a room with no coffee or chocolate and sweat it out of her." He moved from the other side of her desk to pace around her living room.

Seth lowered his face closer to hers. "Don't think we wouldn't do that if you were in trouble."

She didn't think that for a second. "Don't you guys have a job or something?"

Joe came back, carrying a shirt. "Thought you said you weren't dating anyone."

She looked up to see Wes's shirt, which she had left on the couch. With a deadpan expression, she said, "I'm not. I just have sex with a different man every night and steal their shirts. But I don't date them."

Joe blinked like someone had suddenly turned a strobe light on him.

Seth choked on his coffee.

Holly said, "Any other questions? Or do you think I can go to work now? I need to drop that shirt off to the man I borrowed it from and then do some surveillance."

Joe tossed the shirt at her. "Surveillance for your new case? What's the case about?"

Holly caught the shirt and set it on the desk. "A cheater. I'm getting evidence so the man can invoke a clause in his prenuptial that will seriously reduce the wife's payout in the divorce."

"Domestics can get ugly," Seth reminded her as he walked back from getting a third donut.

"This one is pretty basic. Except the husband had the wrong man. But I found the right one last night." Holly caught them up on the book club. She explained about Tanya and Cullen. "I staked out her car last night." Glancing at her notes, she read, "Cullen dropped Tanya off at her car in the public parking lot behind the bookstore at ten-thirty P.M. The two of them played tongue hockey for fifteen minutes, then Tanya got in her car and drove away at ten-forty-five. I followed her home and watched her go inside the house. I stayed another twenty minutes, but she appeared in for the night. I'll have all the photos and reports I need on this one inside of a week or so. They aren't even hiding the affair."

Seth said, "Standard boring stakeout stuff. Let's talk about the dinner with this bookstore owner. You ended up with his shirt how?"

Holly just shook her head at her brothers. What had she expected? They were men. "I held my gun on the bookstore owner and made him take his shirt off. It's my hobby. And if you two don't leave, I'm going to get my gun and start shooting."

Joe picked up his coffee cup and looked at Seth. "I think we should leave before she gets in a bad mood."

Seth laughed. "Ever seen her in a good mood?"

Joe studied her. "Now that would be scary." Grinning, he lifted his cup. "I'm taking my coffee with me."

Holly waved him away. "Whatever. You both still owe me a hundred bucks. Don't think I've forgotten!"

Joe looked back at her. "We said six years."

Holly narrowed her gaze. "You said five! You said I wouldn't last five years as a cop. I lasted five and a half years!" Her brothers had predicted that Holly was too much of a rule-breaker—as she remembered them saying, *"a kick-ass rule-breaker"*—to deal with the rules and regulations that govern a police officer's actions.

Joe shook his head. "Six. But math never was your

strongest subject, now was it, Holly?" He turned and strode
out the door, with Seth following behind.

She waited until the door closed before she smiled. They'd
had this same argument for years, ever since Holly quit the
sheriff's department and started her PI agency. But her brothers knew how much her PI agency meant to her. They knew
she had nothing else—and she never would. Any dreams she
might have once had about a husband and family . . .

Holly shut down that train of thought. The O'Man's blog
was still up on her computer screen. She looked it over and
got the gist of it—a knuckle-dragger bragging that he could
seduce any woman based on her "type." A couple types he
listed were Anti-Princess, Invisible Woman, Wonder Woman,
Barbie Babe, Cat Woman. Holly stopped reading. She wasn't
interested in the women he supposedly seduced, but in the
man's real identity. She couldn't help it—it was her nature to
want to solve mysteries. What made a guy want to hide behind a ridiculous nickname on a Web site and try to convince
the world he could seduce any woman? Holly sighed and
closed down the Web site. She had her own work to do.

She turned her attention back to her case. She planned to
follow Tanya today, starting with Tanya's yoga class at eleven.
Holly didn't expect to find Cullen at the yoga class, but she
wanted to cover all her bases. Still, that left her an hour and
a half before the class started. She could go into her office
and catch up on a few things.

Her gaze caught on Wes's shirt sitting on the desk next to
her mouse.

Or she could run by the bookstore and return Wes's shirt
to him. Last night, she'd been caught off guard by the sexual
attraction between them. She'd meant to use him for information and had been shocked at the strength of her reaction
to Wes's sex appeal.

This morning, she wondered what the big deal was. She
hadn't had sex in a while. She liked sex. She liked men. She

just didn't want a relationship. What was the harm in a couple of dates, maybe a couple of passionate nights, as long as she kept her priorities in place? Wes didn't seem like he was looking for anything more than a few laughs and a sex partner.

She stood up and grabbed the T-shirt. What harm could it do to drop by the bookstore and return the shirt? See where things went from there?

A half hour later, Holly was balancing two cups of hot takeout coffee, with Wes's shirt hanging over her arm, as she walked toward the bookstore. She caught Wes just as he was unlocking the door to Books on the Beach. He looked suave and sexy in a pair of well-cut slacks and a black button-down shirt. His hair had a touch of shower dampness darkening the sun streaks. A thread of desire tightened her stomach at the sight of him. "Hey, book boy."

After sliding the key out of the lock, he turned and the morning sun sparkled in his green eyes. "Ah, my favorite stalker." He held the door open for her.

Holly walked past him, very aware of him watching her. Since her plan was to put Tanya under surveillance, she'd dressed in a pair of jeans, tennis shoes, a black T-shirt, and twisted her hair up into a clip. She had a moment of self-consciousness, then shoved it aside. She wasn't here for his fashion opinion.

He walked toward her, took the coffees from her, and set them down. Taking hold of her bare arms, he leaned down and slowly kissed her. Then he lifted his head and crinkled his eyes with a sexy smile. "Good morning. Tell me you're stalking me for a second date."

That molasses kiss moved languidly through her veins until it hit her heart and kicked out a rush of adrenaline-laced desire. Holly took a deep breath and reminded herself she was going to take control. She knew what she wanted. "I came to return your shirt." She pulled it off her arm and handed it to Wes.

He took the shirt and tossed it on the counter without looking. He kept his green gaze on her. "And?"

Damn, he wasn't buying her excuse and unaffected demeanor. "And to see if the puppy is okay."

He grinned at her. "If you want to know, you'll have to come over tonight to see for yourself." He rubbed his right hand over her bare arm. "I'll take you to dinner wherever you want to go. Then we'll go back to my house, take the puppy for a long walk on the beach, put him to bed, and then I'll have you all to myself."

Holly was surprised to see he'd been thinking about her as much as she'd been thinking about him. Only tonight she planned to do this on her terms. "No."

"No?" His hand froze on her arm.

She shook her head, taking a step back to lean against the counter. She slid her purse off her arm and set it down. "We'll do pizza and a movie at my house." He wouldn't have her so off-balance and overwhelmed if they were at her house. And the silly little puppy wouldn't tug at something she didn't want to feel.

He surprised her by laughing. Sliding his hand up over the curve of her shoulder, he said, "Are you asking me on a *date*, Hillbay?"

The feel of his hand on her skin was warm, sensual, and way too sexy. But if she shrugged his hand off, he'd know he was getting to her. As if she hadn't felt his good morning kiss arrow right through her center and make her want more. So much more. Instead she kept her breathing even. "You don't get out much, do you, Brockman? If you want to call pizza and a DVD at my house a date, knock yourself out."

He dropped his hand and reached past her over the counter to grab a pad of paper and a pen. Handing them to her, he said, "Write down your address." He picked up one of the coffees and took a drink.

She wrote down her address and handed it back to him. To show him her indifference, she said, "Seven o'clock or I'll eat all the pizza myself."

Wes took the pad but his gaze stayed fastened on her. "It's a *date,* Holly. I'll be there and I'll bring the wine."

His words were low, full of promise, and they tightened her gut with anticipation. How the hell did he do that? She turned around and watched as he walked around the counter, tore off the paper where she'd written the address, and stuck it in his shirt pocket. She was trying to think of a reply when she realized that Wes's gaze had caught on something behind her. A faint frown line burrowed between his eyebrows. Her cop instincts automatically kicked in. "What's wrong?"

His gaze swung to her, but the sexual promise had vanished. "The door to the meeting room is closed. It was open when I left last night." His shoulders tensed and faint worry lines shadowed his mouth.

She turned and looked behind her. The door was closed. Seeing him start to move around the counter, she walked over to block him. "Wes, are you positive you left the door open?"

He stopped and looked down at her. "Yes." He set his hands on her shoulders. "Don't get in the way. Stay here."

She was aware of his strength, and the worry tensing his hands. "Listen, let me—" She was talking to herself. He was fast, damn fast. He stepped to the side, walked around her, and headed toward the door.

Holly reached inside her purse on the counter and got her gun out. By the time she unlocked the safety, she reached Wes's side. As he pushed open the door, she stepped in front of him and raised her gun.

But the man on the floor had already been shot. From what she could see, he had a head and a chest wound. *Professional,* she thought. Instinct and training took over and she started assessing the danger.

"Holy Christ, that's Cullen," Wes said, so close his words tickled her neck.

Quickly, Holly looked around the room. She didn't see anyone else. From memory, she knew there was a small bathroom off to the right and another door next to that. It had been closed last night so she didn't know what was in there. To Wes, she ordered, "Stay here."

Carefully, she walked into the room and went straight to the bathroom. It was clear. She went to the second door and eased it open. It was a combination office and storage room. No one was in there, and the back door that led to the alley behind the store was still locked from the inside.

Then she went to the victim. The entry wounds in his head and chest didn't look too bad, but she knew the exit wounds in his back would be a lot worse when the coroner turned him. Blood had seeped and stained the carpet beneath him where he lay between the meeting table and the storage room/office door. From the way he was positioned, she thought he must have been shot while standing and facing where Wes stood. She knew he was dead, but she crouched down and put two fingers against his throat anyway. Then she stood up, engaged the safety on her gun, and moved to Wes. "He's dead."

Wes ran his hand around the back of his neck, then dropped it and locked his gaze onto her. "No shit. I can see that for myself. The question is, who the hell are you?"

"Don't freak." She knew it was a fair question since she had just pulled a gun out of her purse. But his attitude was cold and accusing, probably because he hadn't thought he was dating a woman with a gun. He'd thought she was a nice, tame real estate agent. "I'm an ex-cop, now a private investigator. That's why I was at your book club last night. I didn't realize it until then, but Cullen is connected to the case I'm working on."

Suspicion coated his voice. "Does this case you're working on have anything to do with me?"

Jeez, there was a murdered body ten feet away and he was making it about himself. "No. At first I thought you were the man my client's wife was sleeping with, but I soon realized it's him." She tilted her head toward the body.

Wes turned to look at Cullen, then back to her. A beat of time passed. He stepped toward her, putting both hands on her arms to stare at her with his steely green gaze. "How do I know you're telling the truth?"

Uneasiness sliced her professional calm, but she didn't let him see it. "Since I have the gun, I guess you're just going to have to trust me."

An aching silence hung between them. Finally, he let her go and said, "Looks that way, doesn't it? I'll call nine-one-one."

Chapter 4

"You're shitting me. Dude, take off," George said. Wes was on his cell phone outside the bookstore, and looked through the window at Holly, who was talking to a detective from the Santa Barbara Sheriff's Criminal Investigation Division. "No. I'm sticking."

George made a rude sound. "You think this is a fucking coincidence? You said the stiff was shot in the head and chest—a hit. In your bookstore. What? You want them to write you a message in black marker on your walls? It was a warning or a screw-up. Don't wait around to find out which!"

"I'm done running. I ran three years ago for a reason." *His sister.* God, he missed her. He knew he'd done the right thing then by disappearing. The thugs had used Michelle as a punching bag to try and convince Wes not to testify. Even now, rage roared through him at the memory. Michelle had been furious, too, and had told him he'd become the very thing their father had fought against—corrupt. Wes couldn't let her get hurt, or worse. He'd gotten her safely out of the way, done what he had to do, then he'd gone surfing one morning and disappeared, leaving his surfboard to wash up on the shore. His only regret was any grief Michelle suffered, but he stayed the hell away from her to keep her safe. His sister deserved her life. She deserved happiness. Once the people after him had realized he'd either died or bolted, they left his sister alone.

"Look, Wes, don't go noble on me. I hate noble."

He laughed. "Yeah, sure." George was not quite the badass he wanted Wes to believe he was. "I'm sticking. Cullen was a slug, but I doubt he deserved to die. I might be the reason he's dead. I'm staying."

George wasn't stupid; he knew Wes's weaknesses. "Yeah? What about your two clerks, Jodi and Kelly? What about your friends? The other members of the book club? What if they get killed?"

"And what if I leave and they get killed? We don't know what's going on. I'm going to find out." He watched through the window as Holly appeared to describe something to the detective. "And I know just who is going to help me."

"Are you out of your—"

Wes hung up the cell. Then he turned it off. George could scream at his voice mail. Sticking the cell in his pants pocket, he studied Holly. *An ex-cop. Damn.* And yeah, he believed her now that he'd seen her with the cops that had screamed up with lights and sirens blaring from his nine-one-one call. Wes knew cops.

His dad had been a well-known journalist with a nationally syndicated column, *Cop Scan*, dedicated to exposing police corruption and brutality. He'd grown up seeing the dark side of the thin blue line. His family had not been a favorite of the cops. Oh yeah, Wes knew cops. As a rule, he didn't like them, but he needed Holly. He headed back into the bookstore.

The detective saw him first and strode toward him. Lois Rodgers was a small woman with dark hair cut short to frame big brown eyes living in a serious face. But it was her vibrant energy that commanded attention. Stopping in front of him, she said, "Mr. Brockman, how do you think the victim got into your bookstore? Did you meet him here last night?"

Wes wondered what Holly had told her. "No. Cullen left right after the book club meeting was over. I didn't see him after that. I have no idea how Cullen got into the bookstore. The front door was locked when"—he glanced at Holly leaning against a bookshelf—"we came in this morning."

"Do you have an alarm system?"

"Yes. With a code. My employees and I know it, and both of them have keys."

She made notes on a five-by-seven yellow pad. "I'll need you to write down the names, addresses, and phone numbers of all your employees and anyone else who has the keys and alarm code."

"My two part-time clerks, Kelly and Jodi, both went to San Diego for a few days' vacation and to catch a concert. I'll give you their cell phone numbers, but they weren't even here. What else?"

Lois Rodgers looked up. "We'll need your fingerprints. For elimination purposes."

"There are thousands of fingerprints in the store. How will that help?" He wasn't sure how far his identity would hold. But he didn't think his fingerprints were in the police files anywhere under his real or fake name, so it really didn't matter.

She arched her brows with an accusatory gleam in her brown gaze. "You don't want to cooperate?"

He smiled. "Of course I do, Detective. I didn't realize pointing out obvious facts was uncooperative."

She narrowed her gaze, then said, "Do you have a gun, Mr. Brockman?"

"No." He didn't own a gun, but George had taught him to shoot. In the first months after he'd disappeared, he'd kept one of George's guns in the beach house, but over time, he'd gotten out of the habit.

She wrote another note, then asked, "Where were you last night?"

"Home all night."

Looking up, she asked, "Anyone see you?"

Wes kept his answers bland, ignoring his impatience. Holly must have told her. "Holly saw me until she left around ten. I read for a while and went to bed."

"Let's go back to Mr. Vail, the victim. Did you have problems with him?"

He thought about how to frame his answer. "Cullen was starting to cause tension in our book club by dating and dropping several of the women. However, it wasn't anything I couldn't handle. Otherwise, I didn't know the man well enough to have problems with him." That should cover anything that the book club members said. And it was the truth.

Rodgers zeroed her gaze in on him. "Did he date the same women you were interested in?"

Finally, his patience snapped and he looked down his nose at the small woman. "I'm a thirty-two-year-old man, Detective, and this isn't high school. I let a woman decide if she wants to date me, I don't compete with other men."

She didn't flinch or otherwise recognize his cold tone. "Good for you, Brockman. Now lose the attitude. I'm conducting a murder investigation and offending you is not my biggest worry."

He almost liked her. Lifting both hands with his palms up, he went for charm. "I'm trying to be helpful, Detective . . ." He trailed off when he spotted Holly heading toward the door. He brushed by Rodgers. "Holly, wait."

Holly stopped in the doorway.

"Brockman," Rodgers said, "we're not done."

Wes looked back at the Detective. "I'll be back in a minute."

Rodgers strode toward him, her short legs eating up the floor. "It's procedure to—"

Wes ignored her, took hold of Holly's arm, and they both walked outside. When Rodgers started to follow, he glared at her. "Detective, I have several lawyers on retainer. Up till now I haven't seen any reason to call them since you're just doing your job and I want this murderer caught. But if you start infringing on my rights, I will call all of them."

She stopped, her intelligent brown eyes reflective as she thought it over. Then she said, "Five minutes. And if you take off, I'll find you and drag you to the station in handcuffs."

"Threats," he sighed. "And not very original threats, either." He turned his back on her and looked at Holly.

Her light blue eyes were icy, her back was rigid, and she rocked slightly on the balls of her feet with edginess. "Let go of my arm and talk fast."

He dropped her arm, reading her impatience in her tight posture. She wasn't classically beautiful; she was attractive in an active, powerful way. It was her strong face, sexy body, and get-out-of-my-way attitude that he liked and admired. But right now, he had to concentrate on finding out what was going on. He decided to go on the offensive. "You're the one who used me, what are you all bent out of shape for?"

She stood still and raised her eyebrows. "What did I use you for?"

"Information on Cullen." He leaned casually against the side of the building. "And sex. You came to my store this morning hoping for a date to score with me tonight."

Her blue eyes thawed slightly. "You must feel so cheap. I was gonna buy you a pizza dinner first."

God, she made him want to laugh. She *had* used him—not that he cared. She'd been doing her job, and he was willing to sign up for her to use him sexually anytime she wanted to. But he needed to use her, as well. "Too late for that, but I have another proposal that will make an honest woman out of you."

Holly's mouth twitched. "You want to marry me?"

That slammed his brain with a case of shock and horror. "Hell, no!"

"No? Gosh, book boy, you really know how to make a girl feel special."

He thunked the back of his head against the wall. She was yanking his chain and he, like a total dumb shit, fell for it. "I want to hire you to find out who murdered Cullen, but I need to be in on the investigation. Sort of like partners."

The cloudy blue color in her eyes iced over. "No. I don't work with a partner." She reached into her purse.

Wes pushed off the wall and frowned, wondering what she was looking for in her purse. "You aren't going to shoot me, are you?"

Holly pulled her hand out, holding her car keys. "Don't be stupid, Wes. I'd never shoot you with all these cops around."

That's why he wanted Holly on this. She was smart, determined, and no one pushed her around. She'd proven to him the lengths she'd go to get information—infiltrating his book club and dating him. But he needed to accompany her as she investigated because she didn't know the truth. He did. And damn it, he'd been forced to run last time to keep his sister safe.

This time, he was going after the problem and resolving it. Wes wanted his life back—wanted his sister back. But he had to make sure it was safe before he approached Michelle. And he needed Holly to help him do that. Of course, he wasn't going to tell her anything about Michelle or his past, unless he had to. Distrust of cops was too ingrained in him. Instead, he used a more reliable method to get her cooperation. "I'll pay you double your rate."

She had started to walk away. Now she turned back. "Why? Rodgers is a damn good cop. There's a good chance she'll solve this case and you won't have to pay anything."

He shook his head. "I don't think so. Holly, what was Cullen doing in my bookstore? How did he and the murderer get inside? It was locked. You saw me lock the door last night and unlock it this morning. Your detective buddy is going to look for the easy answer, and that's me since it's my store."

He took a breath and added a little raw honesty. "I want to know. I have to know. Is that so hard to understand?"

She dropped her arm to her side with her car keys hanging from her fingertips. "You want to know bad enough to pay me double rates? Why not just hire another PI?"

He took a step closer. "I want you to investigate." He touched her face. "I know which women Cullen dated from the book club. Since he was murdered in the meeting room, it could be linked to that." He had no idea if that was true but it sounded good. "And they're more likely to talk to you if I'm there. Plus I know"—he paused as he tripped up on the tense—"or *knew* Cullen, so I might spot something you don't." Then he smiled at her. "And I like you."

Her face hardened. "This is business. I'll take the job with the terms that I decide how involved you will be."

Wes nodded, figuring that was the best he would get from her at the moment.

Holly reached back into her purse and pulled out a business card. "Call my cell when you're done here and we'll arrange a time to meet. Right now, I have to go see a client." She handed him the card.

Wes snagged her wrist, tugging her toward him. "This is about more than business." Then he let her go and turned back to his bookstore.

He heard Holly huff and stomp off. She really didn't like not having the last word.

Holly's eyes burned from doing computer searches on Cullen Vail. It turned out that Cullen had a record—he'd done some fast-talking swindling of women for a get-rich-quick pyramid scheme that caved pretty early into the game. That little escapade earned him probation and restitution.

Holly leaned back in her chair, tapping her pencil on her desk while looking at her poster from the old *Moonlighting*

TV show. She'd loved those shows when she'd been growing up. PIs got the job done that the cops couldn't.

And they didn't follow the rules.

Holly wasn't big on rules either. Neither, apparently, had been Cullen. So what had he been doing in that book club? Trolling for women? Maybe. A guy like him would probably buy into the stereotype that a bookish woman didn't get many dates, therefore she was an easy lay.

She couldn't think of any other reason he'd be there. He didn't seem the book-loving type.

So she could assume he was there to pick up women. And it was a fact that he had a record as a swindler. What if, Holly thought, she put those two things together, and someone from the book club was one of Cullen's past victims? That woman waited for the opportunity and killed him in revenge.

She liked it. That was a place to start. With the murder occurring not just in the bookstore, but the meeting room of the book club, on the very night of the last book club meeting, it was a logical leap that someone from the book club could be the murderer.

So was Holly really going to take the case? Hell yes. Double the money was a damn good offer, and she needed the money since losing one of her big clients. Her PI business was in the black, and she meant to keep it that way. If she didn't succeed as a PI, that left her nothing. She'd be the failure her mother believed her to be.

But Holly wasn't a failure. She was good at her job and this case was the perfect opportunity to prove it. It wasn't every day that a murder in a locked bookstore came her way. It was the kind of case that would require all her skills. It caught her interest.

As did Wes Brockman. He looked like a rich playboy who had a bookstore as a hobby. But she didn't think that was the full truth. So what was his story?

She looked at the clock in her office. It was just after seven. Wes still hadn't called. He could be tied up or he could have changed his mind. But she had enough to get started on the case if he did call.

It had been a long day. After finding Cullen's body and giving her statement, she had finished up her report on Tanya Shaker and met her client, Phil, at his lawyer's office. Since Cullen Vail was dead, she gave them what she had on Tanya and Cullen. The lawyers decided it was enough to invoke the clause in the prenuptial.

Once she had closed Phil's case, she'd written a report for another client, then she started her research on Cullen. It was time to go home.

After shutting down her computer, Holly gathered her purse and started locking up her office. She was starving, so she ran into the kitchen and grabbed a Milky Way bar from her stash in the small refrigerator. She kept them in an old orange Tupperware container that her brothers wouldn't bother to look in. She tore off half the wrapper, tossed it in the trash, and turned off the light.

Outside, she held the candy bar between her teeth, the scent and taste of chocolate and caramel tormenting her as she pulled the door closed behind her and locked it. Then she grabbed the wrapped end of the bar, took a bite, and turned to walk to her car.

Someone screamed and launched themselves at her. They slammed into her face and chest, shoving Holly back against the wall, where she landed on her butt. *What the hell?* Throwing down the chocolate bar and her purse, she shoved the person off her and jumped to her feet.

"You bitch! You ruined my life!"

This time Holly was ready as the woman sprang at her, trying to grab her hair. Holly turned, caught her arm, and threw her to the ground, wrenching her arm up behind her back. She knew who it was now.

Tanya Shaker.

"Let go of me! I hate you! You had no right to spy on me and Cullen! He loved me!"

The back of Holly's head hurt. She felt warm blood running down her left arm and her Milky Way was smashed on the sidewalk. Damn, she'd really wanted that candy bar. Tugging Tanya's arm up a tad higher, she said, "Shut up and listen, bimbo. You just had your free pass. You get up and stay the hell away from me or I'll have you arrested. You've got five seconds to make up your mind."

Tanya started to cry.

Holly let go and straightened up. "For the love of God, have some dignity."

Tanya rolled over, rubbing her shoulder where her arm had been pulled back. "My husband wants a divorce!"

Why were they always surprised? "You were sleeping around on him, honey. Don't do the crime if you can't do the time." Holly looked sadly at her mashed Milky Way. Should she go back in the office and get another one? Or go home before this day got any worse?

"It wasn't like that! Cullen loved me! And now he's dead!"

"Cut the shit, drama queen." Seriously, how stupid could she be? "Your knight in shining condoms had a record. He was after you for sex, or maybe money. But it wasn't love."

Tanya stared up at her with black mascara running down her face. "You're mean."

"You think?" Holly was fighting an urge to laugh when a male voice startled the crap out of her.

"I would say she's cutting you a break, Tanya. Most people would call the cops and press assault charges."

She turned around. "Wes." He wore jeans, a surfing T-shirt, and an intense look in his green eyes that seemed to sink inside of her. What was he doing here? She told him to call, not show up right after she had a minor brawl.

He reached out and took hold of her arm, turning it slightly so he could see the elbow. "You're bleeding."

"Yeah, but the real tragedy is my candy bar. I don't think I can save it." She glanced down to see the crime of mushed chocolate and caramel.

"Hey! What about me!" Tanya got to her feet.

Holly looked back at her. "Go stay with a friend. Get drunk, then get up tomorrow and stop screwing up your life."

"You're a big help," Tanya said. "I don't even have a job."

It was the candy bar that made her feel pity, not Tanya. That annoying pity softened the words in her mouth to, "Are you going to look for a job?"

Tanya made some weird faces as she struggled to unglue the drying mascara on her eyelashes. Finally she blinked. "Guess I'll have to."

Clearly, chocolate deprivation was making her hypo-glycemic. "I'll ask around to see if anyone I know is hiring. Call my office tomorrow." Now why had she said that? Why was she helping this bimbo?

Maybe because she recognized a woman so desperate for attention she wanted to believe that Cullen loved her?

Tanya stood up straight. "Really? Okay! I'll call you to-morrow. And, uh, I'm sorry for attacking you. Sort of."

"Next time, wait until I've eaten my candy bar."

Tanya nodded very seriously then wandered off. Holly sighed and said to Wes, "Do you think she's okay to drive? I suppose I could give her a ride home or wherever she's going."

He still had a hold on her arm. "She'll be fine. She really attacked you?"

Her brain finally engaged. "Get over it, Brockman." She yanked her arm from his hold. "You know I'm a PI. It's not always a pretty business." Or dainty, feminine, or classy.

He dropped his arm to his side, but kept his gaze tuned to her. "Amazing."

She hated feeling defensive. Holly liked who she was and she didn't have to explain it to the rich book boy. "What?" Why did she even ask?

"You still have the chip on your shoulder. Takes more than a body slam to knock that off, huh?"

She'd have smacked him but his grin was just too damn sexy. "It's my Milky Way. I really wanted that Milky Way."

Wes glanced down at the sidewalk. "Lost cause, Hillbay."

She had to agree. "What are you doing here? You were supposed to call me, assuming you still wanted to hire me."

He stepped closer. "Consider yourself hired."

Chapter 5

Holly led Wes through the garage door to her kitchen and set her purse and keys down on the counter. Her galley kitchen wasn't very big, but Wes's presence made it seem smaller. Having him in her condo reminded her that she'd gone to his bookstore this morning to invite him over this evening for a night of pizza and sex.

Instead, they were going to work on a murder case. Better for her career, but Holly had a sneaking suspicion that her libido was pouting. *Stupid, slutty hormones.*

She went to the refrigerator. "Want a beer? Maybe a sandwich?" They were here to work, so why was she trying to feed him? She had suggested they go to her house so she could change her shirt after her scuffle with Tanya, and then they could get to work.

He moved up behind her. "Still not over the Milky Way, are you?"

His warm breath skittered down her bare neck since she had her hair clipped up on her head. "No. I'm starving."

He looked over her shoulder. "Not much in here from the look of things. Yogurt, apples, bread, chocolate milk, beer, eggs." He reached past her and pulled open the meat drawer. "Cheese and ham. I can work with that." He closed the drawer then put his chin on the curve of her neck and shoulder. "Go take a shower, or whatever women do after they've finished wrestling, and I'll make something to eat."

She twisted away from him, ready to insist she was fine the way she was. Then it hit her—damn, he was right about the chip on her shoulder. Between this morning when he'd been shocked, maybe appalled, to find out she was an ex-cop, and then him catching her taking down Tanya made her feel defensive. It was stupid. Forcing a smile, she said, "Thanks. I'll just be ten minutes. Make yourself at home." She slid past him, went out of the kitchen and down to her bedroom.

Automatically, Holly turned on the TV mounted on the wall opposite her king-sized bed to a movie channel. Her bedroom was painted a pale green that didn't clash with the hunter green bedspread. That was pretty much the extent of her ability to decorate. Otherwise she had a serviceable dresser and nightstands made out of oak. On the dresser was a twenty-year-old picture of her family. It had been the last family picture taken before her mom left them. She opened a drawer to get out a pair of panties and wondered why she kept the picture.

To remind her that she had never been the daughter her mom wanted?

Holly grabbed the panties and slammed the drawer shut. She gathered up a spaghetti-strap T-shirt and a pair of shorts then headed to the bathroom.

Getting under the warm shower spray, she washed off the blood and her long day as quickly as possible. Leaving her hair wet, she pulled on her clothes and brushed her teeth. After dragging a comb through her hair, she left it down and hurried back out to the kitchen.

Wes was at her stove, whistling a tune as he lifted two sandwiches from a flat skillet. He picked up the plates. "Good timing."

In her bare feet, she walked up to him. "Grilled cheese?"

"Grilled ham and cheese. With potato chips and apple

slices. Take these to the table." He handed the plates to her.

Her stomach rumbled loudly. She took the plates and went to the table at the end of the kitchen.

Wes opened the freezer and got out two bottles of beer, then followed her to the table. She sat down and said, "Guess you like your beer cold."

He took a seat next to her, then opened one bottle and handed it to her.

She took a drink and had to admit that it tasted icy and perfect. "Thanks."

As he opened his bottle, he asked, "Did you put antiseptic on your elbow?"

Holly bit into her sandwich. It tasted almost as good as the beer. "No. It's just a scratch. I'm going to need the names and contact information for all the members of your book club." She told him the preliminary research she'd done on Cullen.

Wes appeared thoughtful as he chewed an apple slice. "I have a copy of the list I gave to the police with me. But wouldn't Cullen have recognized someone he swindled?"

She shrugged. "Depends. He could have worked with a partner so he might not have met all the victims in person. The woman could have changed her looks. Or he did recognize her and thought she didn't recognize him. Or he just didn't care. There are numerous possibilities." She had another theory, a simpler one. "It's also possible that the murder is not tied to his past crime, but one of the women in the book club got pissed off enough to kill him after he dumped her."

Wes finished his sandwich and pushed his plate back. "That's possible. But how did they get into my store?"

"Either Cullen or the killer had a key and the alarm code. They're not that hard to get. They could have picked the lock, but it's easier to steal a key, or in Cullen's case, talk one of your employees into making him a copy."

He shook his head. "Kelly and Jodi wouldn't do that."

Holly rolled her eyes. "Didn't you say they're young? In college? Wes, they didn't betray you, they fell for Cullen's charm. And when we talk to them once they get back, they'll tell us."

He pulled his mouth tight. "You seem so sure."

"I am. But I could be wrong. I'm more concerned with why someone wanted to kill Cullen in your bookstore then how they got in there." She looked down at her empty beer bottle, trying to see it. "It could have been sheer opportunity. They knew they'd be alone with Cullen, late at night, no one would likely hear the shots. But they reset the alarm and locked the bookstore." That had been swirling in her brain all day.

Wes sat up straight. "You're saying it's personal?"

Holly didn't know yet. "I'm saying it's something to keep in mind. Are you sure you and Cullen didn't both date the same woman?"

"Positive."

She stared at him. "How can you be sure?"

"Because I haven't dated anybody in a while."

She shut her mouth before she asked him why not. She hadn't dated much because she'd been busy with work. She moved on. "It could have been simple opportunity, but then we're dealing with someone who kept their wits about them after committing murder." Holly stood up, collected the plates, and went into the kitchen to load them in the dishwasher. "Let's see the list of the book club members. We'll start with the ones that Cullen dated, the ones you know of, anyway. And we'll talk to your clerks."

Wes stood, pulled a sheet of paper from his front jeans pocket. "The first five names are the women Cullen dated. The rest don't seem to be connected to him at all."

Holly closed the dishwasher and wiped her hands on a dish towel. "Good. There's a chance one of them is the murderer and we will solve this quickly."

Wes gathered up the beer bottles and walked toward her.

Holly opened the door beneath the sink where she kept the trash. Wes dumped the bottles in, then stood up. He was inches from her. "You believe me, don't you?"

His green eyes had hard points of yellow, and he leaned slightly toward her. Needing her answer. Needing something from her. Something she might not be able to give him. That caused her stomach to tighten, her shoulders and neck to tense. "That you're not the killer? Yes, I believe you." She kept her voice cool. "The double fee you're paying me is very convincing." She wanted him to know she was all about work. Money. Tangible success. Solving cases. Those were the things that made sense to her, where she could understand what was expected from her and provide them.

He closed his eyes for a brief second, then opened them. "You're telling me that you follow the money?"

She hated this. There was some underlying emotion or need in his question. But she couldn't grasp it and didn't want to. How was it that she'd known him for a day and a half and already the usually thick, bold black lines that kept her life clean from emotional issues were blurring? "I have bills to pay, Brockman. Most people do."

She turned away, grabbed a bottle of dish soap to wash the pan he'd used to grill the sandwiches. All she had wanted was a night, or even a couple nights, of sex. Uncomplicated sex. Sure, she liked a man's arms around her, liked the slide of his body pressed up against hers. The scent of a man when his skin was hot with desire and slick with sweat. Sex was about pleasure and maybe a little comfort, where no one got hurt.

She could have had that with Wes, she was pretty sure, if they hadn't found a murdered body in his bookstore. The shock and trauma seemed to have ripped away a cool layer from Wes, the layer that projected easy playboy charm. Now he was more exposed, vulnerable. She stuck the pan under the stream of water to rinse the soap off and refused to feel bad for telling him the truth. She did work for money.

The fact that she didn't believe he had killed Cullen had nothing to do with money and everything to do with her observations mixed with instinct. Wes had clearly wanted Holly to stay with him last night, and that led her to believe he had not set up a plot to lure Cullen to his bookstore to murder him.

Wes wasn't stupid, she knew that for sure. He wouldn't have killed Cullen in his own locked bookstore. Or if he had, he'd probably have called the cops right away and claimed Cullen broke in and the murder was self-defense. Plus, she had been with Wes when they found the body. He'd been solely focused on her until he realized the door to the meeting room was shut. So many little things . . .

Yeah. She believed in him but she wasn't going to make a big thing out of it. It was business.

Wes took the pan from under the stream of running water. "It's rinsed." He picked up the dish towel she had set down and dried the pan.

Holly realized she had stood there staring out the small window into the black night. Shutting off the water, she took the dried pan from Wes and put it away. Then she went back to the counter to pick up the list and study it.

Bridget O'Hara

Nora Jacobson

Maggie Partlow

Helene Essex

Tanya Shaker

Seeing Tanya's name, she said, "I followed Tanya all the way home last night and saw her go into the house. I waited around for twenty minutes and saw the living room light go out, and a light go on in the back of the house. My sense was that she was in for the night, but we'll talk to her again.

Maybe she knows what Cullen was doing at the bookstore after she left him." She was really irritated that she hadn't asked Tanya that after their scuffle earlier.

Wes folded the towel. "Is that why you offered to help find her a job? Befriending her so she'll confide in you?"

Holly glanced up. "I would have if I had thought of it."

Wes cracked a grin.

She tried to ignore the warmth his smile sparked inside her and looked down at the list. "Nora is the one who said the anthology was about more than sex . . . something about the relationship building during mysterious circumstances."

"That's her, and the two women sitting by her were Maggie and Helene. The three of them have recently bonded."

"Like the Dumped By Cullen club?" She remembered their reaction to Cullen in the book club meeting.

"That'd be my guess. Bridget, the first one on the list and the first one I realized Cullen was dating, she talks to anyone. She doesn't seem to be part of the Helene/Nora/Maggie clique."

"Okay, I'll talk to Tanya when she calls. First thing in the morning I'll track down Helene and I'll work backwards. I'll need to talk to your two clerks, as well." Holly turned to walk out of the kitchen and made a left into her home office. She set the list down on her desk, then stepped back.

And bumped into Wes's chest. He put his arms around her, lowered his face to her nearly dry hair, and inhaled. "I've wanted to do this all night. You look hot, Holly. Sexy. Shorts that reveal your long legs, no bra beneath the top."

He changed so suddenly, she could barely get her breath. "You're my client now. I—"

"Shut up." He moved his mouth down over her ear, into the curve of her neck. His mouth was warm, his breath hot. Her nerve endings sizzled, her body felt soft and tight with need at the same time. She should stop this. "Wes—"

He slid one hand down her side, cupped her hip, and pulled her back into his groin to feel his hard dick straining against his pants. "I'm not going to listen to logic. Not tonight." He slid one thin strap down her arm.

It was hard to think with his mouth moving over her shoulder and his hard dick pressing into her backside. So she drew her line. "This is just sex."

"Oh yeah. Sex. Making love. Screwing. Call it whatever you want." He moved his left hand to slide her ribbed cotton top over her nipple. His right hand went down to her thigh. "Just as long as I get to do this." His fingers skimmed up her thigh, under her shorts, under the elastic of her panties.

Holly wasn't worrying about word choices anymore. She leaned back, farther into him, giving him better access. Turning her head, she reached up to bring his mouth to hers. He tasted like beer and pure wet heat. She wanted more instantly, and slid her tongue over his, then deeper to taste all of him.

Wes made a noise, then slid his finger deeper until he plunged inside of her. He lifted his head, watched her as he stroked her.

A loud knock startled both of them.

Wes stilled, but kept his finger inside of her. "Expecting someone? Now is not a good time."

"I don't know who it could be. Unless . . ." She was going to kill them. Shoot them with her gun. Then kick them.

He pulled her tighter against his chest and whispered into her ear, "Stay quiet, they'll go away." He shoved her shorts and panties farther over to slide in a second finger.

She nearly came right then. Except that a dead man yelled out, "Hey! Holly, you in there? We got pizza."

"Fuck," Wes snarled in her ear. "Boyfriends?"

She put her hand on his wrist, forcing his hand out, and rearranged her panties and shorts. She couldn't do anything about her erect nipples. She took a step then turned around. "Worse, brothers," she answered, and immediately saw that Wes had a bigger problem than she did.

Much bigger. His erection shoved against the front of his

jeans. If her soon-to-be-dead brothers weren't standing at the door—God, she was going to kick both their asses. "Go in the kitchen, or bedroom, I'll get rid of them."

Wes looked at her like she'd grown a third boob. "No."

She looked down. "Uh, Wes . . ."

His expression turned pained. "Seriously, Holly, do you think I don't know that I'm sporting a massive boner? So how many brothers? And no," he said when she opened her mouth. "I won't hide like a teenaged horn dog."

"Okay." She wasn't sure what to make of that. A small part of her was pleased, but most of her was sexually turned on and ready to kill her stupid brothers. "Two brothers," she added, and walked to the door as Seth pounded again.

Holly yanked open the door. "Get lost. I'm busy."

Seth put his hands on her shoulders and walked her backwards to unblock the door while Joe carried in a large pizza box. Seth said, "We heard about the murder." He stopped short five feet into her living room.

Joe stood next to him with the pizza box.

Holly glared at their backs. "Leave. Now. Or I'm getting my gun."

Joe turned around and leveled his blue gaze on her. "Date?"

"Out!"

Seth glanced back over his shoulder. "Dad's worried about you, AP. He's having a bad day, so Joe and I said we'd check on you."

Holly rolled her eyes. "You're a lying sack of dog shit, Seth. Dad's on a fishing trip with three buddies, and I talked to him on the phone twice."

Seth grinned. "He could still be worried. Maybe I talked to him on the phone, too."

Joe turned back to Wes. "Are you staying for pizza? I'm Joe, Holly's brother. This is Seth." He walked by Wes into the kitchen.

Wes turned and followed Joe. Holly heard him introduce himself but she was busy trying to think of where she could bury Seth and Joe's bodies.

"Might want to close the door, Hol. Probably too late to put on a bra." Seth went into the kitchen.

Holly slammed the door. Hard.

The next morning Wes arrived at Holly's condo around ten A.M. Holly opened the door wearing a pair of low-cut jeans and a black tank top. Her hair was scooped up on her head, making his hand itch to let it down. He wanted to touch her everywhere. Sexual frustration was screwing with his concentration. Her brothers had made damn sure he left before they had last night.

Without waiting for her invitation, he stepped in, pulled her to him, and kissed her. "Good morning." He looked down at her silver blue eyes.

"If you're done playing around, we have work to do."

He grinned. "Cranky in the mornings, are we? I didn't notice it when your tongue was in my mouth."

Holly pushed him away, shut the door, and stalked over to her computer. "My brothers didn't leave until one A.M. I'm too tired to figure out the best way to kill them. I'll do it tomorrow."

Wes moved up behind her. "Holly, they were just concerned about you. In case I turned out to be a deranged killer who offs people in my bookstore."

She lifted a cup of coffee off her desk and sank into her chair. "That's what pisses me off. I don't need bodyguards or baby-sitters."

"Can't really blame them. Monty and I went by the bookstore this morning to make arrangements to have it cleaned." His gut tightened in anger. Was Cullen's murder connected to his past?

Holly said, "There are special cleaners who handle crime scene cleanup."

He nodded. "I know. They'll be there later today. I cleared it with your friend, Detective Bulldog. I'm going to keep the store closed at least until next week." Since he didn't know what was going on, he had to protect his customers.

She lifted her blue gaze. "You said you went to your bookstore with Monty? Who's that?"

Grinning, he said, "The dog. Remember? The one you rescued from under my deck?" He certainly did. He'd had the wicked pleasure of watching her curvy ass as she crawled under his deck.

She furrowed her forehead. "Monty? What kind of weenie name is Monty?" Then she widened her eyes. "Where is the dog? He's not in your car, is he?"

"Monty is with my neighbor until I get home." Fixing a stern look on his face, he added, "Monty is not a weenie name. Take that back. You don't go insulting a man's dog."

Lifting her brows, she said, "If you can't take the insults, don't give your dog a weenie name. Duke is a good name. Or maybe Boss. Or Sabbath. Or Rock. Those are tough names."

He leaned down, putting his face right up to hers. "But you didn't want the dog, remember? Or any animals." He lifted his head to crane his neck in an exaggerated attempt to look around her condo. "Hell, I don't even see a fish or a hamster."

"What do I look like, book boy, a pet store owner? I'm a PI. I work. I can't worry about feeding a stupid fish."

With his nose an inch from hers, he said, "Commitment phobia?" He wanted to know more about her. He wanted to know everything about her. What had formed and cemented the chip on her shoulder? What made her need to be so tough? And yet he'd had glimpses of Holly's softer side. She'd cut Tanya some slack, and she'd helped rescue Monty. Then pushed Monty away, when Wes had practically felt her longing to hold and play with the puppy.

She narrowed her eyes. "Been watching too much Dr. Phil, Brockman? Newsflash, women don't find pop psychobabble sexy."

He put his hand on her thigh. "You find me sexy. Want me to prove it?"

She grabbed his wrist and moved his hand. "You're paying me to work." She turned and studied her computer screen.

Wes knew he was getting to her. But she was right, he had to focus on finding out who killed Cullen in his bookstore and why. He turned to look at her computer monitor. "What's this?"

She sipped some of her coffee. "Some asshole's Web site. He goes by the name The O'Man. He does podcasts on Thursday and Sunday on his site. Looks like he hasn't gotten the podcast up for today, since it's Thursday and I don't see a new one posted."

Wes looked at the front page, which read "*Women Are Easy If You Have The Right Tool.*" He shifted his gaze to Holly. "Any particular reason you're reading this guy's blog? Is it connected to Cullen's murder?"

A guilty little grin slid over her mouth. "No, nothing to do with the case. I was taking care of a little personal business before getting to work."

Wasn't this interesting. "You have personal business with this blog?"

"It's my brothers' fault. They sent me this blog to annoy me, and now I'm curious who this guy is. But before checking this Web site this morning, I spent a few minutes signing my brothers up for e-mail newsletters from Web sites on how to get in touch with your feminine side, an erectile dysfunction support group, freedom from the closet, transvestite tips, and a few other fun sites. Then because Joe and Seth are the ones that showed me The O'Man Web site, I went on to see if I could find any clues to The O'Man's identity."

"Because?" Why did she want to know his identity?

She shrugged. "If he really dated and slept with these women, I doubt they realize they are being talked about on his blog for public entertainment."

Ah. Justice was important to Holly. So was revenge, he

had to grin at her methods of getting back at her brothers for interrupting them last night. Ignoring the Web site, he looked at Holly. "My sister would have signed me up for the erectile dysfunction group and beauty tips for babes." He couldn't help the nostalgic smile as he thought of Michelle. She and Holly had some similar traits. Neither one were pushovers.

"Would have?" Holly leaned forward and set her coffee cup on the desk. "Is your sister dead?"

Christ. He was usually much more careful. To give himself a minute, he picked up her cup and drank some of the coffee. Then he said, "We had an argument and don't talk now. We should get going."

Holly touched his leg for a moment, then stood up. "I'd like to talk to your two clerks first."

His throat felt strange at her quiet sympathy, or was it understanding? Wes hadn't had that kind of intimacy with a woman in years. He hadn't realized how goddamned much he had missed it until Holly. He drank more of her coffee to wash down the feeling, and said, "Kelly and Jodi are coming back from San Diego today. We'll have to wait until they call me when they're back in town."

She nodded. "Helene, then. Let's go. I'll drive."

Holly drove her white Nissan Maxima fast and skillfully through the town. Goleta ran along the edge of the Pacific Ocean, with the Santa Ynez Mountains rising up on the other side. It was a beautiful town that offered crisp beaches, a rich history, and a comfortable lifestyle. Wes was thinking about how little he missed the cutthroat world he'd left behind in Los Angeles. Who would have thought that he would end up owning a bookstore in a beach and college town? Holly's voice broke into his thoughts.

"What does Helene do?"

He had to think about that for a few seconds. "She calls herself a gift consultant, for corporate and personal occasions. I believe she works out of her home and has a presence on the Internet. She's been in the book club about four months."

"What does she talk about?"

He shrugged. "Mostly books or movies. Sometimes sports. She likes baseball and is a Giants fan. I've heard her talk about hairdressers, clothes, TV shows, and that kind of thing with the other women, general chitchat."

"What's your impression of her overall?"

Wes noted that she asked good questions. "Helene thinks well of herself, but she's nice enough."

Holly thought about her own impression of Helene from the book club. "It looked like she belongs to the country club."

"She has a bit of the money look, but she would need it for more upscale clients. She has to visit clients and make the right impression to get them to trust her to come up with the right gifts." Wes looked over at her. "The corporate world spends a lot of money on gifts."

Her gaze sharpened. "Do they? You've had experience in the corporate world?"

He closed his mouth. *Idiot.* What was it about Holly that made him reveal parts of himself that he'd had no trouble keeping quiet in the past?

She turned on the correct street and parked in front of Helene's house. "Her home is modest."

Wes agreed. It was a one-story white house with a brick chimney and blue shutters.

She turned to him and said, "I want you to let me do the talking. You're just here to reassure Helene so she'll talk to me."

He kept a straight face. "Yes, dear."

She put the car in park and turned a serious gaze on him. "You hired me to do a job, Wes. Let me do it."

"I intend to. But I know Helene and I'm sure she'll talk to me. I think you're tough enough to deal with that." He turned and got out of the car, thinking that Holly really liked to be in control. On the other hand, she had no way of knowing that Wes had years of experience in schmoozing and persuading people to do what he wanted. He met her on the sidewalk and they both headed up to the front door. Holly rang the doorbell.

Finally Helene answered the door. "Wes, what are you doing here?" Helene swept her cool gaze to Holly. "And you, Holly is it?"

Holly stepped forward. "Holly Hillbay. I'm a private investigator. Wes has hired me, and we'd like a few minutes of your time."

Helene looked right at him. "I have nothing to say to you, Wes. My lawyer will be contacting you if you keep bothering me." She slammed the door.

Chapter 6

Holly turned from Helene's freshly slammed front door to smirk at Wes. "I know Helene, I'm sure she'll talk to me," she mimicked. "What did you do to put a bug up her ass? Why is she invoking lawyers?" Bringing lawyers into any conversation always made Holly suspicious.

Wes looked puzzled. "I have no clue. Maybe she's mad because I told the police that she dated Cullen?" He shook his head.

Oh man, he looked so bewildered that it was hard to hold onto her tough girl game. But she managed with, "Get lost, Brockman. Let's see if Helene will talk to me."

He didn't budge. "Maybe I can talk to her, find out—"

Holly shook her head. "She's mad at you. Now skedaddle and let the professional work here." She was so enjoying this. She'd told him yesterday that she worked alone, but no, he had to tag along and already he was causing trouble. She loved it!

He cocked his head, amusement softening his features. "Having a good time, Hillbay?"

"Wonderful. Best time all week." She pulled her keys out of her purse and dangled them. "Go get my car washed for me. Or you can just drive around the block a couple times. Take your pick."

He closed his fingers around her wrist and pulled her closer. "Payback's a bitch, Hill*baby*. You might want to remember that." He snagged the keys from her fingers and walked toward the car.

Her smirk flattened into a tight line of annoyance. "I have a gun," she reminded his back. Hill*baby*. No one called her that. It was . . . yuck. She ignored Wes's soft chuckle as he headed toward her car and pounded on the door to get Helene's attention.

Helene pulled open the door. She wore tan pants, a shell-pink top, and an air of importance. "If you bother me again, I will—"

Holly stepped into the doorway to stop a replay of the Dramatic Door Slam and talked fast. "Knock it off, Helene. That little scene might have worked with Wes, but I'm not buying it. You're trying to scare him off, why?"

Helene didn't soften her stance, but she did answer. "Simple. I don't want to get involved in a murder investigation. I don't want to be called as a witness and I don't want my name associated with a man who is being investigated for a murder in his bookstore. I'm building a business in Goleta and I don't want my name dragged through the mud of Cullen's murder."

That kind of reaction wasn't uncommon. Holly said, "But you dated Cullen. Surely you want his murderer caught."

She tilted her head, her carefully cut hair swinging around her face. "That's not my problem. I've already told the police what I know, which is next to nothing. Now get out of my doorway."

Holly didn't move. "Where were you last night after you left the book club?"

Helene's eyes widened in amusement. "Isn't that adorable, just like the PIs on TV. I was with friends, which I told the police. I have an alibi. Now why don't you move your ass out of my doorway and go ask Wes where he was?"

Hmm, this woman had some serious ice in her veins. Holly was impressed. "Care to tell me the names of your friends and where you went?"

"Now where's the fun in that for you? I'm sure you'll be able to find out that information using your investigative skills. In the meantime, I have work to do and I'm done being polite." She started to swing the door shut.

Holly might have blocked the door, just on principle, but her cell phone rang. She stepped back and watched the door close while she pulled her phone out of her purse. She didn't recognize the incoming number. While walking to the curb, she answered, "Hillbay Investigations."

"Holly? Hi, uh, it's me, Tanya. You told me to call today. You know, about a job?"

Holly spotted her white Maxima parked a few houses down. She walked to the passenger side of the car while remembering her disgusting moment of weakness after Tanya had attacked her. "Right. I'm out in the field right now, Tanya. I haven't been to the—" She pulled open the door and stopped as her brain shifted into gear. Tanya was the last one to see Cullen alive aside from the murderer, and she might have answers. "That is, I'd like to meet with you. Where are you?"

"At a friend's house. Do you want me to come to your office? I could be there in, like, twenty minutes. But I'm not dressed up for a job interview or anything."

She folded herself into the passenger seat and pulled the door closed. "It's not a job interview. I thought we could talk about your qualifications and what kind of job you're looking for. I'll see if I can help you find a job. But I need a favor, too."

There was a few seconds of silence. "What?"

"We'll talk about that at the office. See you then." She hung up, stuck her cell back in her purse, and finally realized where she was—in the passenger seat of her own car. Turning to Wes, she said, "Switch places with me, I'm driving."

He flashed a grin at her and started the car. "Too late, you gave me the keys. What did Helene say?"

She debated kicking his butt right out of her car, but decided it wasn't worth the effort at the moment. She yanked the seat belt over her chest and said, "Helene refuses to get involved in the investigation into Cullen's murder, and she's dropping her membership in your fan club. Drive back to my place so you can pick up your car and be on your way."

Wes put the car into drive and pulled away from the curb. "You're slick, Hill*baby*. Luring Tanya with a job to cross-examine her."

Clenching her jaw, she took a breath. "Do. Not. Call. Me. That."

He looked over at her. And smiled. Big, huge, bare-assed grin.

"Stop that." He was worse than her brothers. "And get off your moral high horse, Brockman. I do what it takes to get the job done."

"Which is why I hired you," he said mildly.

She studied his profile. Who was he? Where did his money come from? A bookstore did not usually generate the kind of income that allowed for a nice beach house, and the ability to double a private investigator's salary at will. What did he really think about her, and her methods?

And why did she care what he thought? Annoyed at herself, she said, "I want you to call me the second you hear from your two clerks. We need to find out if one of them gave Cullen, or maybe even the killer, the key to your bookstore." Turning to watch the road, she realized where they were. "You're almost to my office. I told you to go back to my house."

Wes did that wide grin again. "I know you're after my body, but we have to work first." He turned onto Hollister. "What did you think of Helene?"

He was an amusing guy with a very hot body. She had no problem admitting she wanted to get naked with him, to herself anyway. Turning her mind to business, she answered, "She seems strong-willed, determined, and focused as a business-woman. She didn't let me intimidate her. And she amuses herself with her wit. She did tell me she was with friends and had an alibi for Cullen's murder." She knew Wes would enjoy the next part more than she had. "But she told me I could use my investigative skills to find out the details."

"Did she slam the door?" He glanced over at her with a half grin, then turned into the parking lot. He found a space close to her office.

"No. Which is a good thing since I was standing in the doorway. But she did start shutting it to force me to move." Holly got out of the car, took the keys from Wes after he locked her car, then strode up to her office door.

"So I guess she didn't confess to murder, huh?"

Unlocking the door, she went in and held the door for Wes. Recognizing frustrated sarcasm for what it was, she touched his arm. "We're just getting started, Wes. It takes time to develop and follow the clues."

He nodded.

She dropped her hand from his arm and flipped on the lights. Then she went into the small kitchen and started making coffee.

Wes followed her. "What does AP stand for? Your brothers kept calling you that last night."

She pushed the button to start the coffee brewing and turned around. Wes stood at the archway between the kitchen and her large, bedroom-sized office. "Family joke."

She went to the refrigerator next to him, pulled it open, and brought out the orange Tupperware. She opened the lid and held the container out toward Wes. "Want a candy bar?"

He snatched the Tupperware container from her hands. "What does AP stand for?"

Damn him, he was fast. "Give that back!"

He held it up over her head. "When you tell me what AP means."

She could just slug him—then he would drop the container. But she'd already lost one candy bar to violence last night. "Anti-Princess. Now give me my candy bars." She grabbed it as soon as it was in her reach, stepped back, and took out a Milky Way bar. "You don't get any."

He grinned at her. "Anti-Princess, huh? Fits you. What about your parents? Your dad's a cop, right?"

She went to the fridge to hide her stash. "My dad's a retired cop."

Wes shook his head sadly. "What, is being a cop your family business or something?"

Holly closed the door and studied Wes. "You don't like cops much, do you?"

"Haven't had much use for them, I guess."

Yeah? What was that about? "What did your dad do for a living?"

His green eyes had a challenging gleam in them. "Journalist."

She knew he was being purposely vague. It was time for her to do some serious background on Wes Brockman. She was sure he hadn't murdered Cullen, but what if his money came from a career that cops frowned on and that was why he had no use for cops? Damn it, her hormones were overruling her common sense. "Where?"

"I grew up in Los Angeles. I didn't follow my father's footsteps into journalism."

Holly leaned against the refrigerator and studied him. "What is your degree in?"

He put one hand on the wall over her head. "What makes you think I have a degree?"

She laughed. "Come on, book boy, you have education and money stamped all over you."

He stared at her for a few seconds. "Okay, I'll make you a deal. I'll answer this one and then it's your turn. I majored in business."

She knew she'd been had somehow. Holly opened her mouth to figure it out but Wes cut her off.

"My turn. What about your mom? Is she in your cop family business?"

Holly froze for a second, her shoulders going tense. Then she forced herself to relax. "She's not a cop." Ducking beneath his arm, she unwrapped her candy bar and headed for her desk. "I have to get ready for Tanya."

He stepped in front of her, blocking her in the kitchenette. "What does your mom do?"

"Dances." She bit into the Milky Way and turned to slide by Wes.

He let her go. "Professionally?"

Holly felt better once she settled behind her desk. It made her feel real and valuable. "My mom teaches dance. Now drop it, I have work to do." She pulled out a pad of paper and started making a list of questions to talk to Tanya about.

A cup of steaming coffee slid in front of her. "Is your mom here in Goleta?"

Wes had obviously found the cups. She sighed to reveal her annoyance. "Why do you care, Brockman?"

He sat down in one of the two chairs facing her desk. "Because you went all icy-tough on me when I asked."

"And you tricked me when I asked you about your degree," she shot back.

He did his smug smile. "Nope, it's the truth."

Wagging the pencil at him, she asked, "How many degrees do you have?"

He shook his head. "It's my turn. Is your mom here in Goleta?"

She dropped her pencil to pick up the coffee and take a sip. "My mom left when I was seven. She moved to San Diego, married a rich guy, teaches dance, and belongs to the important clubs. She has two daughters and they can both dance. They are one big happy family. End of story." She set the coffee cup down, downed the last of her candy bar, and picked up her pencil. She got real busy starting a list of questions for Tanya.

What the hell had she told him that for?

Ignoring the silence, she focused on the questions.

"I have a law degree."

Startled, she looked up, meeting his green eyes across her desk. She could hear the hum of the fluorescent lights overhead. She could feel her blood pumping in her ears. He was a lawyer? But he didn't practice? Hell, that explained the money. And if he had been a defense lawyer, they made entire careers out of destroying cops, so maybe that explained his apparent dislike of cops.

But all of that was background noise in her brain. What was real, vibrant, and taking up all her breath, was the way he'd told her. It had cost him something to tell her, she didn't know what, but she had heard it in his voice. And he'd done it in return for her little speech about her mom.

The door opened before she could think it out.

Holly got up, relieved that Tanya had arrived and the moment was broken. She walked around her desk and noted a big improvement. Tanya wore her hair straight, her makeup a little on the heavy side but not as thick as it had been at the book club. She wore a T-shirt that skimmed the top of her jeans. "Tanya, come in and sit down."

Wes stood up. "Hi, Tanya, can I get you some coffee?"

She looked at Wes. She appeared a little confused.

Holly said, "I'm doing some work for Wes. That's one of the things that I wanted to talk to you about. Do you mind if he's here?" She should have made Wes go home. Tanya wasn't the only one he confused. She amended that—she wasn't confused. It was the attraction between them blurring the lines.

Tanya answered. "No, I don't mind." She looked at Wes. "Can I have coffee with sugar?"

"Sure."

"Sit down," Holly said, and went around her desk. She gave Tanya a moment to get settled then got down to business. "So what kind of work experience do you have?"

"Not a lot. I've been a waitress and a sales associate for retail stores." Tanya looked up when Wes handed her the coffee. "Thanks."

"You're welcome." Wes went to the couch against the wall and sat down.

Holly went on. "Okay, what about office work?"

"Uh, not really. I can use a computer at home."

"Okay." She made a note on her pad. "Any other skills?"

Tanya sat forward. "I learn fast and I'm willing to work hard." She looked around the office.

Holly wasn't sure what she was looking for. Her desk took up about a quarter of the space. The couch and filing cabinets brought that up to half the space. The kitchen was in a small alcove, and there was a bathroom and storage area behind that. She picked up her coffee, letting Tanya finish her inspection.

"I could work for you. Answer phones, type stuff, handle your schedule, maybe"—her voice thinned—"like, you know, do little things like, um, help you investigate."

Holly choked. Her nose burned and her eyes watered as the hot coffee spread in the back of her throat, then finally went down. She stared at Tanya.

"I know! You found me cheating on my husband. And I did sort of attack you. But I could be your secretary or assistant. I—"

Holly shook her head, struggling to find her voice. After a few seconds, she said, "I don't have an assistant. I'm a one-woman operation." That was the way Holly liked it, both at work and in her personal life.

Tanya's shoulders seemed to deflate beneath her pink T-shirt. "Maybe I could try out? For free? See if you like having an assistant?"

This was what being soft brought. She should never have offered to help Tanya. She should have kicked her ass as soon as Tanya jumped her. She should have—

"You could put her on my payroll. Just while you're work-ing on my case." Wes stood up from the couch and walked over to stand at the end of the desk to look at Tanya. "It'd be temporary while Holly's working for me."

She was getting a headache. "That won't work."

Tanya ignored her. "Oh! Thank you! You'll see, Holly, I'll be really good. I can organize your files, handle your phone calls, um, clean the office . . ."

"Just don't touch my Milky Way bars." God, how did she get into these things? And why wouldn't Wes just shut up?

"Tanya," he said, "you can get started by helping us figure out who killed Cullen."

Her bottom lip slid out like a three-year-old kid's did, and her big blue eyes pooled.

That was it. Holly slapped both hands onto her desk and snapped, "Stop that right now. In this office, we don't cry over dumb-ass men! You can throw something, call him names, or just be damned glad the bloodsucker is out of your life, but we don't cry."

Tanya's eyes rounded. The she sniffed once and said, "Okay."

Holly nodded, purposely refraining from looking at Wes, who was standing by her desk. He might not like her meth-ods, but she didn't care. To Tanya, she said, "Good. Now get it through your head that Cullen used you. He didn't take one look at you across the table at the book club and fall in love. That is not the real world."

"But—"

She glared at her. "No buts!"

Tanya sat back in her chair. "Stop yelling at me. I get it." She looked down at her lap. "Last night was the first and only time I slept with him. He spent a week making me feel like I mattered to him."

Holly rolled her eyes and sighed.

Tanya looked up and said, "I know he seduced me for sex and nothing more."

That was better. "Good. Now tell us about Cullen. Did he have any plans after you left him last night?"

Tanya picked up her coffee then sat back. "No, I assumed he would go back to his boat. I thought I wore him out."

Ugh. Holly took a drink of her coffee to try to burn that image out of her brain.

Wes jumped in. "Can you think of any reason he would be in my bookstore that late at night?"

She shook her head. "He never said a word about your bookstore or meeting anyone."

Holly cut in, "I saw Tanya leave and followed her. I think we have to assume that Cullen must have gone into the bookstore right after dropping Tanya at her car. He was right there."

Tanya went a little pale. "You followed me home? Isn't that kind of creepy?"

What did the chick think investigating was? "Creepy or not, I'm the one who told the detective that I watched you go into the house, turn out all the lights, and stayed for another twenty minutes to make sure you didn't leave again."

"Oh." Tanya looked sheepish. "My alarm system for the house records when it's disabled. It showed that once I came home, it wasn't turned off until the morning. But thanks. I wouldn't want to be a suspect." She shuddered.

Wes got her focused again when he asked, "Any idea if Cullen might have gotten a key to my bookstore? Did he have a key you didn't recognize with him when he dropped you off? Anything like that?"

Tanya shook her head. "He had keys on his key ring, but I didn't know what they were all for. Sorry."

Holly decided to try another tactic. "What did Cullen talk about that night?"

Tanya thinned her lips and said, "He talked about himself.

Well, first he talked about me, how beautiful and special I was." She dropped her eyes to the cup in her hand. "But once we were done with sex, he was fiddling with his laptop and talking about making it big as a radio personality. Like a Howard Stern kind of shock jock."

This time Holly did look at Wes. "Did you know this?"

He shook his head. "First I've heard of it."

Holly wrote down notes and asked, "How was Cullen going to do that?"

She compressed her lips in thought, then said, "He didn't really say. Just that he had big plans."

Wes asked, "What did he say specifically?"

"Just what I told you, and he kept paying more attention to his laptop than me."

She tried to make sense of it. "What was he doing on his laptop?"

"Don't know. I asked him, but he just laughed, looked at his watch, and said it was time to get me back to my car. He shut down his laptop and we got dressed and left."

That struck her. "Time? Like he was meeting someone?" she said thoughtfully, not expecting an answer. She added that to her notes, and included questions about what was on the laptop, and how Cullen had planned to become a radio shock jock. Then she looked up. "What about friends? Do you know who Cullen's friends were?"

"No."

"Family?"

"No. Wait, I remember he said something about his family being in Oregon. And maybe something about a cousin in Southern California, or used to be in Southern California . . . something about a cousin, I think." Tanya shifted in her seat and set her cup on the desk. "I really was stupid thinking it was love. If we'd been in love, I would have known these things."

Holly met her gaze. "You're not the first. What do you know about the other women he dated in the book club?"

"Bridget, Maggie, Nora, and Helene." Tanya's blue eyes sparked in anger. "He made a point of telling me they had all wanted him. But that he wanted me. Shit." She turned away.

Cullen had told Tanya what she wanted to hear, Holly thought. He'd used her to get sex. It was an old story that got repeated way too often, because it worked.

"So do I start today?"

Holly blinked. Hell. "Don't you have to find a place to stay? Maybe pick up some clothes from your house? Get a divorce lawyer?"

"Yeah, I guess I do." Tanya got up. "Will you call me later and let me know when to start?"

Holly nodded. "Thanks for your help." She walked Tanya to the door and held it for her while she left.

Then she turned back to deal with Wes. He sat on the end of her desk watching her. He looked good wearing a pair of jeans and a brown and green shirt. But that didn't change her annoyance. She stalked up until she was toe-to-toe with him. "What do you think you're doing hiring her for my office? I don't want help!"

He reached out, took hold of her shoulders, and tugged her toward him. "You're welcome."

Holly brought both her hands up, using her forearms to push his arms away and break his hold on her. "Knock it off." She was not going to be pushed around. Just his touch lit the barely banked sexual fire. Holly could handle that. But somehow Wes made her feel outgunned, as if she didn't have the defenses to handle him. "We don't have time for sex, Brockman." She paced off the distance between her desk and the kitchenette. "We have a murder victim who appears to be a jerk, and he pissed off a group of women. Where's the murder weapon?" She went around her desk and pulled her cell phone out of her purse. She found the name in her address

book and hit send. "Seth, any word on the murder weapon?"
She'd asked Seth to charm information from Detective
Rodgers.

He answered, "No murder weapon, but I do have something interesting. Vail's boat was broken into. The only thing
that appears to be missing is a computer or laptop. There is
equipment that goes with the computer, some kind of broad-
casting shit, printer and scanner unit, that kind of stuff, but
no computer. It's not in his car either."

"When was the boat broken into?"

"Tuesday night, or that's the theory anyway. I assume
Rodgers has a reason to back up the theory. She doesn't believe in coincidence."

Holly wasn't much on coincidence either. That meant the
killer wanted something. Something on the computer? "Any
suspects for the break-in or the murder?"

"Rodgers wouldn't say who she thought looked good for
either. I couldn't get a read on her about Brockman either.
Watch yourself, AP Gotta run."

"Thanks, Seth." She hung up.

"What?" Wes asked.

"Cullen's boat was broken into, and the police can't find a
laptop or computer. Tanya said he had a laptop. So what was
on that laptop? Was it worth killing for?"

Frowning, Wes said, "You think someone killed Cullen
in the bookstore then went to the boat and got his computer?"

Holly didn't know. She played the different scenarios in
her brain. "Could be the killer saw Cullen leave with Tanya.
He or she knows that it's going to take a little time to do the
kiss-and-grope good-bye. They break in, grab his computer,
then drive to the bookstore and kill Cullen."

His gaze grew troubled. "Why not just kill Cullen at the
boat when he gets back? Why do it in my store?"

"Excellent question." She walked to her desk, reached

past Wes and got her tablet. "There's Cullen, the killer, your bookstore, and the laptop. We're pretty certain those are involved." Holly looked at the four items, trying to see a connection.

Wes pulled her down so that she sat next to him on the edge of the desk. Looking over her list, he said, "Tanya said Cullen wanted to be on radio, a Howard Stern type."

Holly looked over at him. "How does becoming a radio shock jock connect to a laptop?"

"Research? Maybe sending out resumes?"

She thought about that. "Applying to radio stations. Hmm, wouldn't he have to have some kind of experience? A portfolio of some type?"

"No idea."

"I'll find out. Damn, I wish we had some way to access that computer." Holly made a note about radio stations, then said, "But now we have more questions for the women. And your clerks." She looked at Wes, sitting next to her. "No word from them yet?"

He shook his head and looked at his watch. "I'd like you to wait until I can go with you to talk to the other women."

That caught her off guard. "What do you mean wait? What are you doing now?"

"I need to go let the cleaners into my store. They're going to be there at one. Then I need to check on Monty and do a few other things. How about we meet around six?"

Once again, she was struck by how little she knew about Wes. She didn't like the feeling that he was keeping something from her, especially when she was busting her butt to help him—for the doubled fee, of course. "What other things do you have to do? You have something more important than finding the murderer?"

He grinned. "Monty. He's important."

Uh-huh. And he was trying to distract her. "After you check on the dog—which, by the way, is why I don't have a dog—what are you doing then?"

"Don't get all huffy on me, I'm not seeing another woman." Wes stood up. "So we'll meet at six. My place?"

Holly stood up and faced him. "Did I say anything about another woman? Rein in your ego, book boy. You can sleep with all the women you want, what I want to know is what you're trying to keep a secret." It was all she could do not to poke him in the chest. Okay, so his "other woman" comment had pissed her off.

His green eyes got serious. "It's just a promise I made to some people. Nothing to do with the case, I swear."

What was she going to do, hook him up to a lie detector? He was paying her the money whether he screwed up the case or not. She waved her hand. "Whatever, I have some work to do anyway. Go."

Wes reached out and put his hands on her shoulders. "Nope, I can't feel it." He looked into her eyes. "But I know I heard that chip on your shoulder snarking at me."

"Haha, you are so funny." He *was* kind of funny but she wasn't going to feed his ego by admitting it.

He ran his hands down her arms. "What I am is done being interrupted when I get you alone. Tonight we'll track down every clue we can, then we're going back to my house. Your brothers won't find us there."

She could feel the heat coming off him. Or was that her? It felt like she couldn't get enough air into her lungs. "Pretty sure of yourself there, Brockman."

His smile was wolfish. "You want me almost as much as I want you, Hill*baby*."

"Don't—"

He cut her off by molding his mouth to hers. Then he stood up. "Six P.M., Holly. Don't be late." He headed toward the door.

The fog of lust cleared enough for her to remember an important detail. "Hey, Wes."

He turned at the door. "Miss me already?"

She raised her eyebrows. "Haven't you forgotten something?"

Confusion creased his forehead.

Holly laughed. She wasn't the only one baffled by this raging lust between them. She grabbed her purse and said, "Your car is at my house."

Realization dawned on him. "Damn."

A little bit later, Holly dropped him at his car. She watched him get into his black Range Rover. Her cell phone rang just as he started his car. Getting the phone out of her purse, she answered with, "Hillbay."

"Nice touch to send your brother to charm me, Hillbay."

"Rodgers." Holly repressed a grin. As she watched Wes pull away, she said, "I can't help it if you fall for a pretty face." She tried not to gag at calling her brother that.

"Yeah? Seth tells me you and Brockman looked pretty cozy last night."

"He's a client." The memory of him pulling her against his chest, putting his fingers inside of her, heated up the car. What was it about him?

There was a beat of silence.

Holly's heart stuttered. Rodgers wasn't calling to harass her over siccing Seth on her. What did she want?

"Wes Brockman only existed until three years ago. Then nothing. Nada."

Her heart picked up speed and slammed against her chest. "You sure?"

"Yes."

"He's not the killer." Shit. She wanted to thunk her head on the steering wheel for saying that. It was some kind of reflex she didn't entirely understand.

"As it happens, I don't think so either. No gunshot residue

on him, or the clothes we analyzed. We looked through his house yesterday with his permission. Nothing. Either he's innocent or he hired a hit."

Tightening her fingers around the cell phone, a heavy weight settled in Holly's chest. *Who was Wes Brockman and what did he have to do with the murder?*

Chapter 7

Wes pulled up to the park and saw George waiting for him. He had spent the last few hours in the store doing some work while the cleaners did what they could to remove the blood and gore of murder from his meeting room. He spent much of that time declining comments to the media over the phone and keeping them out of his store. But seeing George with the team baseball cap pulled down low on his head, expensive shaded glasses, and overall I'm-a-badass demeanor cracked his gloomy mood. He grinned as he got out of the car. "Good, my assistant coach is here."

A bark brought George's head up. "What the hell is that?"

Wes pocketed his keys, then leaned back in and scooped up the puppy. "This is Monty."

George stared at him. "A dog? You brought a dog to practice?"

"Yes." Wes headed to the back of the Range Rover to start unloading equipment. A baseball rolled out and Monty fell all over himself trying to chase it. Laughing, Wes turned and fished out a tennis ball. "Monty!"

The dog turned and looked at him.

Wes lobbed the ball at him. Monty tried to catch it but missed. The tennis ball bounced and Monty barked happily and chased down the ball.

"A dog," George announced again. "Do you really think

the boys are going to pay attention to baseball practice if there's a puppy around?"

Wes turned to George. "If they don't want to run laps, they will." The boys all knew that Wes was a tough Little League coach, and they respected his rules. Seeing George's serious expression, he said, "Relax. The kids will be fine. They love playing baseball. They can play with Monty after practice." Wes handed him a bucket of balls.

George's expression remained stern. "I have news."

Wes's grin died and he looked around. Normally five or six kids were already at the field and rushed up to help unload. He didn't see anyone. Monty came loping up with the tennis ball in his mouth. Looking back to George, Wes said, "Yeah? What news?"

George dropped his chin and looked over the rim of his glasses. His eyes were dark pools of trouble. "Bart Gaines was murdered in prison last year."

Wes gripped a bat, holding onto something familiar. Bart Gaines was the catalyst that had sent Wes's life straight to hell. And Wes was the reason Bart had been in prison.

He looked down at the bat in his hand. For years, Wes had been a top sports agent at Apex Sports Agency in Los Angeles. He had represented major league baseball players, many of them high-dollar stars. Bart had been a sports fitness trainer, and Wes had sent many of his clients to him. Wes had discovered that Bart was doping players with anabolic steroids after one of Wes's baseball players died. Pulling himself back to the present, Wes leaned down and picked up the ball that Monty was dancing and barking around. He threw the ball and said, "Who killed him?"

"Mob."

"Fuck." Adrenalin rushed his body and buzzed his nerves. To get some relief, he hefted the bat into a batter's grip and swung. Again and again as his mind sorted through the information. Finally, he dropped the bat to one hand. "How would the mob get into my store? Why kill Cullen? Are the mob and Cullen's murder even connected?" All these questions had been beating at him for days. That was why he'd hired Holly, to find out. But somehow it hadn't seemed really possible. Until now.

George said, "I can't find any connection between Cullen Vail and the mob." He shook his head. "It's not adding up. I don't think it's the mob. The only reason they went after you in the beginning was to keep you from testifying against Bart."

"Because Bart and Apex had the stronger connections to the mob. And once law enforcement tugged that thread, it all came tumbling down." Wes hadn't been the real threat to the mob—hell, he hadn't even known the mob was connected to Apex until after he'd contacted the DEA about his suspicions that the trainer was giving the players steroids. Wes stared blankly at the equipment in the back of his car. "So Bart squealed?"

George bent over, picked up the ball Monty brought back, and tossed it. "Yep. All kinds of indictments for the gambling and doping. You know Apex was destroyed."

He nodded, feeling another stab of guilt. He hadn't been there to guide his clients, help them find another agent. He felt like he had abandoned them. But he had been more afraid the mob would kill him or his sister in revenge once he testified. He said, "Then who is behind the murder of Cullen? Holly was leaning toward either a pissed off lover, or someone from his past that he swindled. He had a record."

George was watching Monty as the puppy tried to skid to a stop by the ball, but ended up tumbling over his big paws. "It wasn't a crime of passion, not with that professional double shot, one to the head and one to the chest. Someone had some training."

"But Cullen is only connected to me through the book club." He agreed with Holly in that respect, since Cullen was a book club member, and the murder was committed in the meeting room.

Two cars pulled up, distracting him from his train of

thought. He was surprised to see Holly's white Maxima. She was supposed to meet him at his house at six. How had she found him? Dumb question, she was a private investigator.

The other car belonged to Nora Jacobson. Four boys spilled out, rushed up to say hello and grab equipment to set up practice. Wes glanced at his watch. Five minutes after four, and only four boys had arrived so far?

Monty came running back with the ball in his mouth.

"Coach, you have a dog? Cool! Can he come with us while we set up?" Nora's son Ryan asked.

Wes nodded.

George turned and herded the boys and dog out to the field.

"Hi, Wes." Nora walked up wearing a pair of jeans and a beige T-shirt.

She looked like Sally Field from the movie *Norma Rae*. But unlike the woman from the movie, Nora tended to be quiet and slightly timid. She owned a bakery and he could personally vouch for her cakes. "Hi, Nora. It looks like we're going to be late getting started today." He glanced around, catching sight of Ryan and the other three boys arranging the equipment. Monty thought it was a cool game and raced around them with the tennis ball hanging out of his mouth.

Nora followed his gaze, then she pushed a loose strand of hair back into her ponytail. "Uh, I don't think any more boys are coming today."

Wes noticed that Holly had gotten out of her car and walked up behind Nora. She stayed quiet. Absorbing Nora's statement, he waited until she finally met his gaze. "Why is that?"

She played with her hair, then locked her hands together in front of her. "Some of the parents have heard rumors. You know, the murder. They, uh, they just . . ."

A cold feeling iced his gut. "What rumors?"

"Love triangle," she mumbled, looking at his right shoulder.

"*What?*" What love triangle?

Nora stepped back. "I tried to tell them . . . I mean, I don't believe it. Most of the parents have been calling me all day since they know I'm the team mom and that I go to your book club. They're hearing rumors that you and Cullen fought over a married woman and you killed him. I know it's a lie! I told the parents, and the police when they came to my bakery today, that it's a lie!"

Getting himself under control, he said, "Sorry, I didn't mean to yell. I just don't know what that means, Nora. I haven't even dated in months." His gaze slid up to Holly.

She stared at him with a hard, impassive expression. He couldn't read her and a chill loneliness rolled through him. What was she doing here? Had she followed him? Maybe she didn't believe him after all?

He looked back at Nora. "Who is spreading these rumors?"

She flushed and tugged at her shirt while staring at the hem. "Don't know. It's just going around. Everyone is edgy."

Holly stepped up beside Nora. "Hi, Nora. I'm Holly. Remember me from the book club?"

Nora turned to her, looking a little surprised. "Yes, sure."

Holly smiled. "I'm a private investigator working on this case. I'd like to ask you some questions."

The flush drained, leaving her skin white and strained against her dark hair. She looked around and shuffled back a bit. "Oh no, I can't, that is, I don't have time. I told the police everything. I have to go back to work." She glanced at him. "I'll pick Ryan up at—"

Her words were drowned out by the screech of tires as an oversized Hummer roared into the parking lot and swung to a stop at an angle. The motor kept running as a large man jumped out. He stormed up to Nora and leaned into her threateningly. "What do you think you're doing bringing Josh here? I don't want my son around this adulterous, murdering son of a bitch!"

"Hey." Wes stepped between them, literally pushing Nora to the side, closer to Holly. "You have a problem with me, talk to me. Don't yell at Nora. She was just doing you a favor like she does every week by giving Josh a ride." His temper shot up into the high scoring zone.

"Get out of my face, Brockman."

Wes didn't know Josh's dad's name, although he recognized him from some games the man occasionally showed up for. "You want to take Josh home, then do it. But don't upset the other boys or cause trouble."

His face got red. "*You* leave. You're not coaching these kids. We've heard all about your sleazy little games." He grabbed Wes's shirt. "And if I find out you've messed with my wife—"

Wes felt his temper crack, but struggled to hold on because he figured the boys could see them. "Get your hands off of me."

The man snarled, "Tell me! Did you mess with my wife?" He shoved Wes back against the Range Rover.

Wes bounced off the rear of the car and came back ready. He measured the guy at about six feet and two hundred fifty pounds of furious testosterone.

The guy took a step, drawing back his right fist.

Wes went in low and shoved his fist into the guy's gut.

"Ooof." He doubled over.

Wes's ears rang with pumping rage. He wanted to slam the prick into the ground and make him eat dirt.

Then he remembered the kids.

Trying to control his temper, Wes stepped back and gave the man room. "Leave." He could barely get the word out. Sucking in air to counter the effects of the adrenaline coursing through him, he added, "Don't make this worse. Take Josh and leave."

The other man straightened up. "Cops are gonna fry your balls anyway." He stormed to the field.

Wes turned around and saw that George had moved the

kids behind the dugout to throw the ball for Monty, preventing them from seeing the scene. At least one thing went right.

Nora said, "I better take the other boys home."

Wes looked at her. "Nora, do you know anything about this? What was Cullen doing that got him killed?"

She shook her head, sidestepping toward the field. "No. Nothing."

Holly started to follow her. "You dated him, Nora. What are you hiding?"

"I can't help you. I don't know anything!"

Holly didn't let up. She walked closer. "Where did you tell the police you were after the meeting Tuesday night?"

Nora stopped scooting away to turn and face Holly. "Helene, Maggie, and I went to dinner, then they came to my house and we watched *The Notebook*. It was after midnight when Helene and Maggie left. I told the police all this. Now I have to go." She turned her back on Holly and jogged across the field.

Wes stared after her. Nora was a single mom who worked hard, and she was team mom for their baseball team. She tended to be quiet and he could understand why she was spooked. Especially since Josh's dad just got in her face.

But it still felt like he was losing another friend.

"Hey, coach, you gonna reschedule?" Ryan asked as he stuffed some of the gear back into Wes's car, while holding Monty under one arm.

Wes took note of Josh's dad hustling him into the Hummer. Josh was a nice kid, a good outfielder. Too bad his dad was an asshole. Looking back at Ryan, Wes took the equipment and set it in the back of his car, then slung his arm around the boy's shoulder. "Sure, Ryan. I'll call your mom and we'll figure it out. In the meantime, you keep working on your swing." Ryan was raw, but he had some real muscle in his swing. He could be a powerhouse slugger one day.

The boy looked up at Wes with his mom's big brown eyes.

"Yeah, I will. Coach, I'm sorry about that guy in your book-store."

"Us, too." The other two boys stored the rest of the gear.

Wes and the boys all loved baseball, and that had formed a bond between them. When he was on the field with the boys, he felt more at home than he had anywhere else in a long time. All he could say was, "Thanks, guys."

Ryan held out Monty, who dropped his ball in an effort to lick the boy's face. Laughing, Ryan pushed Monty's face away and said, "Rad dog. Wish we could have one."

Wes took Monty. "You can play with Monty anytime." Then he watched the three boys get in the car with Nora and leave. None of this made any sense. Why would someone spread rumors about him and a married woman? Was it Tanya they were talking about? It had to be.

Holly moved up to him. She wore the same clothes she had earlier today, but something about her had changed. Closed off. Suspicious? Angry? He knew she'd come out swinging, so he started with, "I haven't been involved with a married woman and I never fought with Cullen over any woman." He was damned tired of people not believing in him. His wife hadn't believed in him, not when he'd decided to do the right thing. Nor had his sister.

She took a deep breath. "I came here to tell you I quit."

It felt like he took a fast pitch to his chest. He set Monty in the back of the Range Rover with his ball. Then he stared Holly down. "So you're a quitter?"

Her expression didn't change. "Depends."

He felt George walk up behind him, but he was focused on Holly. What was she after? More money? It wouldn't be the first time some woman figured out he was rich and decided she should get a cut. "On?"

"The truth. Who are you? Why is it that Wes Brockman didn't come into existence until three years ago? I didn't find any evidence of Wes Brockman passing the bar exam in

California." She looked around the empty field. "And why would you keep the fact that you coach a Little League team a secret? Who the hell are you?"

A vicelike tension gripped his lungs and guts. How much did she know? Obviously she'd done some research. Was she truly pissed off? Or was she using this to force him to pay her more money? "What do you mean?" He felt George stiffen behind him.

Holly narrowed her gaze. "I should just walk away. You are really pissing me off, but I'm going to give you some free advice before I wash my hands of you. You don't want to trust me, fine. I don't give a shit. But you'd better get your ass down to the police station and tell the truth to Rodgers." She stopped talking, her chest heaving with anger or some other high emotion.

George shifted next to him and said calmly, "Holly, what does Wes owe you for the work you've done? We'll pay you now and you can forget all about Wes."

"Shut up," Wes snapped. No way in hell was he going to let George pay her off. They had an agreement and she was damn well going to fulfill her end of it. He needed her. She had the inside with the cops so he could know what their investigation turned up. "She's not quitting, she's negotiating."

Holly cut her gaze to him. "Have a good life, Brockman, or whoever you are." She turned to leave.

It was so easy to slide back into his old skin and play hardball. "Hillbay, if you walk away now, I won't pay you anything. Not a penny."

She stopped walking.

He felt a wave of smug relief, and something else, some vague disappointment that annoyed him. What had he expected? Ethics to outweigh money? Crossing his arms over his chest, he waited. She didn't make him wait long.

Holly walked up to him, tilted her face up, and speared him with her silver blue gaze. Her voice cracked like ice. "Come again?"

He stared right back at her. "You told me yourself that you follow the money. I have the money. And I'm not going to pay you any more than double your standard fee, plus expenses, which we agreed on."

Color flooded her face, making her skin glow and her eyes shimmer with fury. "You really think I'm negotiating here?"

He didn't say a word. Just let the silence stretch out. She was good, but Wes had negotiated with the best and beat them.

Finally, Holly said, "Here's my final offer, book boy. Take your money and shove it up your ass."

Wes stayed at the baseball field and gave his arm a workout throwing the ball for Monty. The puppy loved the game, trotting after the ball, then racing back to drop it in front of him.

He couldn't believe Holly had walked. Just like that.

The ache in his shoulder warned him he was pushing too much, but Wes threw the ball hard. Monty scampered after it, his gold ears flapping as he barked his happiness at chasing the ball.

A slow burn replaced the ache. He was going to have to ice the damn shoulder. The baseball field was quiet, except for his heavy breathing and Monty trotting back with the ball. He dropped it at Wes's feet with his sides heaving.

Wes picked up the ball and headed for the dugout where he'd left a couple bottles of water.

Monty barked and ran around his legs, trying to convince him to throw the ball.

"Give an old man a break, Monty." He couldn't help but laugh at the puppy. He had to be thirsty and exhausted but he still wanted to play.

That was how Wes had been about baseball. He'd loved the game, lived for it. It had all been taken away in a nightmare of bullets and blood.

And cops who got there too late.

Wes took a deep breath and forced the memories back. They wouldn't help him now. He had needed Holly, needed her inside connection to the police investigation while he and George dealt with the possibility that the mob had murdered Cullen and was after him.

But she had bailed.

Maybe she did have ethics after all. But that didn't make him feel better. She'd never really given him a chance.

Monty followed him into the dugout. Wes grabbed a bottle of water, took the batter's helmet he'd gotten out of the baseball gear, turned it upside down, and filled the bowl with water. Then he crouched down and held it out for the dog.

Monty stuck his gold muzzle in and drank, wagging his tail and wiggling his whole body.

"Are you in witness protection?"

Startled, Wes dropped the helmet and shot up to his feet.

Holly stood in the entrance to the dugout. Chunks of her dark blond hair had escaped her clip to frame her face. Her mouth was serious, her eyes cop-blank. She leaned her bare shoulder against the fence. Casual, and yet he could feel her intensity.

Monty picked up the ball and ran to Holly. He dropped it at her feet and barked. When she didn't move, he nosed the ball toward her and snorted.

She ignored the dog. "Are you?"

A feeling he barely recognized damn near cut off his breath—*hope*. He hadn't realized how hopeless, how unfeeling, his life had been for three years. Until the moment Holly had walked into his book club and rocked his life. She had shaken up his world and made him realize he'd just been existing, not living.

And now she was waiting for an answer.

He walked toward her. "No. I wasn't a big enough fish to go into witness protection." He was close enough to smell her scent, the scent that was pure Holly, citrus with a softer, almost powdery smell. To distract himself, he scooped up the ball at his feet, stepped out of the dugout cage, and threw it.

Holly whistled. "That's some arm you have there, book boy."

He turned around. "Once I could throw a ninety-four-mile-an-hour fastball strike."

Holly linked the fingers of her right hand through the fence. "You played pro?"

He had a choice to make. Could he trust Holly with the truth? Was she here because she realized that twice her normal fee was a good deal? To negotiate more money? Or for some other reason? He surprised himself by telling her, "I signed the contract, but I never made it to spring training." Reaching out, he curled his fingers around hers from the other side of the chain-link fence. "Why did you come back, Holly?"

She said bluntly, "I want this case. I think I can solve this murder."

"Ambition, huh?" Wes wanted her. His life was on a greased road to disaster and he couldn't get his brain out of her pants. He was attracted to her hot body, pretty face, and kick-ass attitude. And the need in her gaze, the need she worked so damn hard to cover up. He'd seen it the first night at his house when she'd held Monty to her chest. He'd seen how much she'd wanted the dog. Then fear had hardened her face and she'd claimed she didn't have room for an animal or anyone in her life. She stayed quiet so Wes added, "If that little stunt you pulled back there was your negotiating method, you suck. You don't come back less than a half hour after walking. You make the other side come to you."

Her entire body, including her slender fingers beneath his, stiffened. "I am ambitious, I told you that. I took the case for the money, I told you that. I am honest, Brockman, unlike you. I'm not looking for more money, I'm looking for the truth."

That feeling again—a flash of warmth in his gut. Hope. "And you came back for?"

"For the truth." She tightened her fingers around the chain-link. "Who are you? Wes Brockman is not a lawyer in California. Was that a lie?"

Monty came trotting back with the ball in his mouth. He dropped it on the ground and barked to let them know it was time to throw it again.

Wes ignored him. It all came down to choices. He chose. "No. Nicholas Mandeville is a lawyer. Or was, at any rate."

Chapter 8

Holly stared at Wes, feeling the warmth of his fingers covering hers through the chain-link fence on the baseball field. He claimed he was Nicholas Mandeville, not Wes. She would check it out. But if he was telling the truth, there was a story there, she could feel it. "Why are you pretending to be Wes Brockman?"

He blinked, let go of her fingers, and bent over to pick up the ball.

Monty barked and turned in circles, clearly encouraging Wes to throw the ball. Wes obliged. Then he crossed his arms over his chest. "I'll tell you, but I need you to swear first that you won't tell the police."

She considered that with an edge of suspicion. "I'm not a lawyer or a therapist. I'm not going to agree to keep your secrets if you've broken the law. And don't think I won't check out your story."

For the first time, he grinned. "I know you will. The only trouble I might be in is for the name change. But I'm willing to deal with that if I can resolve the situation that brought me here. Deal?"

Holly looked him over through the fence. He wore a pair of black sweatpants and a white T-shirt that showed his powerful shoulders and flat stomach. The late afternoon sun caught the streaks in his brown hair, and brought out the dots of yellow in his intense green eyes. Oh yeah, he was sexy. But what tightened the ball of lust low in her belly was something she couldn't quite define, an intensity deeply ingrained in his character that he covered with easygoing charm. But she didn't think with her libido, she thought with her brain. It was a fair deal. "Okay. So start talking."

Monty came back with the ball. Wes reached down, scooped the dog up in his arms, and rubbed his head, careful of the healing cut on one ear. "I disappeared to protect my sister, Michelle."

"Michelle . . ." She drew the word out, a memory surfacing in her mind. "Michelle Mandeville? The surfer who has been in all the magazines and on talk shows? She's your sister? You told me this morning that you had an argument with your sister and don't talk to her now." She didn't have enough pieces yet to make the puzzle fit.

A small smile of pride warmed his face when he looked up from Monty. "Yes, she's my sister. And we did have an argument. Let's go for a walk."

The abrupt shift in topic took her a second. Then she nodded. She fell into step next to him as they walked from the baseball diamond toward the playground. There were a few kids running around, but it was mostly quiet. She glanced over to see Monty try to lick Wes's face.

"No, Monty," he said, and gently pushed his face away.

The dog rested his head on Wes's arm. He had to be worn out from chasing the ball. They were following the sidewalk path around the park.

Finally Wes said, "Three years ago, I was married, a very successful agent for some top major league baseball players, and pretty much had a charmed life."

Holly said, "I thought you said you were a lawyer? And what happened to your pro baseball career? Why didn't you make it to spring training?" She knew she was trying to catch up on years of Wes's life in minutes.

"I had an injury to my right shoulder that ended my career. So I went to law school. From there—"

Holly interrupted. "What kind of injury?"

"Gunshot."

Holly stopped walking. She saw Wes go a couple more steps, then turn back to look at her. Monty had fallen asleep, his head thrown back and his tongue hanging out, totally trusting Wes to hold him. A thick feeling clogged her throat looking at them, so she shifted her gaze to his face. "You were shot?" She knew he didn't like cops. Had she made a mistake about him? Maybe he'd been shot by the police?

He walked back to her until she could feel Monty's fur tickle her arms. "Home invasion robbery at my parents' house. The robbers didn't know I was there. They tied up my sister and mom to keep them under control and were beating the shit out of my dad. They thought he had money because he was semi-famous."

"Your dad the journalist?" She could feel the old anger in him.

"Yes. He had a column called *Cop Scan*. He exposed corruption and brutality within the police and sheriff's department in Los Angeles. Sometimes he went on assignment to other locations. The robbers followed him home one night, came in through the garage with guns. Two of them. I was in the closet under the stairs looking for something in the boxes my mom had packed away. I called the police on my cell phone when I realized what was happening. I told them to hurry, and no lights or sirens." He stopped talking, his gaze moving to the brightly colored jungle gym on the sand.

Holly knew he wasn't seeing the playground, but the memories. "What happened?"

"It seemed like hours. I heard my dad explaining over and over that all they had was what was in his wallet and my mom's purse. The robbers thought he had a safe. He didn't. We weren't rich, just average middle class. My dad was trying to stay calm . . ." Monty made a low whining sound in his sleep. Wes soothed him by gently petting his head and saying, "It's okay, boy."

Holly wondered if the dog had nightmares about nearly drowning. Or the people who tried to drown him. She felt pity for the dog but she was more interested in Wes's story. "What happened when the cops arrived?"

His gaze settled on her. His eyes were the color of heavy, wet moss. "It took the police eleven minutes to get there *with* lights and sirens. But I'd already had enough. I went out of the closet with a bat. I tried to circle around the back of them, but the police sirens startled them. One of them turned and saw me—he fired. The other one fired on my dad. I caught the bullet in my right shoulder. My dad was shot right through his heart. He died within minutes. Maybe seconds."

Holly didn't know she'd reached out until she felt his tense forearm beneath her hand. "I'm sorry." What he had described sank in. "They came with lights and sirens? Are you sure you told the nine-one-one operator the situation?"

"I'm sure." He bit the words off. "There was an investigation and it was deemed equipment failure. The nine-one-one operator claimed her equipment to dispatch the call had failed for a few minutes. And the lights and sirens were a miscommunication."

"But you think it was some kind of payback against your dad? Revenge?" She couldn't imagine that happening. Not in an emergency. Besides, if they knew who Wes's dad was, wouldn't it make more sense to get there as quickly as possible and prove the cops were the good guys?

Wes shrugged. "It was a long time ago. After that, my pitching career was over so I went to law school." He turned and headed to a cement picnic table set under a tree. He sat down and shifted Monty to sleep on his lap.

Holly sat down next to him. "How did you become a sports agent?"

"I was recruited right after I graduated law school by the

Apex Sports Agency. They wanted me to represent baseball players. This was my chance to get back into the game I loved. After seeing what had happened to my dad, I was determined to become powerful, so powerful that people like the cops couldn't just ignore me." He looked over at her "I was going to make and break careers."

There it was, Holly thought, that intensity and determination in him. "Did you?"

He grinned. "Oh yeah. Turns out I was even better at negotiating than pitching a fastball. For years, I lived the high life. I made it to all the A-list events, I went to the best restaurants, parties, et cetera." He turned to look at her. "Amazing how a life like that would just fall into my lap, huh?"

She knew she was wearing her skeptical expression. "Too good to be true?"

He nodded. "I was so focused on my life, on attaining more and more. I never wanted to be as devastated again as I was when my dad was killed and my lifelong dream of playing baseball shattered. So I kept collecting better and better players. I had an uncanny ability to sign the powerhouse sluggers." He shook his head.

Holly didn't flinch. "So what happened?" A beat of time passed, as if he had to summon up the answer from a dark corner in his mind.

Then he answered, "Conrad Nader. He was an okay outfielder, but man, that guy could hit. He was on his way to breaking homerun records. Then his wife came into my office one afternoon. Lacey was a very nice woman and good for Conrad. He adored her, and she kept his ego in check. But that day, she was in tears. She told me that she thought Conrad was showing symptoms of being on anabolic steroids. She begged me to help him before he died." Monty snorted and snuffled in his sleep. Wes looked down at the dog, rubbed his belly, and went on. "I told Lacey that it was my job to take care of my clients and not to worry. Then I ushered her out the door."

"You didn't believe her?"

His green eyes were filled with guilt, regret, remorse . . . some strong emotion. "I didn't *want* to believe it. And looking back, I think that's why Apex recruited me. Somehow, they knew I'd let the money and power buy off my ethics." He looked over at Holly. "I never even talked to Conrad. I told myself that I'd know if one of my players was in trouble. He died two weeks later in a hotel room while on the road. I still refused to acknowledge the truth. At the cemetery after Conrad's funeral, I was huddled with some players, and in the back of my mind I was thinking about who I was going to replace Conrad with."

"Jesus, Brockman." Holly pulled back, feeling the cold cement of the bench beneath her butt. Wes was describing exactly the type of rich, powerful man she detested. A man like her ex fiancé, Brad, who would stop at nothing to get what he wanted.

His mouth went flat and hard. "Can't handle the truth, Hillbay? I'm not telling you this to get your absolution. I don't need your forgiveness. I knew what I had to do and I did it. Now I live with the consequences."

Holly absorbed his words. It didn't take any deep insight to feel his pain, grief, and regret. "How long you been hiding that chip on your shoulder, book boy?"

His shoulders relaxed a little. "Touché."

"Go on, tell me the rest." Holly really wanted to know.

"A couple people were escorting the widow away from the casket to the limousine when she spotted me. She shook off their support and walked over to me with her head held high. I'll never forget it. She looked tired but dignified in her simple black dress. She said, 'You lied to me and you failed Conrad. You're no better than a murderer.' That was it. She turned and walked away." He sighed and added, "She was right. If she had screamed at me, hit me, anything else, I'd have continued in my delusion. But her quiet, dignified anger and grief broke through my denial and I knew she was right."

Holly could almost see the scene. "So what happened?"

"I started digging around. Soon I learned that the elite trainer our sports agency sent our top athletes to was giving them steroids, sometimes in double or triple doses. Remember, this was before baseball was forced to do any real, significant testing. They were doping *my* players to turn them into power-house, record-breaking hitters. No one seemed to care that a man was dead."

Bitterness thickly coated his last sentence. "What did you do?"

He swallowed, as if forcing down a bad memory. "I decided to turn the trainer in. My wife begged me not to, she said I would destroy our lives and it was the baseball player's fault for taking the steroids."

Holly couldn't contain her own sarcastic tone. "Nice. Did Conrad know?"

Wes shrugged. "I can't be sure. Probably at some point, he did. But the competition is so fierce, Holly. And he was just a kid, really. Besides, that's not the point. The trainer was push-ing dangerous drugs on these guys, and my agency, which was supposed to be advocating and protecting our players, sent the athletes there knowing that. Later I found out why."

Oh boy, she could see it now. What had Wes said—amaz-ing how he kept signing powerhouse sluggers? "Gambling?"

He blinked in surprise. "Yeah. The mob had very strong connections to the agency. But I didn't know that then. I by-passed the local police and went to the DEA, and together we set up the trainer. And got him."

This was the man Holly was attracted to—the one who did the right thing even at a personal cost to him. "The mob didn't like that, I take it."

"This is the part where it gets confusing. See, I knew nothing about the gambling or the mafia's connection. I had a really bit part in this, just exposing the doping. I had nothing to do with the gambling and racketeering charges that followed later."

"What about your wife? Where does she factor into this? Was she threatened or anything?"

"She left the day I went to the DEA. I had some threats, phone calls, my ex-bosses warned me I was in danger and shouldn't testify. But I was never actually confronted by someone representing the mob. My wife was out of the picture and left the state. But eventually the mob found my sister and beat her up to send a message to me."

Her stomach turned. "I'm sorry, Wes. That had to be awful."

His green eyes collided with her gaze. "You have no idea. Michelle was furious and scared. She was only about twenty-two at the time. So young. She told me I'd become exactly the type of man that my dad had exposed in his *Cop Scan* columns, that I had abused my power and now a baseball player was dead and people were getting hurt."

That had to be brutal. "But she came around, right?"

He took a deep breath. "I didn't wait to find out. I had to make sure Michelle was safe. She was all I had left—our father had been murdered and our mother had died a few years before. I had failed to protect my family from the home invasion, then I failed to protect my client, whom I was making a shitload of money off of, and then my sister was beat up. It was time for me to step up and take action. So I sent Michelle to Australia until the trial was over. I put enough money in Michelle's bank account to keep her comfortable for years." He turned back to look at the playground. "I testified. I had to. For my dead client and for his wife. The morning after the guilty verdict came in, I went surfing and purposely disappeared. Nick Mandeville was dead and I set up a new identity as Wes Brockman. I knew Michelle was going on a surfing tour for months and should be safe. I never contacted her. She probably assumes I'm dead."

Holly's brain had been working the puzzle as he gave her the pieces. "And now you think the mob has found you? Why would they kill Cullen in your bookstore?"

He looked over at her. "It's possible they found me, but it

seems unlikely. If the mob wanted me dead, I'd be dead. I'm sitting here now out in the open. Anyone could shoot me. It doesn't make any sense."

"But you are sure it was the mob that beat up your sister?" Holly wanted to clarify her facts.

"Michelle didn't get their names and social security numbers. Mob was my best guess."

It didn't add up, in Holly's mind. The mob could have killed Wes—or Nick, as he'd been back then. They hadn't needed to bother with his sister. And he was right, if they had found him now and wanted him dead, he'd be dead. Still . . . "Cullen's murder did look professional with the twin shots in the head and chest."

He looked over. "So you think it is the mob?"

She shook her head. "No, I think it was someone who knew how to kill, someone who had some training. Besides, the victim was facing his killer. A lot of hits for show have the victim on his knees and shot from behind. Cullen didn't leave any signs that he'd been afraid of the killer. No struggle. He'd been shot while casually standing there watching the killer come in the doorway or something like that."

Frustration coated Wes's words. "Then what?"

She kept thinking it through. "It's possible that a pissed off lover or a revenge-seeking victim of Cullen's earlier scams did it. But the murderer planned it. It was not a heat of the moment, passion-driven killing. And the fact that it was in your bookstore brings you into the equation." Holly took a deep breath and said, "If you are telling me the truth, I think someone is setting you up. Maybe for revenge. Someone is destroying your life."

He looked stunned, then recovered enough to say, "So you'll stay on the case?"

Holly made herself stand up. "I'll let you know."

Holly had spent a solid hour and a half at her office, running searches and checking all her sources. Wes's story held up. She believed him. That was why she was standing in his kitchen watching him pour Monty's food into a bowl while the dog did a clumsy dance in anticipation.

Wes set Monty's bowl on the floor by the sliding glass window. In his eagerness, Monty skidded on the tile, fell over, then got up and finally made his way to the bowl.

Holly had to clamp her lips to keep from laughing. The dog radiated happiness. It was revolting in a sort of cute way.

Wes stood up, picked up two glasses of wine, and handed one to Holly. "I'm glad you came over."

She took the glass. "Tell me who George is?"

He looked away from her, his shoulders tensing. "A friend. That's all. Just a friend."

She set her glass down and said, "This is exactly the kind of evasion that's going to stop. I can't work with half-answers."

Wes picked up her glass of wine and looked her in the eyes. "Holly, George made a bundle of money by doing security work for very wealthy clients. He's retired, and does occasional consulting. That's all. We've been friends for three years. He's the only one who knows the truth about me." He held out her glass. "Until now."

That rang true, or nearly true. Holly wondered if George had done a little corporate espionage and was now keeping a low profile. She took the glass. "I'm keeping my eye on him." But near as she could tell, George had no connection to Cullen, and no reason to kill him and destroy Wes.

"He's not involved," Wes repeated.

She ignored that. "Let's get to work. We need to figure out who killed Cullen and why." Feeling a little edgy, she took a healthy swallow of the wine. Being in the same room with Wes had that effect on her. She needed to clear up one more point. "If we find out there's some kind of hired killer in Goleta . . ."

He cut her off while absently rubbing his shoulder. "We'll tell Rodgers. She's running her own investigation, too. But we both agreed it wasn't likely a mob hit. You said maybe it was revenge, but why kill Cullen to get revenge on me?"

Seeing him massage his old injury, she felt a heavy ache behind her breastbone. Sympathy wasn't useful so she ignored it and answered him. "Did you see what happened at your baseball practice today? Killing Cullen in your locked bookstore puts suspicion squarely on you. And now rumors are being spread about you. It looks like your life is being systematically destroyed. And I'd say that whoever is doing it—and my bet is *so* on a woman—is just getting started."

He dropped his hand and stared at her. "You believe me."

Holly shifted on her feet, feeling like she was losing control of her boundaries. Of course she believed him, he was her client. If she didn't believe him, she would have cut him loose. But something about his tone, his gaze, made her feel . . . needed in more than just a professional way. "Bet your ass, book boy. I might be street educated, but that means I know a setup when I see one." She set her wine on the table and went to his refrigerator and opened it. "Where do you keep your candy bars?"

"Don't have any."

Disgusted, she shut the door and opened the freezer. "Any ice cream?"

She felt him move up behind her and put his hand on her shoulder. "Have you eaten since your last candy bar? Let me find something to make for dinner."

She shut the freezer door and turned. "Forget dinner." She needed to focus on work. "Let's look at suspects. How pissed was your wife? What did she think you ruined by going to the DEA?"

He slid his hand to the back of her neck and massaged her tight muscles. "Our lifestyle. Tiffany liked being the wife of a powerful man. I knew that, I married her because she was perfect for the job, designer-clothes thin, charming, and willing to let me be the family star. Then I changed the rules. I saw myself in the eyes of a woman who called me a murderer and I didn't like it much."

Holly tried to keep her mind on the job. "Where did she go? What happened?" His hand was still on her nape, his long fingers caressing her. It felt too good to make him stop.

"She moved to New York and divorced me before the case came to trial. She started dating other powerful men before the divorce was final."

She wondered how much that had hurt. "That's cold."

Anger thinned his mouth. "You aren't being fair to her. She had no control over what was happening. I screwed up, and believe me, she was furious about that. But what tore her up was that I wasn't putting her, and our life together, first."

She rolled her eyes and put her hands onto his chest to shove him away from her. "Don't make me hurl, Brockman. That's a load of crap and exactly why I don't get involved in romantic relationships."

He turned away from her. "Not every woman's cut out to be a hard-ass."

Nice direct hit. She had to admire it. Wes had accurately pointed out that she was more of a hard-ass than a woman. *Big deal.* "This hard-ass is trying to find out who is screwing with your life, so you might want to get over the disappointment." She walked to the table where she'd put her laptop and her wine. "I'm going to do a search of Tiffany Soft-Ass's current address."

"Holly."

The whole point of being a hard-ass was that it didn't matter and it didn't hurt. So she looked up. "What now?"

He moved toward her. "I'm a huge admirer of your hard ass."

She put both hands on her hips, trying for a casualness that had deserted her. "You're just trying to charm me into keeping your secret. Now go away so I can work."

He shook his head. "You gave me your word. I'm not worried. You won't break your word unless you have to."

Her chest hollowed out at his words.

His hand slid around the back of her neck, pulling her to him. "I told you earlier, in your office, no more interruptions."

She tilted her head back. "That was before I knew who you were."

He lowered his head until she could just feel his breath. "What name are you going to call out when I'm stroking you into an orgasm?"

A tremor of longing traveled down her spine and spread until she throbbed between her legs. Her belly was on fire and she pressed her hips against him instinctively. She didn't know if she was answering him or protesting when she said, "Wes."

"Damn right you are." He took her breath away by skimming his mouth over hers, starting at one corner and sliding to the other side. Chills and heat collided. He moved his free hand to her butt, cupping her and pulling her into his hard-on. She couldn't stand it and opened her mouth, sucking his lower lip between her teeth.

He tightened against her, his dick pulsed against her belly, and he gave a sensual little sex-growl deep in his chest.

His obvious desire ripped through Holly, increasing her desire. She didn't lie to herself, she knew people reacted to stress and danger with heightened sex drives. But his drive grinding against her belly showed her how sex was getting in the way for both of them. They both wanted it. The best thing to do was get the sex out of the way and get back to work. "Let's do it, Brockman."

He lifted his mouth from hers. "Hill*baby*, you have the soul of a romantic." Shifting, he lifted her into his arms.

"Bite me." She let him carry her. Why not? If he wanted to play caveman, she'd show him what a cavewoman could do.

Rolling out a killer smile, he said, "Absolutely." He walked through the living room and made a left turn into the master bedroom, which had a view of the beach. He set her on her feet next to his king-sized bed.

She watched him walk to the French doors to the left of the bed and open them. The deck wrapped around the back of the house. Damp salt air breezed in.

"Take your hair down." Wes stood a few feet away, watching her. He was backlit by the dying light as the sun sank into the ocean. She couldn't see his eyes. But she could see him fist his hands at his sides, struggling to control himself.

There was nothing as sexy as making a man want her, crave her. Reaching up, she took the clip from her hair. Then she pulled her shirt off and let it fall to the floor. Kicking off her shoes, she unbuttoned her jeans, shimmied them down to her ankles, and stepped out of them. Leaving her in a black, lacy bra, and barely-there panties.

Wes made a sound, then he pulled off his shirt, got rid of his shoes, and shucked his pants and his boxers. She had a full ten seconds to take him in, and wow, he was worth looking at. His shoulders rippled with the strength to throw the fast pitch she'd seen today. She shifted her gaze to the old scar on his right side. The bullet must have shattered the bone, but he had healed and the scar almost blended in. She lowered her gaze to skim over the flat waist that narrowed to his hips, full-sized erection, and powerful thighs. Then her viewing time was up and he came to her naked and said, "God, you are hot."

"You're not bad yourself. For a book boy." He'd kept himself in shape from his athlete days. She touched the pads of her fingers to his chest and ran them down to his iron-hard abs. She felt his muscles twitch and jump.

"Before I totally lose control, do we need a condom? Or are you safe?"

"Safe." She dropped her gaze and wrapped her hand around his penis. The warm swollen length of him pleased her. Especially when he thrust into her hand.

Sucking in a sharp breath, he said, "My turn." He pulled her hand away from his cock and went to work on the front clasp of her bra. He slid it off her shoulders and let it fall.

She ached for him to touch her. She ached for him to slide inside of her. He wrapped his left arm around her waist and cupped her breast, gently massaging and squeezing, then teasing her nipple. The sensations arrowed through her, and this time it was her arching into him.

He took her mouth and slid his hand down her belly. She wanted him bad enough to beg. Thrusting her tongue against his, she tilted her hips, waiting for his touch through, or under, her panties when she felt him freeze.

Shit.

"What is this?" Wes lifted his mouth from hers.

Holly met his gaze. "It's an old scar. Just ignore it." She used the back of her knuckles to stroke across the head of his penis. A shiver rocked him.

But Wes clamped down on her hand, holding her in place while he stepped back. He dropped his stare down her stomach to the scar that ran across her lower abdomen and into her pubic hair, under her panties. He fingered the scar.

She hadn't thought about her scar since it didn't usually bother men. But now she was acutely conscious of it. Damn it, his scar didn't bother her. "I don't have time for squeamishness. Do you want to do it or not?"

Snapping his head up, he pulled her against him. "Don't be an idiot." Lifting his hand from the scar, he laid it against her cheek. "What happened?"

"A knife happened. I was a cop, it's a hazard of the job. And let me just say, Brockman, that you are the biggest mood killer I have ever had sex with." She wanted to look away from those green eyes boring into her. It was easier to have him look at her scar than to let him study her face and eyes. "Let go of me."

Very softly, he answered, "I'm not done with you."

She hated feeling this vulnerable, this exposed. "Wes, the

moment is over. Don't make me hurt you." She sucked in a breath.

"Hill*baby*." He lowered his head to breathe against her face. "We are going to do something about that chip on your shoulder." Before she could react, he pushed her back on the bed.

She fell flat on her back and bounced once.

Wes pulled her panties off of her, stepped between her legs, and dropped to his knees. "Still want to argue?" He slid his hands under her butt and tugged her toward him.

Not so much, Holly thought as her lower body clenched in anticipation. His hot breath teased her thighs. Her muscles contracted while her clit swelled and ached. When he brought his mouth down on her, she raised her hips, going wild. He squeezed her ass, holding her to him while tonguing her— dipping inside of her, then swirling around her clit. No longer caring about anything but the pleasure rolling through her, she grabbed handfuls of his comforter and fought to climax. He kept her just at the edge, and in torment.

He chuckled lightly, then raised his head. "Say please, Hill*baby*."

God, he was annoying. Lifting her head, she looked down at his sizzling green eyes and the wicked grin on his wet mouth. "Payback's a bitch, Brockman. Remember that, *please*."

He laughed, then lowered his head, sucking her into his mouth and lightly running his teeth over her clit at the same time that he penetrated her with two fingers.

Her orgasm blasted over her and she stopped thinking under the waves of intense pleasure. Before she could catch her breath, he lifted her hips and thrust his dick into her. Her body clamped down around him. He leaned over her, covering her body with his, and demanded, "Take me, Holly."

His jaw was tight, his body gleaming with the sweat of blazing hunger. He held himself up on his elbows, and drove his hips into her with a hard, primal rhythm. Her body responded, as pleasure shivers raced through her, building higher with every thrust. "More." She wanted it all.

He plunged deeper and harder. "Say my name." Then he pulled out and thrust back into her, his entire body bowing as he climaxed.

She lost control, wrapped her arms around him to get closer as another orgasm rocked her. "Wes," she said into the curve of his neck and shoulder.

Wes rolled off her and onto his side. Holly lay still on the bed. *Damn.* That was . . . *damn.* "You have control issues, Brockman."

Rising up on his elbow, he looked down at her. "Because I didn't let you take charge of the sex?"

It took a little work to get her defenses up. "Not every woman likes the forceful caveman approach."

He brushed her hair back from her face, then skimmed his fingers over her cheek and down her jaw. "I don't like half-assed sex and neither do you, so cut the crap." Sliding his hand lower, he settled it over her right breast.

"Whatever." Holly lifted his hand off of her breast to roll off the bed.

He caught her, pulling her back against his chest. "I make you nervous, why?"

His strength kept surprising her. But he was gentle as he placed one arm under her to pillow her head, and curled the other arm possessively around her waist. The answer came to her fast and easy—because he didn't give a shit for her boundaries. She explained, "Wes, this is about lust. Danger and fear ramp up lust. Both of us are highly sexual people. This is a side effect."

She could feel his chest expand against her back as he breathed. Then he said, "It's a hell of a bonus, this side effect."

She relaxed a little. "Bonus. Right. Temporary bonus."

His hand drifted lower to trace her scar. "It's been a long

time since I've been able to tell someone the truth about who I am."

Looking down, she watched his finger etch over the scar. That felt more intimate than when he'd had his fingers inside of her. Holly tried to reestablish her boundaries. "As long as we're on the same page, book boy. It's just sex."

Chapter 9

The ring of the phone cut through his sleep. He must have dozed off. After frowning at the empty space next to him where Holly had been, Wes glanced at the bedside clock to see it was after seven and grabbed the phone. "Hello?"

"Wes, it's Jodi."

He sat up. "Hi, Jodi. Are you back in town?"

"No. We're still in Ventura. We had an accident and—"

Getting off the bed, he grabbed his boxers and pants. "How bad? Is Kelly hurt? You?"

"We're okay, Wes. Kelly's right here talking to a cop. A guy in a white truck hit us and we went off the freeway into an embankment. Hit and run."

His gut went cold. Leaving his pants undone, he said, "Are you sure you're okay? Did you get a license plate?" Had someone tried to kill them? Because they worked for him? He had to get them somewhere safe.

"I'm sure we're okay but we didn't get a license plate number. It's going to be a while before we get home."

"Listen, Jodi. I don't want you to come back here. I'll put you and Kelly up in a hotel there in Ventura until I figure out what is going on."

"Why? Wes, I thought the police wanted to talk to us?"

His gut twisted at the uncertainty in her voice. Jodi was twenty, and Kelly was nineteen. Just kids. Good kids in college. Their respective parents sent them to the University of Santa Barbara and both girls had part-time jobs to help pay expenses. They were good students, nice kids.

And he might be putting them in danger.

Holly walked in while he said, "Jodi, I'll handle the police here. They can go talk to you at the hotel. But with Cullen's murder in the bookstore, I'm not going to take any chances with you or Kelly. I'll cover getting your hotel room, and you two can put food and anything else you need on the room. In fact"—he looked at Holly—"I'll drive up tonight to see you. I'll get whatever you girls need from your apartment. I don't want you two to worry about anything." They rented an off-campus apartment with two other girls.

Jodi answered, "You're really serious about this, aren't you?"

"I'm not taking chances with you and Kelly. I'll find a hotel, book a room, and call you back. How bad is the car? Do you need a rental car?"

"I don't know. The car is in the ditch, they have to tow it out."

He could hear tiredness in her voice. "Honey, it's okay. It was probably just an accident and I'm being a cautious old man."

Holly sat on the bed next to him. "Ask her to let me talk to the investigating officer."

Wes relayed the message then gave Holly the phone. In two minutes, she had established that the car was not drivable and that the cop would make sure Jodi and Kelly got safely to the Holiday Inn Ventura Beach Resort. She even had a phone number so Wes could make a reservation for the girls.

He quickly made the reservation and arranged to have a rental car delivered to the hotel for them. Then he looked at Holly. "I need to leave as soon as I grab a quick shower." Remembering he had a dog to think of now, he added, "Can you watch Monty while I'm gone?"

She made a rude noise. "I'm not a dog-sitter. Besides, I'm going with you. Pick me up at my house." She stood up and looked down at him. "I'll call Rodgers and let her know the situation."

"My neighbor will take care of Monty." Rising, he added, "You don't think it was an accident, do you?"

Although she had dressed, Holly had left her hair down and it swept her shoulders as she shook her head. "I don't like coincidences. I think you're the target of a seriously pissed-off killer."

"It was intentional." Kelly's blonde hair was wet from the shower. She wore a pair of gray sweatpants and a green T-shirt.

Wes could feel her anxiety and put his arm around her. The two of them sat on one of the two double beds in the room. Holly sat across from them, and Jodi was perched a few feet away at a pressboard writing table.

Holly had a pad of paper on her lap. "What exactly did you see, Kelly?"

"I saw him following us in the rearview mirror for miles. I don't know how long. I moved over to the far right lane 'cause Jodi and I were going to get off and find a Starbucks. The truck moved to the second lane next to us. Then he just suddenly veered right and slammed into us. I lost control of the car and we ended up in the ditch."

Jodi set a bottle of water down on the writing table. She had on a dark blue pair of loose-fitting shorts and a long-sleeved T-shirt. "A witness told the police it looked intentional. And that once the guy straightened out his truck, he sped away." She shook her head in frustration. "I didn't see anything. I was navigating because I thought I remembered a Starbucks in the area." She reached back and rubbed her neck.

Wes narrowed his gaze. "Sore?"

She smiled weakly. "The cops said we'd be sore but we're not hurt."

"Maybe we should have you two looked at anyway." Wes didn't want to take any chances.

Holly said, "I think they'll be okay, Wes. They just need to take some Advil or Tylenol and get a good night's sleep." She turned back to Kelly. "Detective Rodgers will call the two of you in the morning. She said she may be able to get what she needs from you over the phone."

Kelly looked up sharply. "What kind of questions will she ask?"

Wes rubbed Kelly's shoulder to reassure her.

Holly answered, "She's trying to find out how the killer or victim got into the locked bookstore. Since you two both have keys, she'll ask if you've given the key to anyone."

Kelly shook her head hard enough for Wes to get a mouthful of her wet hair. "I don't give the key to anyone."

"Neither do I," Jodi added.

He started to reassure them but Holly cut him off. "That's exactly what you need to tell her. Then she'll probably ask you to think about who might have access to the key. We know you are both very careful, but maybe there's something that you were sure was harmless? Like maybe you had to make a class so Cullen stayed behind to lock up for you?"

"No." Jodi had dark hair and very expressive eyes. "Wes warned us about Cullen. He didn't want us in the bookstore alone with him, or to let him give us rides home or anything like that."

Kelly nodded her agreement.

Holly looked at him.

He shrugged, a little embarrassed. "The girls tease me about being overprotective. But I worry about them. I rarely let them stay alone in the store at night, that kind of thing." He couldn't help it, he had a little sister. That kind of protectiveness was in his DNA.

Jodi cracked a smile. "When my parents call the store and I'm not there, Wes gives them an update on my life. I think they call him to check up on me."

"Mine, too," Kelly said with a sigh.

Wes grinned. "You both asked me to talk to your parents about this trip to San Diego and the concert. They weren't too sure about it. Who talked them into it?"

Kelly sighed. "Yeah, well, they only let us because you promised our parents you'd make us call you every day."

He looked at Holly and winked. "There are worse things then having parents who love you."

"So you've told us." Jodi rolled her eyes. "So how long should we stay here? We have classes next week."

He needed to keep them safe, but they needed to get back to school. "I know. I'll figure something out."

Holly said, "They can stay with me."

Wes cut his gaze to Holly.

She went on. "We'll figure it all out. But my brothers can hang around if I can't. Between all of us, we'll make sure nothing happens to them."

Kelly turned her body so she was facing him. "What about you, Wes? Are you in danger?"

He could see she was tired. They were both worn out from the combination of the trip and the shock and fright of the accident. "I don't want you worrying about me. I'm paying my PI to do that." He glanced over at Holly, then at Jodi. "You girls get some sleep."

Holly stood up. "We'll stay the night then take you back to Goleta in the morning. We can get whatever you need at your apartment, then set you up at my house. And tomorrow, after you've gotten some rest, think about how someone might have gotten the key and alarm code to the bookstore."

Wes hugged both girls and they left.

In the hallway, he looked at Holly. She had worn her usual jeans and tank top, but she had added a brown suede jacket. When he'd shown up at her condo, her hair had been wet from the shower. Once it dried on the drive, she'd clipped it up and out of her face. "Thank you for letting the girls stay at your condo. You didn't have to do that."

She turned away and walked toward the elevator. "You're paying for it. Just like you're paying for a couple more rooms tonight."

She was playing hard-ass again. His PI didn't want his thanks, she wanted those girls safe. Admiration for her welled up in his chest. He knew she wouldn't want that either, so he stopped beside her at the elevator and said, "One room with a king-sized bed."

The doors to the elevator slid open. Holly went in and said, "Are you cheap or horny?"

Wes had refused to answer Holly until they were inside the room. Another thing he liked about her—she wasn't a hypocrite. She didn't once say that she couldn't sleep with him. Or that it wouldn't look right. Or that she needed her space.

She was honest about sex. She liked it, wanted it. She just didn't want him getting too close to her emotionally.

While Holly dumped her suitcase and went in the bathroom, he looked around the room. Big king-sized bed in the middle of the room with a muddy green spread. Same color drapes, but they were open to reveal the lights of the city through the beige sheers. There was a low dresser with a TV on top and two nightstands. The usual generic hotel room. He took off his shoes and put them in the mirrored closet by the door and across from the bathroom.

The bathroom door opened just as Wes shut the closet. When he looked into the mirror, he saw Holly's image. "Holy Christ."

She leaned against the door frame wearing another bra and panty set. This woman had some serious underwear issues. This set was red.

Jesus. He swallowed.

He couldn't look away from the red triangle over her mound attached to red strings that arced over her hips. He was fairly sure that if she turned around, he'd see that red strip disappear into her ass and he'd probably drool. Her puckered nipples showed through her red bra—hell, it set him on fire. All the skin in between drove him crazy. Finally he was able to drag his gaze from the mirror long enough to turn around and face her. Even better.

She said, "Cheap or horny?"

His dick was so hard he wasn't sure he'd be able to get his zipper down. There was no way he could look casual with a straining hard-on, but he made the attempt. "Haven't decided." He brought his hand up, stuck out his index finger, and drew a circle. "Turn around."

Her blue eyes dropped to his bulge. Her smile reminded him of a cat. But she turned around.

Wes forgot to breath. There was a strip of red across her toned back from her bra. Below that, her back narrowed to her waist, then flared to her full hips, where her thong slid between her two rounded butt cheeks. He moved up behind her, put his hands on her shoulders, then slid them all the way down her back to cup her ass. Leaning close to her ear, he said, "Horny." Her skin was smooth, firm, and God, he wanted to bury himself inside of her. Her shampoo smelled of some kind of tropical fruit.

She moved into the bathroom and said, "I can feel that, book boy. Take off your clothes and we'll discuss solutions to your horniness."

Wes looked past her to the mirror on the wall of the bathroom. It was a large, floor-length vanity mirror. To the right was the long counter with the mirror over that. He ignored the toilet and shower to his left. "Is this about me taking control of sex earlier?"

"You make it sound like a power struggle." She smiled, then ran her hands from the undersides of her breasts over her flat belly.

"I'm inclined to let you win." His voice sounded hoarse in

his own ears. He pulled off his shirt and tossed it toward the bedroom.

Holly had moved a few steps into the bathroom while he stood just outside the door. She ordered, "Pants."

He looked up at her. A light flush stained her nose and cheeks, and spread over her chest. He wasn't the only one who was horny. Keeping his eyes on her, he unbuttoned his pants and said, "See how hard I am for you? Are you wet enough to take me?" He slid his pants and boxers down his hips.

Her flush deepened and she moved toward him. "I'll need a closer look."

Wes kicked his pants away and forced himself to stand perfectly still. He'd let her think she was in control.

For a while.

He knew she wanted to keep control so she could have herself a nice little orgasm without too much threatening intimacy. But he had gone too long without intimacy. Without the give and take that took sex to the next level. He wanted to know about this woman whose body he was possessing. He wanted to discover every mark on her and learn the story behind it.

Her blue eyes now had wisps of smoke gray and her smattering of freckles stood out against her skin. She wrapped one hand around his cock, and slid the other between his legs to cup his balls. Wes slapped his hand against the wall as pleasure rolled through him.

"You look very hard." She lifted her gaze to his. "Very excited."

He had to swallow before he could remember the thread of the conversation. He moved his free hand to touch her through the strip of red panties. "Hot and slick." He lowered his head to kiss her.

But she ducked him, dropped to her knees, and ran her tongue over the head of his cock. He shuddered and braced himself with both hands on the doorjamb. *Baseball. Try to think about baseball.* But all he could think about was the feel of her tongue, her mouth. "Holly." He moved his hands to her shoulders. "Come here."

She rose into his arms. He pulled her close, lining up their bodies and kissing her. Connecting with her. Finally, he looked down into her smoky blue eyes. "You are beautiful, exciting, and I love the way you hide sexy underwear beneath your street clothes." He didn't think she knew how much that told him about her. His tough PI had a soft side she kept hidden. It made him feel hot and protective of her at the same time.

She looked a little annoyed. "Can you stop talking and do it?"

He smiled, knowing his words made her mad because they meant something to her. "No. I'm going to tell you exactly how much I want you as I make love to you. Over here." He pushed her toward the counter. Meeting her gaze in the mirror over the sink, he asked, "Okay?"

She didn't answer, but slid her panties down to the floor and stepped out.

He moved up behind her, enjoying the feel of her bottom against him while he reached around to unhook her bra at the front. Kissing her shoulder, he looked into the mirror. "I want to see all of you."

She shrugged off the bra.

He palmed her breasts then gently squeezed the engorged tips. She responded by arching her head back. He could feel her muscles going taut with need. He dropped one hand from her breast to slide it between her legs and feel her slick, wet heat. Even though she was ready, he still pressed two fingers deep inside of her just to feel the most intimate, sensual part of her. She moved against him, her gaze watching him in the mirror.

His need ramped up to desperate. "Bend over, Hill*baby*. Let me in." When she did, he bent his knees and guided his dick into her. He buried himself as deep as he could.

Then he looked in the mirror. She was braced on her arms,

looking down with her dark blond hair falling around her face. He wanted to see her face as he thrust into her. "Holly, look at me. Let me see you."

She canted her hips to take him deeper inside of her. Then she lifted her gaze to him. "Touch me."

Her words were hoarse and honest. And her eyes were locked onto his in the mirror, just as he'd asked her. His balls drew up and the need to climax gathered in unbearable pressure as he pressed himself inside of her. He kept one hand on her hips so he wouldn't ram her into the counter. With his other hand, he used his index finger to find her swollen clit. Swirling around that nub of flesh, he felt her body tighten around his dick. He saw her mouth fall open, her face soften, and then her gaze lose focus.

"Wes . . ."

Her climax triggered his orgasm. He plunged farther in, needing to ejaculate as deep inside of her as she could take him.

Holly woke up Friday morning to the phone ringing and a naked man in bed with her.

"That your cell?" Wes's voice was sleep-husky in her ear. He was curled around her back.

"Uh, yeah." She reached for the nightstand and picked up her cell. The readout told her it was Detective Rodgers. "Hillbay."

Rodgers didn't waste time. "Turn on the TV. Bradley Knoll has called a news conference."

"You're shitting me." Stunned at the name, Holly grabbed the remote, turned on the TV, and started flipping channels.

Wes sat up. "What's going on?"

Rodgers sighed loudly into the phone. "Sleeping with the enemy, Hillbay?"

She ignored Rodgers and Wes as she found the channel with Bradley. The sight of him ripped open her old wounds. He looked like Mark Harmon in a designer suit, but she knew he had the soul of a jackal. She shoved her emotions aside and focused. Bradley stood at a microphone with four women behind him. She recognized Helene and Nora. To Wes, she confirmed, "That's Maggie on the right?"

"And Bridget on the left."

"Hell." She shut up and listened.

Bradley waited for complete silence, then announced, "We are filing a civil suit for unspecified damages against Wes Brockman and the Books on the Beach bookstore for sexual harassment. He clearly used his book club to lure women for sexual purposes. And after the murder of Cullen Vail, Mr. Brockman hired a so-called private investigator, one Holly Hillbay, to stalk and harass my clients. These women are victims. First of Wes Brockman and his sex games. Then, after Mr. Vail was murdered, by the County of Santa Barbara, who harassed them all over again by forcing them to relive, over and over, their sexual encounters with the deceased. And at least one of these women had to describe fighting off Mr. Brockman."

"Bullshit." Wes threw back the covers, climbed over Holly, and snatched his cell phone off the dresser.

Rodgers said in her ear, "Holly, this thing is exploding. Either you get Wes and his two store clerks to the police station ASAP, or I'm arresting all of you." She hung up.

Bradley called an end to his news conference. She watched him, thinking that he looked the part of a rich philanthropist these days. Bradley loved the camera because it didn't show the money-hungry shark beneath the smooth executive's clothing. The last time she saw him in person, she'd still been groggy—

"Do you know him?"

Holly dragged her gaze from the TV. Wes stood five feet from her, naked and furious. There was no reason not to tell him the truth. "I dated him a long time ago."

He moved closer and sat on the edge of the bed to face her. "How long ago?"

She didn't see why that mattered. "About three years. Rodgers wants you, Jodi, and Kelly at the police station right away. You'd better call your lawyer."

He watched her carefully. "Already did." He reached out and took hold of her hand. "I never dated, or tried to seduce, any of those women, Holly."

The job, she had to focus on her job. Not sex, not feelings, not the *need* in Wes's green eyes, but her job—to find out who murdered Cullen Vail. She took her hand from his.

"It's not me you have to convince. Bradley will file the lawsuit, which will further damage your reputation. Let's get dressed and get on the road."

Since Wes sat on top of the covers, he had her trapped on the bed. "I want you to drive the girls to Goleta in the rental car. I'll take my car. I'm going to meet with my lawyers before talking to Rodgers."

Was he running? He'd run before. Damn Bradley—seeing him had stripped away her self-confidence and the ability to trust her own gut. And she hated that she let him. She wasn't being fair to Wes—she'd seen his reaction to Jodi and Kelly's hit and run. He had been concerned about them and immediately took care of them. Wes wasn't running, he was dealing with tough problems. "Are you going to tell Rodgers the truth about who you are?"

He took a breath. "I'm going to have to, but first I'm going to make sure my lawyers set the conditions to protect Michelle. Rodgers is going to have to agree to keep my identity quiet before I tell her anything. This killer can't find out where Michelle is. And Michelle can't find out that I'm alive, or she'll come find me."

"That's such a bad thing?" Holly asked. It was clear that he missed his sister. In spite of her frequent desire to kill her brothers, she'd miss them if they disappeared from her life.

His green eyes hardened. "If whoever killed Cullen ran Jodi and Kelly off the road to get at me, imagine what they'd do to my sister. Remember, the mob sent a goon to smack her around as a warning to me."

"We both agree that it's not the mob this time, but I see your point." She considered all the angles. "The thing is, Brad is ruthless and we're going to need all the information we can find to fight him. I was just thinking that maybe your sister might know something, remember something or someone who could be behind this. And we could protect her—"

"Hell, no. No." He leaned back, away from her. "I trusted you enough to tell you who I am and about Michelle. You have to swear you won't contact her or—"

"All right. Chill, dude. I was just thinking out loud. This isn't just a murder anymore. You are being targeted and I'm going to find out who is doing this. This bogus lawsuit is part of it." Bradley was not going to jump into this thing and make it all about him. He would fling mud-coated accusations until no one knew the truth anymore. She hated that, hated that he didn't care about justice.

"Chill?" He took a breath, expanding his impressive chest to visibly get control. "She's my sister, not some faceless clue in your investigation. It's that lawyer, isn't it? He's the reason for the huge chip on your shoulder. And the reason you're suddenly willing to risk my sister to solve this case."

She'd let him too close and he didn't like what he saw. *Tough shit.* Sitting naked in the bed, she didn't try to cover herself. He'd seen her, he'd simply have to deal with it. "That's who I am, Brockman. A hard-ass PI. And that's what makes me worth every penny you're paying me. I will find the killer and I will stop him from hurting anyone else. Isn't that what you want?"

He kept his jaw rigid as he said, "Keep my sister out of it."

She nodded and refused to let herself look away. "You're the boss. I'll take Jodi and Kelly home and then to the police station. After that, I'm going to track down the women and try to talk to them. I might be able to get one of them to slip up and tell me what was on Cullen's laptop that was worth stealing and/or killing for. And I'm going to try to find a connection between the players—Cullen, Helene, Maggie, Nora, or Bridget, and your past." She felt a little better, on a little firmer ground. She had a plan and work to do. After taking a breath, she added, "You need to have your lawyers call Rodgers now and set up a meeting. I'm going to take a shower. Move."

He shifted on the bed, his jaw relaxing. "Holly—"

She didn't want to talk. "Don't. Sex is a bonus, the rest is business. Don't make it a relationship. Now get out of my way."

Chapter 10

Several hours later, Holly sized up one of the book club members, Maggie Partlow, through the front window of Maggie's business. She wore a tailored suit and two cell phones on her expensive belt. Her black hair was no-muss short, her makeup efficient, and her eyes were constantly on the move.

She matched the research Holly had done on her and the other three book club members this morning—after getting Joe to meet her at the police station. She'd made arrangements for him to take the girls to her condo when they were done and for him to keep an eye on them. Rodgers had confirmed that Wes's lawyers had made an appointment for late morning to meet with her.

Holly had been working nonstop, running backgrounds and looking for a connection between Wes when he'd been Nick Mandeville in L.A., the four book club women, and maybe the trainer who went to prison then was murdered, Bart Gaines.

Maggie was an upscale wedding planner. Her office looked like a high-end travel agency, with a reception desk buried in lush carpet, fancy chairs around an antique table where Maggie sat with two women and a mound of photo albums, some kind of blueprint or sketch, and a laptop computer.

So far, they were so absorbed in what they were doing, they hadn't seen her looking through the window.

Time to shake some trees and see what fell out. Holly walked in.

Maggie looked up, her professional expression melting into a frown. "Excuse me," she said to the women at the table and stalked toward Holly. "You'll have to leave. My lawyer said—"

Holly cut her off. She hadn't been served with anything legal yet, so she was free to conduct an innocent investigation. "Your lawyer is a camera-loving weasel. Feel free to tell him I said so."

Maggie's dark eyes narrowed. "Leave, or I will call the police."

Nice. "Go ahead, call them. Then we can all get together and talk about what's on Cullen Vail's laptop computer."

Maggie's mouth tightened and a beat of time passed. "Get out."

Holly looked over at the two women sitting at the table. Mother and daughter, probably all giddy about the daughter's wedding. They looked familiar.

It hit her.

She turned back to Maggie. "You're planning the Evans wedding?" They were a prominent Goleta family. Country club to the bone. "Do they know about your sordid little affair with the murdered man?"

Color flooded Maggie's face. "Are you threatening me?"

Holly smiled coldly. "That was a question. Here's another one: what were you doing on Tuesday night after the book club meeting?"

"I'm calling the police." She pulled one of her cell phones off her belt.

Holly walked over toward the two Evans women. "Hi, I'm Holly. I'm thinking about hiring Maggie, but you know, I heard—"

A hand clamped around her arm

Holly smiled. "Be right back." She turned and followed Maggie across the room.

"This is harassment!" Maggie hissed.

Holly pressed her. "Where were you after book club?"

She answered tightly, with a fake smile that looked carved in wax. "Helene, Nora, and I went to dinner at the Elephant Bar. Then we went to Nora's house and watched *The Notebook*. We left well after midnight. Now get out." She was starting to shake with anger.

Convenient how that story matched Nora's. "First tell me what was on Cullen's laptop."

"I don't know."

Holly pushed harder. "You're lying. Just like you lied about my stalking and harassing you. I've never even talked to you before today. I saw you at the book club, but I didn't say a word to you. For the record, you might want to know that I keep excellent records and will be able to easily prove that in court. Now what was on that laptop?"

"I'm not talking to you. I'm calling my lawyer." Maggie yanked her cell phone off her belt again.

Holly figured she'd pushed as hard as she could. "People always run for their lawyers when they have something to hide. Wonder what that is?" She turned and left.

After getting into her car, Holly made a few notes in her notebook, then started the car and pulled out. She was just a few minutes away from Nora's bakery.

Her background check had turned up some interesting information on Nora. Finding the location, Holly parked her car, got out, and headed up to the bakery. She walked in to the warm scents of vanilla, butter, cinnamon, sugar, and chocolate. The first thing she saw was a little girl eating a huge cookie. She couldn't look away. The child took a big bite, saw Holly and waved with a big crumb-grin.

Holly forced herself to breathe and turn away. She studied the bakery cases and shoved the little girl out of her thoughts. One case was filled with decorated cookies and desserts, and another had cakes.

When she heard the door open, she assumed the little girl and her mother had left. Breathing a sigh of relief, she saw Nora walk out from the back wearing an apron over her street clothes. She looked at Holly and slowed her walk, her face draining of color. Then her gaze shifted past Holly, and she said, "Wes, what are you doing here?"

Huh? Confused, Holly turned around, and to her surprise she saw Wes come in the door. He wore a pair of gray slacks and a blue polo shirt. She hadn't talked to him since they'd all left the hotel this morning.

What was he doing here?

Wes met her gaze, then looked at Nora. "I've got three missed calls from you on my cell phone. I thought maybe you needed to talk to me."

Well, that was interesting, Holly thought. She wondered how it had gone for Wes at the police station. Obviously Rodgers hadn't arrested him, not that Holly had thought she would. Had Wes told Rodgers the truth about his identity?

Nora looked around again. "No. I don't think . . . I have three cakes to get done. Big party tomorrow. The Evans's engagement party."

Wes walked up to the counter, standing next to Holly. "Nora, let me help you. You were calling me for something."

She stared at the door. "I wanted to tell you that Ryan's, uh, falling behind at school so I'm taking him out of baseball."

Yeah, right. Holly didn't buy that for a second. "Cut the bullshit, Nora."

Wes whipped his head around. "Holly—"

This was her job, not his. "You're lying through your teeth. You didn't sign on with a scum-sucker like Bradley Knoll to destroy Wes, and then call Wes to politely let him know you're taking your son off his baseball team." Putting her arms on the Formica top of the counter, she leaned in. "Stop lying. Tell us what you know. Like what was on Cullen's laptop computer. Did he figure out who you were? Was he blackmailing you?"

Nora's Sally Field girl-next-door look blanched. "No!"

She pushed harder. "Then what was on that computer?"

Nora shook her head. "Nothing. I just dated him a couple times, that's all."

That whole beaten kitten look was really grating on Holly's nerves. "Tell me, Nora, did you know Wes back when you lived in Los Angeles?"

Shock froze her face. She glanced at Wes then back at Holly. "How do you . . . ?"

Oh for crying out loud, she was a private investigator. Hadn't anyone heard of background checks? It wasn't like Nora had really covered her trail. "Know that your husband is in prison for embezzling? Know that you changed yours and Ryan's last name from Fargo to Jacobson, your maiden name? It's my job. And if I can find out, maybe Cullen found out . . ."

"No." Nora shook her head. "No, I'm sure he didn't. He called me The Invisible Woman, but he never—" She cut herself off then looked at Wes. "I'm sorry. I didn't want to hurt you . . ." Her words trailed off when the door behind them opened. Her face went from tight regret to surprise, then to a mask of nothing.

Holly and Wes both turned, bumping shoulders as they faced the door. She said, "This ought to stir things up."

Bradley Knoll and Helene Essex walked in. Helene went around the bakery cases, put her arm around Nora, and ushered her into the back of the bakery, like she was saving her from seriously unpleasant customers or something. Brad the Cad zeroed in his superior gaze on Holly. Then he puffed up his chest, rooster-strutted up to her, and looked down his nose. "Maggie called me and told me you went to her place of business and made threats. I can get your PI license pulled for that. You never learn."

Standing next to Wes in the bakery, she looked up at the man she had once thought she loved enough to put her own dreams on hold for. He still had the baby blue eyes and handsome features. He still smelled good.

But he made her stomach turn.

Forcing a smile, she said, "No, you can't. Jesus, you are still a blathering, pompous windbag. And it's so damned disappointing after I spent all those thousands of dollars putting your ass through law school." She hadn't planned on that little speech, but what the hell.

Brad pulled his full mouth into a grimace. "And you are still a low-class tart."

Wes shifted next to her but Holly cut him off before he said anything. "Yeah, yeah, I know. Heard it all before. Do you have something to say that has an actual point?"

Helene walked out of the back by herself, leaving Nora in the back. "Maggie told us how you threatened to bad mouth her to her clients. That is harassment."

Brad picked up his cue. "You will both cease and desist immediately. Maggie Partlow, Nora Jacobson, Helene Essex, and Bridget O'Hara are my clients and all of them claim you have been harassing them."

Holly laughed. "I've never even met this Bridget O'Hara, how can I possibly be harassing her?"

Brad's entire body tightened. "Just stay away from my clients." He looked over at Wes. "Both of you. Leave now. You don't have business with this bakery."

Wes said, "I've used this bakery many times, Knoll. If you have legal business with us, you'll go through my lawyers, do I make myself clear?"

Brad said, "I will absolutely contact your lawyers. We are filing our civil suit against you, your store, and your questionable private investigator on Monday morning. In the meantime you are not to go near my clients."

Wes turned to Holly. "You're right, he is a blathering, pompous windbag."

She cracked up. "Always was. Thinks he's fooling the world into believing he's a prep school graduate. Somehow he got the idea that talking out of his ass passed for high class."

Wes grinned.

Brad glared at her. "I've waited a long time to see you get what you deserve, Holly."

She turned to Brad. "I got that the day you walked. I probably forgot to send you the thank you card."

He wasn't going to let that go. "Thank God you aren't the mother of my child."

It took all her cop training to take that hit without flinching. Although her mouth was dry, she said, "See there, two things I have to thank you for."

Helene stepped up. "Touching. Now why don't you two leave before I call the cops."

Holly tore her gaze from Brad's furious face. Looking at Helene, she said, "Hiding behind lawyers and cops just makes me want to dig harder to find your secrets. And since you have a big, gaping two-year hole in your address history, I think I'll start there." She shoved forward, forcing both Brad and Helene to move or she'd knock them over. She stormed out the door and headed for her car, taking deep breaths to get her anger under control.

Wes caught her arm before she reached her car. "Are you all right?"

She ignored that question and tugged her arm from his hold. "Nora seems scared and I need to figure out how to use that. I have no idea what Bridget is to this little group of liars. I'm going to figure out how to cross her path."

Wes said, "I know how to do it."

"Really?" She looked at him and felt the ping of her hormones and something else—something softer and deeper that she didn't like. Wes kept working his way into her head. She needed to keep her mind on business, not Wes. "Well, if you know, book boy, spill it."

His square jaw firmed with determination. "I'll tell you once you catch me up on everything. I want to know about the background checks you've done on the book club members. I want to know about Jodi and Kelly." He moved closer, bringing his face two inches from hers. "And most of all, I want to know what you ever saw in Bradley Knoll."

His green eyes burned like gemstones. She realized he was angry and . . . what? Surprised? Appalled? "Two out of three is all you're going to get, book boy. If you want to work, then meet me at my office." She turned and hustled to her car.

Away from his questions.

Wes watched Holly moving around the kitchenette in her small office and wondered when he had lost his mind. Holly was an ex-cop, from a family of cops, and blindly ambitious. He was trusting her with the safety of the one person he loved the most, his sister.

He'd seen the way Brad pushed her buttons. And Holly had let it spill that she'd paid for much of Brad's law school before they broke up. Wes knew much of the chip on her shoulder was due to Brad Knoll.

And he knew in his gut that she had something to prove to him.

But here he was, believing she would keep her promise not to reveal his identity or contact his sister.

It wasn't just sex clouding his mind, it was Holly herself. So determined to make it on her own and so willing to stand up to any challenge. She was so alive, vibrant, and sexy. Ever since the day Holly Hillbay had walked into his bookstore, Wes Brockman's world had become a less lonely place.

And a hell of a lot more complicated.

Holly handed him a cold soda. "What's your plan to get close to Bridget?"

That was his PI—all work. He was going to have to do something about that. Perched on the arm of the sofa in her office, he watched her ass in her jeans as she went to her desk just a few feet away. "Let's start from the top. What's your background on the four women?"

Holly opened her can of Pepsi. "Short version: Bridget grew up in Goleta and has a yoga/Pilates studio. Maggie opened her wedding planning business six years ago and is very ambitious. Nora has the past in Los Angeles. Her husband was convicted of embezzling from an accounting firm. She changed her last name to her maiden name and moved to Goleta two years ago. She quickly worked her way up to buy out the bakery. And Helene, now that's an odd one." She sipped her soda.

"You mentioned a two-year gap in her address history."

She nodded. "She's from Riverside, California, and she used to be a human resources manager for a big factory there. Then she suddenly left that job, moved out of her house, and there's nothing for two years. Like she disappeared. Then she turned up in Goleta eight months ago as a gift consultant." She picked up a pencil and tapped it against the soda can. "Could be that she moved in with someone else while she got the cash together to launch her gift consultant business. She could have paid cash and not left a trail."

"Makes sense," Wes agreed. "She looks like she comes from money."

Holly raised her eyebrows. "She does have that look, doesn't she? Daddy's princess type?"

"But?"

She got up from her chair and went to the side of her desk to sit on the edge. "Guess I thought she was more the L.A. type than Nora." She shrugged. "Rodgers might have info on Helene's missing two years. I'll try her. But I'm also thinking we should ask around. See if anyone knows. Which brings us back to your plan."

He liked making her wait. "We have to go in order. What about Jodi and Kelly?"

"They're at my house. My brother Joe is baby-sitting." Her smile rolled out wickedly. "You're paying his hourly bodyguard rate."

"More cops. I just can't get away from cops," he muttered. "And now I'm paying them. Great."

"You're welcome." The gleam in her blue eyes warned him. "You may end up paying my brothers for more work than bodyguarding. If I can't get the women to tell me what they know, I may send Seth after them. He can charm words off paper. I need to figure out which of the women will be the most susceptible. I suspect Nora is our best bet since she seemed scared, and you had the missed calls from her on your cell, which might mean she was trying to reach out to you." Her mouth pulled tight. "But Seth can't let Brad see him."

Wes was fascinated by the way her mind worked. Devious. *But what was Brad's problem with Seth?* "Because?"

The light left her blue eyes. "Seth and Brad had a run-in that left Brad bruised and bleeding."

Dark suspicions rose. "A little street justice while on the job?"

Her face hardened. "My brother is a good cop. His dispute with Brad was . . . personal."

"Personal?" He was instantly swept back in time to his sister showing up at his door with a black eye. Wes would have killed the man who smacked Michelle around to threaten him, except he had no way to find him. After seeing Brad and Holly at the bakery a little while ago, it was clear Brad had deeply hurt her. Had Brad hit her? Instantly he doubted that, but something had happened to get her brother riled up. Wes stood up and closed the distance between them.

She watched him with a guarded look. Wisps of hair fell from her clip, softening the hard look she tried to achieve.

He wanted to push the hair back just to touch her. He kept his hands at his sides and stopped in front of her. "What did Brad do to you?"

She raised both her eyebrows and shrugged. "Old story, sort of the cop version of the hardworking nurse who puts the doctor through school, then the doctor dumps her. I put Brad through law school. Once he got that degree in his hand, he walked. Pathetically clichéd."

Ouch, but there was something more. Something that haunted her silvery blue eyes, something that cemented that chip on her shoulder. "Your brother went after Brad for that?" It was enough, and he supposed it explained her driving ambition to succeed and make money.

Her eyes slid away from him. "My brothers are interfering, testosterone-driven idiots. What's your plan for getting us close to Bridget?"

It was the same look in her eyes as when he'd found her scar. Like he'd found her weakness and would . . . what? Use it against her? He trusted her with his secrets. It bothered him that she didn't trust him. "I want to talk about you." He lifted his hand to slide his finger along the chunk of hair that had escaped her clip. "You can trust me, Holly."

She leaned back. "You're my client, Brockman. Not my partner. Now either talk business or get out of my way."

He dropped his hand. "Do you ever get tired of that massive chip on your shoulder?"

She stood up and forced him back a step. "I'm not one of your Barbie girls, Brockman. I'm the PI you hired to find out who is destroying your life. The chip on my shoulder keeps me focused, so either deal with it or get out of my way."

His mask of anger slipped in incredulousness. "Barbie girls?"

She rolled her eyes. "I saw a picture of your wife on the Internet, and the women you dated before her. Barbie girls. Sticks with boobs. Ornaments for successful men. Professional

140 *Jennifer Apodaca*

clothes hangers looking for a man to keep them in clothes. Barbie girls."

"Barbie girls. Damn." He'd never thought of the women he'd chosen that way.

Exasperated, she said, "What now?"

Even though she irritated him, he couldn't help grinning. Holly's way of looking at the world intrigued him. "Where'd you ever get that term?"

She looked confused. "Uh, I think it was that blog, the O'Man's blog. But if the shoe fits . . ."

His grin widened. "I've sworn off Barbie girls. They want a man to make them happy. Been there, done that, failed miserably. Now you, you're a different sort. You don't need me to be happy. You're just using me for sex. Right, Hill*baby*?"

She looked uncertain for a second, then the steely determination took hold. "Yes. And, as you said, been there, done that, and now we have work to do. Your plan?"

To get her back into bed ASAP. "We're going to an exclusive engagement party at the Biltmore tomorrow evening. Nora is doing the cakes, Helene is selecting the gifts for the bridal party, and Bridget is the bride's yoga guru. They're all guests who will be schmoozing for more business. Want to guess who is the party-slash-wedding planner?"

"Maggie, I know, I ran across the bride and her mother in Maggie's office." She shuddered. "The Biltmore in Montecito?" Then she lifted her face to him. "You're invited?"

He grinned. "Yes. I'm not sure how they'll feel about having me there now with all the rumors circulating, but they won't be obvious about it."

Thin tiny lines formed between her eyes.

"What?"

She sighed. "I can't think of a better way. I guess we'll have to go. But I'm not wearing pantyhose."

Wes did his best not to laugh. "Uh, no one under forty wears pantyhose, Hill*baby*."

"Shut up, book boy." She turned to walk toward the door and muttered, "What the hell do people wear to engagement parties?" As she paced back toward him, a horrified expression dropped her mouth open.

Her disgruntled expression amused him. "A cocktail dress. You do own one, right?"

"I own a gun."

"Guns are out of style this year."

They both turned when the door opened. Wes recognized Holly's brother ushering in Jodi and Kelly.

"Joe, what's up?" Holly asked.

"Got called into work," Joe said. "I tried to call but you're not answering your cell." He strolled up to Wes and held out his hand.

As they shook hands, Wes said, "Hi, Joe. Thanks for looking out for my two top employees."

"No problem." Joe turned and grinned at the girls. "They like movies so we spent the day kicking back."

"But now we're bored." Jodi crossed her arms over her chest. "Wes, seriously, a bodyguard? You're worse than my dad."

Kelly chimed in. "We don't need a bodyguard. Jodi and I want to go to the movies. It's Friday night."

No way. He thought fast, trying to . . . "I have an idea." Holly was standing next to him. He'd have to take his chances that she wouldn't slug him. "Holly needs a new dress. We're going to an engagement party tomorrow."

"Shopping? Cool," Jodi said.

Kelly moved closer to examine Holly. "Maybe some highlights?"

Holly glared at them. "No. But I will take you guys to the movies."

Wes was having way too much fun. "But you need a dress, Holly. A cocktail dress. And shoes. Maybe you should get a pedicure."

She turned and pierced him with her icy blue gaze. "Eat dirt and die, Brockman."

"Come on, Holly, it'll be awesome!" Kelly grabbed hold of her arm and tugged her toward the door.

She looked back at Wes. "You are so dead, book boy."

Joe burst out laughing.

Chapter 11

Wes hadn't seen Holly since the night before in her office, and he missed her. He'd spent the day working his bookstore, chatting with customers and chasing off the press. A murder, four women, and a lawsuit brought out the vultures.

He knocked on Holly's door and wondered what she would be wearing. Nothing would surprise him. Knowing Holly, she might just go to the party in jeans.

And she'd still be a knockout. In fact, he'd probably spend the whole night wondering what kind of smokin' hot underwear she had on.

He pulled his brain out of his pants as he heard the door open. Holly stood in the doorway and she was dressed to kill. Or drive him insane. She wore an ice blue dress that matched her eyes. The halter top hugged her breasts, skimmed the curve of her hips, and stopped midthigh.

From there, it was smooth tanned legs all the way down to silver high heels that revealed naked toes.

Oh God.

He looked up. Her hair hung down in soft curls. "You look . . ."

She lifted her chin. "Can't run worth shit in these heels. And I had a hell of a time getting my gun into my purse."

For the first time, he noticed the silver purse hanging off

her shoulder. He grinned at her. "You look beautiful. Can you walk in those heels?"

"I'll manage." She stepped out of the house and pulled the door closed. "Once I corner Bridget, and maybe hover around to eavesdrop on the other women, we're leaving. I'm not standing in these shoes for a minute longer than I have to."

He took her arm. "I like your shoes." He had a mental picture of her in the shoes and a thong. Damn, he had to stop thinking about her shoes. And underwear. And body. And her scent—no perfume for her. She smelled like soap and lotion. When they reached his car, he reached past her and opened the door.

"Knock it off, Brockman. I'm not a Barbie girl. I can open my own door."

"But I want to watch your dress hike up your thighs when you climb in."

She shoved her elbow into his gut, then she climbed in.

He didn't care. It was worth it to see the blue material slide up to the top of her thighs. Holly didn't have skinny stick legs, she had curves . . .

"Snap out of it."

He raised his gaze to her and grinned. "Being sexy and beautiful really makes you uncomfortable, doesn't it?"

"Bite me."

Wes drove the twenty minutes or so to the Biltmore Hotel considering her demand. Biting her, licking her . . . If he didn't get himself under control, he was going to spend the night hiding his erection.

After he gave his car to the valet, he escorted Holly into the hotel. The Santa Barbara Biltmore was done in the Spanish Colonial style with red tile and beautiful archways practically on the shores of Butterfly Beach. Located in exclusive Montecito, the hotel catered to upscale businesses and the affluent.

Walking in was like going back in time. He could feel himself sliding back into the skin of Nick Mandeville, hot shot sports agent. It was a little nostalgic, a little unsettling. He didn't want to be that man—not the one who let a man die from steroids. Not the man who put his own sister in danger. But he had loved doing the deals, and the adrenaline high.

"Fancy."

He looked down at her. "Never been to a Four Seasons?" Wes had stayed at many of them. But when he'd been Nick, he hadn't ever been to Santa Barbara. That was one of the reasons he'd picked Santa Barbara—when he became Wes he doubted anyone would recognize him. But it was beginning to look like someone had recognized him.

Holly frowned. "No. Why would I?"

Putting his hand on her bare back, he felt her tension. It annoyed him that his self-confident PI let this place intimidate her. She didn't show it, but he knew. "We're going to the Loggia Ballroom." He kept his hand on her back as they went in.

The party was in full swing with at least eighty people there. Holly didn't react, but he knew she was taking in the large room with crystal chandeliers, a large fireplace, and French doors that led to a patio. A dance floor and band were set up in the middle, and round tables covered with linen cloths and exquisite flower arrangements were scattered around the perimeter. Wait staff milled around with trays of appetizers.

On a dais at the end of the room was the head table for the engaged couple and their family. Below that was the cake table.

The cakes were there, which meant Nora was around somewhere.

"How did Nora manage to do the cake? Doesn't the Biltmore have a master baker or someone?"

"Pastry chef, and there's always a way to get what you

want. If they're having everything else catered, the hotel probably allowed it. The bride and groom's families are both well off."

"How do you know them?"

"Golf. Let's go get a drink at the bar." He led her to one of the two open bars.

"You play *golf*?"

The horror in her voice caught his attention. "It's not like kicking babies. Yes, I play golf. A lot of business is done on the golf course. And rich people really like to stay up on the latest trends in books." He guided her to the front of the line. "What would you like to drink?"

"Coke."

He handed her the drink and said, "There, I see Bridget. She's with that balding man next to the dance floor."

Holly looked that way, then said, "Oh, shit."

"What?" Wes looked down to see her frowning in the direction of Bridget and her date.

"That's Phil Shaker."

He stared at the man. "Tanya's husband? The one who hired you to prove she was cheating?"

"Pus-sucking little weasel. That's him. With his hand on the blonde's ass." She took a deep breath and started walking toward him. "He won't get away with this."

"Holly." Wes took hold of her elbow. "What are you going to do?"

She turned her frosty blue gaze on him. "Tell him he's paying Tanya her full share of the prenuptial, that's what I'm going to do."

He tried to defuse her agitation with a reasonable suggestion. "Do you think this is the best time to do that? We need to see what we can get Bridget to tell us. Not antagonize her and her date."

She tilted her head back. "I see, so I should just ignore the fact that I helped that moralizing jackass screw Tanya?"

Her voice rose so he dropped his to get her to calm down. "No, I'm saying that we'll pick a better time."

She turned around, clearly ignoring him to march forward on her mission. She took two steps and stopped.

Wes bumped into her back. "What now?" He wanted her to listen to reason.

"Double and triple shit."

"Hmm, that sounds ominous." He looked over her head in the direction she indicated. "Uh-oh."

Tanya Shaker entered the ballroom through the same door they had come through earlier. She wore a black and silver spaghetti-strap T-shirt, a tight black skirt, cowboy boots, and an expression of utter rage that colored her face deep pink. She stood out in the crowd of well-dressed men and women as she stopped and looked around.

"I'll head her off," Holly said. "You go warn shit-for-brains Phil."

She did have a way with words, Wes thought. And she moved fast in those high heels when she wanted to. He turned toward Bridget and Phil and got within five feet of them when he glanced over and saw Holly reach for Tanya's arm and miss.

Tanya had spotted Phil. She fast-walked over and plopped herself in front of Phil. "You two-timing, double-crossing, no-haired, mini-dick weasel! I let you make me feel like a tramp when the truth is that you're a middle-aged man desperate to get a hard-on!"

Phil blinked like an owl behind his glasses, and rubbed his hand over the four or five hairs left on his head. "Tanya, you're making a fool of yourself. Show some dignity."

Her eyes widened to twin disks of brown-eyed fury. "Dignity! You threw me out of my house! Probably so you could screw Barbie Babe over here!"

"Hey!" Bridget said. "Take that back!"

Tanya whirled on Bridget. "You'll spread your legs for anything with money. Cullen Vail knew it and laughed about it because he did you and he didn't have money."

Bridget screeched and threw her drink at Tanya.

Tanya lunged forward, grabbed Bridget's hair, and both of them slammed to the ground in a tangle of bare legs and foul words.

Wes sighed and started to move forward to separate the women.

Holly beat him to it. She grabbed a pitcher of ice water from a passing waitress and dumped it over the two women. "Get! Up! Now!" She yelled the order like a cop on the street.

Both women sputtered.

Phil reached a hand down. "Bridget, I'm so sorry."

Tanya scrambled to her feet. "You're going to be sorry! I'm hiring a lawyer! And I'll hire my own private investigator!"

Phil turned on her. "You'll get nothing because you are worth nothing. You worked at a grocery store when I met you." He grabbed her arm and shook her.

Wes hated men who roughed up women. He took a step, intending to put a stop to it. "That's—"

But Holly moved in front of him, got into Phil's face, and said, "Let go of her."

Phil ignored her to yell at Tanya, "I'm not going to let you ruin me!"

Before Wes could reach out and move Holly aside, she grabbed Phil's free hand and twisted his thumb back.

"Owww!" He dropped Tanya's arm and sank to his knees. "You're hurting me!"

The silence was worse than Phil's whiny cries. Holly felt the stares of the high society guests in the ballroom of the Biltmore. Guess they weren't used to a woman in a cocktail dress and high heels dropping a man to his knees. Sighing at the situation, she released her hold on Phil's thumb and said, "Get up and stop acting like an ass."

He got to his feet and turned on her. "You work for me! You got the pictures to prove Tanya's a whore. What are you taking her side for?"

She fought to control her temper, and to remember the well-dressed crowd around her. "I *worked* for you, Mr. Shaker. As in past tense, because the job is done. But I don't like injustice, and it's starting to look to me like you used me to cheat your wife out of her half of the prenuptial settlement." Holly glanced over at Bridget, who had three men hovering around her with napkins to help dry her off. Stupid men. She turned back to Phil. "How long have you been doing your midlife crisis over there?" She craned her head toward Bridget.

Tanya scrubbed her hands over her eyes, smearing mascara into dark wet streaks. Water dripped from her hair and shirt. "Yeah! How long have you been screwing my yoga teacher?"

Holly knew this was going to deteriorate into another brawl. "All right, enough." She turned to a still dripping Tanya. Clearly, most of the ice water had landed on her. "Go home and dry off. I'll call you tomorrow and we will talk."

Tears welled up and spilled over her eyes. "But—"

She held up her hand and said, "Stop." Holly didn't want to feel the sympathy pooling inside of her. Tanya looked cheap and blue collar because she was. There was no crime in that, but men treated her like she could be used and thrown away. And that royally pissed her off.

Tanya dropped her shoulders. "Okay." She turned and left.

A new voice said, "Well, that was quite entertaining."

Holly turned around and saw Brad standing with the engaged couple and their families.

Brad smirked at her. "Looks like you're having trouble

with your business, Hillbay. Of course, you always did like a good street fight followed by a six-pack of beer."

Would *fuck off and die* sound crass? She stared at Brad. "Don't you have an ambulance to chase somewhere?"

The charm spread out over his Mark Harmon face hardened.

"Holly." Wes put his hand on her elbow.

"What?" She turned and stared at him, catching the wary look in his green eyes. Hadn't she told him over and over that she was a kick-ass PI, not a Barbie girl?

Brad laughed. "Good luck, Brockman. Our little Holly doesn't know the meaning of manners or restraint."

That did it. She glared at Brad. "Fuck off and die, windbag." She ripped her elbow from Wes and strode toward the nearest bar.

For a beer. She wondered if they had a six-pack.

"Hey." Wes was right behind her.

She kept walking. "I'm getting a beer."

"I need a scotch." He moved up beside her.

She went up to the bar and placed their orders. Then she turned to Wes. He looked like he had walked off a magazine cover. Rich, suave, charming. "Bet that's an expensive suit."

He reached past her to get the drinks and took them to a quiet spot at the end of the bar. After handing her the beer, he said, "You're too smart to let your old boyfriend goad you like that."

Holly looked into Wes's gaze and felt something move inside of her. Maybe if she told him the truth about her breakup with Brad, he'd understand. She wanted him to understand—and that scared her. That kind of emotion with a guy led to desperation and trying to be something she wasn't. She lifted her chin and said, "Weren't you paying attention, Brockman? That's why he dumped me." She drank some of her beer and looked around. The large knot around the dance floor was breaking up. Many of them looked her way. She saw Maggie talking to the Evans family, probably trying to smooth things over.

"Cut the shit, Holly. You're just giving Knoll exactly what he wants when you lose your temper like that. He's trying to embarrass you."

She settled her gaze on Wes. "I'm not embarrassed. If you are, then that's your problem. You hired me to find a killer, not be your escort to snobby events."

He thunked his glass of scotch down on the bar. "I'm not embarrassed, Hillbay." He leaned closer. "In the old days, I destroyed people like Knoll before breakfast. But he's distracting you from the job. And that is what I'm paying you for."

Shit on a stick, that hit home. She hated feeling vulnerable. She had been an embarrassment to her mother and nothing more than a means to law school for Brad. And after her last experience with Brad, she had decided to accept who she was and never again pretend otherwise. She would never again try to get a man to accept her. The pain and price were just too high. But she had been acutely aware of Wes standing there when Brad mouthed off. She took a deep breath. "You're right and it won't happen again. Nothing will distract me from the case." She shoved down on the hard knot of emotion welling beneath her breastbone.

He reached for her. "Holly, I didn't mean . . ."

She stiffened. "Yes, you did. You want your life back, and my job is to solve this murder so you can get on with it." She turned and nearly collided with Rachel Evans, the bride-to-be.

Wes stepped up next to her and smoothly said, "Hello, Rachel." He leaned down and kissed her cheek. "You look beautiful."

She smiled. "Thanks." She turned and smiled at Holly. "Hi. I'm Rachel. I was impressed with the way you handled that problem back there."

Was she serious? "Hi. Congratulations on your engagement." She judged the woman to be in her mid-twenties. She
had her brown hair swept up on her head, intelligent brown
eyes, and a pleasing face. Her dress was black and tasteful.

Rachel turned to order a glass of wine from the bartender,
then looked back at Holly. "Thank you. It's nice to meet a
woman who has the guts to speak her mind."

Shrugging, Holly sipped her beer. "I was a cop for over
five years. Some things just stick." Like taking control of a
confrontation immediately. And sounding like you meant it
when you gave a command. For a woman, that often meant
deepening her voice and increasing the volume.

Rachel directed her gaze to Wes. "You hired her?"

He nodded. "She's the best. I always hire the best. After
all, I hired you."

Rachel turned to Holly. "I designed the Web page for his
bookstore." She sipped her wine and seemed to study Holly.
Then she added, "This whole mess with Cullen Vail being
murdered in Wes's bookstore is awful. Then the lawsuit . . ."
She sighed.

Holly's mind jumped around. "Did you know Cullen Vail?"

Rachel's brown eyes measured Holly. "I met him once at a
party. He wanted me to design a Web site for him that would
showcase his talents. I declined."

What was Rachel trying to tell her? "You didn't like him?"

She had a very professional smile. "Not much. I never did
find out exactly what kind of Web site he wanted, but he had
told me the Web site would make him famous. My impression was that he thought he could seduce me and get me to
design his site for free."

Had he? So Cullen had a Web site? Holly hadn't found it
using his name as she knew it. "Did he ever have a Web site
designed? Do you know what he called it?"

Rachel shook her head. "No. I didn't think about him
again until I read in the paper that he was killed in Books on
the Beach."

Holly shifted to let a group of people by. Rachel seemed talkative so she decided to try to get as much information as she could. "This is a lovely party. Did Maggie arrange this, too?" Holly had seen Rachel and her mother in Maggie's office. Would she remember?

Nodding, Rachel said, "You didn't look like you were there to hire her yesterday."

She did remember. "No. I had some questions for Maggie."

After a beat, Rachel said, "People don't like to get involved. Professional women have to be especially careful. That's why Maggie and the others went on the offensive and hired a lawyer."

A very greedy offensive, Holly thought. "Painting themselves as women who were silly enough to sleep with a man who sexually harassed them is their strategy?"

Rachel smiled. "It's better than being considered a murderer. And they are going to belabor the point that if it's okay for men to satisfy their sexual needs, why can't women?"

That was a truth not everyone wanted to hear. "No arguments from me. Have you known Maggie long?"

"She's done work for my dad. He's an investor in various things. Parties like this"—she lifted her wineglass to indicate the room—"these are business opportunities for him."

Okay, Holly was seeing the kinds of problems that a professional woman like Maggie might face when she was linked to a murder. Being a sexually active female was okay; being involved with a murder would kill off her business. Word of mouth was how she stayed in business.

Which also meant that if Cullen had something on Maggie, something that he kept on his computer, then Maggie had a pretty good motive to kill Cullen and steal that computer. "Did Maggie ever say anything to you about Cullen?"

She crossed her arms, careful of her wineglass. "No. I see someone I need to say hello to. Enjoy the party." She headed off.

Holly watched her walk away in her stunning black gown. "What was that about?"

Wes said, "Support. She was showing her public support and she really wants to help."

Holly could still see people covertly watching them. Not rudely staring, but watching just the same. She ignored it and thought about the case. "So Cullen probably had a Web site. I didn't find it in any of my searches." Maybe the Web site was connected to the disappearance of his laptop? She couldn't make the connection in her mind.

Wes touched her bare arm.

Startled, she looked up at him. His fingers on her arm were warm and sensual.

"Dance with me, Holly."

"What the hell for?" Recovering from the surprise, she shook her head. "Not gonna happen, book boy. I don't dance." To keep from seeing his expression, she lifted her beer and drank. She hated dancing. *Hated it.* Her mother had forced her to go to dance classes when she was a little girl. It took her mom a couple years to figure out that her daughter was not a dancing princess.

Then her mother had left.

Wes skimmed his palm up and down her arm. "You don't embarrass me, Hill*baby*. In the last few days, you've made me feel more alive than I have in three long years. You're right, I do want my life back. And I want you in it."

He had to be drunk. "Look around you, book boy. This is your life. Money, power, fancy parties . . ." She returned her gaze to him. "My life is work and beer. We had great sex, but it was just sex, not a relationship. You can pick one of these Barbie babes for that once we find the killer." She set her beer down and turned to leave.

Before she took a step, she caught sight of two sides of beef in suits striding her way, followed by Maggie Partlow. Holly recognized security coming to toss her out. Guess

Rachel's show of support hadn't worked. She lifted her chin, acutely aware of Wes behind her.

The two men stopped, assuming the wide-legged tough-guy stance while Maggie slid around them. She appeared confident and competent in her long gold skirt paired with a cream top, and holding a very official-looking walkie-talkie in her hand. "You both are no longer welcome at this party. Please leave now."

Holly quickly scanned the room. From different spots, Brad, Helene, and Nora watched. Bridget was busy fawning over Phil, not yet realizing that he was going to be seriously poorer once Holly was done with him. But Brad, Nora, and Helene were part of this tossing-out ceremony. What was the deal with them?

"I'm going to have a word with Frank Evans," Wes said.

Maggie glared at him. "I don't think so." She looked over her shoulder. "Gentlemen, please see these two out."

Considering her options, Holly decided to retreat. "We're going." She took a step, forcing one of the security guys to move aside and bringing her next to Maggie. She turned and looked into the woman's eyes. "I have what I need anyway. All this over a Web site? Is it really worth it?"

Maggie's voice was cool and efficient when she said, "I have no idea what you are talking about."

Chapter 12

Holly adjusted her seat belt and kept her gaze on the road while her mind tumbled over the night's events.

"What was that about a Web site?"

She looked over at Wes's profile as he drove through the night toward her house. "Shot in the dark. Remember Rachel said Cullen asked her to design a Web site?"

He nodded.

"His boat was broken into and his laptop appears to be the only thing missing. Someone wanted that laptop, most likely for what was on it. So I thought maybe Cullen has a Web site and it's connected." She couldn't quite put it together. The pieces of information in her brain just wouldn't line up in the right order. Biting down on her frustration, she said, "I took a shot to see if I could ruffle Maggie."

"Didn't look like it worked." His jaw tightened. "Doesn't seem like anything ruffles her."

She wasn't so sure about that. "Her left eye twitched."

"Really?"

She smiled. "Oh yeah, I got to her. But I don't know why. A Web site—what would Cullen put on a Web site? He wanted to be a shock jock, or that's what he said to Tanya. What could he put on a Web site? His resumé? No, that wouldn't make him famous." She shifted in her seat. "What would make a woman desperate to kill him and steal his computer?"

"Blackmail?"

She frowned as she considered that. "You think he was blackmailing the women? Like what? Threatening to tell Tanya's husband about their affair? But she would have told me that, I'm sure of it. She wouldn't have had anything else to lose since her husband already knew she was sleeping with Cullen."

"He had just seen Tanya the night he was murdered. I doubt he'd had time to blackmail her yet."

She saw his point. "Okay, then what would he use to blackmail the other women?"

Wes slowly took his eyes from the road and looked at her. Even in the dark night, she felt his gaze.

Then he said, "Pictures. He could have been taking naked pictures of them, or pictures of them during sex, and threatening to sell them."

Her heart started pounding. "Like digital pictures on a computer." She used a digital camera. It was possible. She looked out the front windshield, thinking. Would one of the women kill to stop Cullen from selling the photos or putting them on his Web site? *Maybe.* "But why kill him in your bookstore?" Was there a connection, or had it just been sheer opportunity?

Wes tapped the finger of his right hand on the steering wheel. "I don't know, but . . ." He shifted his glance to the rearview mirror. "Shit."

Holly twisted around and saw the flashing red and blue lights behind them. "Were you speeding?"

He shook his head and pulled over to the right. The headlights from the police cruiser lit up the interior of Wes's car as the cruiser pulled up behind him.

"Keep your hands out where the police can see them." Holly left her purse on the floorboard. Cops were very cautious with traffic stops. They never knew when some thug was going to pull a weapon and shoot.

Wes rolled down the window then kept his hands on the steering wheel.

"Good evening, sir." The deputy moved his flashlight around the interior of the car. "Holly," he said in surprise.

"Yes, Parker, it's me." She'd known him for years. He was in his thirties and a career cop. "What's the problem here?"

"I'm going to need you both to step out of the vehicle," Parker answered.

Not good, she thought. "Okay. Just so you know, I have my gun in my purse at my feet. I'm going to leave it there and step out." She got out and went to the back of the Range Rover, where another deputy waited. She stood there while Parker directed Wes to turn off the engine and get out. They both walked back to the front of the cruiser. The cruiser's headlights provided light. "Parker, what's this about?"

"An anonymous tip about a weapon in the car. We're waiting for a search warrant." He looked at the other officer. "No need to put them in the car. Holly is an ex-cop."

A trap. It had to be. Had someone planted the murder weapon in Wes's car? She looked over at him. His face was tight, and in the cruiser's headlights she could see the frustration and anger in his eyes.

Parker's radio crackled. He walked away and took the call. Then he came back with his cop face on. "A judge signed the warrant and Rodgers is on her way."

Wes shrugged. "Go ahead, search it."

The deputies got to work.

Left alone between the two cars, Wes said, "They're looking for the gun used to kill Cullen, aren't they?"

"That would be my guess." She dragged her gaze from the car to Wes. "Someone is seriously out to get you."

He reached out and took her hand. "Thank you."

Huh? "What for?" The warm feel of his hand around hers was comforting. Which was just stupid.

"Believing in me." Keeping hold of her hand, he turned to watch the cops search his car. "Let's hope whoever did this didn't plant the gun, or I'm going to jail."

Ten minutes later, they still stood in the same place when Parker walked up. Holly snatched her hand away from Wes.

Parker didn't seem to notice. "Mr. Brockman, we're finished."

Wes said, "No gun?"

The deputy shook his head. "No. I'm sorry for your inconvenience but we have to follow up on these tips."

Holly was relieved that the gun wasn't in the car. But Parker had obviously found something. "What's that in your hand?"

"Just an old magazine." He lifted his hand to give it to Wes. "It slid down the side of the backseat."

"That's odd." Wes reached for it, then angled it in front of the car headlights to see the magazine.

Holly saw shock briefly blank his face before he tightened his jaw and looked up. His voice was casual. "I guess I left it in my car. Any other problems?"

Parker shook his head as another car pulled up behind the cruiser. "No. That's Detective Rodgers. I'm going to go talk to her, then we'll be on our way."

The two deputies walked around the cruiser to where Rodgers parked. "Come here," Holly said, and walked to the passenger side of the Range Rover. Whatever it was, she didn't want to chance Parker thinking something was wrong. She opened the door so the dome light went on, then she looked at Wes. His face was pale and tight. "What is it?"

He lifted his gaze to her. "It's an old surfing magazine." Holding the spine of the magazine in one hand, he used his other hand to flip the pages until it fell open to an article. He held it in the light so she could see. "That's Michelle."

Holly saw a picture of a young woman with dark hair and vivid green eyes in one shot. In another shot, she was surfing. "Your sister? The article is about your sister? Is this your magazine? Did you forget about it?"

He shook his head. "No. I bought this car after I moved here. Anything I have on Michelle is in a safe deposit box. And look." He turned the page and showed Holly a sentence marked with yellow highlighter that read: *My brother Nick taught me to surf.*

Anger brought color to his face and made his eyes flash. "Someone planted this in my car then called in that tip. Whoever it is knows who I am, and who my sister is."

It was well past midnight when they got to Holly's condo, after going to the police station with Detective Rodgers. They had showed Rodgers the magazine and told her their suspicions. Rodgers was going to have it dusted for prints, but Holly knew that wasn't going to turn up anything but Wes and Parker's prints. Whoever planted the magazine was smarter than that.

She undid her seat belt and said, "No need to come in. I'm going to do some research tonight then we'll get an early start in the morning."

Wes leaned across the seat, lifted her, and pulled her toward him.

She sucked in a breath in surprise. "What are you doing!" Why did she keep forgetting how strong he was?

He settled her across his thighs. "I want you in my lap where I can talk to you and touch you at the same time."

Wes had stripped off his coat and tie, and rolled up the sleeves of his expensive shirt, yet he still looked like Mr. GQ. But his eyes didn't look rich and sophisticated, they looked hot and a little desperate.

It was that desperation that tugged at her.

She shoved it away. "You're thinking about sex again."

He dropped his gaze to her breasts. "Hell, yeah, I've been thinking about sex since I first saw you tonight." He put his right hand on her bare shoulder and ran his palm down her arm.

The intensity of his touch, of her reaction, startled her. It was as if she craved his touch, craved his nearness. Her body wanted to lean into him, to snuggle up to his incredibly strong chest . . .

What was wrong with her? She didn't *snuggle*. She wasn't a cuddly woman. *Ick*. She was a tough, hard-assed kind of woman who took what she wanted, and on her terms. "Fine. You want a quickie, let's do it."

His mouth twitched. "Maybe I just want to touch you."

Damn it, this was some kind of power struggle she didn't understand. "Your hard-on says different." She wiggled her butt around just to torment him. And herself. Already, she was growing wet and swollen for him. She'd gone too long without sex and now her hormones were doing a little sex-me-now dance every time she saw Wes.

He leaned his face close to hers, while dragging his fingers back up her arm, across the halter strap of her dress and into the V of her breasts. "Hill*baby*, you do live dangerously." He used his free hand to pull her mouth to his.

Holly tried to take control. She angled her mouth to drive him crazy, then slid her tongue along his. When he made a deep sound in his throat, she knew she was gaining the upper hand.

Wes lifted his head and looked down into her face. At the same time, he dipped his thumb and first finger into the cup of her dress to grasp her nipple. He pressed gently, with just enough pressure so that her nerves screamed, *Yes!* She resisted the urge to lean back and give him better access. Returning his stare, she said, "I have to go in. My brother is staying with Jodi and Kelly until I get in there."

He tightened his arm around her back. "You aren't running away from me this time. I want to know everything about you, Holly." He stroked her nipple back and forth. "Like why you don't dance."

She tried to follow his question, but he was making her hot and restless with lust. "I don't like dancing. We should stop. Somebody might come by and see us."

Wes withdrew his hand from her breast.

Holly had the sudden urge to slug him. Or grab his hand and put it back. Obviously she must be tired and frustrated from the case and it was making her too needy. She started to scramble off his lap.

Wes held her fast. "No one is around. And no one is going to see me touching you." He put his hand on her thigh.

She took a breath, blew it out, and faced him. "Wes, let me go."

He studied her face. "First tell me why you don't like dancing."

She didn't know what he wanted. But she did know his long, warm fingers were sliding up her thigh. She could stop him, she was sure of that. But the blunt truth was that she didn't want him to stop. When Wes touched her, it drove away the deep feeling of loneliness for a while. His touch made her feel whole, sexy, and very female. To remind herself of who she was, she answered, "Because dancing is stupid."

His green eyes heated with tiny yellow dots. He brought his hand to the hem of her dress and drew circles on the skin of her thigh. "Lying will cost you, Hill*baby*." He lowered his face. "You know you want me to touch you. You want to spread your legs and let me move aside your panties. Then I'll play with your clit until you're squirming and begging. You'll be so wet, I'll be able to thrust two fingers inside you. Maybe three fingers. And then, just when you can't take it, I'll slide my thumb over your clit and you'll come." He kissed her nose. "Unless you keep lying to me."

He was taking her breath away. Confusing her. She squeezed her thighs together. "What makes you think I'm lying?"

He drew his finger up the seam of her pressed-together thighs. "You told me your mother teaches dance. And you looked like you had bitten into a rotten apple and found a big worm when you said it." He softened his voice. "I want to know."

It stunned her how much Wes saw about her, and that he even remembered what she had told him. Especially with the trip to hell in a handbasket his life was taking. And in the faint light from the parking garage, she didn't have the strength to lie. "My mom forced me to take dance classes when I was little. I hated them and I sucked at it. According to her, anyway. I just wanted to go play with my brothers. Cops and robbers was my favorite." She shrugged. "That's it."

Ignoring her closed legs, Wes moved his hand around the back of her thigh and higher to cup her butt cheek. "Anti-Princess, that's why your brothers call you that. You were a tomboy instead of a princess."

Her stomach went cold. "I'm done playing twenty questions." Grabbing his forearm, she tugged at his arm. His muscles bunched and he squeezed her rear, but didn't move. "Knock it off, Wes. I'm not going to make out in a car like a pair of horny teenagers."

He slid his hand out and let her go. "What's the matter, Holly? Am I not playing it your way? Quick and hot orgasm with no intimacy?"

She scrambled off his lap to the passenger side of the car and grabbed her purse off the floorboard.

He went on, "Or am I right? Is that it, Hillbay? I'm getting too close to your secrets so you have to run?"

She closed her fingers on the door handle and looked back at him. His face had hardened from sexy, teasing charm to unyielding stone. "It's a job, Brockman."

He raised his eyebrows so that scorn poured from his green eyes. "Right, the job. Your career. It's you against them, *against us*, the men who screw you over. Is that it?" He jerked his body around and started the car.

She got out of the car and turned to face him. "The job is who I am, Brockman. And this little scene is why I don't work with partners. So just back off, and stay out of my way while I find out who is pissed off enough at you to go as far as murder while they methodically destroy your life." She slammed the door.

Wes whistled as he flipped the pancakes. He was an idiot, of course, as he was certain Holly would point out.

Loudly.

When she found him in her kitchen, cooking breakfast with Jodi and Kelly.

But like it or not, Holly had a partner, for now at least. And he was not afraid to fight for her, or fight with her, whatever it took to know her.

His life was a mess, his sister might be in danger again, and he very well might have been set up for Cullen's murder. And he'd had to take a very soapy shower last night to resolve his raging lust. Yet he was happier than he'd been in years.

Holly would probably add *lunatic* to her insults.

"You're in a good mood." Jodi looked over the top of the book she was reading at the table. She wasn't a breakfast eater and had told him so. But then she'd eventually brought her book into the kitchen to watch him and Kelly cook.

Wes smiled at her. "I like breakfast."

"Uh-huh. I think you like Holly." She stuck her nose back in the book.

"Is that it?" Kelly asked as she moved crisp bacon from the frying pan to drain on paper towels. She had her long hair pulled back in a ponytail, wore shorts with a teeny little top, and chattered nonstop. "Do you like her?"

Wes added the last batch of pancakes to the plate staying warm in the oven. Shutting the oven door, he looked at Kelly. "I like her enough to cook breakfast for her. If she ever gets her butt out of bed."

"Her butt is out of bed. But what the hell are you doing in my kitchen?"

Ah, Holly's snarky morning voice. Wes walked the plate of pancakes to the table, then turned around. Holly was pouring herself a cup of coffee. She had on a pair of running shorts that cupped her delicious ass, and a thin T-shirt. Her hair hung wet around her face. She looked like an engaging combination of hard-ass with her firm body in an aggressive pose and her tough expression, and vulnerable with her bare feet, wet hair, and the wary look in her incredible blue eyes. A protective sensation clawed up from his belly to his chest. "I cooked breakfast. After I went to the store. You might consider going grocery shopping once in a while." He went to the refrigerator to get out the orange juice.

Holly said, "I told you last night—"

Shutting the fridge door, he cut her off. "Not going to work, sweetheart. I'm not disappearing just because you piss me off."

Her mouth fell open. After she snapped it closed, she glanced at the two girls sitting at her table and blatantly watching them. "Don't call me that."

If he laughed at her expression, she'd kill him. "Sit down and eat. You can snarl at me later." He loved bossing her around. Mostly because she would make him pay—life was never boring with Holly. She didn't take crap from anyone. He liked that about her, liked that she didn't expect a man to make the world right for her. But she also made sure to run off any man that got too close, too intimate. He was beginning to understand her.

Her own mother telling her she wasn't good enough. Christ, that thought darkened his mood. He shoved it off and risked turning his back on her to pour the orange juice. He was counting on her not stabbing him with a kitchen knife in front of his two employees.

Holly sat on his left and glared at Jodi and Kelly. "Who let him in?"

Kelly answered with a big grin. "I did. He had food!"

At that, Holly lost her battle with a grin. "Right, food. Some people actually insist on having it." She forked three pancakes onto her plate.

Wes added a couple slices of bacon. "Drink your juice," he told her.

"Your days are numbered, book boy." She dug into her pancakes.

He ignored her and worked on eating his own breakfast until the doorbell rang. Wes set down his fork and started to stand up.

Holly stood and stared down at him. "You stay here with the girls."

He looked up into her silvery blue eyes and saw all cop. She was giving orders and she meant it. "Do you have your gun?"

"I'm covered." She took long strides out of the kitchen.

"Wes?" Kelly said from his right. "Who do you think it is?"

He took her hand. "Probably one of her brothers or another old boyfriend, but we're not taking any chances."

Jodi looked up from her pancakes. "Holly can take care of herself. She's cool."

"Hungry after all, huh?" Wes teased her.

She ignored him.

Wes heard Holly let someone in. "We're eating breakfast. You might as well join us." She came into the kitchen with Tanya following her.

"Tanya." Wes stood up. What was she doing there? He recovered enough to say, "Good morning. Would you like some pancakes?" Tanya was dressed in a pair of stretchy tight black pants and a zebra-striped top that made him dizzy if he looked at it too long. But when he looked up at her eyes, he saw pain and determination.

"I'd just like some coffee, Wes. Thank you."

She sounded tired. Not surprising after that scene with her

estranged husband and Bridget. He went to the coffeemaker to pour it for her while Tanya went around the back of the table to sit on Holly's left. He leaned across the table to hand Tanya her coffee, then sat down.

Tanya turned to Holly. "Do I still have a job with you? Starting tomorrow 'cause, you know, it's Monday?"

Wes turned to watch Holly. What would she say?

Holly set her fork down. "Yes. And first chance we get, we're going to go after Phil. If he was cheating, too, then he can't invoke the clause of the prenuptial for your cheating."

Tanya's shoulders relaxed and her face softened. "Thank you. I know what you must think . . ." Tanya looked around the table, then said quietly, "I just wanted to get Phil's attention. I know that's stupid, and then I fell in love with Cullen."

"Bullshit." Holly held her coffee cup in both hands and stared at Tanya. "You were desperate for attention and Cullen gave it to you. That's what happens when you look to a man to make you happy."

Tanya and Kelly flinched at the harsh words, while Jodi nodded and pushed her plate away.

Wes wouldn't have put it quite that way, but he agreed as far as Tanya went.

Tanya stared into her coffee. "That's what he called me, a 'desperate housewife.'"

Wes felt sorry for her.

Kelly put her hand on Tanya's arm. "Maybe he meant you're hot like those women on that TV show."

Wes smiled at Kelly. She had a big heart.

"No," Holly said abruptly. "No," she repeated, her face flooding with color as she sucked in a breath. "Bridget is 'Barbie Babe.' Tanya is 'Desperate Housewife.' He had a nickname for all the women. He wasn't talking about a TV show, he was talking about his Web site!" She stood up and hurried past him and out of the kitchen.

Wes got up and followed her. He found Holly in her home office signing onto the Internet.

God, she was something. She had one leg tucked underneath her, her gaze locked onto the computer, her expression so intense, he could practically hear her brain working. Somehow, she'd pulled a clue out of Tanya's words and she was going to work it.

Holly had been right about one thing—she was damn good at her job.

"The O'Man. Cullen is The O'Man! Look at these names."

As absorbed as she was in the computer, she'd still heard him follow her. His PI would always have a cop's instincts. He walked over, put one hand on the desk and one on the back of her chair. Looking at the screen, he studied the Web site. "This is the one you were looking at a few days ago."

"Yes." She was nearly breathless with excitement. "See the list of titles for his podcasts?" She pointed to a sidebar.

Wes read:

Coming Soon: Desperate Housewife
O'MAN SEDUCTIONS
Anti-Princess
Invisible Woman
Wonder Woman
Barbie Babe
Plastic Girl
Cat Woman
Batgirl
Black Widow
Electra
Lois Lane

He turned his head and looked at her. "Anti-Princess? Is that you?" His mind tumbled over that. She had appeared to follow Cullen after leaving the bookstore the first night. But she had an explanation for that—Phil Shaker had hired her to find out who Tanya was sleeping with.

Her bright expression dimmed. "No. My brothers thought the same thing. I'd never met Cullen until that night in your bookstore."

Watching her face, he told himself to let it go. But he couldn't. "It wouldn't make a difference to me."

She stiffened. "I don't give a rat's ass what you think, Brockman. This is about your case. Look at this." She pointed to the screen. "This is why someone killed Cullen and stole his laptop."

One thing he knew about Holly, she was honest about sex. She'd just tell him. In fact, she'd use it to push him away. He lifted his hand from the chair to slide it beneath her drying hair. "Don't tense up. Look, I'm sorry. I asked, you answered, and I should have accepted your answer the first time." He rubbed the tension in her neck while directing his attention to the screen. "Invisible Woman. Remember Nora said that Cullen had called her that when we talked to her at the bakery?" It had stuck in his mind because it fit. Nora was just sort of there, nearly invisible.

Holly nodded. "That's right, I remember now."

Gently kneading the tension in her neck, he asked, "These podcasts—they're like a radio show?"

She didn't shove his hand away. "I haven't listened to them, but I assume so. And it fits. Rachel said that Cullen believed the Web site he wanted her to design would make him famous. Tanya told us he wanted to be a shock jock, like Howard Stern."

Her excitement was contagious. He read from the Web site, "Sex is a game. The O'Man plays to win."

Holly added, "His whole site is about how to seduce women. So these names, like Desperate Housewife—"

Wes jumped in. "It's like you said. He identified Tanya as attention starved, paid attention to her, and got her in bed. And if Nora is the Invisible Woman, that would imply she felt invisible and all he had to do was single her out in a crowd to make her feel special." He looked at Holly. "What do you want to bet these podcasts are descriptions of how to seduce these women, and then graphic stuff from the sex?"

She arched her brows. "One way to find out. We're going to have to listen."

"I'll help," Tanya said.

Wes took his hand from Holly's neck and straightened up.

Tanya stood a couple feet away, her face a red mask of anger. When she saw them both looking at her, she lifted her chin. "I want to help. I want to, you know, learn from this. I'm tired of falling for men who don't really care about me."

Ouch, Wes thought. He looked at Holly.

She said, "Okay, I'll get you started. I'd like you to keep notes on what is in each podcast. And as you listen to them, I want you to think about the women we know Cullen slept with. We want to match these nicknames he's using for his podcasts to the real names. Are you up to it?"

Tanya nodded, walking up to look at the screen. "It looks like he's going from the last woman he slept with—me—and I guess he never finished that one since it says 'Coming Soon.' But then that would make Helene the Anti-Princess."

"Yes, and we know Bridget is Barbie Babe. Not counting Desperate Housewife, she's fourth down the list. That fits. But," Holly added, "Rodgers said last night that they have proof Bridget was in Sacramento the night of the murder, visiting a relative. She's not a suspect." She looked back to Tanya. "But we still want to match the real names up to the nicknames, so keep an open mind. Listen to the podcasts and see if it fits."

Tanya stared at the screen. "What a cruel thing to do."

"Yeah," Holly agreed. "And it got him killed." She dug out her iPod. "Can you figure out how to download this?"

"Piece of cake." Tanya sat down in Holly's chair.

"Brockman, you and I have work to do. I need to get one of my brothers over here to keep the girls safe. Then I'm going to get my laptop and we're going to your house."

He assumed that she wanted to work at his house where they wouldn't have to censor anything they said for Tanya, Kelly, or Jodi.

Before he could reply, Tanya jumped in. "Holly, I'll be here. I'll keep an eye out. We'll stay inside, keep the doors locked. If Kelly and Jodi don't mind." She lifted up her purse. "I have pepper spray and I'm not afraid to use it."

Chapter 13

Holly set up her laptop on the kitchen table while Wes moved around his kitchen making coffee. Monty was making a nuisance of himself, running back and forth between them with his ball. His golden face, thick, furry ears, and big, brown puppy eyes tugged at something warm and fuzzy inside of her.

Something dangerous.

Holly kicked the stupid ball just to make the dog leave her alone. He bounded after the ball, his oversized, clumsy paws slipping and sliding on the kitchen floor. She yanked her gaze away to watch her computer boot up.

Why had Wes come over to her house this morning? What did he want? She'd made the boundaries clear last night. She was a PI, and he was her client. The sex had been a side benefit. Once he made it complicated, they were done with the sex.

Monty put his paws on the edge of her chair, and nudged her arm with his cold nose. He had the slobbery ball in his mouth.

"No, Monty," Wes said in a firm voice, saving her from having to deal with the dog's pleading eyes.

Monty dropped to the floor, crawled under the table, and curled up on her feet.

Stupid dog. She took a breath and focused. Her job was to

find the killer. She had it narrowed down to three suspects. "Since Bridget was out of town, our three main suspects are Nora, Helene, or Maggie. If there's only one killer, why would two of them cover for the one who murdered Cullen? They all alibi one another."

Wes reached up over the coffeemaker, got down two cups, and looked over his shoulder at her. "Maybe the three of them plotted it together?"

She considered that. "Maybe. I don't think they were all three in the store when Cullen was killed. The scene is too clean and controlled. Rodgers thinks there was one killer, too. And when I talked to Nora's next-door neighbor, she heard the women arrive at Nora's and a movie being played pretty loud. So until we get evidence otherwise, let's go with the theory that one woman met Cullen at the store and killed him. Then what were the other two doing?"

Waiting for the coffee to finish brewing, Wes leaned his hips against the counter. "Stealing the laptop?"

"Okay. Why? Cullen's Web site is still up, so it wasn't to somehow take the site down." She had to put herself in that woman's head. "I need to think like the killer. She finds out Cullen has a Web site, sees herself in the nickname . . ." It came to her then. "Her real identity, which links her to the nickname, is on the laptop."

Wes shifted to look out the door to his deck, which led to the beach. "They are all three business owners. They may have felt vulnerable about anyone finding out who they are."

Holly sighed. "This isn't adding up. All three of them decide to kill Cullen? What are the chances that they all three plotted to kill him? Would Nora agree to that?"

"Maybe to protect her son."

She stared at the O'Man Web site. "It's all conjecture until we can find a connection. I can start by finding out if any of them has a gun permit." Pushing the computer away, she ignored the puppy sound asleep on her feet and snoring. Holly pulled over her tablet of paper. "We have the three suspects, the murder victim, the bookstore, and we think we can tie those together." She wrote all that down then looked up. "How do you and Michelle fit in?"

Wes turned back to look at her. His green eyes darkened. "Something to do with my past. Someone knows I disappeared to protect Michelle."

Holly shook her head. "Someone from both your past and your present. This killer has not made any assumptions. She knew exactly what would push your buttons—a murder in your bookstore; starting rumors with the parents of your Little League team; running your two clerks off the road; and that magazine article in your car." She made a quick note about trying to talk to the valets. But Holly knew that in an upscale place like the Biltmore, the valets, were all going to deny they'd let anyone into Wes's car, or that they placed the magazine in there for someone. Detective Rodgers would be all over the valets which would scare them off entirely. She looked up at him. "Who knows that you are Nick Mandeville?"

He turned around and poured the coffee. "I haven't told anyone but George about my past in three years. Until you." He set a cup in front of Holly.

She watched him sit down on her left. "What about George? I know what you said before, but how well do you really know him?"

Wes ran his hand through his hair. The longish dark strands shifted and fell over his forehead. "George is not involved in this. You'll just have to trust me on that."

That annoyed her. "Trust doesn't get the job done. How do you know George is who he says he is?"

He leaned back in his chair. "Because the DEA agents I worked with on the case against Bart Gaines sent me to George."

She had been reaching for her coffee, but dropped her hand when she heard his answer. "He's the one who got you the new identity?"

He shook his head. "That's not the point. I needed protection for my sister and George knew how to make it happen. He told me what to do and I did it. If he wanted to hurt Michelle, he could have done it anytime."

She suspected that George wasn't just a security consultant if DEA agents sent people to him. "Is he government?"

Wes locked his jaw.

They both heard a knock at the front door, followed by the door swinging open. Monty woke up, scrambled to his feet, and raced out from under the table, barking.

Holly grabbed her purse from the floor at her feet. She stood up, turned so that she was in front of Wes, and raised her gun to the entryway.

George walked through, holding a wiggling, ridiculously happy Monty. He spotted Holly with the gun and went still. He lowered his head to look over his blue-tinted glasses. "Problem?"

"Put the gun away, Holly," Wes said behind her.

She wasn't so sure. "Who are you?" she demanded from the man calling himself George. He had inky black hair, a slightly dark complexion, dark eyes that were deep wells of experience, and his well-cut clothes didn't hide the lean hardness of his body. His free hand hung loose and slightly away from his body.

Wes put his hand on her shoulder. "Holly, it's all right. He's not in on this thing."

She ignored Wes and focused on George's jacket. When Monty wiggled, moving the jacket, she could see the bulge. "You have a gun."

"Yes." His gaze stayed on her, his eyes growing amused while he continued to pet the dog. "You're thinking I'm helping the woman doing this to Wes."

"Crossed my mind." She noticed that he didn't look to Wes to help him. No, he considered Holly the threat.

George nodded carefully. "Just as I've considered that you are in on it."

She forced herself to keep her face tight and blank. *Her? Why would he suspect her?*

George enlightened her. "You showed up at the bookstore the night of the murder. You go home with Wes, but leave before the time of the murder. You admit to being at the public parking lot to watch Cullen and Tanya return from Cullen's boat. You show up the next morning at the bookstore before Wes opens it and finds the body." He arched a single dark brow at her as if to ask if he needed to go on.

Rather than explain herself, Holly turned the tables on George. "Someone researched Wes. They know who he is, and what his vulnerable spots are. This killer has known Wes, or they're getting their information from someone who does." She had to take a breath to control her anger. Wes had spent three years trying to fix his screw-ups and his life was being destroyed. He'd give up the one thing he loved more than anything else—his sister—to protect her. He didn't deserve this.

"Holly." Wes gently squeezed her shoulder. "George isn't in on this."

She didn't let Wes sway her. Her job was to protect him, and if that meant challenging the one friend he'd had in three years, she'd damn well do it. "Who are you?"

George moved slowly, raising one hand to slide his glasses back up his nose while hanging onto Monty with the other. "Can I get some coffee first?"

Holly relied on her gut, and her gut told her that George was not a threat to Wes. Lowering her gun, she said, "You can't talk and walk at the same time?"

His lips twitched. "Touché." He set Monty down on the floor. The puppy scampered over to the chew toy by his food bowl and set to work on that. George headed to the coffee-maker and said, "I'm ex-DEA."

By this time, she wasn't surprised. It rang true, as he had the skills from what she could see. She'd seen his expression go "cop" when he'd seen her gun. Even though he had his glasses on, she had seen him assessing the danger and reacting. Plus he knew things, things like how to get Wes a new identity. The question was, "Why did you leave?"

After filling a cup, George walked to the table and sat down across from her. "My identity was cracked and information saturated the Internet. I was, still am, a walking dead man."

Holly sat down and placed her gun on the table within her easy reach. Life sucked sometimes. "So you went underground? To do private security work?" *Got IDs that probably weren't legal but kept people alive?* She didn't bother asking that one out loud.

He nodded. "I'll be moving on as soon as we resolve Wes's situation."

In his dark eyes, Holly saw the emptiness. The vast, deep, and dog tired emptiness. There was nothing left. George had one more goal in life. To help Wes recover a life.

Then he was done. Finished.

She'd seen it with burned out cops. But it was magnified in George. Turning to look at Wes, she knew that he saw it, too.

"Told you," Wes said.

She returned his stare. "No, you didn't. You just said trust me."

Holly felt the challenge in the silence between them until George snorted and broke the moment. She glared at him. "What?"

"I told Wes hiring you was a mistake."

She leaned her head back and stared at the ceiling while stretching her neck. "Like I give a shit what you think."

Laughing outright, George said, "You have a rep of a bull dog. I knew you'd sink your teeth in and pick apart Wes's life. What I didn't know was if he could count on your loyalty."

She lifted her head. "And now?"

He arched both eyebrows over his glasses. "We'll find out, won't we?"

Men. They were both pushing her to be something she wasn't. Wes was looking for the soft woman inside of her, and George was looking for the faithful female lapdog inside of her. They were both going to find out that was all hard-ass PI. "Whatever. Do you have any information that might help the case?"

"Maybe." He shifted his gaze to Wes. "I've been in New York talking to your ex-wife."

That had caught Holly's attention. "What did you find?"

George drank some coffee, then said, "I told her that I was investigating the disappearance of Nick, her ex-husband. She told me that she's had a reporter calling her, wanting to interview her about that. But she declined. She's remarried to a Trump-like businessman and doesn't want the publicity. Nor does she want to hurt Michelle."

Wes said, "How is Tiffany? Does she talk to Michelle?"

"Your ex-wife is fine. She seems happy, though saddened by your disappearance. She told me you were an excellent surfer and swimmer. She doesn't know what to think about the way you just disappeared but your surfboard washed up on shore. Especially since you cancelled your life insurance policy and deposited a lot of money in Michelle's bank account before you disappeared."

Holly surmised that Wes had cancelled the policy to keep Michelle from innocently committing fraud by filing for the insurance, and to keep insurance investigators from actively looking for him.

Wes went on. "What about Michelle?"

"She lives in Hawaii and Australia now. They talk occasionally. Mostly about you. Michelle misses you."

Holly saw Wes look down at his coffee. She took over. "Who was the reporter that contacted her?"

George turned to her. "She didn't remember. But the woman asked about Michelle, said she wanted to get in contact with Michelle to get some kind of permission. That bothered

Tiffany. Michelle has never talked about Nick, or what happened between them, in public. But privately Michelle told Tiffany that the police caught the two guys who beat her up. They weren't hired by the mob, but by some woman."

The connection. Holly sat bolt upright in her chair, feeling the connection. There it was—a woman manipulating Wes three years ago by hiring a couple thugs to beat up Michelle.

But what the hell did it mean?

Wes snapped his head up, his green eyes zeroing in on George. "What the hell? Who did hire them? Did they prosecute them?"

George shook his head. "Michelle refused to come back to California to testify. She did identify their photos but she just didn't want to go back to Los Angeles. They dropped the charges. The two men claimed they didn't know who hired them—a female voice on the phone and a money drop once it was done."

Wes stood up and paced to the door leading to the deck. "Christ. I should have found those pricks myself. And why would some woman hire them to beat up Michelle?"

Holly could feel his agitation. His regret. His love for his sister. "Because even then, this woman knew who you were and your weak spots. She figured Michelle getting knocked around would get you to back off the case." But how did she do this without Wes knowing the woman? She had to be somewhere on the fringes of his life. It was so frustrating.

George nodded his head. "It's done more than you think."

Wes stalked back to the table and stared down at them. "Who is she?"

"That's what we have to figure out," Holly said. She looked at her notes. "It could have been your baseball player's wife. She might have been so angry that you let her husband die that she decided to get revenge."

Wes shook his head. "She wanted me to testify, Holly. It was her husband who died."

Holly met his gaze. "Grief isn't always rational. What we have to do is find the connection between a woman in your book club and the woman in your life three years ago."

"Wouldn't I recognize her? I would recognize Lacey, Conrad's wife. I'm sure of it."

She nodded and made some notes. "Okay. Who else stood to benefit by scaring you off from testifying against Bart Gaines? Bart, obviously, so what woman would he get to hire thugs to beat up Michelle?" Looking up from her notepad, she said, "Was he married?"

Wes nodded. "He was married. I don't remember if I ever saw her. I wasn't in court except when I testified. Her name was . . ." He frowned and looked down into his coffee. "Ashley. She was some kind of executive and always working."

"What did she do? Can you remember?"

Wes shook his head. "No."

"Would Bart have known much about you and told his wife, Ashley?"

Wes considered that. "We didn't hang out in the same social circles. He was a sort of employee. We sent our players to him for training. So I might have talked about a player's conditioning and progress with him, or discussed a strategy to get more power behind a homerun hit . . ." He stopped talking as he realized what he'd said. He was obviously thinking that steroids had been part of the power behind Conrad's homeruns. Then he seemed to push it aside. "But I wouldn't have told him personal stuff."

She nodded. "It could be anyone, but we have to start somewhere."

George said, "I'm in the process of trying to track down the two thugs who beat up Michelle. Just because they didn't tell the police who hired them doesn't mean they don't know or have some clue."

Wes opened his mouth, his green eyes burning with anger.

Holly cut him off. "No, you're not going after those two. Let George handle it. You and I need to talk."

He looked between her and George.

George shrugged. "She's bossy but she's also right."

Holly sighed. "Look, Wes, I think there are two keys to this mess. One is Cullen's missing computer. Whatever is on it might be worth killing for. Second is your sister. I think she may have a missing piece of the puzzle. Maybe she knew Cullen somehow, or she'll recognize photos of Helene, Nora, or Maggie from somewhere. But that magazine left in the car points to a connection with Michelle."

Wes turned to stare at her. "No."

She bit back her annoyance. "We'll keep her safe. I'll track her down and make up a story to get her to talk to me. I'll see what she can remember, show her some pictures. Maybe she even has an idea who hired the thugs to beat her up." She stopped talking, looking at her laptop and thinking of Cullen's. And what George had said. She looked at him. "Did you say that the reporter who called Tiffany wanted some kind of permission from Michelle?"

George nodded. "A 'release' was the word Tiffany used. Tiffany didn't like that idea at all. She seemed genuinely concerned about not causing Michelle any more grief, but she also didn't want the old scandal brought up again and somehow tainting her life with her new husband."

She looked at Wes. "We need to talk to Michelle. Maybe this woman has been in contact with her. Trust me to keep her safe, and to not tell her you're alive until you're ready."

His face hardened and he glared at her. "No. She's safer thinking I'm dead. No one can use her to get to me. If you can't live with the terms, you're fired."

She was infuriated at his stubbornness. Slamming her laptop closed, she said, "The killer left that magazine in your car as a threat. They know who you are, who Michelle is, and the underlying message is that she's not hard to find. The question is, do you want the killer to find her before we do?"

His entire body froze to a rigid statue of anger. "No. Stay away from Michelle. I don't want you near her."

Holly felt that deep in her chest. He didn't trust her. He didn't think she, the blue collar daughter of a cop and an ex-cop herself, was good enough, or that she had the integrity to keep her word. She shoved her gun in her purse, stood up, and said in an offhand tone, "You're the client. I'm going to my office and work the other angles."

Chapter 14

Holly traced Lacey Nader to Washington D.C. where she had been testifying before Congress on steroid abuse.

Leaning back in her office chair, she stretched her neck and tried to think it out. It seemed that Conrad Nader's wife had directed her grief and anger from his steroid-related death into a positive place. She doubted Lacey Nader was behind Cullen's murder.

No, she thought, the killer was someone else. She just had to keep digging to figure it out. Since Wes had barred her from tracking down his sister, she had to go at it from other angles. And that was what she was doing—working.

Not thinking about Wes or about his reaction to her suggestion. He said he trusted her. Except with his sister, obviously. The sound of her office door opening yanked her from her thoughts.

"Got as much as I could on Gaines." Joe strode up to her desk. "He was murdered twenty months into his prison sentence. His parents live in Michigan, and he has a brother there, too. One sister has married and moved to Chicago."

She had called Joe and asked him to talk to any contacts he had in the prison system. "What about the wife?"

Joe sat in a chair facing her desk. "Ashley Gaines. They married in 1997. She was a headhunter with Plum Positions Recruiting from 1993 until just over a year ago when her husband was murdered. She took an early retirement and moved to Riverside, California, where she's living in an apartment."

"Riverside?" That struck Holly. "Why Riverside?"

Joe lifted one hand, palm up. "Don't know. She lives quietly from what I can tell."

"Did you talk to the firm? Do they hear from her?"

"I called and talked to human resources. She said that as far as she knows, Ashley doesn't ever go back to visit old friends or anything like that. She said she left on good terms."

"How old is she?" Something bothered her. Okay, several things bothered her. Wes Brockman, for instance, and the fact that he didn't trust her.

Okay, what *really* bothered her was that she cared that Wes didn't trust her. Why the hell did she care? He was the client, and she'd do the job.

"AP, are you listening?"

She blinked. "Sorry, thinking about the case. What did you say?"

Joe fixed his blue gaze on her. "I said that Ashley is thirty-five years old. I got a picture from her last driver's license." He shoved a photo on her desk.

Holly looked down. The woman in the photo looked past forty. She had brown eyes, brown hair, and a small chin. Not unattractive, but no-nonsense plain. She didn't look like any of the women from the book club. Not close enough anyway. It looked like another dead end.

Frustrated, she said, "Thanks, but it's not one of the women I'm looking at for the murder." She frowned as one of the things bothering her materialized in her brain. "She retired at thirty-five? How did she do that? How can she afford to live?"

"She kept paying the insurance policy she had on her husband. When he died in prison, she got the money."

"So what's she doing now? Playing golf?" Holly studied the picture but no more answers popped. Finally, she pushed it toward the stack of papers on the case and sighed.

Joe sat back. "How'd your date go last night? Seth said you were dressed to kill, but when you came in, you were in a mood to kill."

"It wasn't a date." Damn big-mouthed Seth. He knew it wasn't a date. "And I was in a mood to kill from standing on high heels for hours. You want to try it?"

Joe rolled up from the chair, then came around and sat on the desk. "Why is this case getting to you? Is it because you're sleeping with Brockman?"

It had probably been a new record. A whole five minutes before she had the urge to kill her brother. "Every case gets to me. And who I sleep with is none of your business."

He leaned down, his blue eyes cold. "It is when the bastard is hurting you."

Hurting her? That was ridiculous. She had to care to get hurt and she didn't care. Her anger was professional in nature because Brockman was putting roadblocks in the way of getting the job done. Irritated, she said to her brother, "Get out of my face."

Totally ignoring her demand, he added, "Jodi and Kelly said Brockman came over this morning to cook you breakfast. This guy has it bad for you."

She moved fast and shoved Joe hard in the chest. It caught him by surprise and knocked him off her desk. He landed on his ass on the floor. She looked down at him. "Stay out of my business."

In a fluid, easy motion, Joe stood up. And smiled. "You do like Brockman." He advanced on her.

Holly resisted the urge to get up and put her chair between them. "Are you on crack?"

He put his hands on the arms of her chair and leaned down to her face. "Have you told him the truth?"

She tilted her head back, refusing to show any emotion. "What truth?"

His gaze was hard. "That you can't have children. That truth."

The cold words splashed through her defenses and caught her breath in her chest. She had to answer him, make him understand that she didn't care. Didn't care what Brockman knew. She wasn't ever going to be that vulnerable again. "No. Neither of us are interested in a long-term relationship."

Pity touched his gaze. "Holly, if he cares . . ."

She hated this, hated that her brothers kept trying to protect her. There was nothing to protect her from. It was over and done. "He doesn't care. It was just sex. You and Seth walked in on sex. Big fucking deal. I have work to do. Either do the job I'm paying you for or get out."

He didn't move. "A man who loves you won't walk away for this. Do you understand that?"

Who the hell was he kidding? Brad had claimed to love her and he'd walked away. She'd barely been out of surgery when . . . She clenched her hands in her lap and willed the memory to recede. In her best level voice, she said, "Yeah, sure. Got it. Can we get back to work?"

Joe sighed and stood up. "Stubborn."

Relieved that he backed off, she turned her attention to work. "What about Nora Jacobson's ex-husband? What did you find out about him?"

Joe looked down. "Worked for a CPA firm. The firm did work for Brockman's company, but her husband was never connected to that. He was caught embezzling and arrested at work. You already know the rest—Nora changed her and her son's last name back to her maiden name and moved to Goleta to escape the press and attention. In Los Angeles, her hobby was baking and cake decorating. She turned her hobby into a business in Goleta."

Holly turned to her desk and drummed her fingers. "That's the first connection to Wes I've found, but it's thin. Are you sure that her husband never did any work for the sports agency?"

Joe shook his head. "I'm sure. I talked to receptionist at the firm, though, and she let it slip that there was a rumor that the guy liked gambling on sports teams."

A shiver of excitement rolled through her. "That could be the connection. Maybe Nora blames Wes for her husband's gambling?"

Joe said, "Could be. Who can tell with women?"

An hour later, Holly walked in the door of her condo. Tanya, Jodi, and Kelly were spread out around her living room, each with an iPod and yellow pads. It looked like Tanya had enlisted help to get through all the O'Man's podcasts.

"Holly, hi." Tanya pulled her ear pieces out. "We were just finishing up. Ummm . . ." She looked around at the two girls then back to Holly. "Kelly and Jodi are helping me."

"So I see." She set her purse and files down on her desk. She wasn't sure she liked the girls hearing the garbage Cullen spewed out as the O'Man, but she really couldn't stop them. They were both over eighteen, plus it was on the Internet for anyone to listen to. "What do you have for me?"

Tanya brought her yellow pad over to the desk. "I listened to the first four podcasts: *Anti-Princess, Invisible Woman, Wonder Woman, and Barbie Babe.* It's just like we suspected—Anti-Princess is Helene. This one isn't as icky with sexual details. It's more a . . . I don't know . . . profile. Cullen says she wants to have the same power as men in the world. She's tough, acts like she has balls, might even be a cop or someone in authority. But in the end, she's not a man, can't have the same power as men in a man's world, so she's forced to use men to get things done, and being the woman behind the man. But when the men she chooses fail her, she's reduced to writing a book about a powerful man. To seduce her, act like you're the man who will help her gain power and get what she wants, and she'll put out."

Tanya looked up from her notes. "That sounds just like Helene." Looking back at her notes, she said, "Invisible Woman is Nora. She always blends in but secretly wants someone to notice her. To seduce her, treat her like she's the most noticeable woman in the room. Notice all the things everyone else misses—her eyes, her jewelry—find something special about her personality and comment on it. She won't be able to get naked fast enough."

Holly had to fight a wave of pity for Nora. She had wanted to be invisible after all the negative attention when her husband was arrested and convicted of embezzling. She had even changed her name back to her maiden name. But she was still a woman with a woman's desire to be noticed. But what if Nora kept a low profile to stalk Wes? And Cullen threatened that? Either way . . . "Cullen was a real Prince Charming."

Tanya sighed. "I guess I just wanted to be noticed, too. Sort of like Nora. Desperate Housewife is probably just like Invisible Woman but he didn't want to repeat the titles. I'm glad I didn't have to listen to what he said about me." She turned to another sheet of paper on her tablet. "Wonder Woman is definitely Maggie. She acts like a super hero—the woman who can do it all without help. Tell her how amazing she is, bringing home the bacon, frying it up in the pan, and looking like Wonder Woman while doing it, and she'll spread her cape, and legs, for you." Tanya looked up. "Cullen's words not mine."

Holly sat on the edge of her desk. She thought of Maggie with her duel cell phones clipped to her belt in her office, and the walkie-talkie at the engagement party last night when she had them thrown out. It did sound like a description of Maggie on the surface. "And Bridget?"

Tanya thinned her mouth. "Barbie Babe looking for a rich sugar daddy. Act rich, throw money around, buy her a few trinkets, and she'll pay you in sex." Tanya lifted her gaze to

Holly. "Each podcast starts off with the 'type' of woman, meaning the nickname like Barbie Babe. Then Cullen describes his actual experience, right through the sex, with one of those types. He describes why Barbie Babe is more likely to give head than the others because she knows she has to pay for her trinkets."

"Too bad he's already dead," Holly said. She needed a shower just listening to Tanya describe it.

"Wonder what Phil has given Bridget," Tanya mused out loud. "One thing's for sure. I'm quitting my yoga class. I went there hoping to find some kind of mind-body peace. My yoga teacher dating my husband is not doing much for my mind-body peace."

Holly stood up. "Getting your fair share of the divorce settlement will do a hell of a lot more for your peace than yoga. I'm going to call the lawyers next week and set up a meeting to see if they want to be reasonable or play hardball." One of the reasons that Holly fought so hard for clients like Tanya was that she knew what it felt like to be so blindsided that you couldn't fight for yourself. Like when Brad dumped her. They'd had a deal: she'd put him through law school on her cop's salary. Then once he graduated and set up his law practice, she'd open her PI office, and he'd be one of her clients. As soon as Brad had his degree in his hand, and he'd discovered Holly wouldn't be bearing him any children, he'd walked.

But now she was a PI, and she would fight for her clients when they couldn't fight for themselves.

She realized Tanya was talking. "What if they fight us? Phil and the law firm?"

Holly smiled. "Then we'll fight back and win. The idiot went to a very public party with Bridget. What do you want to bet he's been seen in other public places with her? We'll win."

Tanya nodded. "Okay. Thank you, Holly."

She waved it off. She didn't need thanks. "Good job today. You did great. I'll let Jodi and Kelly catch me up on the other podcasts."

"What about tomorrow? Do I go into the office?"

"I'm not sure if I'll be in the office or not. Why don't you call me in the morning about nine? We'll work something out."

Tanya set her notes down on Holly's desk. She shifted back and forth on her feet. "Did I really help?"

"Yes, you really did. Wes will pay you for the time you worked today. And I'll have something for you to do tomorrow. After that, we'll see. Now go home and relax."

Tanya surprised the hell out of Holly by hugging her. "Thank you." Then she let go, picked up her purse, and said good-bye to Jodi and Kelly and left.

Kelly took her earphones off. "You should see your face, Holly."

Jodi added, "Don't you have girlfriends?"

That simple question stopped her cold. "Uh, sure." She had a beer with her cop friends when they had time. But now that Holly was out of the department, those beers got fewer and farther in between. She had some guy friends, too. She just wasn't into shopping and pedicures.

"Hey, don't scowl, Holly. Jodi and I are your friends now. Tanya, too."

She looked at Kelly. Truthfully, Holly was only about six or seven years older than the girls, but it felt like decades. Going back to her comfort zone, work, she said, "I'm not looking for friends, I'm looking for answers." She walked over to the couch. Kelly was sitting there curled up with her legs beneath her. Jodi was sprawled on the chair with her legs hanging over the arm.

"Answers to what?" Kelly asked.

Sitting down, Holly said, "About who could have gotten the key and alarm code to the bookstore."

Jodi swung her legs to the ground and sat up. "We told you, we never gave Cullen the keys or the alarm code."

"What about the book club members?"

Jodi immediately said, "I think Wes gave George a set of keys."

Since George had keys to Wes's house, she wouldn't be surprised if he had keys to the bookstore. But if George was going to kill someone, Holly had the cold, sure feeling the body would never be found. And certainly not where it could lead back to him. "What about other book club members?"

"Like who?" Kelly started doodling on the pad of paper in her lap.

Holly zeroed in on her. "Like someone who helped you out when you wanted to leave the bookstore early one night. You know, maybe locked up and set the alarm for you?"

Kelly kept doodling.

Jodi didn't say anything.

"No one is looking to blame you two. I promise. Wes won't be mad. We just need to know who you might have given the keys too, even for a short time, and who you gave the alarm code to."

Kelly looked up. "It was me. I did it. I had a date but the book club ran long." She took a breath and started talking faster. "Usually Wes will lock up, but he asked me to that night because he had something to do. He hardly ever asks and I thought I'd have enough time. But a few of the book club members stayed later, just talking and talking and talking."

Holly could see Kelly getting more and more agitated. "Kelly, just tell me. Who were the members that stayed late?"

She brushed her hair out of her eyes. "It was Maggie and Nora. I tried to drop a hint that they needed to go but, you know, Maggie can be kind of intimidating." Her shoulders slumped. "Anyway, Nora caught on. She suggested they leave so I could lock up. But Maggie got all snippy and told me to just give Nora the key. She'd lock up and give it back to me in the morning."

She could just imagine Maggie intimidating the hell out of Kelly. "So you did?"

She wiped the back of her hand over her eyes. "Nora is the team mom for Wes's baseball team! He trusts her. I didn't see the harm . . ."

Jodi got up, went to the arm of the couch and sat down. Putting her hand on Kelly's shoulder, she said, "You should have told Wes the first time he asked. But, Kelly, I probably would have done the same thing. I mean, it's Nora." Jodi shifted her gaze to Holly. "Nora isn't a murderer. She has a son. He's really a nice kid."

Holly guessed that Nora made a copy of the key. Was she holding a grudge against Wes? The thread was tenuous at best. Her husband gambled, which likely led to his embezzling and conviction, and Nora and her son being hounded and maybe ostracized.

Wes's sports agency had some gambling connections and had been using a trainer to give their players steroids, giving the teams that were picked an edge. But Wes had nothing to do with the gambling. He pretty much hadn't known about the steroids until Conrad Nader died. And he didn't find out about the gambling connection until after he went to the DEA.

It was thin. But it was the only connection she had right now. Holly got up and went to the desk. Pulling out the photo of the trainer's wife, Ashley, she returned to show it to the girls. "Have either of you seen this woman at the bookstore?"

They both looked at the picture.

Jodi shook her head. "I don't recognize her."

Kelly said, "I don't either, but I doubt I'd remember everyone that comes into the bookstore. And she doesn't look real memorable."

She was right about that. "Kelly, thanks for being honest."

She lifted her gaze to Holly. "Do you think Nora did it?"

Her gut said no. "I'm going to find out." She wished she could talk to Michelle, Wes's sister. Maybe fax the pictures of Ashley and the three book club members to her.

But Wes had made himself perfectly clear. He didn't trust her with his sister. So Holly would have to find out another way.

It was time to go to Riverside and talk to Ashley Gaines.

Chapter 15

Wes and George worked to track down the thugs who had beat up his sister. One of them was dead. The other one worked in Riverside.

That rang a bell. Wes said, "Riverside. I think that's where Holly said Helene is from."

George had made himself at home in Wes's office in his third bedroom, commandeering the computer to do some searches of DEA files. How George got into those, Wes figured he was better off not knowing. He also used his cell phone and multitasked at a rate that made Wes tired.

Or maybe it was the guilt. He'd pushed Holly to trust him, then he turned on her the second she asked him to trust her.

But damn it, those thugs could have killed Michelle. And Michelle blamed him. She had told him that he'd become corrupt just like the men their dad had exposed in his *Cop Scan* articles. She'd been right. He had to protect her now. Why didn't Holly understand that?

"That's an interesting coincidence."

"What's that?" Wes realized he had gotten lost in his thoughts.

"That Helene is from Riverside and one of our thugs is living and working there."

Wes stood up. "What's his address? I'm going to go talk to him."

George slid his glasses down his nose. "Really? And are you going to tell him you are Michelle's brother? Or that you are Nick Mandeville returned from the dead? What exactly are you going to tell him?"

Wes stared right back. "Maybe I'm not going to talk at all."

George returned to doing something on his computer. "You'll be a big help from jail. Go ahead, kill this guy, which at this point is our only lead. Good plan, Brockman."

Frustration clawed through him. "Then what the hell am I supposed to do?"

George leaned back. "Search Cullen's boat. See if we can find any connections to Michelle, or any information about Nora, Helene, or Maggie, or see if whoever broke in and stole the computer left any clues the police missed." He looked over his glasses. "Try to find out just what got Cullen killed."

"How do we get on the boat?"

"*We* don't. I do and then I call you. I've talked to Cullen's mother—she's his next of kin. We're trying to clear it with the police. I've told her I'm interested in buying the boat."

Wes shook his head. "Amazing. So we wait to get clearance?"

"The police have all they need off the boat by now. I expect a phone call at anytime. Then I'll call you and meet you there."

Wes frowned. "Call me? Where will I be?"

"Has it occurred to you that Holly has made herself very visible? Any idiot walking by the two of you can feel the sex sparks. And she's been pushing some buttons. While you are worrying about Michelle . . ."

His gut turned over. "The killer could go after Holly." The thought made his chest hollow out, then fill with a protectiveness that surprised him. Christ, he'd been a selfish bastard, so focused on fixing his life and problems, never really considering what all this might cost Holly. She'd taken in his two clerks to keep them safe.

Holly Hillbay was not quite the hard-ass that she wanted the world to believe she was.

Then what had he done? Gone and told her to behave better at the engagement party, and to focus on his case. Because he was paying her. Never mind that her boob of an ex-boyfriend was doing his best to publicly humiliate her.

So she shaped up, just like he demanded, then put her neck farther out on the limb by telling Maggie that she knew Cullen was murdered over a Web site.

George asked, "Is that what you had in mind?"

That comment snapped Wes from his thoughts. "Hell, no! I don't want Holly to get hurt. I never thought . . ." He rubbed his forehead.

"So you aren't using Holly to bait the killer?"

Wes dropped his hand and stared at George. "No. I want her to find the killer. I want my life back."

George leaned back in the office chair, studying him. "When I first met you, you didn't care if you were killed. You just wanted Michelle safe."

He shrugged. What had he had to live for? His parents were both dead, his wife had left him, his career was gone, his friends went with the career, and he hadn't liked the person he'd become. But since meeting Holly, he felt . . . hopeful. Alive. He wanted to solve this, find his sister and rebuild their relationship, prove to her he was a brother worth having in her life.

George folded his hands behind his head. "So where does Holly fit into this plan? She's not good enough to be near your sister."

Wes blinked, his mind trying to grasp why George would think that when his own words to Holly echoed in his head, *No. Stay away from Michelle. I don't want you near her.* He pushed up out of his chair. "I have to go."

George dropped his hands from behind his head and waved Wes away. "I'll call you and the two of you can meet me at the boat."

*   *   *

Holly wasn't at her office, so he tried her condo. It was nearly four by the time he got there. He lifted his hand to knock when the door opened and Holly's brother filled the doorway. "Uh, Seth, right?"

"Yep. I'm rescuing two damsels in distress." He turned his head toward the interior of the condo, and yelled, "From the wicked witch."

Seth reached out and caught something in his hand.

Wes looked at the object in his hand and tried not to laugh. "She threw an orange at you?"

Seth grinned and held the door open. "Come in at your own risk." He turned his head and said, "Come on, thing one and thing two. Let's get out of here before the wicked witch decides to eat us."

Kelly walked up in jeans and a frilly lace thing that Wes would classify as underwear, but he bit his tongue. She frowned at Seth. "You are purposely goading her."

Seth opened his eyes wide. "Who, me?"

Jodi appeared in the doorway, wearing a tank top and jeans, and Wes almost grinned. She looked just like Holly. She even had her hair twisted up in a clip. She leaned back into the house. "Sure we can't bring you some dinner, Holly?"

Holly's voice floated out. "No thanks. I'll pick something up on the way."

His amusement vanished. "On the way where?"

Seth stepped outside and said, "Go ask her yourself."

They were the same exact height. Probably close in weight. Standing shoulder to shoulder, Wes sucked in a breath to spread out his chest and shoulders. "She's your sister. Aren't you concerned?"

Seth dropped his gaze over Wes with a measured stare. "If you mean, can Holly take care of herself, she'd better damn well be able to. Joe and I taught her from when she was a little girl. And that gun she carries isn't a fashion statement. She's an excellent shot and she is not timid about using it. But if some *guy* who just wants to jump her happens to hurt her, you bet your ass I'm *concerned*. And my gun isn't a fashion statement either." He followed the girls down the walkway.

Wes decided that Seth might be an okay guy and went into the house. Holly wasn't in the living room, home office, or kitchen. He headed down the hallway to the bathroom and extra bedroom. From all the clothes and girl stuff strewn around, it was clear that Kelly and Jodi were staying in the extra room. He shook his head in amusement and made his way to the end of the hall and stopped at the master bedroom.

Holly had the TV on while she stuffed things into an overnight bag. Her face was tight and determined, her shoulders tense. She knew he was there, but she was ignoring him.

He went into the room. It was so Holly, simple, with the basics of a bed, dresser, nightstands, and the TV. While she walked into what he assumed was the bathroom, Wes looked at the picture on the dresser. It had to be a family portrait. There was an older man who resembled her brothers, two young boys about ten, Holly at seven or eight, he guessed, and a breathtakingly beautiful woman.

Holly's mother. Wes picked up the picture to study it. Her mother had Holly's silver blue eyes and the shape of her mouth, but their facial structure was different. Holly's was a little more squared, and a lot stronger.

He turned his gaze to the little girl. She had a mop of hair held back out of her eyes by two clips with pink flowers on them. Her little shoes had matching pink flowers, and the dress had lace. Holly's expression was mulish.

Grinning, he imagined the battle her mom had getting Holly to wear those clothes. They were so wrong for her. She wasn't the delicate, fluffy feminine type. When it came to dresses, she looked much better, and a hell of a lot sexier, in the ice blue halter dress she'd worn last night.

"Want to look through my underwear drawer, too?"

Wes looked up at her cold eyes and set jaw. He'd hurt her feelings and that made her angry. "Your mother is beautiful."

She turned her gaze to the overnight bag on the bed. "I have to get going. I'll call you when I get back if I have anything new for you."

He set the picture down, went to her, and put both his hands on her bare arms. "Holly, I'm sorry. I don't want any of us to contact my sister because I'm afraid for her, but it's nothing personal against you."

She lifted her arms, knocking his hands off of her. "Nice to know. Now move so I can get going."

She didn't believe him. She was pulling farther and farther away. Comparing him to her ex-fiancé, Brad? He had to make her understand. Watching her start to zip her overnight bag, Wes said, "I think you're going to want to postpone your trip. George is trying to get access to Cullen's boat. Once he has clearance, he'll call us to meet him there and look around. He thought maybe we might be able to find the connection to Michelle, the thugs that beat up Michelle, the women in the book club, or maybe what's on the computer."

Holly stopped. Standing up, she turned to look at him. "George can do that?"

"He's in contact with Cullen's mom, his heir. They're clearing it with the police."

She nodded. "He's good." Then her gaze cleared. "I'll drive separately. Once I've seen the boat, I'm heading to Riverside to track down Ashley Gaines."

She was two feet away and he desperately wanted to touch her. He wanted to pull her into his body and drive away the hurt that made her rigid and closed off. He wanted to break through her protective shell, but he also needed to know what information she had. "Why? What have you found?"

She reached into her bag, pulled out a file, and dug through it. Finding what she wanted, she turned and handed him a picture. "It's Ashley Gaines. Recognize her?"

Wes took the picture and studied it. The woman looked like she was heading to the back side of forty, a plain woman with a small chin. "I don't think so." He lifted his gaze. "I don't remember what Bart's wife looked like, or if I ever saw her. But this woman looks a little old for him. Not his type."

"Why?"

Now he had her full attention. She was all PI, determined to keep him at a distance. He answered, "Bart was big on physical looks. But maybe the trial, imprisonment of her husband, and his murder took their toll on her."

She met his gaze. "Could be. But I thought I'd take a run out and talk to her."

Wes thought about that. "Didn't you say Helene was from Riverside?"

She nodded, took the picture from his hand, and stuck it back in her file.

He knew he'd been right. How did it all fit together? "George found out that one of the thugs that beat up Michelle is dead. The other one lives in Riverside."

"Another connection." She blinked and sucked in her bottom lip as she concentrated. "Damn, it's there, but I just can't see it. I wonder if your sister knows . . ." She shifted her gaze to him, then away.

He saw the regret, the pain, and reached for her. "Holly . . ."

She sidestepped him, the pain gone. Her light blue eyes were full of grim determination. She still held the file in her hand. "I know how one of the women in your book club could have gotten into your bookstore to kill Cullen."

He was torn, needing to make her understand, but this was important, too. She stood by the bed, just a few feet away, but it felt like miles separated them. "How?"

"Kelly gave Nora the key and alarm code one night after the book club so she could go on a date. She got them back from Nora the next morning. It would have been easy for Nora to have the key copied."

As the meaning of her words sank in, he winced. "Kelly should have told me."

Holly softened a little. "She didn't want you to be mad or disappointed in her. She's only a kid. And she really thought it would be okay to give it to Nora." She turned around, leaned over, and put the file back in her overnight bag. Then she zipped it up.

Like he was mad at Holly over his sister? His gaze fell to the curve of her ass. The need, the longing to touch her, ripped through him. He wanted to *possess* her. He wanted to arouse her, drive her to the edge of passion, where she was brutally honest. Where she couldn't hide from him. When he demanded she look at him, she opened her eyes wide and showed him everything she had.

He shuddered as the raw, coursing need for her wrapped around his chest. It was more than lust, it was his need to have real, uncensored intimacy with her. The kind built on trust in your partner. Unable to stop himself, he took a step and wrapped his arm around her waist, sliding a hand along the curve of her buttock. He leaned forward until his mouth was against her bare neck.

She went statue still. "Let go of me."

"No." He felt her stiffen her spine, and draw her right arm forward. Before she could elbow him, he took his hand off her buttock and locked his arms around her. "I'm not letting you go until you give me the chance to talk to you. To tell you I'm sorry for making you feel I don't trust you. Not until I try to explain why I don't want anyone to contact Michelle."

She didn't struggle, but turned her gaze to his and said, "You don't have to tell me anything. You're my client, nothing more."

"I'm a hell of a lot more to you. That's why you're trying to push me away." He let her go and sat down on the bed. Then he reached out to grab her hand.

She resisted.

He looked up into her frosty eyes and reminded her, "We have to wait for George to call anyway. You might as well listen to me while we wait."

She jerked her hand from his hold. Then she leaned her butt against the dresser, folded her arms over her chest, and said, "Talk, book boy."

Damn, she made him want to laugh. But he owed her the truth, and his truth wasn't a bit funny. "Holly, I can't let Michelle get hurt. She's all I have left. Our dad was murdered and I couldn't stop it. Our mom died a couple years later. I'm all Michelle has, and I was supposed to be her big brother and take care of her. I failed. I can't fail again."

Her stare never wavered. "I told you I wouldn't bring you into it."

He got up and moved toward her. "I know, but I can't risk it. What if someone tracks her through you? The whole town knows you're working for me now since your ex-fiancé announced his lawsuit on TV." The thought of Brad Knoll made his blood boil. That man had hurt Holly and Wes didn't think she had fully recovered.

Holly was quiet for a beat before her shoulders relaxed. "I can see your point." She took a breath, then added, "I wouldn't let her get hurt, Wes."

He believed in Holly, but what if he was wrong? He couldn't let his sister pay the price. "I owe it to Michelle to fix my screw-ups before I let her know I'm alive."

She shrugged. "Your decision. But if your sister is smart and tough enough to succeed in competitive surfing, I doubt she's the type who's going to appreciate being protected."

Pride in his sister nearly choked him. "She's one of the top five surfers in the world."

Holly uncrossed her arms and rolled her eyes. "God, Brockman, you are such a man. I meant she'll be furious with you for disappearing to protect her."

He grinned, reached out, and put his hands on her shoulders. "Maybe not all women are as confident and capable as you are, Holly."

She met his gaze. "I don't need a man, so what?"

No, she was afraid to need a man, or anyone. He wanted her to feel safe with him. He wasn't the man he had been in Los Angeles. He had grown, learned, changed. He was a man she could fight with and believe he would come back.

He was a man she could trust.

He ran his hands over her shoulders to her back, and leaned down to say, "How many times do I have to come back for you to believe in me?"

The pulse at the base of her neck throbbed. "There's nothing to believe in."

"Me. Believe in me, Hill*baby*. You can trust me with your truths. I won't use them against you. I won't walk out and never come back." He needed her to know it. Believe it. Hold onto it. Because Holly made him want to live again. She wouldn't turn her back on him when he had to make the hard choices.

Like his wife had. Like his so-called friends had. Even his sister hadn't stood by him when he tried to do the right thing, but Wes didn't blame her. She had been pulled into the situation and beaten up. He had failed her.

He skimmed his right hand up her back to her nape and curled his palm around it.

"What do you want from me?" Her voice was thready. Tense. Uncertain.

He looked at the picture a couple feet to her left on the dresser. "Tell me about that picture of your family."

Little shallow lines of confusion formed between her eyes. "It's the last family portrait before my mom left. Why? It's just a picture."

He tried to imagine how hard it had to have been for Holly. "You must have missed her. Missed having a woman around."

She shrugged. "It was a long time ago."

He rubbed the back of her neck, feeling years' worth of tension and pain knotting her muscles. He tried to absorb it by pressing her body into his. Into her ear, he said, "More, Hillbay. Tell me more. I want to know you."

Her body softened against his. "She left after I had a dance recital. I wasn't good enough to get the lead. It was some dance about a princess—I can't really remember. I just remember trying to twirl and I fell, smacking into the princess and ruining the recital. I was embarrassed and scared and crying. My mother came up on stage and I ran to her."

Wes felt it coming. It knotted in his gut and made him forget to breathe. It took all his concentration to keep his voice gentle. "What happened?" He stroked her back, feeling the line of her bra, and the bulge of her knotted muscles.

She took a breath. "She pushed me away and went to the princess girl. She never said another word to me that night. The next morning, she was gone."

Christ. "You're mother is a class-A bitch."

He felt her laugh against the skin of his neck. "It was a long time ago."

And she hadn't danced since then. No wonder she refused to dance. Everyone, no matter how loving their family was, had scars. Everyone was shaped by family and events. He knew that. But for a woman to be so cold to her daughter was unbelievable. "Look at me." He wondered if she'd do it.

She lifted her head and faced him.

No tears. His PI didn't cry—it would be a weakness someone could use against her, like not being able to dance. But he saw the pain of rejection in her eyes. "One day, you will dance with me. Just me. And you will know that I will be there to catch you if you fall." He meant every single word.

"No." She shook her head. "I'm going to solve this case and you are going to have your life back. We'll be done." She swallowed once. "I'll be done with you."

She thought she'd dump him before he could dump her, or

reject her. "But you're not done yet, are you, Hill*baby*?" He leaned forward to take her mouth.

She wrapped her arms around his neck and opened her hot mouth for him.

Warmth and desire punched him hard, and he slid his hand down to her ass. It had never been like this with his wife, or the women he'd had since then. Honest, real, not about money, power, or climbing the success ladder, but about two people needing sex and comfort. *Intimacy.* He reached for the hem of her shirt, and lifted his mouth from hers to yank it off. He dropped it and lowered his gaze.

A skimpy little jewel green bra. Her nipples were puckered, the rosy tips pushing at the fabric. His mouth watered while his cock pulsed. His throat was thick with need, but he managed to ask, "Panties?" Did they match? What did she have on?

She pushed him so he stepped back, hit the bed, and sat down. After kicking off her shoes, she undid her jeans and shimmied them down her thighs.

His chest locked as he took her in. Jewel green like the bra, but spiderweb thin, exposing her pubic hair and swollen lips. Nearly dizzy, he raked his gaze down to her feet, and back up her long, shapely legs. Then over her belly.

The scar.

He reached out and traced the scar. He lifted his stare up to her breasts, then her face. "Come here. Closer."

She stepped between his parted thighs.

He inhaled, catching her scent mixed with her excitement. Jesus, he wanted her. Leaning forward, he captured a nipple through the silky bra.

She made a noise.

Exciting him more, he suckled harder, feeling her hips move forward, seeking. He wrapped his hands around her waist, and glided them over the smooth swell of her hips, brushing the web-thin panties and down the clenched muscles of her thighs. Her thighs trembled. He knew if he touched her between her legs, she'd be wet. And if he stroked her clit, she'd be swollen. Letting go of her nipple, he ran his hands around her legs to the inside of her thighs. Then he looked at her face. Beautiful. Sexy. Open to him. Her eyes mirrored passion and need. Her mouth was soft. Her neck elongated. "Hill*baby*, tell me what you want, what you need."

She put her hands on his shoulders and lifted her breasts by taking a deep breath of air. "I want to come."

Her simple need. "I know. And you are so close, aren't you?" Just to torment her, he drew his fingers higher on the inside of her thighs. Then he leaned forward to tongue her scar.

She jerked back.

Against the warm skin of her stomach, he snapped, "Don't do that. You won't hide anything from me." One day, he would get to the truth of the scar, but for now, all he needed was her trust. Using the tip of his tongue, he followed the scar down, feeling the jags and lumps that scars formed. At the edge of her panties, he used his tongue to nudge it aside. He skimmed his fingers up her thighs to the edge of her panties.

She groaned, shivered, then tried to shove him backward with her hands on his shoulders.

He contracted his stomach muscles and resisted her. He drew his fingers around the front of her thighs, and took his mouth away. "Take off your panties."

She tried to defy him. "Take off your clothes."

"So you can jump me before I'm done with you? So you can grab your orgasm, fast and hard?" He shook his head. "I don't think so. I want to watch you build and build until you break. Until I give you the pleasure your body begs me for." She was beautiful and sexy and, damn it, he wasn't going to be just another orgasm to her.

Her blue eyes darkened. "I'm not taking orders here, book boy."

She underestimated him. She thought he would do her bidding like a good boy so he could get into her panties. But he meant to have all of her. As she'd never given herself to any other man. Ever. Closing his hands around her waist, he moved her back a step and stood up. Holding her waist, he said, "Take off your panties or I'll do it for you."

It showed on her face. Uncertainty. It almost made him give in. Slide his pants down and fuck her just to give her the orgasm and wipe that look off her face. How was it that she thought being a woman to him made her powerless? It made him angry. "Take them off, Holly."

He watched her struggle and the anger evaporated. Her eyes were her downfall. She wanted the orgasm. She needed him. She feared the intimacy that required trust. And she didn't know how to keep it all under control. He kept his hands on her waist.

She wouldn't give in. "You want them off, you take them off."

Slowly, he sank to his knees, drawing his hands down her waist, then skimmed over the edge of her panties, leaving them in place. He brought his hands to the insides of her thighs and pushed her legs apart.

The thin, delicate strip of fabric between her legs clung damply to her. Inhaling, the scent of her wet desire went straight to his balls. His control shattered.

She wanted the panties on, then he'd go *through* them.

Using his thumbs, he slid them to the tops of her inner thighs and beneath the delicate fabric to rub the pads of his thumbs along her seam. Parting her wet curls, he leaned forward and licked her through the panties.

"Oh."

He heard her bite the word off as she canted her hips forward. "More," he demanded. Sliding one thumb deep inside of her, he used his tongue to press the wet, silky fabric against her clit. It molded to her, creating friction.

Her breath grew harsh. She dropped her hand to the back of his head. "Wes."

Her soft voice rocked him. He'd give her what she wanted, anything. "What, baby? I'll give you the orgasm that you want."

She closed her eyes, then opened them. "I want more than that. I want to touch you, taste you, feel you."

Her courage stunned him. He rolled up to his feet and kissed her hard. Then he stripped off his shoes and clothes. When he looked at her, she was reaching for the front clasp of her bra. Going to her naked, he brushed her hands away. She had met him halfway.

More than that, she understood that he needed more from her.

"Let me." He unhooked the bra and slid it off her. Then he stripped off her panties. When he rose to his full height, he pulled Holly against him, just to feel her skin, her curves in his arms. Dropping his mouth to the curve of her shoulder, he said, "You make me feel alive, Holly. You make me want to fight again. And God, you are so sexy, it makes me want to possess every part of you."

She leaned her head back to look up at him. "I don't have much to give."

That made his heart stutter. "The hell you don't." He lifted her up in his arms and put her on the bed. Following her down, he laid over her and pushed her thighs apart. "You have what I need, Holly." She was so ready, the head of his dick slid inside her. He held himself there, waiting.

Her eyes darkened to middle blue. "This I can give you." She tilted her hips up.

"Keep looking at me." He thrust into her, burying himself deeper than he'd ever been inside any woman. When she gasped, he held himself still. "Too much?" He felt her clench and pulse around him and, God, it was perfect.

"Yes. No. Don't stop."

Like he could. "I won't." He took her mouth and made good on his promise, thrusting deeper and harder as she writhed and arched into an orgasm. He raised his mouth from hers and watched. "Look at me!"

She did, letting him to see the pleasure sweep her away. Allowing him to see the moment she stopped fighting and let herself be vulnerable. *Sexy and priceless* was his last thought as he pressed even deeper into her and came in long, hot, endless vibrations.

Finally able to breathe, he had started to tell her what she meant to him when his cell phone rang.

Chapter 16

The sound of the cell phone broke the moment. Holly had been staring up into Wes's face, into his eyes. She had seen the climax take him, felt him come deep inside of her. His expression had told her that she was special. That sex between them was special. She had to put things right, remind them both that this was temporary.

So she had started to tell him the truth about the scar that he was so strangely fascinated with. But the phone rang from somewhere on the floor where Wes had left his pants.

"It's George, most likely," Wes said. He had his arms braced on either side of her head. He kissed her forehead, got up, and quickly found his pants. Once he fished out his cell phone, he answered with, "So, are you in?"

Holly got up and started dressing while he paced. If George got them onto Cullen's boat, they might find some answers. And when they solved the case, Wes could find his sister. After pulling on her jeans, she picked up her bra.

"Okay, we'll meet you there." Wes hung up and looked at her. "He's leaving my house now so he'll get to Cullen's boat first."

Holly fastened the bra and picked up her shirt. "How did he get permission?"

He pulled on his pants and picked up his shirt. "He contacted Cullen's mother in Oregon and told her he was interested in buying the boat. She was very cooperative."

Holly looked around for her hair clip and spotted it on the dresser. Twisting up her hair, she said, "As far as I know, his mother hasn't come to Goleta to claim Cullen's body, or find out what happened to him."

Wes put on his shoes and stood up from the edge of the bed. "Maybe they're not close. I'm sure the police have contacted her. Why?"

She turned around, looked at him, and felt a hollow place open up in her chest. She hated it, hated the vulnerable feeling Wes exposed in her. "After we search Cullen's boat, I'm going to Riverside. I'll call you if I find anything."

He reached out and pulled her to him, down across his thighs. He pushed his hand deep into her hair. "Thank you, Holly."

She shifted, feeling nervous. "For what? It was just sex."

His smile spread in a warm and wicked grin. "No, it wasn't. It was great sex and more." He leaned his face close to her. "You trusted me."

"Knock it off, Brockman. We need to get going." She levered off his lap.

He grabbed her hand. "Holly, I don't want you going to Riverside alone. If you still need to go after we take a look at Cullen's boat, I'll go with you."

She went still, but her mind raced. "Why?"

He looked up at her with his green eyes. "It could be dangerous."

Was he serious? "That's what you're paying me for, book boy. Don't worry about the danger, that's my job."

Standing up, he kept hold of her hand. "I don't want anything to happen to you. It's called caring. People do it all the time." He leaned down, kissed her, and added, "Let's go. We'll take my car."

They ended up parking in the parking lot behind Wes's

bookstore and walking to the docks. This time it was full daylight on a Sunday afternoon, unlike when Holly followed Cullen and Tanya to the docks after the book club meeting. People milled around, tourists buying food from the vendors and looking at the boats. Holly stayed quiet as they walked to the gate that would let them into the section where the boats were docked. The water below them smacked against the pilings and hulls. The air smelled like brine, old seaweed, and the oily scent of boats.

She took it all in, acutely aware of how vulnerable and exposed Wes was as he walked along beside her. She had her gun in her purse, but now she wished she'd put on a holster and worn a jacket. There was a vibration in the air that she hoped was from the sound of boat engines as they went in and out of the harbor, and not because Wes was in danger.

Two little boys raced past her. She turned to watch them and heard their mother calling out for them to slow down. For a second, her concentration was on the two boys and their bright, laughing faces. When she realized what she was doing, she jerked her head back around, brutally ignoring the regret in her gut, and focused on her job.

She spotted George by the gate waiting for them. Heading toward him, she looked around again. She needed to keep her mind on Wes's safety, on finding the connection that would lead them to Cullen's killer, and the person screwing with Wes's life.

Someone from his past.

"I just got here," George said as they walked up to him. "I stopped by the police station to get the key."

She watched as he turned and inserted the key into the lock. George had shed his coat, choosing to wear a short-sleeved black pullover. She was pretty sure he'd strapped a gun to his ankle. He didn't seem like the type to go unarmed. Like her, he believed Wes was in danger.

George kept scanning the docks just like she did. Habit, or did he feel uneasy, too? Or maybe it was just the knowledge that they were going onto a dead man's boat. While George held the gate, she and Wes walked through.

The slap of the water against the hulls of the boats was louder. Down the dock a ways, a boat was heading in toward the slip. Up on her left, a group of young twenty-somethings laughed as they moved around on a medium-sized boat. George led the way to Cullen's boat, while she and Wes walked side by side one step behind him. From what Holly remembered, the boat was about halfway down the dock on the right.

Wes said, "Did you talk to Rodgers, George?"

They both saw him nod, then he said, "She said she didn't believe I was interested in buying the boat and I'd better damn well tell her if we find anything related to the case." He slowed down as they approached Cullen's boat.

Holly half-smiled at Rodgers' comments while scanning the rows of docks. So many people out on a Sunday afternoon, she thought.

She heard Wes say, "We need to find something, we need a break."

Both men stopped walking, and Holly pulled up behind them. The sun was bright, bouncing off the water and making her eyes water behind her sunglasses. But a sudden glint caught her attention.

Her heart thudded. *A gun!* She wasn't taking a chance that she'd been wrong. "Wes! George! Down!" She turned to look at them while reaching into her purse to get her gun out. They were both standing with their backs to her, looking at Cullen's boat. Wes turned and reached for her.

George turned to scan the same area she had.

The crack froze them all. Holly stared at Wes. Oh God, was he hit? No blood bloomed anywhere on him that she could see. Her mind raced.

George said, "Well, damn," and sank to the ground.

"What the hell!" Wes roared, dropping the hand he'd been reaching for Holly with and squatting down next to George.

"Gunshot." Holly's reactions kicked in. She already had her gun in her hand. She took up a protective stance, trying to keep her body between the two men on the docks, and the area she thought the gunshot had come from. She couldn't be sure where she'd spotted the glint of sunlight off metal as the shooter had raised the gun. It had all happened so fast and a good part of her reaction had been training and instincts. But she thought it was one or two docks over.

She scanned her gaze over everyone, trying to spot the gun. Close by, people realized something had happened and were quiet. A few voices were calling out, "What was that? Did a boat hit?" An older couple appeared on the deck of their boat nearby.

Holly couldn't find any sign of a gun. Where was the shooter? Her heart banged against her chest, blood roared in her ears, but her mind was crystal clear. "Wes, where is he shot?"

"Back of his left shoulder. Lot of blood. I don't think the bullet went in, but it tore an ugly gash."

"It's fine. Help me stand," George said.

She kept scanning, looking for the danger. She saw a speedboat roaring away. Was the shooter on that boat? To Wes, she instructed, "Do not let him move! Both of you stay down!" She was not going to let the shooter finish the job.

Someone from her left shouted, "Oh my God!" Someone had opened the dock gate and people rushed in.

Holly turned. It was two men in their fifties. No gun. "Call nine-one-one and report a shooting. We need an ambulance. Now."

The man who had spoken stared with a blank face. But his companion snapped into action. He pulled out a phone and started talking.

Holly heard the man say into the phone, "A man has been shot." Nodding to herself, she knew that would get the police here with lights and sirens. She turned back to watch the crowd and keep her body between danger and Wes and George.

But she knew the shooter was gone. It was just too freaking perfect. A crowd of people, and she'd bet no one saw the gun. They wouldn't expect it, and it all happened so fast, the shock would blur the details.

And the shooter would get away.

Fury pounded at her as more people approached, sickly curious about the man who had been shot. Voices reached her.

"Wife caught him cheating . . ."

"Business deal gone bad . . ."

She shut it out and asked, "Wes, how is he?"

"Okay."

It felt like hours had passed as she tried to keep the situation under control and safe, but she knew it had only been minutes. She could hear the sirens approaching. "Wes, get George's gun and put it in my purse. I'm pretty sure he has a piece on his ankle. Get the holster, too."

"Smart," George said from the ground.

"Always," Holly shot back, feeling the weight of Wes slipping George's gun into her purse as the sirens screamed closer. Deputies were the first ones through the gate. Holly turned, quickly identified herself, and gave the gun in her hand to the closest deputy.

It was a safety precaution. The cops acted first to ensure everyone's safety, then sorted out the details later. She'd get her gun back once they had a read on the situation. She filled them in. "We were accompanying the victim to look at a boat he was interested in buying when he was shot. I didn't see a shooter, but it seems to have come from one or two rows over."

One deputy took careful notes while paramedics worked on George. They said that when George had turned at Holly's warning, he prevented the bullet from plowing through his back and chest. Instead, it had dug a groove through the back of his upper left side.

Had someone tried to kill George? Why? To torment Wes? Or had they tried to kill Wes and missed?

*   *   *

"I'm not taking drugs." George sat on the couch in Wes's living room. His face was pale and drawn tight.

"Don't be stupid," Wes yelled at him. "The doctor said to take the pain pills every four hours!" He shoved the bottle of pills in George's face.

Monty whined and ran over to Holly. He sat down by her leg and whined in his throat.

Holly rolled her eyes. Men. They were both pissed off. Add to that George's pain from being shot and stitched up, and Wes's fear for his friend, and they were both acting like little boys in the middle of a temper tantrum. They'd stand there all night and yell at each other to keep from thinking about what could have happened.

She pushed off the edge of the fireplace, bent over, and picked up Monty. He licked her face. *Ugh.* Wiping her face with the back of her hand, she stalked over to Wes and snatched the pills from him.

Wes turned to glare at her.

She shoved the dog into his arms. He had no choice but to take the dog. Monty immediately burrowed into Wes's arms, trying his best to make Wes pet him.

Satisfied that the dog would keep Wes quiet for a minute, she opened the bottle and poured out two pills. Then she set the bottle down on the table behind her and picked up the glass of water. When she was ready, she fixed her gaze on George. "You can either take these like a good boy or I'm going to shove them down your throat." She leaned forward to stare at his pain-filled eyes. "You are in so much pain, you can't even lift your arm. Don't screw with me, George, I'm not in the mood." She held out the pills.

He blinked once, then said, "You're a piece of work, Hill-bay." He took the pills.

"Yeah yeah, gutter mouth, I know." She put the glass of water into his right hand. "Just take the pills so we can get to work."

Wes stood at the end of the couch with Monty in his arms and snorted.

George ignored Wes and handed her the water back. "We?"

She knew George's goal was to help Wes. Then he didn't have any more goals. She wasn't about to let Wes lose his friend. "You think one little bullet is a reason to slack off? We need to figure out who knew we were going to be there on the docks. And what they didn't want us to find."

He reached beside him to pick up a pillow. "Detective Rodgers and Cullen's mom knew I would be there."

Holly took the pillow from his hand and walked around the back of the couch, and Wes, since he was standing there. She met his gaze, and saw his relief that George had taken the pills. She reached out and put her hand on the bulge of his bicep. Then she went behind George, tucked the pillow behind his neck and head, and said, "His mom lives in Oregon, I don't see how she could have told anyone that matters in Goleta. Who did you pick up the keys from?"

He rolled his eyes up to her. "Clerk at the police station."

She sighed and walked around the couch. "Okay, so I suppose word could have gotten around. I'll do a little research on Cullen's mother and see what I can find."

"I'll give you what I have. His parents' names are Jed and Peggy Vail. Father's a boat mechanic. Cullen left home young, came to California to make it big."

"Got it. I'll see if there's some trail that might have tipped off the shooter that we were at the boat." She looked at Wes and saw that Monty had fallen asleep. The dumb dog. Wes turned around and walked past the gurgling fish tank into the library, where she assumed he would put Monty in his bed.

"What did Rodgers say?" George asked.

She looked over to see the pain lines were easing on his face. "She said it looked like a nine millimeter bullet that cut a path through you before burying itself in Cullen's boat. They dug two just like it out of Cullen. When they test it, they'll see it came from the same gun." It was past eight, and dark outside. They had spent time giving statements and at the hospital while George was sewn up and disinfected. They never did get onto Cullen's boat since Detective Rodgers immediately took control of the boat again as part of the investigation into George's shooting.

"They'll never find the shooter." George closed his eyes.

Holly shifted her gaze to Wes as he walked back into the room. He looked nearly as bad as George. Watching your friend get shot qualified for a bad day.

Wes ran his hand around the back of his neck. "If you hadn't called our names . . ."

"Good instincts," George muttered.

It was her job to be alert and rely on her instincts. She changed the subject. "George, do you know if Helene, Nora, or Maggie own a gun?"

"Maggie. For two and a half years since she was mugged at an ATM."

"Concealed?"

He was slower to answer. "No."

The drugs were kicking in. She looked back to Wes. "Do you have a guest room with a bed?"

He nodded.

George said, "Are you going to threaten me again?"

Holly grinned at Wes but answered George. "Do I need to?"

George opened his dark eyes. "I kind of like it." He sat up and got to his feet.

She liked George. He was a no-bullshit guy, and from what she could see, a loyal friend to Wes. He'd gotten shafted by the bad guys and forced out of the job she suspected he had loved. But he didn't wallow in pity. Shit happened and he dealt. "Then you'll love me in the morning before I've had coffee." Holly planned to stay the night. She'd called her brothers to bring Jodi and Kelly over.

He chuckled and headed down the hall. Wes followed him.

Holly went into Wes's kitchen and looked in the fridge with the vague idea of making them something to eat.

"Hungry?" Wes moved up behind her.

She looked back over her shoulder. "I thought you might be. I can make something if you're hungry."

He put his arms around her and settled his chin on her shoulder. "You can cook?"

Keeping her gaze on the fridge, she said, "How do you think my brothers, dad, and I managed to keep from starving?"

"Donut shops?"

She had to fight a smile. "I can shake and bake with Betty Crocker any day."

"I don't know if that was a mixed metaphor or just blasphemy." He turned his mouth to the delicate skin on her neck. "I'll be happy to feed you, Hill*baby*. If you're hungry."

Desire raced through her. "Not now. George is . . ." She shivered when he dragged his wet tongue around to her collarbone. "Wes!"

He lifted his head to her ear. "Thank you. You saved George's life today. I was right there with you and I have no idea what tipped you off."

Instincts that she trusted. "Dumb luck."

Wes reached past her for a package of chicken and handed it to her. "I'll start the barbecue. You wash and season these." He pulled her back and shut the door.

She put the cold package of chicken on the counter and asked, "You want to cook all that chicken?" It was a supersized package of chicken thighs—enough to feed a small army.

"Yes. We'll eat the leftovers tomorrow." He went out onto the deck.

Holly found a large platter, washed the chicken, and nosed around until she came across seasoning that she liked.

Wes came back in. "Wine, soda, or beer?"

She turned from the chicken, looked at him, and felt a sudden tightness in her chest. It was hard to get a full breath. Damn it, she liked him. He didn't try to change her. "Uh, whatever you're hav—" Wes's doorbell cut her off.

Holly hurried into the living room, where she'd left her purse by the fish tank, and got out her gun. Wes was already at the front door looking out the peephole.

"Recognize who it is?"

Wes heaved a huge sigh. "Who else? Your brothers, with the girls and someone else I can't quite see."

Curious who the other person was, she yanked open the door—"Dad!"

"Dad?" Wes repeated behind her.

Before Holly could recover, her dad pushed Joe out of the way and engulfed her in a bear hug. "Hey, Princess. I hear you're having all the fun without me."

She felt hot tears sting her eyes. Just his voice could do that. When her mom left, Holly had cried herself to sleep many nights. One night, her dad came home early from a long shift and heard her. He came into her room, scooped her into his arms, and told her that her mother hadn't deserved her. She had seen tears in her dad's eyes then and she knew she had to be strong for him. But she never stopped loving her dad's hugs, his rough voice, or his insistence that she was his princess. She'd never made him cry again until the night in the hospital when they'd all learned she'd never have children.

Careful of the gun she still held, Holly hugged him back. "I told you about the case, Dad. But you were fishing with your buddies."

He raised his eyebrows. "Your brothers tell me you're dating a guy." He turned his gaze to Wes. "Would that be you?"

Wes stepped forward and held out his hand. "Wes Brockman, and yes, sir, I'm dating your daughter. She's also working on a case for me."

"We're not dating." She shot a killer glare at her brothers. "Wes, this is my dad, Eric Hillbay."

Wes said, "Come on in. I was just getting ready to put chicken on the barbecue."

Kelly shifted from foot to foot, looking everywhere but at Wes. "I'll help. Do you have potatoes, Wes? Or rice? Oh, I know, baked beans—do you have some cans of baked beans? I can doctor them up if you have molasses . . ." Her voice slid away as she headed toward the kitchen.

"I brought beer and potato chips." Seth hefted a couple plastic grocery bags.

Holly closed the door as they all piled into the kitchen. She looked down at the gun in her hand. She should probably shoot someone, but she wasn't sure who. Her brothers were usually at the top of her list, but Wes was strong competition.

They were not dating. It was just sex.

Chapter 17

"I'm going to see if George is awake and take him some food." Kelly started putting together a plate of chicken.

Wes shut the refrigerator door where he'd been getting out a second round of beer and soda. Setting the bottles and cans on the counter, he put his hand on Kelly's shoulder.

She flinched.

He felt for her. She'd been scurrying around all night, cooking beans, serving chicken, and picking up empty plates. She was nervous and making herself sick. "Kelly, honey, I'm not mad at you. You had good reason to trust Nora with the key to the store."

Her shoulder shook. "I'm sorry, Wes! I mean, Nora is your team mom, and she's so nice, I—"

Damn. He took the plate from her hands and hugged her. "I know. I'm not sure if Nora's involved. But I'm not mad at you, okay?" He looked down at her head bent into his shirt.

She shuddered and took a deep breath. "I'm sorry I didn't tell you right away."

He pulled her face up. "I know you are. But you have to know you can tell me anything, okay?" He wanted Kelly and Jodi to come to him if they needed help. They were young and away from home. Two smart, pretty, and nice girls. He'd kill anyone who hurt them.

She nodded.

"Go wash your face, then see if you can get George to eat." He let her go.

She asked, "George is going to be okay, right?"

He clamped his jaw, and had to force himself to relax his hands. "Yes. The wound hurts, but it basically just needed a whole bunch of stitches and some time to heal. That's it." He'd been trying not to think about what it felt like when he'd heard that shot and seen George slide to the ground— like he lost a brother. If he had a brother.

She studied his face, then said, "I'll get him to eat after I wash my face."

When he turned around to grab the beers, he saw Holly standing there. She looked . . . odd. Like she'd seen something that made her mad or sick or sad. "Hey, you okay?"

She walked past him holding a bowl. "Yes, I'm just getting more chips." She picked the bag up and dumped them in the bowl.

A thread of anger started inside of him. "You saw me hugging Kelly. You can't think—"

She turned around. "I don't. I think you treat her like a little sister. Like family. You need a family of your own. Which means I have a job to do so you can make that happen." She picked up the bowl and walked outside.

He watched Holly for a second, relieved that she didn't think the worst of him. And yet, there had been something distant or regretful in her voice, something that had slid around her protective shoulder chip. But she was coming to trust him, and in time she would realize she was safe with him. Safe enough to share her truths with him and trust that he would guard them, not hurt her with them.

He grabbed the beers and soda for Jodi off the counter and went outside.

Jodi got up and took the soda. "I'm going to read for a while."

"You and Kelly will be all right sleeping in the third bedroom?" The girls had brought with them their stuff, and the overnight bag Holly had packed to go to Riverside. "The couch in there folds out into a bed."

"We'll be fine. 'Night, Wes."

"Get some sleep. You'll be able to go home to your own apartment soon." He walked out to Holly and her family gathered around the table by the fire pit in time to hear Holly catching her dad up on the case.

He opened his beer and drank it. Life was ironic. The reason Wes had contacted the DEA about the doping death of Conrad Nader was because he didn't trust cops.

He didn't like cops.

Now he had a serious case of the hots for an ex-cop who came from a family of cops. And they were all discussing his case.

The irony was that these cops cared about their jobs like his dad had cared about exposing corruption in those who were supposed to protect and serve the public. Wes and his sister had grown up seeing the dark side of the thin blue line.

It turned out that maybe Wes had missed the point—that most cops cared about the job and really did want to make a difference. Holly had given him the gift of that knowledge. He turned his attention to her father.

Eric Hillbay sat with his arms linked behind his head, leaning back in his chair with his legs stretched toward the fire pit. The flames flickered over his face. Finally he unlinked his hands and sat forward. "What's your next move, Holly?"

She looked around the table. "Nora tried to call Wes a couple times, and we're pretty sure she wanted to talk. But when we saw her, she seemed scared. I think she's our weak link. In fact, I think she wants to tell what she knows, but she's scared."

Her dad said, "Of what?"

Holly started to answer, but Wes jumped in because he'd been thinking about this exact question. "She has a son, Ryan. She'd do anything to protect Ryan. So she might be afraid that she'll go to jail and Ryan will have no one. Or she might be afraid someone will hurt Ryan."

Eric studied him. "You don't think she killed Cullen? Or was part of it?

He shook his head. "No. The Nora I know could not have shot Cullen twice unless her son was in danger. Nothing we've found on Cullen suggests that he was threatening her son. And I doubt she has the skill to shoot George from a distance as someone did today."

Joe twisted off the cap of his beer. "Not bad, Brockman. But she's part of the alibi. In fact, they were all supposed to be at her house when the murder occurred."

He nodded. "I know. And she appears to have gotten the key and alarm code." He had to be clear about this. "Let's look at facts. Her husband was embezzling and she didn't know. She's naïve, she's trusting, or used to be. My gut, the same gut that made me rich doing deals for baseball players, tells me Nora trusted the wrong people and got pulled into a nightmare she doesn't know how to get out of."

Holly nodded. "So she might have gotten the key thinking that one of them was going to meet Cullen at Wes's bookstore for a reason other than murder. Actually, I don't think Nora was at the bookstore at all when Cullen was murdered. I think she stayed home and made it look like all three of the women were there so her neighbors would confirm the alibi."

Wes looked at her. The firelight played off her dark hair, catching the blond highlights. She had it twisted up again. He was starting to realize she wore it that way as part of her effort to keep herself tough and distant. Quietly, he asked, "You think Nora was used?"

Holly met his gaze. "And now she's trapped. That's the only way I can make it work. I think one of the other two went to the bookstore to meet Cullen, maybe to distract him while the third one went to his boat to steal the laptop."

"Where they thought their real names were linked with the

nicknames on the Web site." He thought it over, seeing it line up to a point. "But why was Cullen murdered?"

Holly paused, then said, "Because one of the women had an agenda the other two knew nothing about. Getting revenge on you. And once Cullen was murdered, she controlled the other two by pointing out that they were accomplices to the crime."

The silence was broken by the waves pounding the surf and the fire crackling in the pit. Someone had been coming to his book club and cooking up ways to destroy his life. Who did he know who was that manipulative and cold? "Maggie or Helene?"

Holly said, "I think so. What we have to do is use Nora to find out which one. Once we get Nora to break the alibi, and find out which woman went to the bookstore, the police can take it from there."

Eric asked, "How do you plan to use Nora?"

She folded her hands around her bottle of beer. "Wes and I can't get close to Nora, or Maggie or Helene, thanks to Brad." She picked up her beer and took a quick drink.

Wes could feel her anger, maybe pain. He watched her for a few seconds, cognizant that her family gave her the same courtesy. Given that her brothers liked to torment her on a regular basis, he knew he was right. Brad had hurt Holly and it went deeper than money. The very fact that his kick-ass PI hadn't gone after Brad to extract revenge or justice in some way told him a great deal. He also remembered Holly telling him that Seth had gone after Brad.

Wes liked her brother even more. He hoped Seth had done the job right.

Holly set her beer down and said, "We can't talk to Nora, but Seth can." She looked at her brother. "I think you should use your dubious charm and see if you can get Nora to trust you. Get her to tell you whatever you can. Find out if she has Cullen's laptop or knows where it is. Anything that will help us."

Seth leaned forward. "What kind of woman is Nora?"

Holly made a face. "Much as I hate to say this, I'm going to borrow the O'Man's description. She's the Invisible Woman. No one really notices her. She wants it that way, because of her ex-husband's embezzling conviction. That was enough negative attention for her. But she's still a woman. And Cullen was able to pinpoint the loneliness and need in her then exploit it. It's on his Web site, The O'Man. He made her feel singled out, like he could see something special about her that everyone else was missing."

Seth nodded. "I can do that."

Joe said, "I'll snoop around the other two, see what I can come up with."

Holly nodded. "The name Hillbay will tip them off, so maybe you should . . ."

Joe grinned at her. "Lie?"

Seth slapped him on the back. "Give it a try, Joe. The truth hasn't been working for you."

Holly snorted. "Shut up, both of you. I don't know what women see in you two. You're both ugly and dumb as bricks."

Eric broke up the bickering by saying, "I'll go by in the morning and see all my old friends at the station. Find out what the scuttlebutt is on this case." He stood up and looked at his sons. "We're leaving."

To Wes's surprise, Joe and Seth both got up and followed their dad out.

A half hour later, Wes finished loading the dishes into the dishwasher. The girls were asleep. Holly was making notes and working in the living room. He shut the dishwasher and went in to coax her to bed. He was glad she was staying the night. People he cared about were developing a nasty habit of getting hurt.

He walked past his fish tank and turned toward the couch. Then he smiled. She was sound asleep, her files and yellow tablets spread out over her lap. She had taken out her hair clip and hooked it on the edge of one of the tablets. She'd been sitting straight up, but her head had fallen to the back of the couch. He walked over and picked up her notes, papers, and pictures, and put them in a neat stack.

He looked down at her. He'd never forget the protective stance she'd taken over George once he'd been shot. She was not going to let the shooter get a second chance. Beautiful and street smart, she had a heart of gold that someone had cut deeply. It made his gut turn over. Reaching down, he lifted her into his arms.

"Hey." She tried to force her eyes open. "I'm awake."

He laughed. "Go back to sleep, Hill*baby*. I've got you." He took her across the living room, and turned down the hall into his room, which faced the beach. After laying her on the bed, he took off her shoes. Then he reached for her pants.

"I can do it."

He looked up at her sleepy eyes. "I know." He tugged her jeans down and caught sight of her green panties. Ignoring his dick's reaction, he pulled her to a sitting position to strip off her top and bra. Then he pulled the covers back, lifted her up and set her on his sheets. "Go back to sleep." He covered her up, kissed her forehead, and headed into the bathroom. By the time he came out, she was asleep again.

Wes didn't mind. He got under the covers, pulled her into his arms, and closed his eyes.

The feel of someone stroking his cock made him rock hard. He woke up instantly. It was still dark, early morning, but there was just enough light for him to see Holly sliding down his chest. Her warm hand was wrapped around the base of his dick.

Either he was having a sizzling sex dream, or he'd just woken up to a fantasy come to life. Her hair was spread out on his belly as she scooted lower. He touched the back of her head. "Holly?"

"Hmm?" She flicked her thumb over the sensitive tip of his penis.

He jerked and felt the rush of hot sperm flood his balls. He looked down at her, at the slope of her shoulder, the curve of her back, the fall of the one breast that he could see, and further down to her butt, barely covered in green panties. Was she horny? Deciding to get him so hot that he wouldn't demand so much from her? Trying to get his brain to work, he said, "You could just ask if you want sex."

Her warm breath teased his dick. Then she said, "I'm taking what I want, Brockman." She leaned her head lower and licked him. Then she said, "Unless you object?"

His cock screamed at him to lie down and shut the hell up. "No objections."

She cupped his balls and covered him with her mouth. The combination of the warm, wet pull of her sucking and her tongue sliding along him drained any blood left from his brain. Pleasure raced through him. He ran his hand over her hair and any place he could reach just to touch her. Her clever mouth worked his dick while her hands fondled his balls.

He grabbed a handful of the sheet and moved against her. Lifting his head, he saw her taking him, suckling him. Then she raised her blue eyes, dark with need and something else.

Something sweet and giving.

Heat gripped from his lower back, raced down his balls, and he exploded into a climax.

Holly loved the feel of Wes in her mouth, of his hand stroking her head. He never pushed her head, the way men did to control a woman. Instead he stroked her, touching her face, moving over her shoulder and back to her hair.

Like he just wanted to touch her.

She'd woken up this morning and seen him sprawled

naked on his back with a morning erection bringing him to half mast. And she'd felt that odd catch in her chest. She didn't want to identify her feelings. She just wanted Wes for the short time they had left. She knew she was getting close to breaking the case.

She decided she'd have him for the little time they had together. He seemed to accept her as she was, flaws and all, and she wanted to give him something back. His life had been ripped apart, his best friend shot, and Wes still worried about others, like Kelly's feelings. He cared about others besides himself.

She could give him this. A pleasant morning wake-up, and maybe a good memory of her.

Wes tugged at her arm, got his hands under her shoulders, and pulled her up to him.

She looked at him and grinned. "Now you can go back to sleep."

He stroked his hand over her hair and down her back. "Why would I want to do that, Holly?"

She laughed. "Every man does."

"You think so?" He kept touching her. "What if I have a burning question that keeps me from being able to go back to sleep?"

She relaxed against him. "Do I know the answer?"

"Oh yeah."

She'd play along. "What's your question?"

He brought his hand around to cup the side of her face. Even in the dim light, she could see the intensity of his green eyes. "Did sucking me make you wet? Horny? If I touch you, am I going to feel your creamy excitement?"

She shivered. She hadn't expected this. "I wanted to do it."

He smiled. "I believe you. I asked you if it made you hot."

"Do you have a problem with early morning gifts, book boy?"

He looked startled. "No. God, no. Holly, I loved it." He lifted his head to kiss her. "But I still want to know."

Yes, damn it. And he was making her hotter now. "Yes. It made me so hot, my panties are probably soaked. Is that what you wanted to know?"

He seemed to miss a breath. "Damn right." He swallowed. "Show me."

"Show you what?" What was this between her and Wes? How did he touch something so deep inside of her?

He held her gaze. "Give me your panties."

"And then?"

He arched both eyebrows. "Did I stop you from taking what you wanted?"

She shifted and wiggled until she'd slid her panties off and handed them to him.

He tossed them aside and kissed her. Driving his tongue in deep, sweeping over the roof of her mouth, playing with her tongue. He held her mouth to his, and stroked his free hand down her side, around her hip, then to the front where he pushed apart her legs. Breaking the kiss, he slid his fingers over her folds and inside her. "Mouthwateringly wet. Just the way I like it." His breath shuddered once as he locked his gaze on her. "Bring it up to me, Holly."

She nearly came right then. But Holly waited until he used his mouth to drive her to an incredible release.

Holly walked into Wes's kitchen to the smell of coffee but no sign of Wes. She turned and headed down the hallway, stopping first at the third bedroom/office. She quietly edged open the door and saw Jodi and Kelly sound asleep on the double sleeper sofa. Pulling the door closed, she guessed maybe Wes was in George's room.

Nope, George was asleep, too.

Frowning, she headed back to the kitchen when she heard Monty barking. She looked out the sliding glass door, past the deck, down to the sandy beach. Wes bent over, wearing only a pair of shorts, and picked up the ball.

Monty barked, did a little puppy dance, then stared at the ball.

Wes drew back his arm and threw the ball.

Monty dashed after it, his gait strong and his golden ears flopping.

Wes rotated his arm, stretching the muscles. With the morning sun warming his body, he was fit, tanned, and she could see in him the younger man who had wanted nothing more than to be a baseball player. It had all ended one horrible night with a home invasion robbery.

Her chest constricted. She blinked, the morning sun making her eyes burn.

Either that or she was in trouble. Because her feelings for Wes just might be a little stronger than professional. "Shit." She stood there, frozen to the spot, wondering how she could be so incredibly stupid.

Monty came bounding back with the ball in his mouth, but Wes turned his head and looked at Holly.

She felt it right down to her toes.

Wes reached down and scooped Monty into his arms and headed toward the deck to come inside.

Holly turned and went to the coffeepot. She found two cups and poured the coffee. She heard the slider open and Wes come inside. She kept her eyes on the coffee.

What the hell did she do now? The only thing she could do, tell him the truth. End it. She was a PI, a damn good PI. She wasn't ever going to be a mother or the other half of a partnership and that was fine with her.

Wes must have put Monty on the floor because the dog bounded over to her. He set the ball down by her foot, then barked softly.

She looked down at the dog. He had such sweet eyes, and a gentle, intelligent face. Leaving the coffee cups, she bent down to pet him. "Out getting your morning exercise?"

He bent his nose and pushed the ball toward her.

Holly laughed. "Hey, I'm not the pitcher around here."

"Monty," Wes said, "come eat." He poured food in the dog's dish.

Monty picked up his ball and trotted over to his food bowl.

Holly stood up. She took a breath and reached for a cup to hand it to Wes.

But he moved up behind her, put one arm around her waist, and used his free hand to move her hair and kiss her neck. "Good morning, Hill*baby*. I like your hair down."

His bare skin was warm and she could smell his soap. "I like it up."

He took the coffee from her hand, set it on the counter, and forced her to turn around. "What's the matter, Holly? You looked upset when I saw you standing in the window."

She lifted her head to stare into his green eyes, and frowned. "You couldn't possibly have seen my face that clearly."

"It's the way you were standing. Your shoulders were raised and you had a hand on your stomach like you were ill."

He knew her that well? "I'm not a morning person. I haven't had my coffee yet." And he was distracting her with his naked chest.

He dropped his hands from her shoulders, reached behind her, and picked up both cups. "Out on the deck, Hillbay."

She didn't move. "Giving orders, Brockman?"

Holding both cups, his shoulders and neck bulging with tension, he said, "Either out on the deck where no one will wander in and hear us, or right here. But either way, you're going to tell me what the hell is bugging you."

The seconds stretched out as they stared at each other. She could leave, but she'd be leaving Wes and the others unprotected. Okay, she'd be running. Finally, she stalked over to the slider, opened it, and walked out to the table by the cold fire pit. It was surprisingly brisk out there. And quiet, except for the rhythmic crashing of the waves and the occasional call of a bird hunting for breakfast. She heard Wes say something to Monty, slide the door closed, and then he set the coffee down in front of her.

Wes sat down on the bricked edge of the fire pit with his back to the ocean and his knees touching hers. He sipped his coffee, set it down on the bricks next to him, then looked at her. "You were fine when we were making love this morning, and you were asleep when I got in the shower. So what happened between now and then?"

"Reality check." She reached for her coffee.

He caught her hand. "Look at me and tell me, Holly. What scares you so much about us?"

That was damned annoying. "I'm not scared." She didn't bother trying to jerk her hand from his warm hold. "I'm realistic. I'm not looking for a relationship. I don't want one. I have my business to build, and you don't trust cops anyway."

He rubbed his thumb on her palm and looked thoughtful. "You're an ex-cop, sweetheart. You and your irritating family have shown me the other side." He flashed a grin. "Maybe most cops aren't dickheads."

God. She wanted to laugh and cry, and that was just so not like her. But Wes took her breath away. For most of his life, he had believed he couldn't trust cops, and now he was changing that view. People rarely did that. Just like he changed the man he was. He hadn't liked who he had become as Nick Mandeville so he became Wes Brockman. Yes, she knew he disappeared to save his sister, but it was more.

"You're overthinking this. The way this works is you have something on your mind, you tell me what it is. Because I'm a man, I'll try to fix it. Then you'll get mad at me because you don't want me to fix it. You're capable of fixing it yourself. See?"

Her mouth twitched because part of her wanted to laugh. But Holly prided herself on dealing with life. Time to deal. "You can't fix this, Brockman. We had fun. The sex was nice. But there's no future." She took a breath and held his gaze. "I can't have kids. Ever."

Chapter 18

Wes stared at Holly and tried to understand. Then it hit him. "The scar."

She pulled her hand from his. Shock had slackened his grip. "Yes." She stood up and looked down at him. "I'm going to the office. Take the girls with you to work. I'm going to get some patrols to drive by the house and keep an eye on George."

Wes stood up so that he was toe to toe with her. Did she think he couldn't see the pain etched so deep into her heart it had grown into a chip on her shoulder? His shock was giving way to anger. "So that's it? You drop your little bombshell and walk out? And I what? Go find a woman who can breed? And while I'm at it, I might as well find one that can dance, too." He heard what was coming out of his mouth, but he couldn't stop. "Is that it, Holly?"

Her eyes widened and her face went pale, showing her freckles and her sorrow. She put her hand over her stomach as if she might be sick. Then she dropped it and got a hold of herself. "Yes." She sidestepped to get away from him since the chair behind her blocked her in.

"No." He said it softly, ashamed of his anger at her. It didn't take much to guess how hard it was for her to tell him. It shouldn't have been, but it was. "Holly, don't leave me. Don't walk out on me." Christ, he didn't mean to say it that way.

But it stopped her. She turned back. And stood there, looking as helpless as he'd ever seen her.

He pulled her into his arms, folded her into him, trying to protect her. She was stiff, and damn it, he could feel her shaking. He ran his hand over her back, trying to soothe her. "This isn't a deal-breaker, baby." He smoothed her hair down and added, "I love you, Holly."

She melted against him. The breath flowed out of her body and she settled into his arms, leaning on him. He had never felt more powerful than this moment, when he had won Holly's trust.

He pulled her head up to look at her face. "Tell me what happened. I assume you had a hysterectomy?"

She met his gaze. "I want my coffee."

Wes blinked, then laughed and let her go. She was his PI, tough, determined, and prickly. He picked up her mug and handed it to her, then got his own, took her hand, and pulled her with him to the edge of the deck. They leaned against the deck rail and watched the waves. Some early morning surfers were out.

She asked, "Do you still surf?"

"Yes." Wes waited. His mug was empty so he set it aside and folded his arms on the rail. He didn't need to push her. She had accepted his love for her, he had felt it. In time, she'd accept that she felt the same way about him. He had to believe that. He watched the waves, thinking about how much Holly believed in him. She was the kind of woman who would believe in him even when he made mistakes. She would believe that he would fix his mistakes.

"Three years ago, I got pregnant."

He nodded without looking at her, and did the math. "Brad?"

"Yes. I was working a lot of overtime, trying to pay off the bills for his law school. We were living together. Anyway, I had pains but Brad wasn't concerned."

The coffee turned to acid in his stomach. He unfolded his arms, reached over, and took Holly's hand.

"One day I was working a double shift, but I was getting sicker and sicker until Rodgers took me home early from work. I was too sick to drive. I called Brad and he said he'd come home and take me to the hospital."

His voice was flat. "Did he?"

"I guess not. I waited, he didn't come home. I must have passed out and my dad found me." She looked over at him. "Rodgers had called my dad and told him she thought something was really wrong. My dad came over, found me, and called the paramedics. It turned out to be an ectopic pregnancy, you know, where the egg settles outside the uterus. I got an infection and they had to do a hysterectomy to save my life."

Wes let go of her hand, put his arm around her shoulders, and pulled her into his side. It was all he could do to control his rage at Brad, the asshole. "I'm glad they saved your life. Did Brad ever show up?"

"When I was coming out of anesthesia. He broke up with me then. He said he needed a wife who could have children and provide the right image for his career."

Blood pounded in his ears. He fought to keep his breathing even. "And Seth beat the shit out of him." It wasn't a question. Wes would have done the same thing if Holly had been his sister. He wanted to do the same thing right now, track down that sniveling bastard and kick his ass.

"My dad pulled Seth off of him. Dad had gone to our apartment to get me some clothes and found Seth doing his best to kill Brad."

"Brad didn't prosecute?" From what Wes had seen of Brad, that didn't sound right.

"Nope, because my dad told him we'd tell the world what a slime bucket he was. We came to an understanding. I wouldn't go after him for the money his law degree cost, et cetera, and he wouldn't prosecute Seth."

That sounded just like Holly. She ate her hurt and pride to keep her brother from getting fired and possibly going to jail. No wonder she had reacted so strongly to Brad's needling her in public. And no wonder she needed to succeed on her own so much. She had to prove to herself and Brad that she could do it. That she was valuable, even if she'd never be a mother. As long as she didn't involve his sister, he was going to help her solve this case. Her first murder case as a PI. She'd have people fighting to get her to take their cases. He pulled her closer.

She took a breath. "For over two years, Brad stayed away from me and kept his mouth shut. But now he's looking to destroy me."

Wes didn't like this. "Why? What do you mean?"

"I had a client I did regular background checks for. A manufacturing plant. They suddenly cut me loose when they said they found out I had been asked to leave the sheriff's department." She turned her head and looked at Wes. "There's only one person who would tell a lie like that."

"Brad?"

She nodded. "And I think the reason he jumped at representing the women in your book club is to raise his profile."

He thought about that. The fact that Brad used Holly to put him through law school, then dumped her when she'd lost their child and endured a hysterectomy, would damage him the most where? "He's going to run for political office."

She shrugged and looked out to the ocean. "It was his long-term plan. So he needs to destroy my credibility. But I'm not going to let that happen. I am a good PI—no, an excellent PI—and I will prove it."

He smiled over at her. "After you kiss me, then you can prove it."

Holly got into her office in time to answer the phone. "Hillbay Investigations."

"Still answering your own phone," Brad said into her ear.

This morning, Holly was in a good mood, so she decided not to slam the phone down. "Why, Brad, how nauseating to hear your voice. Are you dying and calling so I can throw a party?"

"Bitch. I thought I'd give you the heads up that I'm serving your boyfriend official papers this morning at ten-thirty."

Curiosity got the best of her. "Brockman has lawyers out the wazoo, so why are you telling me?"

"You really are inadequate at your job, aren't you, Holly? Most PIs appreciate professional courtesy." He hung up.

Holly set the phone down. "Courtesy, my ass. You're up to something. I just bet it has something to do with a camera." Maybe he leaked the information to the newspapers or local TV news. And he thought getting her there would make her look bad.

But she was going to solve the case, and she was ninety-eight percent sure one of Brad's clients was going down for murder.

Hearing her office door open, she looked up and winced. "What are you wearing?" Holly picked up a big stack of papers and stuff from her desk and walked to the small table in the kitchenette that was doubling as a desk for her assistant.

Tanya grinned and did a little twirl. Her orange and green striped skirt swirled around her legs. Her orange jacket top had a green trim. "It's my version of a power suit."

"I need shades to look directly at you." Holly dumped all her notes and papers on the table. There were notes from Tanya and the girls about the O'Man's podcasts, Holly's log sheets, pictures, all the stuff she compiled for cases. "Organize these for me. I want a suspect folder, clues, and notes in some kind of order."

"Sure." Tanya opened the refrigerator and pulled out a soda. "I heard about Wes's friend George getting shot. That's terrible."

She grimaced at the memory. "He's okay. He was sore and crabby this morning, but okay. Wes and his two clerks are going to the bookstore today. I'm going to head over there in a little bit, since it looks like Brad Knoll has some kind of show planned. After that, I'm going to go to Riverside to find Ashley Gaines. Will you be okay here?" She hadn't told Wes yet that she was going to Riverside. She'd tell him at the store.

Tanya sank down in a chair and said, "You're leaving me in your office? Alone?"

She grinned at that. "And giving you a key to lock up. Unless that's a problem? It's not like I keep money or my expensive diamonds here." She went to her desk to get the extra key. "I'll leave you my cell phone number and my dad's number. He helps me out sometimes so he can answer most questions if you can't reach me."

"Wow, you have a dad. That just sounds so weird."

Holly couldn't help it, she laughed. "I wasn't hatched from an egg." Dropping the key on her desk, she added, "Both my dad and brothers are doing a little work on the case, so they may be checking in at the office. Have them call me on my cell if they have information."

Tanya sat back. "You look different. Softer."

Holly stared at her. "I do not. I just look normal compared to your blinding outfit." She went to her desk and got her purse. She checked her gun, fished out her keys, and headed out the door.

Fifteen minutes later, she walked down the street towards Books on the Beach. She was still annoyed by Tanya saying she looked softer. Ex-cops and PIs did not look soft. Stopping at the door to the bookstore, she glanced in the window to see her reflection.

She looked the same. Tough. Satisfied that Tanya was a head case, she went inside the store and stopped in surprise. There had to be ten or fifteen customers milling about. Was that usual for a Monday before lunchtime? Jodi was behind the register while Kelly and Wes helped customers find selections.

Wes spotted her, said something to the older woman he was helping, then walked over to her. "Hey, what's up?"

There was no denying that Wes Brockman was a tasty-looking man. He wore a pale blue shirt that made the green in his eyes look deeper. There were faint tension lines around his mouth, but the way his eyes crinkled slightly when he smiled at her was real. Genuine. And damned if it didn't make her feel softer. "Uh, well, Brad called to tell me that he's serving you with his bogus lawsuit at ten-thirty."

Wes's smile faded. "I'll handle Knoll. You don't have to be here."

She narrowed her eyes. "Why wouldn't I be here? Do you think I can't handle Brad?"

He reached out, cupped the back of her head, and pulled her nose to nose with him. "I know you can handle him. But this is my bookstore, my turf, and I will not be played by that sniveling prick. And I won't stand by and watch him hurt you. I'm on your side, Holly, so deal with it."

He startled the hell out of her. Wes had a core of absolute steel, but she had been so busy convincing herself that he was a *harmless*, charming, playboy bookseller, she hadn't paid enough attention. But the truth was that Holly couldn't love a man who was too soft. She needed a man who was as strong as she was. And Wes was that and so much more. However, that didn't mean she was going to let him fight her battles. "Back off, book boy. Don't make me hurt you."

His smile was slow and wicked. "You can try, Hill*baby*, but you'll end up on your back and begging."

She rolled her eyes. "Why do men turn everything into a sex joke?"

He laughed and let her go.

Holly looked around, trying to find her bearings. "You're pretty busy in here."

"Yeah, not bad. They're buying books to hide the fact that they're here to get gossip. Word spread that George was shot and I was there. Want some coffee?"

"Hey, Holly." Kelly walked by with a customer.

"Hi, Kelly. Busy morning, I see." Holly smiled, then turned back to Wes. "Coffee sounds good. I'll get it if you're busy."

He leaned close to her. "Hill*baby*, I'm never too busy for you."

Warm pleasure skimmed along her insides. Jeez, he *was* making her soft. But before she could think of a response, he walked away toward the coffeemaker.

She took a few seconds to admire his butt in his dark slacks. The man had a seriously fine ass. And thighs. And package. And arms. But what she really liked about Wes was . . . just him.

Enough! She was turning into a marshmallow. *Ugh.* It was damned embarrassing. She really needed to get her edge back before Wes had her cooking him dinner and washing his socks. She waited for two women to pass her on their way to the cash register, then started walking toward Wes and the coffee.

She heard the door open. Was it more customers or Brad with his nasty paperwork to sue them? She glanced over her shoulder. A woman. Not Brad. She turned back to see Wes fill up a second cup of coffee then set the carafe back. She took a last glance at his backside and walked over to get her coffee.

A female voice behind her said, "Nick? It is really you?"

Holly stopped and blinked, feeling the weirdest sensation run along her back. Her heart started to pound. Her brain whirled. She looked at Wes.

He turned, holding two cups of coffee. His gaze hit her first, then shifted to the door. It looked like he stopped breathing, like his entire body just froze in time. Finally his mouth moved, then formed the low-pitched word, "Michelle."

Kelly rushed up to Wes and grabbed the two cups of coffee. "Wes, are you okay? What's wrong?"

He didn't acknowledge Kelly, just stared right over her.

Holly turned and took a second look at the woman. She had long, dark hair, even features, a tan, and looked just like the picture Wes had showed her in the surfing magazine.

Wes's sister. What was going on? How did she find Wes?

While Holly watched, tears welled up and spilled down Michelle's face. "Nick, oh God, it is you!" Michelle ran toward him.

Everyone in the bookstore stared in frozen fascination. The tension was so thick, it was hard to breathe. Kelly was the only one who moved, stepping back from where she'd been standing in front of Wes.

Michelle flung herself at Wes, forcing him to catch her. "You're alive. I knew you were alive!" She sobbed, her whole body shaking in reaction.

The pain etched on Wes's face shifted him from shock to torment. He pulled Michelle against him, but it looked like it was involuntary. His love for his sister won out over his angst.

It hurt Holly just to see Wes's anguish and struggle.

Taking a shuddering breath, Michelle stepped back and smacked Wes on his arm. "Why? Why would you leave me?"

Holly's throat filled for the old sorrow and anger in Michelle's voice.

Wes's voice was thick. "Michelle, I had to. I couldn't let you get hurt anymore."

"It wasn't your choice to make!" she yelled at him. Her lip and chin quivered again. "I'm so sorry, Nick. I didn't mean what I said. Please forgive me."

Wes pulled his sister back into his arms. "What are you doing here, Michelle? It's too dangerous." He closed his eyes. His entire face was nearly gray with his inner turmoil.

She leaned back over his arm and looked at her brother. "I had to come. A private investigator e-mailed me. She said you were in trouble and gave me the address of this bookstore. She told me what time you'd be here. Here's the e-mail and the picture of a Little League team with you as the coach that she sent as proof you were alive." She held out two pieces of paper.

Wes looked over his sister's head to Holly.

Sick at the accusation stamped on his face, Holly took a step toward him. "No." It came out a whisper. He couldn't believe she would do that. She got a hold of herself and started toward him. He had to know her better than to believe she would contact Michelle behind his back.

Especially after this morning.

But a blinding glare of light stopped her. Holly turned and saw a TV camera on a man's shoulder and a woman rushing toward her with a microphone. "Holly Hillbay?"

The light zeroed in on her. She heard herself reply automatically, "Yes?"

"Excellent. Stand here." The woman turned to stand next to her, raised her mike, and starting talking while looking into the camera. "Holly Hillbay has solved the three-year-old mystery of what happened to hot shot sports agent Nicolas Mandeville. And she brought Michelle Mandeville, Mr. Mandeville's sister, who is very prominent in the surfing world, here for a reunion."

The camera swung to capture Wes and his sister.

Then it swung back to her. The woman shoved the microphone in her face. "Ms. Hillbay, how did you crack this case?"

"Get away from me!" This was freaking unbelievable. She didn't know what the hell was going on. Holly felt the danger but didn't understand it. This had to be another threat against Wes. Someone got his sister here. She scanned the bookstore, squinting from the glare of the camera lights, trying to see if she could spot a weapon or a suspect. Trying to make sense of it, she recognized a familiar, and hated, face.

Brad. He strolled in wearing a designer suit and a shark's smile. "I'll be happy to tell you how she did it." Brad adjusted his tie as he seamlessly glided in front of the camera. "Holly Hillbay has always had a thing for powerful men. She knew who Nicolas Mandeville was, then she saw a picture of a Little League team in the local newspaper, and recognized Nick, aka Wes Brockman, as the coach. So she infiltrated the book club at this bookstore, owned by Wes, and eventually seduced him into telling her who he really is—Nick Mandeville. Then she tracked down his sister and used this scene to get on the news to advertise her PI agency."

Her mouth went dry and her gut burned with rage. "What have you done?" she demanded of Brad.

He turned to look at her. "Me? Holly you're the one who cracked this case. Smile for the camera."

She didn't care about him. Didn't give a rat's ass about Bradley Knoll. The man she cared about was Wes. She whirled around to find him. He would believe her. Wes talked about honesty—told her he wouldn't walk out on her just because he was mad. He had told her that not being able to have children wasn't a deal-breaker. He had told her he loved her. She could make him understand that they'd both been set up.

She'd find a way to protect both Wes and his sister.

Holly spotted the news reporter shoving her microphone in Wes's face. "Mr. Mandeville, why did you fake your death?"

"No comment," Wes said, and used his shoulder to nudge the woman aside. He was trying to shield his sister from the camera as they walked to the door. "Jodi, close up," he told her when he got to the counter.

"Wes." Holly caught his arm. He had told her to trust him. She did. She would.

The camera turned on them.

She didn't care. The memory of this morning rushed through her. Of making love early in the morning, of realizing she was falling for him, of screwing up her courage to tell him the truth, knowing that he'd leave her. But he hadn't left her, he loved her. She trusted that he'd never use what they had against her.

He wouldn't hate her. It squeezed her chest until it was all she could do to remain standing. He had to believe her. He'd said he wouldn't turn against her. Beneath her hand, his arm clenched to the feel of solid rock. She hurried, trying to get the words out. "I didn't do this." Her dry eyes stung and her throat hurt. "We're being set up."

Letting go of Michelle, he grabbed her hand and flung it off his arm. She could feel his pulsing anger. He literally took a step back to keep control. "I told you I won't be played in my own bookstore." His green eyes burned into her, then he curled his arm protectively around Michelle and moved away.

When Wes and his sister got to the door, he looked back. "You're fired."

Chapter 19

He knew.

Holly was frozen to the spot with the echo of the door slamming still ringing in her head. Wes knew she hadn't sent that e-mail, and that they were being set up.

I told you I won't be played in my own bookstore.

He had turned the tables on them, letting Brad, and whoever put the dumb shit up to this, believe that he'd fired her.

Someone touched her arm. She turned to see Jodi's strained, pale face. "Holly, what's happening?"

She stared at Jodi's face and thought, *What if I'm wrong? What if Wes really doesn't believe in me?*

From where he stood behind her, Brad cut in. "You're finished, Holly."

She whirled around and realized a stark truth—she had let Brad turn her into a coward. Instantly, she made a decision. She chose to believe in Wes. He had done his part in this little scenario, now it was time for Holly to step up and do her part. She knew Brad was nothing more than a puppet; she had to find out who was pulling his strings. "Who put you up to this, Brad?"

He smiled with practiced arrogance. "You should have stayed in uniform. You'll never be more than a grunt taking orders. You are in way over your head."

She fought down a wave of frustrated anger so powerful

she had to squeeze her muscles to keep from slamming her fist through his face. Wes's sister arriving in this highly orchestrated show was no accident. The danger was escalating and she couldn't see where it was coming from.

"Holly?" Jodi sounded lost.

Brad looked past Holly to the girl. "Holly won't tell you what she did, so I will. She betrayed a client, your boss. Do your boss a favor and throw her out. He'll give you a raise."

She couldn't see Jodi, but Holly felt the girl straighten up and say, "I don't believe you. Holly wouldn't do that."

Brad laughed at Jodi.

Anger rolled through her. "Don't talk to Jodi like that. She's a hell of a lot smarter than you could ever hope to be. She knows what Wes wants done, he told her." She turned her gaze to Jodi. "Close the store. You and Kelly are coming with me."

Jodi stared back, then nodded and went to talk to Kelly.

Because Jodi believed in Holly. Even in a moment when she couldn't be sure, she believed. That humbled Holly, and gave her courage to press on. This setup was supposed to destroy her and Brad was there to enjoy it. *Okay*, she thought, *let's see what shakes out.* "Brad, don't you understand? We're being used. You're being used. Just like everyone else. One of the women in the book club murdered Cullen, and they're planning something with Wes and his sister. Who is it?"

Brad shook his head. "You really thought you were the only one who knew who Brockman was, didn't you? But someone else knew, and they have a book already written and ready to go. And now that Brockman knows just what you are"—he looked down his nose at Holly—"he and his sister will take the offer and sign the release."

"A book?" Her mind skittered back to George and his conversation with Wes's ex-wife. She said someone called her, wanting to find Michelle, and something about signing a release . . .

"Thinking small again." Brad shook his head. "A book, movies, and so much more." Then Brad's face grew serious. "I'm warning you, Holly, I won't let you get in my way. I have plans. Plans that take money and backing."

She ignored the threat. "Who is it, Brad? Who wrote this book?"

He shook his head while holding his gloating little smile. "You're out of the game now. You're nothing. And if you ever open your mouth about me, everyone will know that you're a pathetic little woman who couldn't ever hold onto a man or a job."

It made her sick. "You stupid SOB! Cullen Vail was murdered! Do you think they won't kill you when they're done using you? You don't know what you've gotten involved in!"

His expression shifted to distaste. "Vail was a small-time scammer. He was bound to get popped sooner or later."

"Jesus, Brad, pull your head out of your ass! Someone shot George yesterday by Cullen's boat. This person is playing for keeps. They will murder anyone in their way."

He shook his head in that same patronizing way. "I always knew you were stupid. I've heard rumors about George. No one really knows his business—probably drugs. But that's the type of bottom feeder you associate with, isn't it?"

It was like trying to swim to shore in a riptide. Brad wouldn't listen. She was wasting her time. For the first time in three years, her hate withered into a lump of aggravation. "Just tell me who it is!"

He plastered on a smug smile and walked out.

Wes got his sister into his Range Rover and drove away.

"Nick, talk to me. The e-mail said you are in danger!"

He looked over at his sister, and felt his throat tighten. In spite of everything, a thread of happiness unrolled inside of him. She'd found out he was alive, possibly in danger, and had dropped everything to find him. Even after his decision to blow the whistle on the doping had led to Michelle being beaten up, and even after he had disappeared leaving Michelle to believe he was dead. "That e-mail was a fake. But I am in danger, and so are you. Holly didn't send that e-mail." Wes had known it the second he saw the e-mail.

Just as Wes knew Holly loved him. He just hoped she understood what he had done. Would Holly realize that he was trying to turn the tables on the person behind this whole mess? Would she trust him?

"Who did send the e-mail?"

He sighed. "I don't know. Someone from my past is screwing around with my life, and yours. I'll try to fill you in but I have a couple calls to make." He picked up his cell phone and dialed.

George answered. "What?"

Wes summed up the scene in the bookstore.

"No shit?" George only took a second to process it, then said, "Whatever the plan is, it's going to happen soon. Someone is separating you from everyone that will help you."

"They meant to shoot you yesterday." Until now, Wes hadn't been sure if that shot had been meant for him or George.

"I think so, too. In fact, I'm going to call Cullen's mother back and have a chat. Later." He hung up.

Michelle put her hand on his arm. "Is this related to the guy you put in prison?"

God, he had missed her voice. He'd missed everything about her. "I think so." He put off calling Holly to explain as much as he could to Michelle before they pulled up in front of his house. They got out of the car.

"You live at the beach," she said as they walked up to the front door.

Both of them had loved the beach while growing up. Wes had learned to surf with his friends. Then he'd taught Michelle. He put his arm around her shoulders and took her in the house.

Monty bounded up to them. Spotting Michelle, he turned

circles in excitement, then he dropped his ever-present ball at her feet and barked.

Michelle bent down and scooped him into her arms. "Well, who is this?"

"Monty. Holly and I found him half drowned one night." The first night he had met her. He had to call Holly as soon as he talked to George again. He didn't see him in the living room. "Let's go to the kitchen." Wes led his sister past the gurgling fish tank into his kitchen.

George wasn't there either.

Michelle carried Monty to the sliding glass door and looked out at the ocean.

George walked into the kitchen. He had on a black shirt, sweatpants, and his right arm in a sling. His blue glasses slid down his nose and he fixed his gaze on Wes. "I talked to Cullen's—"

Wes frowned, seeing that George was staring at his sister. "Michelle, this is George."

She had turned. "Hi, George."

Wes's cell phone rang before he could prod George into finishing his sentence. Pulling it out, he saw it was from Holly. He needed to hear her voice, to know that she was okay and that she understood what he had done in the bookstore. Putting the phone to his ear, he asked, "Where are you?"

"My fee has quadrupled, Brockman."

Wes closed his eyes for a second. "I knew that e-mail was a fake, Holly. The second I saw it. Believe me, baby." He needed her to believe in him. He needed her.

He only heard the sound of the waves from outside, and he felt both George and Michelle staring at him. Then Holly said, "You knew I could handle Brad."

He smiled, and wished like hell that she was right in front of him so he could hold her, touch her. "Just as long as you left him alive. I have a score to settle with him." He knew it was a primitive caveman urge, but damn it, that bastard had hurt Holly on so many levels. And Holly could have died if her dad hadn't gotten there in time, since Brad had been too busy to bother going home and taking care of the woman carrying his baby.

"Street justice, book boy? Isn't that what you accused my brother of?"

He remembered when she had told him Seth and Brad had a dispute. Because of the work his dad had done outing abusive cops along with abuses in the system, he'd thought the worst. But he knew better now. "I'd give your brother a medal," he said softly. "And your brothers aren't the kind of cops who deal in street justice. That was a brother taking care of his sister."

She snorted. "You are so full of shit." She paused, then added, "I couldn't get Brad to tell me who was behind bringing Michelle to Goleta. He doesn't realize he's just a puppet in a game."

Wes got serious. "Someone is pulling a lot of strings. So what did you find out?"

"That someone else has known for a while who you really are, and they've written a book. They have big plans for the book."

"A book? About me? All this for a book?" Wes tried to make it work in his mind, but it didn't make sense.

Her voice was ripe with sarcasm. "Brad, the imbecile, believes the whole reason the person got Michelle here was to convince you two to sign a release."

Wes shook his head. "Doesn't play. Hell, people write unauthorized biographies all the time. And if I'm missing, they could write a book about me easily. They don't need a release."

George had been listening intently. Now he interrupted to say, "Wes, put Holly on the speaker for a minute."

He nodded to George. "Holly, I'm switching you to the speaker. George has something." As soon as he did it, Wes set the phone down and said, "Can you hear okay, Holly?"

"Yes. What's up, George?"

George moved closer to the phone. "I called Cullen's mom back. I explained that there was an incident at the dock that prevented me from seeing the boat, but I was still interested and hoped to look at it soon."

George's voice was a little strained—from what he'd learned or pain from his bullet wound?

"What did she say?" Holly asked.

"That her niece is going to buy the boat. She talked to her niece on the phone right after she talked to me." George paused and looked up at Wes. "It seems that Cullen and his cousin were close when growing up in Oregon. They used to go hunting together. But Cullen didn't have the stomach for it like his cousin did."

Christ, Wes thought. He stared at George. "Who is it?"

"George, who?" Holly reiterated the question.

"Ashley Gaines."

Michelle walked over from the sliding glass door. "Ashley Gaines. Isn't that the wife of the trainer your testimony put in prison?"

Wes put his arm around his sister. She was hugging Monty to her chest. The dog lapped up the attention.

"Michelle," Holly said from the phone. "Did you ever meet Ashley?"

"I remember her from the trial."

Wes looked down at her. "That's right, you went to a lot of the trial."

"Wes, get your sister to my office," Holly said. "Ashley Gaines is connected to this, and obviously she has skill with a gun if she grew up hunting. And she's got a plan, that's why she got Michelle into town for that show at the bookstore. I have some pictures I want to show Michelle."

Wes hesitated. "I have to keep her safe."

Michelle overruled him. "We'll be there, Holly. My brother needs help, and I'm here to help."

"If he gives you any trouble, Michelle, I have a gun you can use." Holly hung up.

Michelle laughed and looked up at him. "I'm going to like her, aren't I?"

He rolled his eyes. "I'm afraid so."

Holly figured Wes and his sister, and probably George, would get to her office in about ten minutes. "Tanya, pull out the picture of Ashley Gaines."

Tanya found it quickly and handed it to Holly. "I noticed her picture when I organized all the files. This woman does not look thirty-five, she looks ten years older. I, uh"—she started tripping over her words—"you know, I saw the birth date on her driver's license and noticed she looked older than the date."

"Very observant," Holly said and took the picture, looking at the face. She was a no-maintenance kind of woman. She had store-bought brown hair, a small chin, and brown eyes that didn't quite look at the camera. She narrowed her gaze. "Who are you? I'm betting you aren't Ashley Gaines."

"So who is Ashley Gaines?" Tanya asked.

Holly sighed. "One of the women in the book club. But which one?"

"I might have a clue," her dad said as he walked into her office. He looked around. "Where are Jodi and Kelly?"

"Seth picked them up and took them to my house. He said he hadn't connected with Nora yet, but right now, I want him to keep an eye on Jodi and Kelly." As her dad sat down, she added, "This is Tanya, my assistant."

"Hi, Mr. Hillbay," Tanya said.

"Call me Eric, Tanya. Nice to meet you."

"What do you have, Dad?" Holly was edgy, but she'd feel better once Wes and his sister got there.

He didn't waste any time. "I went to the station to chat with old friends and heard the news—Nora Jacobson has a gun."

Holly blinked. "George checked and only Maggie Partlow

has a gun permit." How had they missed this? Holly should have checked herself.

"The gun belonged to her ex-husband. Remember, she changed her name from Fargo back to her maiden name of Jacobson after the divorce."

Holly wanted to smack herself. "Stupid oversight," she said through gritted teeth. "A nine millimeter?"

Her dad nodded. "Rodgers is out looking for Nora to have a chat."

She checked her watch. "Wes and his sister should be here soon. I want to see if his sister can recognize a picture of Ashley Gaines, the woman I think is behind this. Then I'll call Rodgers and get her up to date."

Her father put his elbows on the sides of the chair and tented his fingers. "Maybe it's Nora, even though you and Wes didn't think so last night."

Holly's gut went tight with tension and worry. "Maybe. The quickest way to find out is for Wes's sister to identify a picture. I did backgrounds on the three women from the book club, but I didn't do identity checks."

"Ah," her dad said. "It's possible that Wes isn't the only one hiding behind an identity he wasn't born with."

She heard the door to her office open. Looking up, her breath caught as Wes walked through the door with his sister and George. Wes wore dark slacks, an expensive green shirt that matched his eyes, and his sun-streaked dark hair framed his handsome face. He looked like he'd just walked off a glossy magazine. And it hit her—Wes loved her, she believed him. But he'd been on the run for the last three years, ripped away from his fancy life and his sister. The bond between her and Wes had been forged in a time of stress.

Would it hold up to everyday life? Was living in a beach and college town, running a bookstore, and loving a beer-and-pizza PI really going to make him happy?

Could he really live with not ever having a child?

She realized she was staring when her dad stood up and said, "Wes, this must be your sister."

Holly recovered while Wes made introductions. She had the stack of pictures on her desk. Standing up, she picked up the four pictures and held them out. "Michelle, here are the pictures I'd like you to look at. Which one is Ashley Gaines?"

Michelle took them. She looked down at the first one and shook her head. "Not this one."

Holly knew which one was on top—the driver's license photo of the woman that was supposed to be Ashley. Damn. Her stomach tightened as Michelle flipped through the remaining three. Was she in there?

Wes walked over to stand between Holly and Michelle. He reached out and settled his hand on Holly's shoulder.

"This is her." Michelle held up a picture.

They all looked at it and Holly said, "Helene Essex. Well, well, it looks like Ashley Gaines found someone to switch identities with."

Michelle said, "Really? She used to have lighter colored hair and hazel eyes, but it's her."

"Her eyes are brown now," Wes said.

Holly felt the tension in his hand. "Contacts. So if Helene is really Ashley, the woman in the Riverside apartment is Helene. Ashley is here in town, going to your book club and stalking you."

Wes frowned. "How did she find me?"

Holly turned and looked at him. "Well, I thought about that. Brad gave it away at your bookstore when he said I recognized the picture of you coaching the Little League team. So I did a Google search of Little League coaches and your team picture popped up in the newspaper. You're recognizable in that picture."

George shook his head from where he sat on the couch. "Told you not to get involved in stuff like that."

Wes shot him a look. "You're the assistant coach."

George did his usual arrogant look of gazing over the top of his glasses. "Only 'cause I had to protect your ass."

Wes looked at Holly. "You gonna let him get away with that?"

"Me? Hey, fight your own battles, book boy." She ignored him and sat down behind her desk. "So Ashley went looking for you." She waved her hand toward Wes. "Then got a new identity, moved to Goleta, joined your book club, and killed Cullen."

"Who is her cousin," George added.

"Yeah, what's the connection about?" Holly got back up and paced past them to the kitchenette. "I mean, what's the end game here? She's done all this work, getting Michelle to Goleta and isolating the two of you." She turned to look at them.

"Revenge?" Michelle asked.

Holly didn't know. "Brad said something about a book. But I can't believe all this is over a book."

"Doesn't make sense. She could publish the book without Michelle's or my consent. Unauthorized biographies are published all the time."

"Don't forget, Nora has a gun," her dad said.

George sat up. "What? There's no gun permit registered to Nora Jacobson."

Holly turned and looked at George. His face was tight, probably with pain. "Rodgers found that Nora's ex-husband, whose last name is Fargo, has a gun registered to him. He didn't take it to prison with him, so we're assuming that Nora still has it. A nine millimeter."

George's gaze drifted to Michelle. "Could be the women are in this together. Maybe they know who Helene really is. Maybe Nora does have a grudge against Wes, believes he is somehow responsible for her husband's sports gambling, which led to him embezzling."

"What would Maggie have against Wes?" Holly turned to look at him.

He was standing by Michelle, catching her up on details. He met her gaze. "Nothing that I know of. Unless she blames me for letting Cullen into the book club."

"Then maybe we need to talk to Maggie. The whole law-suit was bogus, just a way to get on TV. Dumb-ass Brad fell for it, of course. But I'm sure he's just another puppet. And I think Helene . . ." She paused and added, "I'm just going to keep calling her Helene to keep it straight even though we now know she's Ashley Gaines." Another breath. "I think Helene is the puppet master. Maybe Maggie needs to be in-formed that Helene is playing her."

Her dad said, "Detective Rodgers needs to be informed that Helene is really Ashley Gaines."

Holly nodded. "I'll call her." Then she turned. "Or can you do it, Dad? I really want to go talk to Maggie. Catch her off guard."

"I'm going with you." Wes turned from Michelle to Holly.

"I'm going, too," Michelle added.

Wes started to argue with his sister but Holly cut him off. "Both of you go to my house and stay there."

Wes shifted around and took a large step toward Holly.

She held up a hand. "We can't tip our hand, Wes. Right now, you've convinced Brad at least that you fired me and walked away. If you and I show up together, and Maggie's in on it, she'll know I'm still working for you."

His eyebrows drew together and he flattened his mouth into a tense line. "I am not going to sit in your condo while you're in danger!"

Holly pasted on a smile. "I'm no threat if they believe you hate me."

"She's right," George pointed out.

"Shut up," Wes snapped.

"Nick." Michelle touched his arm. "Holly will be in less danger if we aren't with her."

She watched Wes struggle. "I don't like it."

She met his gaze. "You don't have to like it, Brockman. You just have to keep your sister safe."

Tanya's voice broke through the tension. "I found it."

They all turned to look at her. Tanya had sat down at Holly's desk and held up a page of hand-written notes that she must have gotten from the files she had organized for Holly.

She looked up at Holly. "I remembered a reference to a book in the podcasts from the O'Man's Web site that I listened to. Here it is. It's the podcast about Anti-Princess, who we all thought was Helene."

The back of her neck tingled. "I remember," Holly said. "Read it."

Tanya said, "These are my notes after listening to the podcast:

> *"Anti-Princess is Helene. This one isn't as icky with sexual details. It's more a . . . I don't know . . . profile. Cullen says she wants to have the same power as men in the world. She's tough, acts like she has balls, might even be a cop or someone in authority. But in the end, she's not a man, can't have the same power as men in a man's world, so she's forced to use men to get things done, and being the woman behind the man. But when the men she chooses fail her, she's reduced to writing a book about a powerful man. To seduce her, act like you're the man who will help her gain power and get what she wants, and she'll put out."*

It felt like someone walked over her grave. "Cullen knew about the book. He was threatening Helene with that podcast. So she killed him."

Michelle tilted her head. "What does this Cullen look like?"

Tanya paged through the files and pulled out one of the

pictures Holly had of the death scene. She silently handed it to Michelle.

Michelle looked down at it. Her face paled and her breathing grew rapid.

Wes put his arm around his sister's shoulder. "You okay?"

She looked up at him. "I dated him. Just for a couple weeks, right around the time you graduated law school."

Holly felt her own pulse kick up. "She knew who you were." She turned to Wes. "Ashley Gaines had her cousin date your sister and learn everything about you, even back then."

"Why?" Wes ran his hand through his hair, his voice thick with frustration. Then he straightened up and added, "She sent the thugs after Michelle. To stop me from testifying against her husband."

Holly crossed her arms beneath her breasts, struggling to get the facts to line up. Helene/Ashley had played people in Goleta for months. So it stood to reason she always had done that. In Cullen's O'Man blog, he said she wanted the power of a man, and used men to achieve it. She shifted back to Wes. "How did you get your job at Apex Sports Agency?"

"They called me."

"Based on what?"

He shrugged. "Holly, I signed a major league contract before I was shot. People in baseball knew who I was."

"And didn't you tell me once that Helene is a baseball fan? That you two sometimes talked about baseball?"

His green eyes burned. "Shit. She worked for an employment agency. She recommended me, probably got an under-the-table finder's fee."

She kept his gaze. "Because she assured the partners in your firm that you'd look the other way when her husband doped the players. She knew you wanted to succeed bad enough to ignore it."

"But why track me down now?"

It was beginning to make a twisted kind of sense. "Because if she wrote an explosive enough book, she wouldn't need a man anymore. She would be famous and powerful in her own right." She took a breath. "We need to find that book. Dad, you call Rodgers." She turned to George. "Armed?"

He nodded.

"Get them to my house." She turned again. "Tanya, that was brilliant of you to remember the podcast. Thank you. But I want you to go home now. I want you out of this in case it turns ugly."

Tanya stood up from the desk. "Are you sure, Holly? I'll stay, do whatever you need."

"I'm sure, Tanya. You did great. Go home."

Tanya nodded and started gathering up her belongings.

"Dad, you lock up."

He nodded.

Holly started toward her desk to get her purse and her gun, but Wes stepped in her path. She looked up at him. "What?"

He didn't say a word, just pulled her into his arms and pressed his mouth against hers. When he let her go, he said, "If you don't call me the second you leave Maggie's office, I will find you, Hill*baby*."

She opened her mouth.

He cut her off. "I mean it, Holly. I want to know exactly where you are, and if I think you're in danger, all bets are off. I'm coming after you."

"Damn it, Brockman, I keep telling you that you're paying me to handle the danger." He made her feel protected. Safe. And it was pissing her off. She took care of herself.

"And I keep telling you that I love you. If I think you need me, I'll find a way to get to you." He let her go and said, "George, Michelle, let's go before she finds her gun and shoots me."

Chapter 20

Holly walked into Maggie's office to find her consulting with a young couple at a table piled with photo albums. Maggie looked up, her brown gaze narrowed, and she said to the couple, "Excuse me." She wore slim, charcoal gray tailored pants, a pearl-colored top, and a furious expression framed by her perfectly cut black hair as she stalked over to Holly. "What are you doing here? I'm going to call my lawyer—"

"Cut the shit, Maggie. Brad never filed the lawsuit. There is no lawsuit. You've been played."

Maggie's fury melted into confusion.

Holly was pretty sure that was a rare look for Maggie, aka Wonder Woman.

Recovering, she glanced back to see the couple engrossed in the photo albums, then returned her glare to Holly and said, "You're lying to save yourself. Get out."

Holly took a shot. "I'm not lying and I'll prove it. There's a book on Cullen's computer. Give me his computer and I'll show you."

Maggie touched one of the cell phones clipped to her waist. "Book? I don't know what you are talking about."

"I'm sure you don't." Holly noticed she didn't say anything about Cullen's computer. If Helene murdered Cullen, and Nora stayed at her house to provide the alibi—although she thought the alibi was to cover the theft of the computer, not murder—then Maggie must be the one who went to Cullen's boat to steal the computer. "Helene wrote a book about Wes, well, about Nick Mandeville." She wanted to see what Maggie knew about that. Of course, it had been a couple of hours since the scene this morning, so word had to be out.

"I heard about Wes being that sports agent, but that doesn't have anything to do with us or our lawsuit." She pulled a cell phone off her belt. "If you don't leave, I'm calling the police."

Holly folded her arms. "Good. Do it. I have my associate calling the police, too, specifically Detective Rodgers. She's going to be very interested in hearing how you and Nora helped Helene murder Cullen."

Maggie stared at her.

Holly inclined her head toward the phone. "Go ahead, call. I'll wait." She was done playing.

Maggie dropped the hand holding her phone. "You're not bluffing, are you?"

"No. Brad thinks he's going to help broker a book deal for Helene. He doesn't give a rat's ass about a lawsuit when he can represent Helene in a huge book deal." Was the book on Cullen's computer? Holly thought it probably was. "What did you do with Cullen's computer after you stole it from his boat the night Cullen was killed?"

Maggie whipped her head back to look at her clients. They were engaged in a whispered argument. She walked over to them and said, "I'll be right back." Then she gestured to Holly and went into her office.

Holly followed. Maggie's office was as tailored as the woman herself. A sleek desk with a sleek computer monitor. Tasteful filing cabinet. Lots of custom-framed pictures of big parties and receptions that Maggie had planned. Holly took it all in automatically—her real attention was focused on Maggie, who sat in the chair behind her desk, where she felt in control.

She looked up at Holly. "I am not going to admit to a crime, Holly. So what are you here for?"

To save Wes and his sister. "Okay, here it is. I think you and Nora wanted your names off Cullen's computer so no one could ever link you to the things he wrote about you in the O'Man blog and the podcast recordings. You are Wonder Woman, and Nora is the Invisible Woman. But I don't think you knew Helene was going to murder Cullen."

Maggie didn't move. "Hypothetical. What's your point?"

The woman had ice in her veins. "I need to find the computer."

Maggie leaned back in her chair. "If I were going to steal a computer like you say, to get rid of evidence, I would get rid of it. I wouldn't keep it around."

Holly felt like a door had been slammed in her face. "Permanently?" She was sure the computer would tell her what Helene was up to.

Maggie fingered the arm of the executive chair. "A boat has a lot of water around it."

Shit. What now? What next? So Maggie had gone to Cullen's boat that night, found the computer, and dropped it in the ocean. A team of divers might be able to find it, but it would take too long and there was no guarantee they could get the information off the computer after it had been submerged in salt water. Holly looked around Maggie's office again, noting the way everything was placed with precision. Maggie was efficient and organized . . . An idea hit Holly. "Backup?" That's what Holly would have done. She'd have taken a copy of the computer hard drive for herself in case she ever needed it.

Maggie's brown eyes widened slightly. "I am not going to incriminate myself."

The gloves were coming off. Holly sat forward. "Helene Essex is not who you think she is. Her real name is Ashley Gaines. Her husband went to prison for doping baseball players. A player died from the steroids. Guess who was that player's agent?"

Maggie's gaze sharpened. "Wes. Who is really Nick Mandeville."

Holly nodded. "Wes blew the whistle and testified against Ashley's husband. At first I thought all this was revenge. But Ashley didn't attain a new identity and go through all this just for revenge. She's doing it to get famous in her own right. She's tired of being the 'woman behind the powerful man.'"

It was as if a string yanked Maggie straight up from her leaning back position. "That's exactly the way Helene talks about men. But I thought she was just angry because she'd hit the glass ceiling in her job in human resources."

"She was never in human resources. That's the real Helene, who Ashley traded identities with. Wes's sister identified Helene's picture as the real Ashley Gaines."

Maggie took it all in, keeping her body still, but it was obvious that her mind was working. "So what does Helene want? What does the book have to do with it? And Brad?"

"Brad's an idiot." Holly shoved that down. It didn't help. "I think Helene maneuvered things as dramatically as possible. She set up Cullen's murder in Wes's bookstore, and made it look like a mob hit. Drama for the book. Then she arranged to have Wes's sister show up in his bookstore with an e-mail from me. Wes gets angry and fires me in front of Brad and cameras. More drama."

"He fired you?"

Holly ignored that. "A book that's going to make Helene/Ashley famous has to have a big dramatic finish. So what's the real reason she has Wes and his sister in one place?"

"To murder them."

Chills ran down her back and arms. "I have to see the book. Brad said it's finished. I think she's already written the ending. Now she just has to make it happen." Holly was convinced that Maggie had backed up the computer's hard drive before throwing it in the ocean, as a sort of insurance.

Maggie studied Holly. "How do I know you aren't setting me up?"

Damn it. Holly didn't have time for this shit. She didn't care about Maggie's worries of prosecution. She had to keep Wes and Michelle alive. If Michelle was hurt or killed it would destroy Wes.

If Wes was hurt or killed, it would destroy Holly.

She leaned her hands on Maggie's desk and looked her in the eye. "If Wes is murdered because of you, I will personally make sure you go down for it. I will do whatever it takes to secure you a place in prison for the rest of your days."

Maggie believed her and said, "Flash drive. My lawyer, Bradley Knoll, has it."

Wes's cell phone rang while he sat around Holly's condo and tried to control his impatience. He yanked it out and looked at the name on the screen. He looked across the living room to George. "I don't recognize it."

Seth stood behind the couch and said, "Answer it."

Wes put the phone to his ear. "Hello."

"Brockman, it's Brad Knoll."

Wes mouthed, "Brad Knoll," to Seth and George. He saw Seth's face tighten with anger, but the man got it under control. Wes leaned back, falling easily into the role he'd played for so many years: ruthless negotiator. "Knoll, what do you want?"

"I have a deal for you."

"Not interested in any deals with you." Wes hung up.

"What the hell did you do that for?" Seth asked, keeping his voice low.

Wes glanced at the doorway to the kitchen. Michelle was in there entertaining Jodi and Kelly with her adventures in surfing while Kelly cooked to soothe her nerves. They heard bursts of laughter every few minutes. The sound of Michelle's easy laugh tugged hard at his gut. He turned his gaze back to Seth. "I know what I'm doing. Brad is the puppet, and probably not smart enough to realize I wouldn't walk on the same side of the street as him. But Helene, aka Ashley, is. If she's there . . ."

"She'd expect you to be uncooperative," Seth finished.

"I'm not so sure, but we'll see how it plays."

His cell rang again. Wes lifted it off his thigh and looked at the display screen. Same number. He answered, "Knoll, do I have to get my lawyers on you?"

"Brockman, you'd be wise to listen to me. I am going to make you rich."

Look at that, three years out of the game and the lines were still the same. Bored, he said, "I'm not having money problems."

"Do you want Holly to get rich off of you?"

Well now, the boy had some balls after all. He felt George and Seth's stares on him, and caught sight of Michelle walking out from the kitchen. To Brad, he said, "How would Holly get rich off me?"

"She used you. You know it. She exposed you to build her PI agency, and now she's going to use that to get on TV, book deals, anything she can milk it for."

Wes had to admit, if he had been dumb enough to believe Holly would betray him, Brad would have his attention. "I have lawyers who will—"

Brad cut him off. "Beat her at her own game, Brockman. I have a client who has a book about you ready to go. And she's willing to cut you and your sister in on the deal."

Wes said, "What kind of book?"

"A biography. She wants to meet with you tonight in my office. Say five-thirty. She'll have a copy of the book for you to review and we'll discuss terms. We'll get this book out before Holly can do anything. She'll be left in the dust."

Wes stayed quiet. Thinking, and letting Brad stew. Holly had been right, there was a book. But Wes didn't believe for a second Helene was going to share profits. He was pretty sure there would be a nasty surprise waiting at the office when they got there. It was a setup, and the beauty of it was that if Wes had believed Holly had betrayed him, he might have been pissed off enough to fall into their trap.

Brad said, "Brockman, at least come and listen. What will it hurt? Both you and your sister. She's part of the deal."

"We'll be there." He started to hang up.

"One more thing," Brad said.

"Which is?"

"We want to keep this quiet. We don't want Holly or anyone finding out and getting the jump on us. Just you and your sister."

"I'm not signing anything until my lawyers look at it." Not even Brad could be that much of a moron. He was a lawyer.

"Of course. You can take a copy of our offer to your lawyers first thing tomorrow."

Might be hard to do, Wes thought, if he was dead. "Five-thirty," he said, and hung up. Quickly, he filled in Michelle, George, and Seth on the parts that they missed.

"What now?" Michelle asked.

Wes went to her and put his arm around her shoulders. But before he could reassure her, the front door opened. Holly came in, followed by her dad. She said, "We both got here at the same time. Do I smell cookies?"

Before Wes could respond, Jodi and Kelly walked out from the kitchen carrying a plate of sandwiches, chips, paper plates, and another plate filled with cookies. They set it all down on Holly's coffee table.

Kelly pushed her hair back and blushed at everyone watching her. "In case anyone's hungry. I also found slice-and-bake cookies, so I, uh, made them." She hurried back into the kitchen.

Jodi looked at Wes. "She cooks when she's nervous."

"Nervous or scared?" Holly walked over and helped herself to a sandwich.

"Both," Jodi said.

Holly nodded and touched Jodi's arm. "Nothing wrong with that." Then she turned to George. "Do you want a sandwich?"

"And cookies."

Jodi laughed. "I'll get them and something for you to drink."

Five minutes later, everyone had food and was crowded into the living room. Wes told Holly about Brad's call, and they all agreed that it looked like Helene/Ashley was using Brad to lure Wes and Michelle into one place, probably to kill them. Then he listened as she filled them in about Maggie making a copy of Cullen's hard drive before dumping the computer in the ocean.

Holly turned to her dad. "What did Rodgers say?"

Eric wiped his mouth. "It took me a while to track her down. She wants to talk to Nora about the gun, but can't find her. She also can't find Helene. Maggie told her she refused to answer questions without her lawyer. Right now she's confirming that Helene is really Ashley Gaines. She said to keep her in the loop."

Wes didn't like it. "Where's Nora? Where's Helene?"

Holly said, "I'm going to try and talk some sense into Brad and get him to let me look at the flash drive."

Wes shook his head. "He won't, Holly."

She opened her mouth but a cell phone's ring made them all jump.

Wes realized it was his. After looking at the screen, he said, "Unbelievable. It's Nora." He put the phone to his ear. "Nora, what's up?"

"I'm in trouble, Wes." Her voice shook.

The room had fallen deadly quiet. Wes kept his voice sympathetic. "What's the matter?"

Her voice edged up to panic. "It's gone, Wes. I've looked everywhere! I don't know what to do!"

He looked at Holly and said into the phone, "Nora, let me help. What is gone?"

A beat of silence, then she said, "My gun."

"Your gun is missing?" He repeated it so the others would understand.

"What will happen to Ryan if I go to prison?"

Wes could practically feel her dark desperation for her son coming through the phone. Gently, he asked, "Nora, did you kill Cullen?"

She started to sob. "No. I didn't even know she was going to do it. What do I do now?"

George said, "How long has her gun been missing?"

Wes asked, "Nora, when did you notice your gun missing?"

"A few days ago. When I tried to call you. But I got scared. What do I do? Where do I go?"

"Nora, if we tell the police—"

"No! I can't go to prison! You have to help me."

Wes took a breath. She'd called for a reason. "How do you want me to help you?"

"Where is she?" Seth whispered.

Wes added, "Tell me where you are, Nora. Let me help you."

"That detective has been to my house and work. I had nowhere to go. I don't know what to do. I want to make this stop before it gets worse. But the police won't believe me."

Wes used his most reasonable voice. "They'll believe me, Nora. And I have a group of lawyers that will help you." He looked over at George, who nodded for him to keep going.

Nora said, "I'm hiding. And I have something else. Maggie gave me a copy of what was on Cullen's computer. Wes, you have to help me make the police believe me."

Excitement and nerves ramped up his adrenaline. Once he'd lived for this kind of high—doing the deal. Now he was fighting for his and Michelle's lives. Wes turned his gaze to Holly. She was what he wanted, not the excitement of the deal, the power of his old position, not superstars on his speed dial. He wanted the woman that he loved. But first he had to resolve this nightmare, and the answer was on that flash drive Nora had. "I'll come to you, Nora. We'll work it out together."

"What about your sister?"

Word had spread. "I'll come alone," he assured her.

"Just you and your sister. Don't leave your sister alone, Wes. She's not safe. Neither of you are. I can't live with anyone else getting killed!"

"My sister is safe where she is."

Nora's voice rose. "You don't understand! You can't trust anyone. Keep your sister with you."

Everyone leaned forward.

Wes believed that Nora was desperate, and that she had the flash drive and knew what Helene was planning. "Where are you, Nora? I'll help you, I swear."

Her breath did that odd hitching thing women did when they were crying. He waited her out and she said, "I'll meet you at your bookstore in an hour." She hung up.

Wes put his phone away and relayed the information.

"I'll go with you," Holly said. "Michelle stays here."

Michelle leaned around Wes and said, "I'm going with Nick. I'm not taking a chance on losing my brother again."

Wes took her hand. "I'm not going to disappear on you this time."

Her eyes glittered like emeralds. "I'm going with you."

Holly stood up. "Let's get going. We want to get there first and be prepared." She looked at her dad and Seth. "You two stay here, okay?"

Eric looked at Holly. "You have to call Rodgers."

"I don't want to scare Nora off. Once she's there, I'll call her."

Wes agreed with Holly.

George leaned over, undid his ankle holster, and held it out to Wes. "Take it."

Wes took the gun, ignoring the cop looks passing between Eric, Seth, and Holly. He pulled up his pant leg and strapped on the gun.

"This isn't a good idea," Holly said.

He looked up at her. "Afraid I can outshoot you, Hill-*baby*?"

She met his gaze and said, "No, I'm afraid you'll shoot your dick off."

George laughed. "Relax, Holly. Wes can shoot. I taught him myself."

She whipped her head around and glared at Wes.

"Hey." Wes held up both hands. "You never asked me if I could shoot. You just assumed a bookstore owner would be harmless."

She blinked. "Damn."

Chapter 21

Holly kept checking the area while Wes parked in the lot behind the bookstore. It was about three o'clock in the afternoon. She didn't see any reporters, thankfully. She did see the usual assortment of afternoon shoppers, and people heading down to the beach.

They got out of the car and rushed down the alley behind the bookstore. "Hurry." Holly would feel better once they were inside. After all, someone had shot George when they were walking to Cullen's boat. Nora insisting that Wes bring Michelle with him could be a real concern. Or there was the possibility it was a setup to get them out in the open where Helene could shoot them and get away. Wes reached the door first and slid his key into the lock.

Holly stood in front of Michelle, practically smashing her against the wall next to the door. Her adrenaline pumped, making her stomach burn. Something about the key nagged at her. As Wes pulled open the door, Holly took her gun from her purse and stepped into the doorway that led to the small office and storage room. It was dark. She moved toward the outline of a desk and said, "Get the light, Wes."

She heard the door close behind them at the same time the overhead fluorescent light flickered, caught, and flashed on.

Holly's hackles rose on the back of her neck. Damn it, the key! They knew Nora had a copy of the key made!

Before she could adjust her eyes enough to make out Helene standing in the doorway of the meeting room, she heard the other woman say, "Drop the gun, Holly."

Holly hesitated, trying to assess the danger and their options.

A loud pop startled her. Then hot pain brutally arrowed into her right arm. The impact knocked her back a step. She heard her gun hit the ground. She heard screaming. Was it her? She didn't scream. It would be so embarrassing if she screamed just because she was shot. There was a roar, too. Sounded like her brothers when they were pissed off.

Get control of yourself! She had to focus. Keep Wes and Michelle alive. It was Michelle who was yelling. She looked back. "Stop that screaming." She had to think.

"Don't move!" Helene snapped.

Holly turned back, keeping her body in front of Michelle and Wes. She forced herself to bring up her left hand and clamp down hard on the wound in her right arm. Christ, it hurt like a bitch. But her brain was clearing enough to realize that Helene had warned Wes not to move. He was trying to get to her. He needed to stay back and behind her. Holly took a steadying breath and said, "It's not going to work, Helene." She refused to feel the hot blood pouring over her hand.

Helene kept the gun on Holly, while taking two steps toward them. She used her foot to kick the gun back to the meeting room door, and said, "Stupid bitch. Now I have to write you into the ending of the book. God, I hate rewrites." She backed up to the doorway, carefully squatted down, picked up the gun, and stuck it into the waist of her pants.

"Excuse me if I don't exactly sympathize." Holly tried to take in her surroundings. How could she stop Helene? How could she keep from passing out? She had to. There was a desk and filing cabinets on her left. On the right were metal storage shelves with the usual office supplies, and an open space next to that where a couple stacks of boxes were probably filled with books. A glint of silver caught her eye on top of one of the boxes. A utility knife, used to slice open boxes. Unfortunately, it was too far behind Holly for her to get to it. Her right arm was useless.

Helene regained her attention. "Get into the meeting room." She took a step back, indicating they should proceed her into the room.

Holly wanted to keep Wes and Michelle near the door. How to give them a chance to get out? Maybe if she caused a distraction, but what? Could she trip into Helene?

Would Wes leave her, knowing she was shot?

To save his sister, he would.

She didn't have time to debate. She took a step, doing her best to look shaky. She took another step and threw herself into Helene.

Holly hit the ground, and white hot pain exploded in her entire right side. It sliced deep into her, making her roll on the carpet, clutching her arm. She had missed Helene, but had Wes and his sister gotten out? She opened her eyes, but all she saw were wavy lines and black dots.

And a pair of shoes.

Instinct warned her and Holly rolled away, ending up taking a kick in the middle of her back. A groan tore loose from her throat. Nausea rolled up and sweat coated her body. She fought to move air in and out of her lungs.

"Stop it!" Michelle screamed.

Holly heard Wes say something else, which meant that he and Michelle were still in the bookstore. Now she had to live through this just to yell at him for not being fast enough to get him and Michelle out of the bookstore. She focused on that, narrowed her mind down to one thought: *Wes.*

She stayed still on the floor. The spots faded, and the pain lifted to mere agony.

"Get up," Helene said.

"Let me help her," Michelle said.

"No."

Holly rolled to her back, seeing Helene standing two feet to her right. Too close to her injured arm. Holding the arm, she used her stomach muscles and sat up. She took a breath to control the wave of dizziness. Then she got her knees under her and stood up.

She was facing the door that led to the bookstore. Slowly, trying to control the pain, she turned around.

Now Helene was on her left. Nora sat at one of the four tables arranged in a rectangle, tears rolling down her face. Wes and Michelle stood in front of Holly a little to the right. Wes had put his body between Helene and Michelle, and closer to her.

She knew the gun was strapped to his right leg, but how could one of them get it? It must not have occurred to Helene that Wes might have a gun. Holly searched Wes's face, seeing that his jaw was clenched tight and his green eyes blazed on her, while a nerve jumped in his left temple. He was furious, barely in control.

For her? What was he telling her? Anything? Or was he just angry?

Wes had had the courage to tell her he loved her. She hadn't been able to do that. She regretted that now, hated that she hadn't given him the words, when he'd given her so much more. He had taught her to believe in her own value as a partner. She dropped her gaze from his face and noticed that he had both his fists clenched.

A glint of silver peeked out of his right fist.

Holly didn't let her expression change, but what was it? She could only see the smooth, curved edge . . . The utility knife! Quickly she looked back up.

His green eyes were glued to her face. Willing her to stay alive, trust him, and work with him.

She turned and looked at Helene. "The police have been looking for both you and Nora. Everyone knows who you are, *Ashley.*"

She smiled, a slow, cold smile. "Good, because when I

wrestle the gun from Nora, who gets shot in the process, they will know that Ashley Gaines is a heroine who tried to save the man who destroyed her husband." She turned to look at Wes. "But I was too late."

Holly's mouth was dry and it was hard to think, let alone talk. "That's a little clichéd. Overdone."

Helene ignored her. "Let's see how Nick likes watching his sister die."

Wes shoved Michelle behind him.

"Okay, your girlfriend, then." She turned the gun on Holly's head.

"No!" Wes roared.

Helene laughed. "Which one, Nick? Your sister or your girlfriend?"

Sweat rolled down Wes's face. "Kill me."

"Oh, I will. After you watch everything you love and worked for die. Just like I did when you suddenly got a conscience. I've been waiting a long time to watch you squirm."

Holly looked over at Nora. She appeared broken. Her hands were tied behind her back and she didn't seem to have any will left. But she looked from Helene to Holly. Then Nora said, "You're a monster, Helene. You stole my gun."

"Shut up, Nora," Helene said calmly. "Choose, Nick. Who dies first?"

"Shoot me!" Nora said, trying to stand up. "Just get it over with!" The chair clanked against the table.

Helene turned her head.

Wes acted, drawing his arm back, flicking out the blade on the utility knife, and throwing it.

At the same time, Holly dropped to her knees, using her left hand and reaching across Wes to get the gun from his leg. She was clumsy and couldn't get his pant leg up. But suddenly the gun was put into her hand.

She looked up and saw Michelle kneeling on the other side of Wes. She put the gun in Holly's hand just as Helene screamed.

Holly didn't try to stand. She stayed on her knees and took

stock. The utility knife hit the mark, slicing Helene's right forearm. She dropped her gun.

But she had Holly's gun in her waist band. She pulled it out, oblivious to the blood pouring from the cut on her arm.

Holly took aim with her left hand and fired.

Helene was thrown back. The bullet hit her in the left shoulder and slammed her on top of the table behind her.

Wes grabbed the gun from Holly's hand, holding it on Helene and starting to walk forward. Behind them, the door burst open. Holly turned just in time to see Joe, in uniform and with backup, burst into the room. "Joe." She was pretty sure she said the word out loud.

Her brother reached her in seconds. "Ah, Holly."

He took hold of her good arm and sat her down in a chair. She looked into his blue eyes. Everything else tilted oddly, but she could see her brother's blue eyes, full of concern. "I'm okay. Tell Wes I love him. I should have told him . . ."

Wes's voice interrupted. "Tell me yourself." He dropped down in front of her and put his warm hands on her thighs.

She was so cold, the warmth of his hands felt good. "I love—ouch, goddammit!" She looked over to see that Joe had a pad of something that he'd shoved up against the wound on her arm. She started to pant, the pain making her nauseous.

"Where are the paramedics?" Wes roared out.

"I hear them," Joe said, but he wouldn't let go of her arm.

Holly swayed on the chair.

Wes took the hand of her good arm. "Look at me, Holly." She forced her eyes to stay open and fix on him.

He smiled. "That's my PI. I know it hurts. The cops wouldn't let me near Helene, or I'd have kicked the shit out of her for shooting you."

She half-smiled. Then remembered what she had been going to tell him . . . "I'm sorry. I should have told you. I—"

The paramedics rushed in.

Wes stood up to get out of their way.

"Wait. Wes . . ." It was too late. One paramedic peeled back the pad Joe had put on her arm, and the other took her vitals. And the cops dragged Wes away to get his statement.

Wes found Holly later that night at her house, surrounded by her dad, brothers, George, Jodi, Kelly, and Tanya. Her face was white with pain and fatigue. The bullet had gone through the outside edge of her arm, missing vital bone, but needing a hell of a lot of stitches. She and George sat on the couch, both looking like hell.

He and Michelle walked in and all talking stopped. Wes told them what he knew so far from his hours at the police station. "Ashley Gaines has been arrested on murder and attempted murder, and they are still adding charges. She's under guard at the hospital. The real Helene has been contacted and admitted to the whole scheme of switching identities. And Knoll did have the flash drive to Cullen's computer, the moron." He said it all as he walked over to Holly.

She looked up at him, her blue eyes fogged with pain medication and maybe a little shock. "Are you in trouble?"

For a second, his breath caught and his chest ached. Seeing that bitch shoot Holly had snapped his mind, and thrown him into an uncontrollable rage. Holly had bared herself to him, body and soul, and as archaic as it sounded, she roused in him a fierce instinct to protect her. If Michelle hadn't stopped him, he'd have gone after Helene in that second, getting them all killed. But his courageous PI kept going after that, working with him until they took down Helene together. And the first thing she worried about was his legal trouble, not the fact that she'd been shot. He leaned over her, putting his arm on the back of the couch behind her left shoulder, and answered her. "Some, but my lawyers assure me it'll be fine. I have to start sorting it out tomorrow, which will mean going back to Los Angeles for a while. But tonight, I'm here to take care of you." Careful of her thickly bandaged right arm, he slid his arms under her and lifted her up.

Her eyes widened. "Wes, put me down. What about your sister?"

He looked back at Michelle, knowing what she'd say because they'd already talked about it. Michelle knew he loved her, and that he'd never disappear on her again. But she also knew that he loved Holly, and tonight Holly needed him.

She smiled at him. "I'm fine. I'll sleep here on the couch."

George stood up. "No, I'll take Michelle back to your house and stay there with her and that mutt you call a dog. We'll be fine."

Wes nodded. George would take care of his sister. He had to take care of Holly. He went down to her bedroom and kicked the door closed behind them. He placed her on the bed and stripped her out of her clothes. Then he went into the bathroom and ran the water, wet a washcloth, and grabbed a towel.

She eyed him as he came back. "What are you doing?"

"Washing the blood off of you." He gently cleaned where the blood had soaked through her shirt and pants. Once he was done, he dumped the cloth and towel in the bathroom. He went to her dresser, found a pair of black panties and a loose shirt he could get over her wounded arm.

She started to sit up. "I can dress myself."

He sat down, reached behind her back, and helped her sit up. Then he worked the shirt over her injured arm, slid it over her head, got her second arm in, and pulled it down. He picked up the panties and grinned at her. "Pay attention, Hill*baby*. This is one of the few times you'll see me putting these on you. Most of the time, I'm going to be doing my damnest to get you out of your panties." He stood, put his hand behind her back, and helped her to lie down. Then he leaned over and slipped the panties over her feet and up her legs. Once he had her dressed, he pulled off his shoes, pants, and shirt. He turned off the light, got in the bed on the left side of her, and pulled the covers over them.

"Wes."

He put his arm under her neck and slid up against her, careful not to jar her, but cradled her against him. "What?"

Her voice was flat. "You have your life back now."

She thought it was going to change things between them. That she had been good enough while he was on the run and couldn't do any better. It made him half angry that she believed that, and half scared to death that he'd lose her. "I've never met a woman like you, Holly. You fought for me from the first day. And tonight you saved our lives."

Her body tensed. "You did. You threw the utility knife. You still have quite an arm left over from your pitching days."

"And you backed me up. Like a partner." He leaned over her and kissed her mouth. No tongue, no sexual tension, just a gentle kiss. Then he touched her face. "I love you, Holly. That's not going to change."

He heard her breathing, felt her heart beating where he'd rested his hand on her chest. She said, "I want you to know for sure that you want a relationship."

"I do." He didn't quite understand what she was so worried about. "It's not like we're getting married in the next couple of days. We'll take as much time as you need."

She shook her head. He felt a wave of pain wrench her body.

"Don't," he told her. "Holly, please, don't hurt yourself. Baby, you're tired, hurt, and lost a lot of blood. Your body went into shock when you were shot." God, he wanted her to keep believing in him.

"Please, Wes."

For the first time since he'd met her, he touched her face and felt tears. *Jesus.* "Holly, don't cry." His own throat closed up painfully. "Tell me what you want."

She took a deep breath. "I want you to take care of everything, get to know your sister again. Take some time. You might find that you want to go back to Los Angeles, go back to your life there. You were rich and powerful, Wes. In fact, you weren't even Wes, you were Nick. I don't want some kind of guilt, or debt, keeping you with me until you can't stand it anymore." In the moonlight streaming through her window, she turned and looked at him with tear-filled eyes. "Take time to think about never having children. Never having a son to play baseball with."

That hurt, surprising him. Somewhere in his mind was an image of him teaching his son to play baseball.

She touched his face with her left hand. "I've had time, Wes. I've come to terms with it. And now that I've met you, I know I'm still worth loving." More tears spilled down her face. "I'd rather you find out what you want, then either come back or walk away clean. Better that than tarnish the memory of loving you by watching our relationship die a little each day because neither of us had the guts to face the truth."

Her courage and wisdom humbled him. She was right. He owed her the truth. Wes leaned over her, kissing her tears. "I'll be back, Holly. I'll always come back for you."

"You don't know that. Not everybody comes back." Her tears dried up. Her words were flat and matter-of-fact. "And that's okay."

He knew she was right. And he did have to go. His lawyers were making arrangements now. He had to clear his name, or names, and resolve everything.

But Holly Hillbay was the one woman who had never walked out on him. He would come back for her. He slid his body closer, needing the skin-to-skin contact with her. "I'll be back."

Chapter 22

Tanya raised her glass of beer. "To Holly! She was awesome today!"

Holly rolled her eyes and drank her beer.

"Tell us again," Kelly said.

Tanya adjusted her black tube top and laughed. "By the time Holly got done castrating Phil with the pictures proving he was screwing Bridget before my, ah, indiscretion with Cullen, his own lawyers told him he was a fool. They added that he had no choice, because of his own actions, but to pay me the entire amount of the prenuptial settlement and Holly's fees for the investigation." Her grin lit up the restaurant.

Jodi looked at Holly. "Who did you get the pictures from?"

She put her beer down. They were at the Elephant Bar, celebrating Tanya's good news. Holly loved this shit, hunting down cheaters, any kind of cheater. "From the flash drive of Cullen's computer. Cullen knew that Phil and Bridget were sleeping together, so he snapped pictures of them making out with his camera phone and e-mailed them to his computer." She shrugged. "Cullen probably planned to use them to convince Tanya to sleep with him, but he didn't need them. Obviously, since he was murdered right after seeing Tanya, the pictures meant Phil and Bridget were doing the deed before Tanya and Cullen were."

Seth shook his head. "Hard to believe Brad did something right."

Holly smiled at the memory. "Brad, the dumb shit, started realizing something was wrong about the time that Maggie stormed into his office and threw him a new one. The two of them made another copy of the flash drive. Brad and Maggie were in Save Their Ass mode. They found Helene/Ashley's manuscript on the flash drive, checked the ending, and realized that Helene planned to murder Wes and Michelle in the bookstore." Holly shook her head, still amazed. Helene or Ashley, whichever name she was called, was a true sociopath, but smart. "Helene knew we'd figure some of it out, so she made it look like the setup was at Brad's office to talk about the book. Then she got Nora in the bookstore, held a gun to her, and forced her to call Wes, planning a dramatic murder, and an ending to her book. The plan had been to blame Nora, saying that she wanted revenge on Wes for her husband's sports gambling, which led to him embezzling. It was crazy in a brilliant way."

Joe's voice was cop-cold. "Brad didn't call the police like he should have."

Holly smiled. "No, but Dad called you and Rodgers. Brad and Maggie were too busy coming up with a story to keep their sorry asses out of prison." So much had happened. It had been a long month. But productive. Holly's arm was healing nicely. She had more work than she could handle. Wes had sent her a large check, and a note telling her that if she didn't take it, he'd just put the money directly in her account.

God, she missed him. But she kept busy and tried not to think about him. Except at night, when she was alone. He was even with her in her dreams. For two weeks, she made herself believe he was coming back.

The third week, it got harder.

Now it was a constant pain in her stomach. But Holly knew she'd be all right. She'd go on. She'd live her life and cherish her memory of the man who loved her exactly as she was. At least for a while.

Seth snapped his fingers in front of her face. "Wake up."

She smacked his hand away. "Don't make me kick your ass in public. I was just thinking."

His understanding blue eyes rested on her face, but he didn't ask about Wes. Instead, he said, "How'd you get Brad to give you the flash drive?"

"The truth. I threatened him. I told him I'd tell the world that he'd dumped me the very day I lost his baby. Oh, and that I paid for most of his law school, ruining the self-made man he liked to brag about being."

Tanya set down her beer. "Holly, I . . . gosh, I didn't know. I'm sorry."

She waved her hand. "It was three years ago. But Brad is desperate to regain his dubious reputation. He gave me a copy of the flash drive."

Her dad sat beside her. "Tell them the rest."

She looked over at her dad. The rock of her life. He had always been there for her. She realized now that her mom may not have wanted her, may have gone out and had perfect daughters to replace her, but Holly got the perfect dad. Her brothers were okay, too, when she didn't want to kill them. "I made the creep crawl back to the human resources person of the manufacturing plant I used to do background checks for and tell them he lied about me. He had told them I was forced to quit the sheriff's department, and they let me go."

Her dad's eyes sparkled. "That's my girl."

She picked up her beer and shrugged.

Nora rushed in, looking frazzled but happy. "Sorry I'm late." She went over to Tanya and hugged her. "I'm happy for you, Tanya. You can go on with your life now. Are you going to keep working for Holly?"

"She'd better," Holly muttered. "I've spent a lot of time training her."

Tanya laughed. "I have to. She needs me."

Nora sat down and ordered a glass of wine. "So, where's George?"

Jodi said, "He's closing up the bookstore. He'll come by."

Holly grinned. "Is he as overprotective as your previous boss?" She ignored the tightness in her chest that came automatically when she thought of Wes. George had offered to run the bookstore and watch out for Jodi and Kelly while Wes was gone. Wes was in and out of town, dealing with the police, the IRS, and his lawyers. He called once in a while, but it was too hard. She wanted Wes to make his own decision.

Jodi rolled her eyes. "Heck, yeah. And he talks to our parents on the phone, too."

Kelly moved her glass of lemonade, smearing the condensation from the bottom of the glass on the table. "Wes is coming home today."

Everyone turned and looked at her. Holly kept her face blank.

Nora saved her. "I have to thank him. I don't know what I would have done without Wes. He got me the lawyer, who negotiated the deal for me. I didn't deserve his help." She blinked back tears and added, "Immunity for turning on Helene. I thought my life was over that day in the bookstore and I was sick for Ryan."

Holly looked at her. "You helped us in the bookstore, Nora. We couldn't have done it if you hadn't distracted Helene."

She nodded. "I watched her shoot you with my gun. I told her about the gun once, and the story of my ex-husband and how Ryan and I were starting over in Goleta. I didn't even know Wes was really Nick Mandeville, and it wouldn't have mattered if I had because I'd never heard of Nick. I never blamed anyone but my ex-husband for his gambling and embezzling." Nora took a sip of her wine and added, "Helene's a monster. She told me that Cullen had pictures of us having sex on his computer and he was going to put them on his blog. I couldn't let Ryan . . ."

Tanya squeezed her hand. "You have friends now, Nora. We all do. If we run into trouble, we know who to count on."

Holly looked around the table, seeing her family and friends. Tanya was right. The gaping hole in her life without Wes was painful, but her friends made it bearable.

Sitting across from her, Jodi said, "Oh, there's George."

He strode up, looking a little less lean. Taking care of the bookstore, and watching out for Jodi and Kelly, had given George a purpose. He came to Holly's side, leaned down, and cupped the elbow of her good arm. "We have some business," he said to the table. "Excuse us for a minute."

George helped Holly out with her PI work now and again. He was a natural at investigating, but he longed for something more. The trouble was that people were still after George. Even Holly didn't know his real identity. She was pretty sure she could find it if she wanted to.

She didn't.

Getting up, she grabbed her purse and followed George outside. They stood on the slab of cement in front of the restaurant. "What's up?"

He smiled down at her. "Go to Wes's house, Holly. Go see him."

Shocked, she said, "Now? What, is he summoning me like an employee?"

"He wanted to come here and get you himself. I told him that if he showed up, it'd be hours before the two of you could get away from the group."

She opened her mouth and almost asked him if Wes was back for good. If he still wanted her. If they had a chance. She shut her mouth and looked down. She wore her usual jeans and a tank top, and she'd added a black jacket for her meeting with the lawyers earlier in the day. She had her hair up in its usual clip.

"Holly."

She looked up.

"Do you want me to go with you?"

She glared at him. "Hell, no. I don't need a baby-sitter."

He grinned.

"Bastard." Her nerves were stretched tight, and George was playing with her.

He slid his glasses down his nose and looked at her. "Make no mistake. If you didn't go on your own, I'd drag your chicken-shit ass there myself. You two are really getting on my nerves." He turned and started for the door of the Elephant Bar.

Holly had to bite back a laugh. Not that she doubted him. "George."

He looked back at her over his mostly healed shoulder.

"Thanks." She turned and headed for her car.

A half hour later, she pulled up in front of Wes's beach house. She had stopped by her condo to get Monty. The dog was growing; his paws were huge now. She got out of the car with the dog and she inhaled the ocean air. George had told her to go up on Wes's deck. She led Monty through the gate to the back of the house. At the steps she hesitated. She didn't hear Wes on the deck, but she heard movement in the house.

Monty got excited and started yanking on his leash, trying to run up the stairs. He must have caught Wes's scent. Holly unsnapped the leash and let the dog go. He barked happily and scrambled up the steps.

A lump formed in her chest. She loved that dog. And damn it, if Wes had decided he was going to move on without her, she was keeping the dog.

She needed a minute to pull herself together. She turned and headed to the ocean. The sun was quickly falling, sinking into the sea, and leaving the water a dark silver color. She stopped a few feet back from the water, crossed her arms, and watched as the reddish orange orb slid down.

She would know soon. Wes would tell her the truth. Could he live without fathering a child? Could he love her? Or did he need something else? Both of them had to be honest.

Monty's excited barking had quieted. She heard the low tones of Wes's voice, then nothing. Music started up behind her. Soft jazz drifted down from one of the beach houses. Had Wes turned on music? She heard him walk up behind her and shivered with nerves. She didn't turn around. "Hello, Wes."

He put his arms around her. "I came back for you." He set his chin on her shoulder.

His warmth surrounded her, his scent filled her. The sun was nearly down, just a rim of light left. And the jazz music wafted over them. She put her hands on his arms. "Are you sure?"

He breathed against her neck. "I am. I missed you every day. But you were right to send me away. I had to clean up my life, resolve my legal problems, and spend some time with Michelle."

She leaned back against him, into his arms. "How is she?" Holly knew how important Michelle was to him.

"Amazing. She's gone back home to Australia to train for her next competition. She'd like us to come see her, and she'll be back out this way in a few months."

"I'm happy for you."

"I know you are, Holly. Before I came home, I flew to Washington and talked to Lacey. I told her that I was sorry I didn't listen to her and do something about it. Conrad was more than just a baseball player, or a homerun slugger, he was a man who touched many lives. She's something else, Holly."

"She forgave you."

His silence settled over her for a full minute. "I won't forget him, and I'll always live with guilt. But she told me she doubted I could have done anything. She carries guilt, too. But the point is, you made me face my ghosts, and come back to you ready for a future." He kissed the curve of her neck, then said, "When I looked out and saw you standing down here in the sunset, I knew I was home." He paused and added, "What about you? Do you want me, Holly?"

That was easy. "I never stopped wanting you." But she had to make sure. She turned in his arms and looked into his eyes. They were a darker green as the day slid into night. And just looking into his eyes made her heart open. Setting her hands on his waist, she said, "Maybe we can adopt or—"

His smile was intimate and easy. "Or we'll be aunts and uncles to your brothers' and my sister's kids. We'll decide together. But for now, I want time with you." He reached down and took her wrists, then paused. "How's your arm?"

She was a little thrown. "Fine."

"Any pain?"

"No."

"Good." He pulled her wrists up and placed them around his neck. He put his arms around her waist.

Holly loved the feel of Wes. Out there on the beach in the silky dusk, with the damp sand beneath them and the crashing waves mixing with the jazz music, she knew that she was home, too. With Wes. She took a breath and told him, "I love you."

His gaze intensified. "And trust me?"

"Yes."

"Then dance with me, Holly." Using his hands on her waist, he guided her into a gentle sway that melded with the jazz music.

She stiffened, her heart rate kicking up. She'd rather get shot again then dance. "That's a sneaky trick." She tried to keep her body from moving.

He took his hand off her waist to cup her face. "No trick, Hill*baby*. It's just you and me, and we're both safe to be ourselves and dance. Close your eyes." He pulled her up against him, fitting her to him, and kept swaying in rhythm to the music floating down from his deck.

With her eyes closed, Holly thought of the man strong enough to face his ghosts. Strong enough to love her. Surely he was strong enough to keep her from falling. She relaxed, melting into the pattern of movements in the safety of his arms.

She did stumble once and snapped her eyes open to see his eyes watching her, full of love and a little smug. "Don't think you're going to make me do this in front of people. I'll shoot you first."

He laughed. "There's my snarky PI with the chip on her shoulder. God, I've missed you."

"Oh yeah? Then show me, Wes." Her breath caught in her throat and she frowned. "Are you going by Wes? Or Nick?"

He pulled her flush against his body with one arm around her waist. He put his hand on her face, and his incredible green eyes bored into hers. "What name are you going to call me when I'm deep inside of you, Holly?"

She shivered with lust and love, but she didn't let his gaze go. "Wes."

"Damn right, you are." He took her mouth, plunging his tongue inside of her with a possessive growl. His hand went to cup her butt and pull her hips into his erection. Then he broke the kiss and swept her up into his arms. He looked down into her face. "How do you feel about sex on the beach?"

"The drink?"

His smile was wicked. "Hell, no."

Turn the page for a first look
at Sylvia Day's
THE STRANGER I MARRIED.
Available now from Brava!

Gray faced her. His eyes knowing. She had not gone undetected.

"I hope one day you do more than watch," he said softly.

She covered the lower half of her face with a gloved hand, mortified and anguished. Yet he was unashamed. He stared at her intensely, his gaze taking in the outline of her hardened nipples.

"Damn you," she whispered, hating him for coming home and turning her life upsidedown. She ached all over, her skin too hot and too tight, and she detested the feeling and the memories it brought with it.

"I am damned, Pel, if I must live with you and not have you."

"We had a bargain."

"This," he gestured between them, "was not there then. What do you propose we do about it? Ignore it?"

"Spend it elsewhere. You are young and randy—"

"And married."

"Not truly!" she cried, ready to tear out her hair in frustration.

Gray snorted. "As truly as marriage can be without sex. I intend to correct that lack."

"Is that why you came back?"

"I came back because you wrote to me. Every Friday the

post would come and there would be a letter, written with soft pink parchment and scented of flowers."

"You sent them back, every one of them. Unopened."

"The contents were not important, Pel. I knew what you did and where you went without your recounts. It was the thought that mattered. I had hoped you would desist, and leave me to my misery—"

"Instead you brought the misery to me," she snapped, pacing the length of the small room to ease the feeling of confinement. "It was my obligation to write to you."

"Yes!" he cried, triumphant. "Your obligation as *my wife*, which in turn forced me to remember that I had a like obligation to you. So I returned to quell the rumors, to support you, to correct the wrong I did you by leaving."

"That does not require sex!"

"Lower your voice," he warned, grabbing her arm and tugging her closer. He cupped her breast, his thumb and forefinger finding her erect nipple, and rolling it until she whimpered in helpless pleasure. "*This* requires sex. Look how aroused you are. Even in your fury and distress, I would wager you are wet between the thighs for me. Why should I take someone else, when it is you I want?"

"I have someone."

"You persist in saying that, but he is not enough, obviously, or you would not want me."

Guilt flooded her that her body should be so eager for him. She never entertained the idea of another man while attached to one. Months passed between her lovers, because she mourned the loss of each one, even though she was the party who said good-bye.

"You are wrong." She yanked her arm from his grip, her breast burning where he had touched her. "I do not want you."

"And I used to admire your honesty," he jeered softly.

Isabel stared at Gray, and saw his determination. The

slow, dull ache in her chest was so familiar, a ghost of the hell Pelham had left her in.

"What happened to you?" she asked sadly, lamenting the loss of the comfort she once felt with him.

"The blinders were torn from me, Pel. And I saw what I was missing."

Here's a peek at
WHO WANTS TO BE A SEX GODDESS?
by Gemma Bruce.
Available now from Brava!

A ndy took her place at the back of the line of Novices and slowly made her way to the front. The name of Dr. Bliss rose from every conversation and floated around the room like an effervescence. Everyone seemed fascinated by the TV guru. She hadn't been at the Welcoming Ceremony, and Andy was curious to see her.

When she reached the head of the line, another purple-sashed priestess gave her a stick-on name tag and a light blue satin sash.

She followed the others into the auditorium and saw Evelyn, Loubelle, and Jeannie sitting near the stage with the other higher ranking goddesses. She found a seat in one of the rows of folding chairs at the back of the room, reserved for the Novices. Peeking over the top of her glasses, she began a systematic search of each row, looking for a tall, auburn-haired, middle-aged stuntwoman—just in case—and came up blank.

She did find Dillon Cross, standing in the line of men on risers at the back of the stage behind a long table that presumably would seat the staff of the retreat. The men were bare-chested and dressed in short white kilts. They were all handsome and fit, though some looked self-conscious and some looked ridiculous.

Unfortunately, Dillon looked good enough to make her

forget her reason for being here. He was also perusing the rows of seats, a slight frown on his face, and she took the opportunity to get a good look.

He was tanned and buff, sleek more than built—like a panther, Jeannie had said. There *was* something predatory about him. A natural grace that was only slightly disturbed by the hitch in his walk. He had long legs and a developed chest that tapered to a narrow waist. A gold braided belt was fixed several inches below his navel.

Andy gave herself a buzz, just imagining what was under that little pleated skirt.

Suddenly he looked right at her. Something zinged in the air between them. He smiled, then shook his head and grinned. Andy shoved on her glasses, chastising herself for being caught ogling her attendant. The world became a blur again.

Conversation abruptly ceased as several priestesses, all dressed in flowing white robes and purple sashes, entered from a side door and took their places at the table on the stage.

Katherine Dane came next and stopped at the podium at the center of the long table. She was wearing an off-white silk pantsuit and no sash, just a purple jeweled pin fastened to her lapel. Two men followed her onto the stage.

The first man, a giant blond with powerful muscles swathed in undulating white pajamas, walked to the far end of the table and sat down. The second man was much shorter, slight, with dark shiny hair that receded from a high forehead. He was dressed incongruously in a pinstriped suit. The overhead lights picked out a sheen of perspiration on his forehead as he sat down.

Ms. Dane signaled for quiet. The rustle of conversation gradually subsided, and the house lights dimmed until only the stage was left in light. She nodded to the audience, welcomed them again, read off a few announcements, and reminded everyone to apprise themselves of the rules of the retreat.

"And now, it is my great pleasure to introduce the founder and guiding spirit of Goddess International, Dr. Fiona Bliss."

At last, Andy thought and removed her glasses to get a better look.

All eyes turned expectantly to the closed door. After a few seconds, the door opened, and Dr. Bliss entered, followed closely by two serious-looking young women in white robes crossed by gold and purple sashes.

The room, as one, sprang to its feet, and deafening applause reverberated through the air. Dr. Bliss walked to the podium, and Katherine Dane stepped into the background. The supreme goddess lifted her hands, palms upward, and though to Andy it looked like a gesture to continue their accolades, the hall immediately became quiet and everyone returned to their seats.

Except for her two acolytes. They stood at chairs on either side of the doctor. There was a brief standoff as the two women eyed each other, and not at all worshipfully. A slight gesture by Dr. Bliss and they sat simultaneously.

Dr. Bliss was close to six feet tall, strikingly poised with classical features and silver hair that was swept back in an elaborate coiffure. She wore a sleek, floor-length caftan decorated in gold braid. She looked magnificent with the row of slaves creating an exotic tableau behind her.

Silence fell over the room, and Dr. Bliss thanked her "dear Katherine" for the lovely introduction. Andy's gaze drifted back to Dillon. He was staring down at the floor, completely motionless.

She turned her attention back to Dr. Bliss, who began talking about finding your inner goddess and how the classes at the retreat would help your self-fulfillment. How women could empower themselves and find satisfaction by discovering their essential woman-ness. The audience hung on her every word.

"Our detractors dismiss the precepts of the goddess program as mere sex therapy." She smiled across the rows of listeners. "But it isn't just about sex . . . It's about power."

Andy could swear she heard eighty slave gonads shrivel up and play dead.

Dr. Bliss began to introduce the staff, starting with the priestesses at the far end of the table. Each stood and smiled and nodded to the audience when her name was called, then sat down as the next one was named.

The pajama-wearing hulk was Hans somebody, the retreat's masseur, and more, if the sighs around Andy meant anything more than wishful thinking.

Then the doctor turned and smiled down at the smaller man. "And this is my husband and help mate, Bernard Bliss, who will be conducting the Eternal Orgasm sessions."

Bernard Bliss stood up and with a deprecating smile, nodded to his high priestess wife. She began the applause that was quickly taken up enthusiastically throughout the room.

Andy stared. There was the sex guru, surrounded by forty half-naked studs, and the nerd with the sweaty forehead was giving her eternal orgasms. Hell. Life was sometimes stranger than the movies.

When the applause finally died down and Mr. Bliss had taken his seat, Dr. Bliss smiled between the two remaining women. "And these are my assistants, Jane Parsons and Carmen Gutierrez."

The two women stood. Jane was a tall, svelte blonde; Carmen was dark and compact. They smiled at their mentor and glared at each other. Dr. Bliss sang their praises, carefully alternating their names as she spoke, meticulously showing no favoritism. Still, the icy looks they reserved for each other boded no good. No doubt about it, thought Andy. There was trouble in Goddess Land.

And now we present
MaryJanice Davidson's latest,
DOING IT RIGHT.
Coming next month from Brava!

Tap-tap-tap.

"What the hell *is* that? Jared muttered, getting up and crossing the room. He had a flashback to one of his literature classes. "Who is that tapping, tapping at my chamber door?" he boomed, pulling back the curtain and expecting to see . . . he wasn't sure. A branch, rasping across the glass? A pigeon? Instead, he found himself gazing into a face ten inches from his own. "Aaiiggh!"

It was her. Crouched on the ledge, perfectly balanced on the balls of her feet, she had one small fist raised, doubtless ready to knock again. When she saw him, she gestured patiently to the lock. He dimly noticed she was dressed like a normal person instead of a burglar—navy leggings and a matching turtleneck—and wondered why she wasn't shivering with cold.

He groped for the latch, dry-mouthed with fear for her. They were three stories up! If she should lose her balance . . . if a gust of wind should come up . . . the latch finally yielded to his fumbling fingers and he wrenched the window open, grabbing for her. She leaned back, out of the reach of his arms and his heart stopped—actually stopped, ka-THUD!—in his chest. He backpedaled away from the window. "Okay, okay, sorry, didn't mean to startle you. Now would you please get your ass in here?"

She raised her eyebrows at him and complied, swinging one leg over the ledge and stepping down into the room as lightly as a ballerina. He collapsed on the cot, clutching his chest. "Could you please not ever *ever* do that again?" he gasped. "Christ! My heart! What's going on? How'd you get up there?"

"Quoth the raven, nevermore," she said and helped herself to a cup of coffee from the pot set up next to the window. At his surprised gape, she smiled a little and tapped her ear. "Thin glass. I heard you through the window. 'While I pondered, nearly napping, suddenly there came a rapping, rapping at my chamber door.' I think that's how it goes. Poe was high most of the time, so it's hard to tell. Also, the man you saw me bludgeon into unconsciousness dropped a dime on you today."

"He what?"

"Dropped a dime. Rolled you over. Put you out. Phoned you in. Wants to clock you. Wants to drop you. Made arrangements to have you killed, pronto. Sugar?"

"No thanks," he said numbly.

"I mean," she said patiently, "is there sugar?"

He pointed to the last locker on the left and thought to warn her too late. When she opened it (first wrapping her sleeve around her hand, he noticed, as she had with the coffee pot handle), several hundred tea bags, salt packets and sugar cubes tumbled out, free of their overstuffed, poorly stacked boxes. She quickly stepped back; avoiding the rain of sweetener, then bent, picked a cube off the floor, blew on it and dropped it into her cup. She shoved the locker door with her knee until it grudgingly shut, trapping a dozen or so tea bags and sugar packets in the bottom with a grinding sound that set his teeth on edge.

She went to the door, thumbed the lock with her sleeve, then came back and sat down at the rickety table opposite the cot. She took a tentative sip of her coffee and then another, not so tentative. He was impressed—the hospital coffee tasted like primeval mud, as it boiled and re-boiled all day and night. "So that's the scoop," she said casually.

"You're here to kill me?" he asked, trying to keep up with the twists and turns of the last forty seconds.

"You're the hitman? Hitperson?" *Who knocked for entry?* he added silently.

"Me? Do wet work?" She threw her head back and pealed laughter at the ceiling. She had, he noticed admiringly, a great laugh. Her hair was plaited in a long blond braid, halfway down her back. He wondered what it would look like unbound and spread across his pillow.

"Oh, that's very funny, Dr. Dean."

"Thanks, I've got a million of 'em." Pause. "How did you know my name?"

She smiled. It was a nice smile, warm, with no condescension. "It wasn't hard to find out."

"What's *your* name?" he asked boldly. He should have been nervous about the locked door, about the threat to his life. He wasn't. Instead, he was delighted at the chance to talk to her, after a day of thinking about her and wondering how she was . . . who she was.

"Kara."

"That's gorgeous," he informed her, "and I, of course, am not surprised. You're so pretty! And so deadly," he added with relish. "You're like one of those flowers that people can't resist picking and then—bam! Big-time rash."

"Thanks," she said, "I think." She blushed, which gave her high color and made her eyes bluer. He stared, besotted. He didn't think women blushed anymore. He didn't think women who beat up thugs blushed at all. He was very much afraid his mouth was hanging open and unable to do a thing about it. "Dr. Dean—"

"Umm?"

"—I'm not sure you understand the seriousness of the situation."

"Long, tall, and ugly is out to get me," he said, sitting

down opposite her. He shoved a pile of charts aside; several clattered to the floor and she watched them fall, bemused. "But since you're not the hitman, I'm not too worried."

"Actually, I'm your self-appointed bodyguard."

"Oh, well, then I'm not worried at all," he said with feigned carelessness, while his brain chewed that one . . . *bodyguard?* . . . over.

 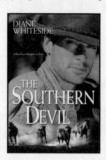